I0640431

A STAR-RECKONER'S
LEGACY
Book Two

AN ILL-FATED SKY
A STAR-RECKONER'S LEGACY #2
ISBN 978-0-9919681-8-3
Copyright © Darrell Drake 2018
All rights reserved worldwide.

Edited by Daniel E. Olesen, author of Annals of Adal.
Cover art by John Anthony Di Giovanni.
Cover design by STK Kreations.

Acknowledgements

For nearly half my life I've been dealing with Pina, and I'm better for it. The book is, too.

Without the company of Merill, nothing would be anchors aweigh. Certainly not this book.

Many thanks to my ragtag group of beta readers: BookWol, HiuGregg, Jen, John MacIntyre, Armani Salary, Tam, Sam Taylor, Marian L. Thorpe, and Travis Tippens.

In editing, Daniel E. Olesen taught me an important lesson: You don't fire an arrow!

Another collaboration between John Anthony Di Giovanni and STK Kreations makes for another superb cover.

Arash Zeini was kind enough to share his expertise in the field of Sasanian Iran, for which I am grateful.

A Star-Reckoner's Legacy

Book One
A Star-Reckoner's Lot

Book Two
An Ill-Fated Sky

Book Three
The Thousand-Notched Axe

I

HONOUR, AT ALL COSTS.

So steadfast in its pursuit, Tirdad had never stopped to consider that anything that had to be done at all costs, shouldn't be done at all. For all his talk of moderation, he had never thought to apply that to honour.

Only now did it dawn on him. Only too late. As Ashtadukht's ragged breathing thinned, as her head began to droop, as an unravelling plait brushed over his knuckles with a gentleness that grief had strangled out of her: only now. He'd never again have the pleasure of proving her wrong.

Ashtadukht had walked the path of the warlord. She had descended upon their homeland cruel with vengeance, as heedless and unforgiving as the procession of the planets. Her div host had defiled the land with greasy stains where families had once thrived. Running her through would guarantee him a lifetime of honour—restore his name if not their House.

She had orchestrated misery. All the same, Tirdad considered himself privileged to have journeyed by her side. He thought of her as a just person who had been backed into a corner.

For many years her annual ritual had claimed another star-reckoner, and in doing so furthered her twisted revenge. She had cursed them for her husband's death because she couldn't bear to curse herself; the loss had all but extinguished her spirit. Tirdad had witnessed firsthand the

5

good she'd done, and he figured her rites paled in comparison, despicable or not.

That sordid night when he'd walked in on Ashtadukht, meaning to apologize for their earlier encounter, he'd interrupted her ritual. Then he'd banished her. In doing so, Tirdad had deprived her of her one coping mechanism. If only he'd been more composed; if only he'd forgone those draughts of wine. Maybe things would've gone differently. This is what troubled him for the years following her disappearance, and what troubled him now.

What is the cost of honour, and at what point is the price too steep?

"I am truly sorry," he said. "It is over now. Find peace, cousin."

Ashtadukht drew her last while hunched against him, having slid further and further down his blade as she faded. She reeked of divs so strongly it made his stomach turn, but he held her a while longer. He recalled their time together, the wonders they'd shared, the trials they'd overcome, and more than anything he feared the finality he now faced. She was gone. So too was any chance of rekindling their bond. When at last he eased her to the floor it was with great reluctance, withdrawing his sword from her heart as he did. So focused on committing her face to memory, he didn't notice the magpie-black oil that clung to the blade until it was pulled free.

"What in the seven climes?" Tirdad muttered, holding the sword out to better examine it. The tar-like glaze swam with iridescence that seemed to suck the life from the already cloud-choked moonlight. Worse, it throbbed in his grasp. Tirdad felt the obscene throbbing—and there was no mistaking its obscenity—emanate from the blade as though he were holding a beating heart. That was enough to convince him to fling it aside, which was the worst possible reaction.

The room he was in retreated from view as if slinking away from the solar system that stormed in with stars and planets blazoned. Some cosmic awareness rushed over him, bringing with it the theatre of the luminaries.

Ashtadukht had explained to him in layman's terms the nature of star-reckoning, had given credence to the celestial battlefield described in doctrine. He'd taken her word for it because she was family, and because she was the star-reckoner. Now and then he'd imagine it while gazing into the night. His imagination had failed him spectacularly.

Tirdad careened through an unfathomable, glimmering expanse girdled by the smoky length of Gochihr, the terrible dragon that will someday collide with the world and drown it in molten metal. He should have been awestruck, but it all came to him with the familiarity of a past life. The faraway clashes of those countless lights reached him as charged sighs—no more than hints at their puissance. Sighs he knew intimately, each and every one.

This transpired as his sword flew away with meaningful revolutions. The first few were harmless enough. But an overwhelming lethargy soon compromised those revolutions, nearly bringing it to a halt mid-air. If Tirdad's consciousness weren't indisposed, he might have picked out a mounting struggle, as if the blade itself were too frightened to go on. A struggle it lost. The blade broke free of his gravity, and in doing so was thrown into the wall with such force that it was buried halfway to the hilt.

That spelled doom for Tirdad.

With neither pomp nor circumstance, Saturn interrupted his heretofore blithe visit. Where there had been empty space, it now hung before him every bit a gas giant.

The planet was more than the manifestation of death. It was the calculated patience of a frost that yearned to consume the universe, a cosmic glacier. Its rings glinted with pride, their sharpness stolen from the constellation of the Lion in a recent triumph. Within its millennia-old storms, trillions of divs licked their wounds, awaiting the next clash. What's more, it hungered with a bided ferocity, as if Tirdad had been keeping it at bay for a lifetime.

He wasn't even a speck in its shadow.

Saturn must have been nonplussed by the appearance of a planet-reckoner besides Ashtadukht, because it hovered there with the planetary equivalent of a creased brow long enough for his eyes to rove over its features. Then it answered his lot.

The wretched hedrons of planet-reckoning violated his mind, leaving permanent furrows wherever their chaotic rattle took them. But he was no planet-reckoner. Saturn had answered his lot fully aware it would end him.

Agony bunched his every muscle. The patient frost of Saturn eased itself into the freshly-carved furrows of his mind, daring him to burn his memories for heat or risk losing his mind altogether. But that was only the beginning. Even the most confident star-reckoners and planet-reckoners used their souls to channel a careful, almost insignificant fraction of the power of the luminaries. It buffeted Tirdad like novae through a nebula. His soul would be eroded long before his mind or body failed.

"Tirdad."

He reeled. If he had ideas about things not getting any worse, they were soon dashed when a star rocketed out of the Lion to take advantage of Saturn's distraction. Their collision lashed at his soul with white-hot intensity. The exchange that followed had the two grappling, Saturn scoring Regulus with its whetted rings, their innumerable forces emerging like a swarm of locusts—divs and yazatas loaded for bear.

"Tirdad."

He was lost in a world of pain. But the voice had as much substance as the theatre, threading its way between the sorties and skirmishes as if it were at home in their wake.

"Tirdad."

He couldn't immediately place it because he hadn't expected his sword to be calling his name. The blade throbbed from a breach it'd carved in the curtain of space, the steady heartbeat somehow reaching him over the din. It beckoned.

"Tirdad."

He struggled to heed its call, a struggle so pitiful it could scarcely be considered a fight. Somehow, he managed to will himself toward the breach. If with only minor headway. The power that buffeted him caused his muscles to knot, his mind to reel, and he could only summon the strength to move during the all-too-brief pockets where the fighting was least fierce. The blade directed him through the thick of the swarm with nudges that came to him like gut feelings.

If it weren't for those nudges, he would have died summarily. Divs and yazatas were at odds all around. Some fought with tooth and nail;

some with sword and shield; some with ideas; some with what he could only grasp as divinity. And there loomed over the fray a planet and star locked in single combat. It was a wonder then that he emerged from the swarm at all.

When at last he reached out and clutched the hilt of his sword, there was no mistaking the voice that followed. It belonged to Ashtadukht, though utterly deprived of emotion.

"Don't ever let go."

Her words had immediate and spectacular effect. The bedroom returned like a sandstorm, swallowing the celestial theatre, snuffing out stars and suffocating planets.

Left with a headache so sharp it'd give the bite of Waray's axe a run for its money, Tirdad collapsed against the wall, a death grip on the sword. Before he had the chance to recover, Ashtadukht's memories flooded his brain like rapids, too quickly and vehemently to make out. Interred in that flood were the remains of every div she'd dispatched, every lonely night contemplating suicide, every meal that tasted like dirt, every star-reckoner brought to justice, everything she'd learned and experienced. Only her final moments came with clarity, though he wished they hadn't.

His lips were warm on her forehead. His sword bit at her chest. A profound sense of failure hung over her.

Tirdad stared at the wall. He knelt in a bed of eggshells, one arm raised to cling to his sword through sheer force of will. All else fell slack. He issued a groan that broke into a sob.

On that ill-fated night, in an estate that would never be a home, a good man would forsake honour.

II

TIRDAD AWOKE TO THE WANDERING, virtuoso performance of a nightingale arrived too early in the year. Its song accompanied a soreness so thorough it afflicted his soul—as if his existence were somehow less than whole. With a lasting wince, he sidled to sit against the wall.

"Looks like someone beat you like a filthy carpet."

Tirdad's thoughts were thick as molasses. He squinted through the dusty dawn light at a figure who leaned against the wall just across the room. The shadows were more resilient there. Only the hint of trousers and boots caught the light.

"Who in the?" Tirdad mumbled drowsily, furrowing his brow and squinting in earnest.

"They box your fucking ears, too?" the man asked, his tone limned with amusement. "Or has a night with her made you forget me that easily?"

The man stepped forward, and the full-toothed smile he wore made an embarrassed shift to a frown. His attention turned to the corpse of Ashtadukht. "Sorry. That was thoughtless." He ran his fingers through his hair, disheveled like the wool of a dirty sheep, and grimaced at his crassness. "You in one piece?"

"Chobin," Tirdad greeted. He had been the only one to sympathize with Tirdad after the news of his cousin's vile deeds had spread. In that way, it was more than his tall, lean stature that earned him the name

'Javelin', it was his ability to sense a person's heart true as a javelin finding its quarry. "Far from it. I don't think I've ever—" The sword!

Tirdad scrambled for its hilt, kicking eggshells in his desperation, and an almost unnatural relief washed over him when he hung from it once more. That brief yet keen surge of fear had the effect of scattering the clouds in his mind.

"I killed her," he uttered, thick with regret. So intent on remembering Ashtadukht yesterday, he couldn't bear to look at her now. "Why'd I kill her?"

Chobin grunted. He'd been nonplussed by Tirdad's sudden clambering, but he knew this mood well. Tirdad had vacillated between depression and anger over the years, though he figured his friend had a damn good reason. No words would soothe him. So he gestured at the wall. "Need help with your sword? How did you manage that?"

With a defeated sigh, and realizing how sorry he must look, Tirdad pulled himself to his feet, muscles objecting all the while. He stared at his blade, which was still choked in magpie-black. "Don't ever touch my sword," he warned, almost threatened. "For your own good."

With that, he began working it out of the wall little by little, relating the events of the night before as he did. He left nothing out. The man behind him had earned his trust many times over. Only when he'd finished did he look at Chobin, who'd listened in silence. "Well?"

Chobin shrugged, thumbs hooked over his belt. His brow was knotted, but with what, Tirdad couldn't surmise. "I believe you. Explains earlier."

"Earlier?"

"Nothing."

Tirdad sighed and held out the blade to demonstrate an iridescence that settled one and unsettled the other. "I don't know what to make of it. I'm sure it has something to do with her. What do you think?"

"Something different about the way you talk." Chobin was examining him rather than the blade, an ear canted his way. "Sounds off."

"You're worse than Waray at answer—" He swallowed the rest of that remark, and it went down with an edge. "Stop tilting your head like that."

Chobin straightened his back in feigned offense, but it only made him look all the more like a dashing marzban, province commander. Tirdad had nothing but love for the man, but he often envied him his military prestige. That might have been him if he hadn't volunteered to ride off alongside Ashtadukht. Instead, he'd been reduced to a lowly mercenary, getting by on the charity of the man before him.

"Always lost in thought. It's a fucking wonder you survived this long."

Tirdad shook his head. He felt as if a part of him were still out there in the cosmos. "Huh?"

"So, what now?" Chobin shifted his weight, a subtle sign of uneasiness that Tirdad had come to recognize.

For the first time since he'd laid her there, Tirdad gave his eyes leave to fall on Ashtadukht. She looked pitiful, an unstrung harp that had never really played in tune. "She was brilliant once," he said soberly. "Brilliant like you wouldn't believe."

He punctuated the pithy elegy with a prolonged silence, over which he watched her world-weary frown and silver-streaked plaits, and as he did, the strangest memory came to him. He remembered watching himself sleep. Just watching. Just the steady rise and fall of his chest. Then as smoothly as it'd arrived, it dispersed. Tirdad blinked confusedly and turned to Chobin. "Have you come alone?"

The marzban met his gaze. "Brought a small detachment. Had no way of knowing what we would find."

Tirdad nodded, then looked again at the corpse. "I'd like to perform the rites. I want to take her to be exposed, observe the mourning period—everything. I'll look into the sword after. You have my word. I realize it's a lot to ask, but—"

Chobin took Tirdad by the head, and pressed his forehead against the once-black hair now banded with grey. "We will find a dog to follow, and a priest to purify the estate. After, you will mourn," he said, then paused as if to contemplate. "I'll make it right with the others." Another pause. "Find you some fucking wine, too."

"This means a great deal to me," replied Tirdad, knowing full well the gravity of that short silence. After the crimes she'd committed, convincing the royalty, nobility, and clergy to allow the rites of death would take some doing. They'd treat her like a div. Although, knowing the marzban he would skip straight to giving the orders. Asking for permission was too much trouble, he'd always say. Forgiveness, on the other hand, made the slighted party feel good about themselves. And people hunger for self-righteousness. "I'll make it up to you," he added at length.

"Hah!" exclaimed Chobin, unable to smother his characteristic joviality any longer. "You are full of tortoise-sodomizing shit. More full of it than a northerner playing at loyalty. What kind of friend accepts compensation?"

"You're a northerner."

"Farther north."

Tirdad grinned, but it strained to reach his eyes, which were still trained on his cousin. What kind of friend kills you?

• • • • •

Tirdad fastened his sword belt over his girdle. He secured a dagger to his thigh, where it was partly hidden by his baggy yellow trousers, then a short sword to his right hip. All that remained was his long sword.

He kept it bedside on a length of bunched silk, the color her tunic must've been before all the dirt and wear. Its narrow golden scabbard was embossed with a feather motif emblematic of Wahram, yazata of victory, and inlaid with garnet and glass. From there, the guardless hilt curved slightly downward to end in a ram's head pommel, and it had been given the same decorative treatment.

Tirdad pensively ran his fingers along the scabbard. He picked it up and unsheathed the blade enough to see the magpie-black. Its throbbing hadn't ceased. He slid it back in, then finished his morning routine by securing it to his left hip. The long sword had come first since his youth; now, it came last. He wasn't sure why he'd made the change.

With a deep, steadying breath, he fastidiously smoothed the front of his poppy-red tunic, then about-faced and started for the exit.

The last thirty days had been devoted to mourning, and rituals before that. Ashtadukht's passing still weighed heavily on his heart. Unlike her, he would not let it consume him.

"You spend too long getting dressed," Chobin chided light-heartedly the moment he stepped outside.

Tirdad shielded his eyes, squinting through the too-eager glare of a sun recently freed from winter. Chobin sat on his horse, the reins to another in his hand. "A military man should have order in everything," he said as he approached.

"Military man, huh? I only see one here." The marzban scratched his beard. "Oh, and some sorry fuck who's been sitting on his ass for a month and more."

Tirdad allowed himself a chuckle. "Yeah, I imagine that's why I'm the one who looks the part. I can't believe you've been in that saddle for a month." He mounted his horse and took the reins from Chobin. "Probably can't tell your cheeks from a bad case of acne."

"Listen here. My cheeks are pristine."

"Well, your clothes sure aren't."

Chobin belted a full-stomached guffaw. "Hah! Do not know what you did in there for a month, but I like it!" Once his laughter subsided, he turned an appraising look on Tirdad. "Seem healthier than I remember. Good. Now, for the love of all that is Truth, would you stop with all this mystery and tell me where the fuck we're going?"

Tirdad rested a hand on the ram's head pommel. "Are you sure about this? You should be with your soldiers."

"Fucking nonsense," the marzban replied. "The divs have scattered, and the nomads' fate is sealed. More importantly, you are a friend. Must we go over this again?"

"Fine. But you're not going to like it."

"I like it already."

"Figures."

"So? Out with it."

Tirdad turned his horse about and urged it into a trot. He had observed the mourning period wholeheartedly, but it bred restlessness. The road called with promises of distraction and, if fortune favoured him, answers. "We're to see a rogue star-reckoner. I think he's our best bet."

"There a reason we need a rogue?" asked Chobin, bringing his mount alongside.

"You know why. They'd have the sword destroyed without a thought."

"Mmn," Chobin agreed.

"And before you ask," Tirdad went on, "As far as I can tell I've never heard of this man. I just . . . I know. Like a gut feeling with detail."

The marzban shrugged. "Did not think to ask. But let me tell you, that does not fucking inspire confidence. Looking forward to it more and more."

"Something's wrong with you."

• • • • •

The pair favoured a westerly course along the Mazandaran Sea, Tirdad savouring its brackish reminder of better times, until they reached the paddy-hugged river delta that, mountains be damned, connected the Mazandaran plain with the rest of Iran. The winding way the water negotiated the range seemed like the tracks left by a leviathan—as if the Great Wall of Varkana had slithered through to reach the sea. The Ivory River carved through the range, and they with it.

"Still a while yet," Tirdad mused as they forded it for the fifth time. The dense beech-dominated forests of the sort he'd haunted as a child would soon give way to oak and juniper, and with them the comfort of relatively level terrain would also pass. "Let's pray the winter was kind to the paths."

"You know," Chobin replied as he swatted at a mosquito, "funniest thing. Almost as if I could have looked into that if you told me where the fuck we were headed a month ago." He slapped at another, and if the dip in his bonhomie was any indication, he regretted removing his tunic. "Fucking mosquitoes."

Tirdad turned in his saddle to look back at his travelling companion, who was riddled with bites. "I keep telling you to take some ambergris."

"I have taken so much ambergris somewhere a whale is checking its pockets." He slapped at the air. "Makes me want a woman with ripe quinces, but does nothing for the fucking mosquitoes."

"Then put your tunic back on," Tirdad said as he turned to hide the grin that had already begun to soften his features. Ambergris increased sexual potency; mosquitoes could love it for all he knew. It occurred to him that he had taken a page out of Waray's book, and just like that his good mood plummeted.

"Better the mosquitoes than roasting in a tunic. A healthy bronze makes me look more muscular besides," the marzban explained, probably flexing.

"Yeah."

"You aren't even looking."

"You never tan." Tirdad reached down to his bow case where it was suspended from his saddle. He drew his lips taut as he counted the arrows. While it had dampened his mood, the unwelcome memory of his single combat with Waray reminded him of the partridges that nested here. "I'll go fetch us some heathcocks."

Bow in hand, he dismounted and secured his quiver to his belt, then headed into the nearest thicket.

While he felt Chobin's eyes on his back, he did not notice the look of defeat with which the man pocketed the ambergris.

· · · · ·

For a pair such as them the only real peril of the road was monotony. Anything else they could either outrun or outfight. So they would pass the time with nard, a game of strategy that sought—and as Tirdad had recently learned, failed—to emulate the celestial theatre. He was the better of the two, but by a small enough margin that a friendly rivalry thrived. When that grew old, or when they were riding, the two would exchange stories while snacking on ragout, preserves, and so much partridge they grew sick of it. It was a journey that would not grace future stories but for the mention of it not being noteworthy.

To Tirdad's unspoken surprise, they reached their destination in the height of summer. What surprised him wasn't when they reached it, but that they reached it at all. He had been nearby once, decades back, when he had been tasked with bringing a rampaging forty-armed div to heel. But this place was foreign to him. And not the sort to be forgotten.

"Castle Dahag," Chobin whispered. "I cannot believe it still stands. The fucker's tyranny ended millennia ago."

"Yeah," Tirdad replied from where they knelt in the shadow of a ridge. A tower loomed far overhead with contours at the same time graceful and disturbing. Rather than standing vigil atop the gorge, it slumped over the edge as if it were crestfallen over being abandoned. No braziers burned in its crenellations; no sentries manned its walls with torches in hand. Only the light cast by the moon described its features, and it did so with the consistency of yogurt spilling languidly over the sides.

"A stork," the marzban said. "Looks like the head of a stork."

"Strange," Tirdad agreed with a nod. "That's a first."

"Why a stork? And why does the light . . . do that?"

"I haven't the slightest. But the star-reckoner is in there. Of that much I'm certain."

"A gut feeling, huh?" Chobin shook his head amusedly. "Certain about a gut feeling. How do you want to do this?"

Tirdad got to his feet and dusted off his knees. His gut told him to stroll in casually, and he found it puzzling that his gut would suggest something so obviously reckless. "I wish I knew how to put it into words."

"Try."

"I've a strong feeling of having been here before, but I'm sure I haven't. It's like salmon finding the spawning ground for the first time."

"Sounds fishy to me."

"I agree," said Tirdad. "But it's also telling me we won't come to harm . . . I think. Whatever the case may be, I suggest we reconnoiter the area above."

With a nod from Chobin they picked a cautious path up the gorge, doing what they could to keep to the deeper shadows. They had no way of knowing that no amount of darkness could have hidden them from the eyes that followed their progress.

Cresting the last rise brought them to the base of a castle that was, as its leading tower had suggested, fashioned in the shape of a stork—a morbid depiction of a stork that had taken some liberties when it came to exposed organs, but a stork all the same. Like the head, its ramparts were smooth, seamless, and graceful, which played a striking contrast to its grotesque features. It was as if the architect had intentionally devised something of beauty for the sole purpose of corrupting it.

17

The pair found it as ostensibly deserted as they had from below. The light that dribbled down the sides disrupted its stillness, but betrayed no activity. Tirdad was beginning to suspect it had been warded against the light. "The door's ajar," he said, indicating the gate. "Do you think it's an invitation?"

"Could be. Could be an invitation to our deaths."

"You were looking forward to this yesterday."

"Still am." Chobin had his jaw set and a wary stare trained on the tenebrous ingress. "Just thought it needed saying for your benefit."

"Sure," said Tirdad, not at all convinced. He drew his sword, and started for the entrance. He and Chobin sidestepped the moonlight that fell in clots from above, and stopped long enough to light a torch. They followed a bare causeway doing what they could to watch for traps, which in truth was very little, until it opened into a cloistered courtyard. All they could make out beyond the reach of torchlight were the patches of quivering yogurt that lived brief lives here and there.

Tirdad glanced at his companion, who just shrugged. He cleared his throat, and called out. "Hello? My friend and I are looking for the star-reckoner who calls this . . . this place home." Uncertainty gripped his voice, but try as he might he couldn't iron it out. "We'd like to talk."

"Just a friendly chat," Chobin stressed.

Dead silence.

Giving his sword an anxious squeeze, Tirdad waited and watched, allowing anyone who might be considering their options time to do just that. After a few steadying breaths and no reply, he glanced back at Chobin with a shrug. "Watch my back," he whispered.

Rather than waltz into the clearing, he nodded to the covered causeway to his left and forged on. Blade interposed between him and whatever lay in wait, he and Chobin crept around the perimeter. Like a thief skulking the shadows, and none too happy about it, they made it to the halfway point where a corridor branched off. A quick wave of his torch illuminated a line of beds caked with what looked to be dried blood. Among them were discarded bandages, open unguents, and what were probably barrels of wine judging by the empty wine vessels scattered about. He and Chobin exchanged a curious look, then they pressed on around the courtyard.

As they neared the exit opposite the way they'd entered, their torch revealed a figure directly in their path. Tirdad halted and brandished his long sword.

"Shouldn't be here mhm," the figure said, accompanied by a low hiss. A div. With its semi-keeled scales and sanguine cuirass over mail, Tirdad recognized it as one of the viper-like Eshm sisters who had proven fearsome in the recent war. She reminded him of Waray. This one was badly injured: she had one arm in a sling, her head and abdomen wrapped in stained bandages. "Shouldn't be here," she repeated.

Tirdad's eyes flicked from shadow to shadow in search of others, but he couldn't pick out anything unordinary. "We don't want to fight."

"Speak for yourself," Chobin said from behind.

"Don't care. You shouldn't be here mhm. Go."

Something more than her injuries gave Tirdad the impression she had no interest in fighting either. He took measure of the div, and when the likely reason came to him, he lowered his weapon. "The war was months ago. You've no doubt been on the run since. Harried all the while, I'd wager." He waved his blade at her dressing. "And those are fresh wounds."

"Go," the div commanded. She unslung her arm, which looked mangled beyond repair, and flexed it with little more than a wince. Then she drew her sword. Her eyes flashed with a visceral hunger he had come to know and respect in his years with Waray.

Tirdad swallowed. Fear swelled in his throat, and his breathing quickened. Adrenaline was quick to follow.

"You tried words," Chobin spoke up from behind. "Doesn't seem like the tortoise-fucker will heed them. Now, we came all this way to see this star-reckoner, so kill the div and move on."

"Don't underestimate her," Tirdad warned. Then to the div, "Do you want to die that badly?"

The div hissed, and what had been a neutral stance shifted to something decidedly more aggressive. She seethed; she bared her fangs. Tirdad hardly had the time to register the host of divs that seemed to manifest out of thin air just beyond the reach of his torch. Then they were on him in a frenzy. Unlike everyday divs, the Eshm sisters fought with brutal finesse and cooperation, weaving in and around one another's attacks like a mass of swiving snakes. It was all he could do to fend off their strikes, and for every strike parried three would connect.

"Not good!" Chobin called out. They were back to back, and the marzban was having marginally more luck both because he had brought a shield and because his lean build belied the strength of a larger man. Every swipe of his shield sent divs flying. But no sooner than they'd hit the ground they were on him again, injuries be damned. "Not fucking good!" he yelled.

"Gathered as much," Tirdad said through gritted teeth. He batted aside one blade, then his frustration drove him to counterattack. That rewarded him another five gashes. And he missed.

"They are—" The marzban interrupted himself with a growl, and three divs were thrown back by his shield. "They're toying with us."

Tirdad had worked out as much. With this many, they could have simply overwhelmed the pair. He'd been given a good twenty light wounds already, most of which could have been death blows. These divs were in a bad way, on their heels for months, and were just now licking their wounds. Issuing threats to such a gathering was beyond stupid. For that, the Eshm sisters were going to pick them apart. "We have to—"

He had meant to direct Chobin somewhere more tenable, if such a place existed. Instead, he was run through. Pain like a firebrand gripped his abdomen, bringing him to one knee. He cried out, but managed to ready his sword for the next attack. None came.

The sister responsible was on the ground in front of him, her shin snapped in half and a failed splint beside it. She made no move to clutch her leg; neither did she give any indication it bothered her. She just sat there wearing embarrassment.

"What the fuck?" The one they'd first encountered marched on the fallen div. "What the fuck was that? We'd only just begun!"

"S-sorry," stuttered the one on the ground. She gestured at her shin as if that were explanation enough.

The leader shook her mangled arm in response. "Like I give a flying fuck about your fucking leg! This is like a fucking . . . a fucking ruined orgasm!"

Meanwhile, Chobin knelt to examine Tirdad. "Got you good," he said. "Put some pressure on it."

"I'm fine," said Tirdad. With the marzban's help he got to his feet and applied pressure to his abdomen. "I'm fine. It caught me off guard after all the nicks is all."

The leader began to whale on her subordinate, so they seized the opportunity to edge their way out of the crowd. The other sisters seemed too absorbed in the beating to pay them any mind. As they crept away, Tirdad counted twenty-three divs, each and every one sporting a mean injury. They hadn't fought like it. "We don't stand a chance," he muttered. "We've got to find another way."

"Yeah," said Chobin. When Tirdad raised his eyebrows, the marzban went on. "Adventure is grand. This is suicide." Then, with a grin, "We need to talk about those gut feelings of yours."

They'd almost cleared the courtyard when the leader once again blocked their path, having cut them off without a sound despite her heavy armor. She had her fangs bared. "You're already dead mhm," she said, her delivery dripping with venom. Her muscles bunched, her legs flexed, and—

"Enough!" The shout spilled over everyone present with almost tangible authority.

—her pounce misfired. "Fuck," she breathed, catching her stumble before it became a fall by driving her blade into the dirt.

A brazier went alight in the centre of the courtyard, rousing a chorus of hissed complaints from the divs. Tirdad glanced over his shoulder. A figure in pristine white robes stood by the fire, a cowl over its face and sleeves to its ankles. It seemed to raise its chin and asked, "What did I say when you stumbled in, pitiful and on the brink of death, seeking the aid of a star-reckoner?"

Tirdad furrowed his brow and turned to face the mysterious figure. His palm came to rest on the pommel of his sword. Whatever it was, it was a star-reckoner, and none too pleased. "I'm not sure I follow," he said.

And he was utterly ignored. The star-reckoner continued without so much as acknowledging his response. "That you could only shelter here provided you behaved. What I see here is nothing short of misbehavior."

"Fuck," the nearest Eshm sister hissed under her breath. More loudly, "They're intruders. We're earning our keep."

"You were intruders until you were not," the star-reckoner replied. Its tone had softened, though a subtle yet unmistakable warning maintained its bite. What followed would brook no argument. "Cause trouble again and you will wish you were out there."

With the Eshm sisters addressed, the star-reckoner finally chose to acknowledge Tirdad. When it strode over, it did so with an otherworldly gait that gave the impression of being too big for its frame—and it stood a few heads taller than Chobin. Upon reaching him, it indicated his wound. "I will heal you," it said in a surprisingly youthful voice.

Tirdad stared at its cowl for a moment, attempting to pick out anything behind the fabric to no avail. He then glanced at the marzban, who only offered a shrug. This was his first venture into Ashtadukht's world without her, and he was already beginning to understand just how little he knew. He swallowed and spread his arms. The star-reckoner uttered an indistinct phrase, lifted its branch-like arms, and just like that his wounds were closed.

"I . . . thank you," he said, his awe evident, as the star-reckoner did the same for Chobin. He thought it was strange that the Eshm sisters came to mind, but he didn't fight it. "Why not heal them?" he asked, gesturing at the crowd.

"You were injured in my home. They were not. They can only afford shelter."

Right. It'd almost slipped his mind that this was a rogue star-reckoner—purely mercenary. "Of course," he said.

"An uncommon question," it mused, its tone briefly betraying curiosity before a swift return to business. "Not what I would have expected. Now, what do you want?"

Tirdad cleared his throat. He felt ill at ease and was having second thoughts about asking a creature such as this for its help. The star-reckoner scarcely breathed, but when it did, those heavy inhalations pulled at his soul. There was no mistaking it: he was in over his head.

Chobin answered for him. The marzban wasn't the slightest bit intimidated, and his flippant tone reflected as much. "So much for hospitality," he said. "My friend here finished off a planet-reckoner. Things got strange as fuck after that. So here we are."

"Go on."

"That isn't quite right," Tirdad cut in, finding his confidence in what he believed to be a disservice to Ashtadukht. He had done so much more than finish off a planet-reckoner. "In my youth, my uncle—a great general if there ever was one—once asked me the distinction between a ram and the ram. 'Exactly that,' he had said. 'Distinction.' So no, I didn't finish off a planet-reckoner. I finished off the planet-reckoner." The passion of his delivery commanded the attention of everyone present.

"With this blade," he said, unsheathing it to reveal its magpie-black coat. Tirdad then related the tale of the night in question. Once he'd finished, he craned to look into the cowl of the star-reckoner. "I need answers. I need to know what happened to my sword. What happened to me."

"I will look," the star-reckoner replied.

A prolonged silence intervened during which a queasy sense of being watched by something hidden and terrible threatened to empty his stomach. It made his hair stand on end. He had had about enough, and was on the verge of making that patently clear, when a power best described as a planet's glower amassed within. It too made his stomach turn, but in a manner he had never thought possible. A pleasant nausea. Then, when it sloshed at the lip of his too-full soul, it surged free. Out of nowhere the star-reckoner was hurled through the crowd and against the ramparts at the far end of the courtyard with such force it cratered the stone. Tirdad made to run over, but the Eshm sisters were once again hankering for a fight. Before they could act on their bloodlust, the star-reckoner spoke up.

"Do not attack them," it said, its voice quaking. With a great deal of effort, legs shaking like a newborn foal, the star-reckoner got to its feet. Where it towered over the sisters, it favoured one side, and its cowl was splashed with blood where its mouth must have been. It shambled over, crowd parting around it. "This will not come cheap," it said. "You could have killed me."

Beetle-browed, Tirdad spread his hands. "I did nothing."

"Was standing by his side the whole time," Chobin added. "He tells the truth."

The star-reckoner tilted its head. "I see. Not directly, but through you. That makes sense. Still, the fee is double."

"Are you fucking kidding me?" Chobin fumed, pointing his sword at the star-reckoner. "Think you can pull a fucking fast one on us because you consort with divs?"

Tirdad placed a hand on his forearm, easing the sword back down. "Don't," he said. "Thanks, but it isn't necessary." He turned a frown on the star-reckoner. "If anything was behind what just happened, I'd wager it was your overconfidence. Now, I've travelled far to enlist your services, and still wish to do so. Are you going to start charging for your reckless-ness? Because word gets around."

After brief consideration, the star-reckoner consented. "Very well. I would however ask that you pay the rate for undertakings rather than divine consultation."

Tirdad nodded. That amounted to a fifty-percent hike, but he had ex-pected those rates coming into this. Ashtadukht had told him that com-petition bade rogue star-reckoners to offer fees similar to what the empire imposed. He untied a pouch from his belt and handed it over, noting the too-long digits that raked the inside of the star-reckoner's sleeve as it accepted his payment. "Forget whatever formalities are involved," he said. The unknown had weighed on him long enough. "I'm interested in hearing it in full. Immediately."

"Here?" the star-reckoner asked, referring to their audience.

"Here's fine."

"I would be remiss in my service if I did not warn you of the danger of this information, especially in the hands of those who would wish you harm."

Tirdad glanced at Chobin, who offered a sinister grin. Of course he would. "Your warning has been noted. Now, if you would."

The star-reckoner took a seat, its slender legs showing signs of giving out as it did, and everyone present gathered around. The Eshm sister with the mangled arm drew up beside Tirdad as if she hadn't just made an attempt on his life.

"It all started with her sacred girdle," the star-reckoner began as if they were sitting around a campfire. "From what I could gather before you kicked me out, Ashtadukht had unwittingly created a phylactery of it over the years. With every knot, a little of her would be tied to the fabric. When you ended her life, the phylactery did what phylacteries do: it set to reviving her. Your blade seems to have obstructed its path, or perhaps it sought your blade because the phylactery was unfinished. That I could not ascertain. What I can tell you is that her soul was redirected partly to you, mostly to your blade. Having said that, I should make this clear: Ashtadukht is no more. You have preserved a mere shadow of the planet-reckoner. Her sentience is lost."

Tirdad interrupted by raising his palm. In the span of a few sentences his hopes had been summarily reinvigorated, then dashed. He turned a pensive frown on the blade, and began tracing it from end to end, watching with intensity as the splashes of iridescence danced at his touch. In a way, it was beautiful. He would have likened it to a black pearl if there were such a thing. He told himself that this was all that remained of her—that what he held was no mere sword, but a relic. Chobin gave his shoulder a squeeze. "Continue," he said without looking up.

The star-reckoner did as instructed. "The events had the effect of investing in you her access to the celestial theatre. Think of it as assuming her stamp seal. But the sword, having inherited the bulk of what was left of her, contains her control over planet-reckoning. Without it, you will be thrown into the heavens head first, and next time you will not be so lucky. So I strongly recommend you do as it said and never let go. Always keep it within reach." A contemplative pause. "You have become a planet-reckoner. I would say an unconventional one, but there is no established convention. So few and far between are they that most star-reckoners of our time are unaware the title exists at all." Another pause. "A planet-reckoner need not be a servant of the Lie."

"Planet-reckoner," Tirdad said. "How's that possible? I couldn't draw a lot if my life depended on it."

"Have you tried?"

"Well, no. But—"

"Do not try here."

"I hadn't planned on it. There's something else, though. I get glimpses of what I believe are her memories."

"What are we but the sum of our memories? She is a part of you, a part of the sword, so it is only natural."

Tirdad applied a white-knuckled grip to the blade, which was all too eager to draw the heat from his blood. "You're positive?"

"Yes."

One such memory had just come to him with excruciating precision. Smell heralded its arrival, reeking of blood and sweat and too much hatred for one person. The stench flooded his nostrils and stole him away like the incense of priests. What followed did so all at once. Blood, unmistakably metallic, clogged his nose and coated his mouth; it gurgled at the back of his throat. Wildfire spread through his lungs, one of which was crushed, shoved aside so that the claw that bore through his back could tease his heart. Pinned against hewn stone, his skull drummed where his many injuries found a splitting juncture. Fingers like leathery spider legs clamped his face in a cage, twisting his head and drawing it back such that he thought and hoped it'd be torn from his shoulders. Beneath them, the tears had become salty tracts, and the one eye he could see out of glared with untrammeled malice at the stars that had forsaken him—stars he had trusted and adored. He cursed them for their mockery, vowed to give their children their just desserts. This failure changed nothing.

He would smear the heavens with their souls, stain the windows an eternal vile. Through the ages, long after he had returned to dust, the stars would still have no choice but to observe the world through the gore of their chosen.

A white cowl leaned into his vision. "Am I losing you yet?" it asked with insincere concern. "Would that I could revive you and start anew— oh, but I guess we have already figured that one out for ourselves." It sunk its nails into his heart. Then the memory absconded, leaving Tirdad to sort through the aftermath.

Rage and hatred swelled within—some belonging to him, some the dream. Tirdad bellowed so loudly it rattled in his throat. He surrendered to the aftermath, and in one swift lunge his blade pierced the star-reckoner's cowl and emerged triumphant from the other side. Sparks popped and sizzled in its sleeves, remnants of a rejoinder that was cut brutally short.

"Good riddance," he spat, then planted his boot on the star-reckoner's chest to kick it free of his blade. The corpse folded backward, and its sleeves caught fire. Without giving it another thought, Tirdad lifted his sword and turned a circle, daring someone to challenge him. As he did, Chobin shuffled in to cover his rear.

"By Ohrmazd," said the marzban, doing his best to watch his half of the crowd, though he would have been fully aware his best wasn't good enough. "You are fucking full of surprises lately. Anything else you want to throw at me?"

Tirdad offered no reply.

The Eshm sisters had drawn their weapons, and though they emanated bloodlust, they were patently distant, heads askew and pupils dilated.

"Think this one through?" Chobin asked as they circled back to back, having found themselves back where they started.

"Less than I've ever thought anything through," Tirdad admitted.

"I can tell. What're they doing? Toying with us again?"

"Haven't the slightest, but it's off-putting."

In a round of hisses, the Eshm sisters broke their trance and retired in the direction of the corridor the pair had passed earlier, cursing and throwing down their weapons along the way. Only the leader remained.

"You're a lucky menstrual-fucker mhm," she said as she eased her arm back into the sling. "Get out of here before . . ." She bared her fangs, but not at anyone in particular. "Just get." She picked up the coin pouch meant for the star-reckoner, looked Tirdad square in the eyes, then went to join the others.

Tirdad wasted no time breaking into a sprint that his feeble torchlight couldn't hope to guide. He had gotten what he came for and more. Now, he wanted to put as much distance between him and this wicked castle as his lungs would allow. Once the head of the stork had disappeared around a bend in the gorge, Chobin took purchase on his arm and stopped him as true as an anchor.

"What the everliving fuck happened back there?" the marzban demanded.

Tirdad spun on him, torch throwing stark shadows on the glower that twisted his face. "Exactly what it looked like, Chobin. I shoved my blade through the skull of a star-reckoner. I smeared his soul across the heavens, and I can only hope the stars were watching."

Chobin wore an incredulousness unlike anything he had ever seen in the man. Planet-reckoner and marzban stood silent for a few heavy minutes that seemed to go on forever. The planet-reckoner was the one to fold.

"That . . . that thing!" Tirdad shouted, thrusting a shaking finger at the castle. Rage still coursed through him, which bled into his delivery. He let out a charged scream that went on until it cracked just to give the rage a chance to escape. With that, and under Chobin's unwavering scrutiny, he deflated. He was being judged. "If you'd seen what I saw," he said, which drew his face into a grimace. "If you'd felt it as if you were . . . as if you were her."

He dug his fingers through his hair, staring daggers at the sky. "What it did—"

Her heart had been in its dreadful grasp. In her chest. Something about that made it so much worse than if it'd been ripped out. The star-reckoner had no interest in killing her; it wanted to violate her.

Tirdad's stomach turned, and he lurched over to wretch, hands on his knees as it splattered the earth. He wiped his mouth on his sleeve without a care for his appearance. "Ugh."

He looked up at the marzban, whose judgment still had not been reached. "The things it did to her, Chobin. I just had to." His tone plainly read that he was sick of explaining himself.

The marzban expelled the sort of sigh a person uses when they have no desire to be cross with a person, but all the justification. He offered his waterskin. "What kind of person wears a cowl backwards?"

Tirdad took a swig, relieved to see the casual amusement once again honey his friend's features, even if they were fraught with concern. "The kind who walks into swords I imagine."

Chobin let out an uneasy laugh and slapped him on the shoulder. "Something is wrong with you."

III

WARAY TRIED TO SUCK IN a breath. And another and another and another. The trouble, she discovered, was in getting them to go down. Suffocating, she panicked, eyes wide and kicking her feet as she frantically scratched at her neck.

Try as she might, she couldn't get in. The gash that had so inelegantly drained her of her life had been reduced to a scar. So she dug her nails into her flesh in an attempt to rip the wound open and free the squirming mass that clogged her throat. Waray struggled for minutes, but the more she panicked, the more her lungs cried out, the less fight she could muster.

It wasn't long before her racing thoughts had slowed to a crawl. Waray pawed weakly at her neck where she had managed to rake out a few maggots. Then tranquility dethroned panic. She stared vacantly into the sun, though she didn't really see it. Her pawing ceased, and her futile breaths grew further and further apart until, quiet and alone, she died again.

Within seconds, her soul was shunted from her corpse. This had the effect of thrusting her into a world swathed in starling-black that stretched for eternity in every direction. Cage might have been a better term for it; it kept her in and everything else out. Waray couldn't see a thing—not even herself—but her connection to the world of the living remained. Through that, she could sense the Nasu buzzing around her.

They were the divs that polluted the body and soul after death if they weren't driven away by priests. She had seen them many times, and they had devoured her other selves after the forty-armed div struck them down. Nasu seemed to her the result of a fling between a crocodile and a fly, though as creative as her mind was she couldn't conjure the image of the two copulating. The logistics were a nightmare. But she had convinced herself that life had found a way. Even life with knobby limbs like runaway gout, soggy wings that had no business generating any amount of lift, and a snout flat and picketed. They buzzed irritably, unable to breach her cage.

Waray sat down, or thought about it anyway. Here, surrounded by curtains of starling-black, things were clearer than they had been in centuries. She remembered. She had been different back then, had—

She coughed up chunks of maggots and dried blood. "Šo-damned—" She cursed when it came back down to land on her face, and bared her fangs at what she believed to be a conspiracy orchestrated to have her eat maggots. Waray rolled over and struggled to get to her hands and knees. "Šo-damned cabal plotting like some . . . like some land over yonder with—"

A coughing fit had her littering the earth with everything she had managed to dislodge before dying, and wheezing all the while. When her esophagus was finally cleared, she threw an irritable hiss at the squirming mess. "—a compost heap."

Next thing she knew the breath was knocked out of her. As she fell over, she realized peripherally that she had been kicked, but was more concerned with losing the air she had finally tamed. She had worked so hard for it, too—died for it. Then it just fled like so much wind.

Having landed on her back, Waray made to spring away, but it turned out dying had done a number on her reaction time. The infantryman who had presumably kicked her was already driving his spear into her gut, which tore through her organs, severed her spine, and lodged in the ground. Pain like a falcon's curved beak ripping at her abdomen shot up her torso and latched onto her vocal cords. But before she could wail, her lineage rushed in.

A wave of heat swept over her flesh, the pomegranate-red of bloodlust swamped her vision, and enough adrenaline for thirty men coursed through her veins. The pain no longer registered. She bared her fangs, saliva dripping from her mouth, and snapped at the air.

"I'll make you slop for the broodmother!" she screamed. "I'll nap in your šo-steamy offal, then I'll shovel you into her gullet!"

"Seems to me it's the one what the traitor killed," said the infantryman. "Must have a phylactery."

"Aye," said another. "Take 'er apart. Legs first. They'll come right off like that."

As they dismembered her, she realized that not only was she speared to the ground, but her legs were paralyzed as well. It was a faraway realization all but drowned by her state, but it did have the effect of amplifying the fight in the parts of her body she did have control over. By time they had finished with her legs, she was gnashing her teeth and flinging drool, struggling with such ferocity that she was tearing her stomach free of the spear. But she was still the same crafty Waray. So when the infantryman slammed his boot into her face in an attempt to calm her down, she let him believe he had succeeded.

Control, even for a few fleeting seconds, didn't come easy; he had just given her blood. Hot, wet, tinny blood. Her mind swam in it.

"Mind 'er teeth," he said, coming to dig his knees into her forearm as if that would contain her. When the axe came down to cleave her arm, her heightened senses were free to roam its every familiar notch. Turned out they were chopping her to pieces with her own axe. Waray canted her head. The meaning of it eluded her, but she would pack it away in one of her many nests to revisit at a more suitable time. Then the axe bit almost clean through her arm.

In doing so, it spurred a spike of adrenaline that sliced through her daze as effortlessly as if it were silk. What followed would have been a blur to onlookers, and the infantrymen may as well have been onlookers.

Waray flexed her abdomen and shot up like the viper she was, just beneath the next swing. She registered somewhere along the way that it put her directly beneath the bit, but she didn't care. More than anything, that was what made an Eshm sister's bloodlust so formidable. Her fangs sunk into his neck, eliciting a muddy cry, while her working hand pulled the axe from his already failing grip. Her attention darted to the remaining soldier, whose second of shocked hesitation would soon mean his end. A grin like a waxing moon soaked in blood reached for one sanguine eye more than the other. Waray's heartbeat drummed madly in her ears, the soldier's failed in her fangs, and despite having torn both her torso free of the spear and her right arm from her shoulder, she felt giddy. She could topple the heavens.

She swung her axe into the infantryman's brow faster than he could react, leaving it there as if she'd just spent the day splitting firewood by the sweat of her brow. Something else to be stashed in a nest for later.

Then she closed her eyes and fell back, taking the soldier with her. She lay there basking in the warmth that showered her face. It invigorated her, but without a drive, her bloodlust was sloughing away faster than it could be sated. And where it retreated, the pain it had held at bay was quick to rush in. So much of her cried out that it all blended together.

Waray emitted a muffled cackle. By the sweat of her brow. Groans were all she had left in her after that, and far be it from the half-div to deny them after they'd queued so patiently. So she groaned and groaned until she bled out.

Until her soul was shunted again into the starling-black cage. Everything was the same as before, besides the sorry shape of her body, which she sensed as an incompleteness and nothing more.

She had been torn about this place the first two times she had waited here while her phylactery worked its magic to put her back together. Now that she was growing used to it, Waray decided she found it disconcerting. She figured no self-respecting cage would suffer an existence without bars. Come the annual cage summit the other cages would surely harangue it into finding some. (Held annually only because she was never certain whether biannual was going for once every two years or twice a year, proper usage be damned. Biannual made her itch something fierce.) This is what she told herself when the fear took purchase on her haunches, which was worsened by the fact that she had no haunches there.

Forgetting isn't about the everyday—everyday omissions are little more than red herrings. Forgetting sustains a person if done right. To not dwell on the tragedies, but to have the strength to remember at times. Those who dwell end up consumed by it. Those who lock the tragedies away do so with a piece of themselves.

Waray had forgotten because she couldn't have lived with the part of her that was responsible. She feared recollection more than any sword or divinity, more than any of her imagined threats. Here, she remembered it all. She was a—

She couldn't feel her legs. "Oh," she said, not bothering to look.

For a time, she gazed into the deceptively placid heavens. She star-hopped from star to flickering star, a method of navigating the night sky Ashtadukht had taught her before their travels took a turn.

"If you can find your bearings," she had said, "the rest will come easier. All you need is that one star you can always rely on. It'll guide you through the others."

Waray pondered those words as she made her way from constellation to constellation—even those with near-forgotten epithets that fought on the fringes of the celestial theatre. Patches in the sky glimpsed a contest of realities: one innocent, the other out for her blood. But she felt oddly reflective, oddly calm. Soon, roving between the insidious patches that prevailed upon the constellations, she began to wonder if the three of them as travelling companions had been her one star.

"Fuck," she said, pushing the body off and sitting up. Waray turned pursed lips on her mangled stubs, then the severed legs not far off. She cocked her head. "That šo-wretched phylactery. Legs are right there. Always knew phylacteries were bad news." She heaved a sigh and tested her reattached right arm. Though sore, it flexed.

She activated the pits in and around her nose, which bled tones of purple into her vision like the ink wash paintings of the Chini, and put them to work in scanning her surroundings. There were a few distant figures with torches that seeped oranges and whites in the breeze. "Bad news, bad news. Maybe." She crawled to retrieve her axe, sliding it into the loop on her belt. "They," she said, flexing her fingers in a claw and swinging it at the diffuse violet around her, "they say you survive with a phylactery. We didn't—" She blinked and knotted her brow. "Didn't need a phylactery until now. Then it goes and puts you together like some—" She planted one hand firmly in the dirt, and with a series of grunts, dislodged the spear that had impaled her earlier. "Like some šo-weary craftsman with his head on his workbench." While she complained, Waray used her trousers to make a bundle of her legs and the spear. "And maybe," she tilted her head, "maybe things aren't going so well. Maybe his shop is in shambles. Used to be a trade hub, but the road was diverted because of . . . don't know. Why's it matter why?" She slid one arm through the bundle and positioned it on her back, then set to crawling through the corpse-laden battlefield one hand at a time. "But a craftsman's a craftsman. Shouldn't forsake the craft. Should put legs on a person."

To anyone watching it would seem as if she were talking to herself. While that may be, her thoughts were directed at the phylactery only she could sense, where it lay at the far end of the field. "Anything less is just—" She posted on one hand, angling her head this way and that to check for warmer brushstrokes, then went back to crawling. "Just a šo-shameful insult to the craft."

Waray paused again sometime later, tongue giving her blood-stained fangs a series of deliberative prods. "Phylactery guild should intervene," she said at length. "Cause a row."

She pressed on until she reached an overturned litter. It had been stripped of its gold, leaving only a wooden frame under which Ashtadukht's belongings were strewn—anything that wasn't of value anyway. Mainly missives and maps. She wasn't interested in the litter so much as the phylactery hidden nearby.

Ashtadukht had bestowed upon her a lapis lazuli girdle that had become Waray's most prized possession. Waray had in turn made the decision to turn the girdle into her first phylactery. The act of vouchsafing a soul in an object or animal came naturally to intelligent divs, but she had never felt inclined to use it. That was until her dear friend had asked for her help, believed in her, and entrusted her with her dream of killing every last star-reckoner—even if it meant starting a war. Waray had wanted dearly to realize that dream because it meant not being alone. Instead, she had betrayed it.

A div had been slain in the vicinity, beneath which she could sense the girdle. That was likely the only reason it hadn't been looted. She worked an arm beneath, and after fumbling around for a moment, pulled the phylactery free. Waray held it up, allowing the moonlight to polish its striking blue gemstones scored with streaks of gold. A few were missing here and there, but it still brought a faint smile to the half-div's face to see those dull crow motifs. Holding it against her chest, she used her one arm to pull herself into the cover of the litter, where the deeper shadows harboured her like they did all of her kind.

"Better right my bum leg," she said as she removed her bundle and arranged her thighs to line up with her stubs. "Won't do to limp. Won't . . . hmm." She canted her head. "Maybe."

As she lay back, Waray wondered whether limps were the trappings of hardened heroes. Heroes who had accomplished much but whose better years were behind them. She was nothing if not old. "Keep the limp," she decided. Then the half-div took her axe in both hands and brought it down on her brow as hard as she could.

For a third time, the starling-black returned. She tried not to think about the bars it had forsaken, and in doing so forsook her distraction. This misstep gave her phylactery leave to fully restore a memory she had fought for so long to forget. It came to her with terrible fervour. She was Shkarag. She was a—

Shkarag stared at an empty, overturned throne. Tears welled in her eyes, and she tried so desperately to liken that throne to the thread of a tale worth spinning. She dragged trembling fingers curled into claws over the scales and scars of her scalp.

"Coward," she finished. She was a coward.

Beneath that litter, overturned like the nest she'd hidden the memory under for lifetimes, she wept from sunup to sundown. She damned herself for not having been the hero her long-dead sister deserved. The only reason she crawled from out her hole the next night was because she yearned for comfort food.

Shkarag didn't bother checking for danger; neither did she bother finding an intact pair of trousers. On her way out, she did take the time to gather the strewn documents into a sheaf, which she shoved between the girdle and her back. Spear over her shoulder, axe by her hip, she made for the hills.

"Eggs," she said as she limped along, snorting snot all the while. "Need some šo-scrumptious eggs."

Movement at the edge of her vision urged her into a crouch, which shot splintering pain down one leg. A grimace soured her features, but she endured it. The half-div cocked her head and cast a sidelong glance in the direction of the movement. Still and silence. Shkarag waited, scratching at the latest scar in her collection where it bifurcated her forehead. If there were something out there, she should have no trouble seeing it. But all the running ink showed her was the tract of shrub- and body-strewn land between her and Nishabhur. She emitted a nervous hiss and pressed on.

The movement returned immediately, only this time it was joined by a host of voices. They all murmured, intoned, crooned, and cried.

"You ran."

"SHE RAN."

"ترســـــو."

"Shewasyoursister."

"SHE'S TREMBLING."

"you ran!"

"CENTURIES.

". . . To betray such a sacred bond . . ."

"Should be agoner."

"Pathetic."

"ترســـــو."

"Coward."

"ترســـــو."

"You-abandoned-her."

"Trustedyou."

"COWARD."

". . . were to look out for one another. Always be . . ."

"lookither."

"You-did-this-to-her!"

"You were one."

"pitiful."

"Youshouldn't exist."

"ترســـــو."

"Coward!"

"SHE'S TREMBLING"

And she was. Shkarag had her spear in one hand, her axe in the other, but she couldn't keep them still. "Stop," came her brittle plea. "Stop . . . stop . . . stop."

Against her better judgment, which was already suspect, she cocked her head to peer into the night. Nothing. Her head fell further into its slant. She tried conventional eyesight.

Close enough for her heavy breathing to excite the worms and grubs that dangled from its porous flesh, a face vaguely like her own hovered before her. It tilted. The starling-black that trickled from its overlarge sockets disrupted the surface like ink encouraging wet paint to run. It tilted the other way. An exaggerated frown pulled at the corners of a maw that hung slack, broken fangs jutting out at unnatural angles.

Shkarag trembled. A hiss that bordered on a whine petered through her lips. She turned her head away, but her eyes were glued to it. It tilted yet again, and the voices redoubled their abuse. "I'm," she stammered, "I'm, I'm sorry. Forgive me."

She tried to back away, but tripped and dropped her weapons in doing so. Her cheek to the ground, one eye forced shut by dust, she still could not look away.

"Forgive you?" the voices said as one. "Sorry?"

The grime-encrusted semi-keeled scales that lined the top of its mask-like face became a chittering cascade. Where they splashed the earth, they transformed into greasy extensions that conspired to be hair but couldn't quite pull off the lie. Then, filthy tresses propelling it like a thousand spiteful snakes, it advanced.

If it were up to Shkarag's mind, she would have lain there paralyzed by a horror that had her heart in a vice. But her body reacted of its own accord, snatching up her spear and axe and high-tailing it for the hills. She didn't look back, not once.

Energized by the same shadows that closed on her, the half-div sprinted, stumbling and falling but never stopping, up the wrinkle of the nearest ridge. She followed crease after crease, maintaining her pace though shifting cobbles threatened to undermine every stride. Oftentimes, they would, but she would scarcely kiss the dirt before she was up again. To Shkarag, her cowardly mistake from so many thousands of moons ago had caught up to her. She had fled. She had betrayed her sister. Now, she fled from her comeuppance. The longer she did, the more the temperature dropped. Every now and then there would arise a lull in the abuse hurled by the voices, but before her exhaustion or the cold could sink in, they would return to grief her once more.

Cobbles and dirt were eventually smothered by the crunch of snow and the pale bite of the higher reaches. The voices faded to background noise. Her stressors came to a head, and cognizance fell by the wayside. Shkarag just went, unaware of her surroundings. The snow reached her bare knees, sinking its icy teeth in, and Shkarag oblivious all the while. She continued through the night, until the cobbles once again reduced the snow to patches that clung to the shadows thrown by the crest of the ridge. When at last the voices relented, the windows of the sky were blanching at the coming dawn. Drenched in sweat, Shkarag collapsed midway down. She was asleep before she hit the ground.

• • • • •

"Nngh," said Shkarag, waking up to an ache like white-hot needles embedded in her right thigh. "Heroes," she complained. "Šo-hardened heroes. A wonder they don't all retire."

She was already beginning to regret her eagerness to keep her limp. It seemed to her it'd gotten worse. Starting at the nasty scar where it'd been severed, Shkarag began kneading the scales and flesh of her thigh while soaking in her surroundings.

"Don't know any heroes," she said. She canted her head at an alpine accentor that darted by, taking note of where it landed. There prevailed a common belief that birds are altogether clever, and Shkarag had always wanted to have a word with the person responsible, because she thought birds were plain stupid. More often than not, she would hardly have to search for their clutches before the birds led her to them.

"Don't know any šo-hardened heroes. Or šo-this or šo-that heroes. Could use some pointers." She spied a bearded vulture circling overhead just outside the glare of the sun. Pupils contracting to a sliver, she glared back. "Not dead. Was dead."

Shkarag gave an exasperated shake of her head. "Vultures. Makes you wonder. Think they have a heroes guild somewhere? All those legends gathered around circling the fresh meat and showing the ropes. Like how to deal with a bum leg. Is there a root to chew?" She paused, cocked her head, then decided, "Maybe."

She stood with an exaggerated groan, though no one was around to hear it. Another glare at the vulture. It had heard. Only with the vulture probably not looking at her did she register that her clothes were in shambles. The infantrymen had cut the legs from her trousers, her tunic had one sleeve missing and a hole in the midriff, and all of it soiled with blood, sweat, dirt, eggs, piss, and shit. She sneered. She hadn't emptied her bowels until she killed herself. If only the phylactery had done its job the first time around.

"Eggs," she said, picking up her spear and setting off for the rock on which the accentor had last alighted. Shkarag poked around in the surrounding tussocks and crevices, eventually conceding what she'd known all along: breeding season was just around the corner. And the vulture would have a range too big to cover. She put her hands on her hips. "That's just as the crow flies," she said, confident in her use of the idiom.

Without the comfort of a fresh egg to sink her fangs into, Shkarag instead sank into a lousy mood. She ambled along, kicking up dust with the toes of her boots, back in the direction of the battlefield. At her pace it would take a few days.

Here and there, her surroundings tilted, demanding she adjust accordingly or suffer the consequences. That emboldened the nagging thoughts; it always did. But enduring the tilt would have been worse. She'd grown accustomed to this over her protracted lifetime, to always feeling as if she were at war with not only her surroundings but with herself. There had been times when even her sister had seemed to plot against her. It could not be overcome. Shkarag had accepted as much. She would endure it, or ignore it where possible. Mostly.

The half-div had never subscribed to the necessity of clothing, thinking it the product of an underhanded marketing scheme spread by tailors and merchants. Nevertheless, she was half viper. While not entirely ectothermic, her body temperature was less stable than that of a human. So she wore clothes, if begrudgingly. How she made it through the snow-capped ridge without so much as a winter cloak was anyone's guess, though it could be reasonably chalked up to fright.

She skirted the higher passes this time, which meant scaling many more ridges than she had during her flight. The first night would come and pass without the faintest whisper, but she maintained her inky refuge all the same. This led her to a slab of igneous rock that was waterlogged with a welcoming yellow. Eager to soak up the heat, Shkarag settled in to weather the cold.

The next day brought a much-needed respite. Not feeling especially vigilant, she hadn't bothered watching for signs of nests or birds to liven her mood. But she happened to drag her downtrodden stare from her increasingly vexing limp at the right time to spot a vulture nest. Disbelief plain, she canted her head and narrowed her eyes. Half-way up a sheer rock wall, the nest clung to an outcropping. She hadn't bothered searching for it because bearded vulture territories ranged hundreds of farsangs. It would have been like searching for a beetle in a salt flat.

A tempered grin coloured her cheeks. She had long ago learned that the world has a habit of throwing you a bone—or an egg—to keep you suffering another day. She had thereafter concluded suffering was the currency of the universe. Why else would the luminaries wage their eternal wars? Or mortals for that matter? Some would claim it is the work of the Lie, of Ahriman, and she surrendered that point. Be that as it may, the nature of the currency went unchanged. What she wanted to know was what was bought with all this suffering. Or did it all go to a nest egg?

Setting that aside with a flex of her fingers, she approached the cliff, hefting her spear for a throw. A vulture with blood-stained feathers stood guard atop a large nest of sticks covered in animal parts. It was situated at a perilous enough height that her phylactery would have to mend her bones if she fell, so Shkarag meant to avoid a fight while dangling from the cliff face. To that end, she drew the spear back, put one arm forward, broke into a trot, then let it fly. And it flew true, skewering the vulture. A clean kill.

Now to snatch the eggs before the mate returned. Shkarag immediately set to scaling the cliff, finding the nooks and crevices she needed to make a hasty climb to the nest. There, she withheld a whoop at her luck, and quickly set to her task. She reached around to pull free the documents she'd taken, then used them to roll up the pair of wheat-colored eggs. She hurriedly removed her spear from the vulture, and used a length of trousers to secure it and the eggs in one package, then stowed that beneath her girdle.

The tangle of sticks, bones, and sun-dried viscera drew a frown. "You're too much," she figured. "Can't dislodge you. Missing tools and time."

Shkarag gave the nest the same wistful caress she would have given a loved one. "Too much." As she did, her chin puckered and her lip trembled. She missed them. Then she was gone, hurrying down the cliff face and breaking into a run the instant her boots hit the ground.

Once she made it over the next crease in the range, she returned to her ambling gait—if marginally less so. The half-div unwrapped the larger of the two eggs with a touch that was trained but not all that delicate. She held it in one hand while the other studied its chalky texture. This one would have been her sister's share. So rather than savour the taste, she bit into it, shell and all, such that the pieces stabbed at her gums and tongue while the contents slid down her throat. It hurt, but she hummed all the same. A brief yet painful treat was right. Shkarag popped the rest into her mouth, certain to chew the shell. Later, she could savour her share.

Content in her small triumph, she pressed on.

The following night wasn't kind enough to afford her a warm slab to sleep on, so she walked through it rather than wallow in an uncomfortable chill. Besides that, she was doubly nocturnal as both div and viper. The bleeding purples and red-violets of ink wash suited her. And when she was feeling more confident, the glimmering of the stars and planets.

"Wonder where Ashtadukht burrowed off to?" she asked the planets. The half-div canted her head, stroking the oblique scar that connected her jaw on one side to her clavicle on the other. "Should find her. Maybe."

For the remainder of her trip, which crested ridge after ridge as if they were waves passing beneath her, she pondered that thought.

Shkarag was relieved to find the battlefield still. The soldiers, looters, and priests must have finished canvassing, because all that was left were the remains of divs. That was all well and good because she had some looting of her own to do, and what she had in mind would be of no interest to humans. She made her way down, the stench of death washing over her a morbid reminder of her childhood, and began her search.

While there weren't many Eshm sisters in the div host, it didn't take her long to find one. Their blood-red armor stood out even amidst the carnage. Shkarag approached the corpse uncharacteristically solemn. She went to her knees and gazed at her half-sister's face. The jaw had been pulverized, probably by a mace or hoof, but she recognized it. Hesitation moored her. So she just stared until the hesitation eased enough for her to lean in and caress the ridged scales above her half-sister's ear.

"Sorry," she said. "Whole šo-wretched universe hates us. Like we're some . . ." She trailed off before she could finish the thought. "I'm sorry."

In truth, her half-sisters had been good to her in their own way. They had accepted her and her sister despite their alloyed lineage. In seeking to extirpate her frail humanity, they had perhaps gone too far in brutalizing her. Had damaged her irreparably. But that's the thing: they hadn't done so out of malice. The Eshm sisters brutalized one another regularly, constantly pounding out any sign of weakness so that they could survive an existence without allies. It was them against the world.

For the longest time, Shkarag had firmly believed that was why she despised them. With her sharpened memories she knew that wasn't the case. All that loathing had sullied their image because every time she saw them she was reminded of how she'd betrayed her sister.

"Sorry," she repeated, countenance strained. "You broom sweepers were good to us. Tried to prepare us for the oncoming storm. I'm the bad egg. Such a . . ." She trailed off again, fighting the urge to ramble, and let out a sigh. Shkarag began stripping the corpse of its gear.

Once that was taken care of, she disrobed—if it could still be called as much with what little remained of her rags. Labouring to keep her thoughts from taking a dive, she focused on the task at hand.

"Trousers first," she decided. The half-div held them out appraisingly. She avoided black for a simple enough reason: she thought it veered too closely to the windows of the night. Something about that didn't sit well with her. As if the colour had designs beyond its station. "You're lucky," she said, extending her arms to get a better view. "The dirt debases you,

I think. Like you kowtowed to the sky. It remonstrated you something fierce, but never let it be said the sky has no clemency." With that, she nodded and slipped them on.

Next came the caftan, which she plucked from the pile without fuss, then swung it by the collar, causing it to billow dramatically as her arms found the sleeves. She fastened one end over the other, then flexed her arms. The sleeves were tight, but not uncomfortable. Shkarag gave it a once over, cocking her head as she did. Caftans were by make form-fitting, but this one hugged her figure with refined sleekness, with a hem that rounded smoothly across the hips. Shkarag cocked her head further and patted the caftan as she had seen Tirdad do during his daily routine. She figured it drove the lice away. "That'll do," she said, bending to retrieve the hauberk. "Bloody caftan, bloody mail, bloody cuirass. What'll they bloody next?"

"Bet," she went on as she pulled the hauberk over her head, "bet they'll want bloody undergarments next. Can't blame em. Nothing beats a šo-good fuck."

She tugged at the cuffs of her caftan to adjust it under the short sleeves of the mail, then did the same with its sweeping hem. A bunched caftan was a maddening caftan.

The cuirass was held at arm's length for a moment of evaluation, but she had already made up her mind. An embossed viper constricted its sanguine gloss, fangs bared where its diamond-shaped head was sculpted into the left shoulder. She strapped it on without further consideration. The bottom rim hardly protected half her midriff, but in doing so it allowed her more maneuverability.

When she'd called the items bloody, she'd meant something more than the river of red that parted around the caftan's diamond motif, or the sheen of the cuirass. For the armor to be crafted, every Eshm sister was charged with providing the blood of both a human and a div with which it would be imbued. That's what gave them their signature colour. And that's why they hadn't been looted.

Shkarag finished with laminated thigh and forearm armor, then tied the ensemble together with her weapon belt and prized lapis lazuli girdle.

She had decided against taking her half-sister's weapons in the event that somewhere out there a lackadaisical phylactery had just remembered its charge. So she did her best to work a sword into each of the cold, scaled hands of the corpse.

Rather than leaving, Shkarag hovered there, head canted and trained on the ruined face.

"Is this all you were after they slaughtered you?" she asked the memory of her sister. "An overripe lime, fallen and forgotten and—"

She clenched her eyes shut to stave off the tears and groped for her vulture egg, rushing to pierce it with one fang. The anxiety that had drawn her muscles taut sloughed away at that first crisp crack. The scraping of the shell along her fang soothed her. It retracted toward her mouth, puncturing a second hole from within. Then she threw her head back and let it hang there, savouring the sliver of yolk that oozed over her tongue.

Once the egg had run dry, she tossed it aside, bade her half-sister farewell with a dismal wave, and set off in search of Ashtadukht.

Thing is, she hadn't the faintest idea where to look.

· · · · ·

Tirdad took a generous draught of wine. Heady and bittersweet, it went down with a warmth that dulled the ache in his bones.

"Almost there," said Chobin, palm out expectantly.

"Almost," agreed Tirdad, taking another draw before relinquishing the wine. He raised his eyebrows and wiped his face. The haze of intoxication had floated in without him realizing it. "I've decided," he said. "I promised I'd discuss it when we returned, and here we are." He spread his arms wide, indicating the sea to his left and mountains to his right, all but invisible on a moonless evening were it not for the profiles that demarcated the sky.

The estate wasn't far off. That struck him as . . . well, he couldn't quite figure how it struck him, only that it did. Had history not veered so sharply in the direction of tragedy, someone else might have called it home. But it had. Ashtadukht's estate belonged to him now. He had no way of knowing how much she'd loathed the place, how often she'd considered torching it.

"And what have you decided?" Chobin asked with a hint of a slur. "Fucking arms out like you are putting on a grand speech. I sure as fuck don't hear it."

Tirdad grinned and tapped his head. "You should've heard it in here. I thought it was mighty convincing, and I'm a tough crowd."

"Now listen here," Chobin said, raising his fist in mock anger. "Been waiting the whole ride back. So help me if you put it off one more minute you will wish . . . you . . ." He squinted long enough for exasperation to kick in. "Fuck it," he said, tossing his hands. "Lost my train of thought."

"A world deprived of the wisdom of the great Chobin, tall as a cypress, strong as a lion, virile as a bull, wise as a—"

"Shut the fuck up."

"—shoot of fig."

"What?"

"I've decided," Tirdad began as he drew his long sword and lay it across his lap, "that I'm a planet-reckoner."

Chobin blew air out his nose. "You decided that?"

"Well, no." Tirdad allowed his fingers to drift over the blade, caressing its heartbeat. "You're right. It was decided for me. But it needn't be a curse. It's what you do with the power that defines it."

An affirmative grunt to his side.

"I'll use this sword to carve out some good in the world. That's what she did before things went . . ." He gestured vaguely. "Before."

"And the planet-reckoning?"

"I'll figure it out."

"How?"

"It'll come to me."

The look that Chobin threw Tirdad's way spoke for how full of shit he sounded.

"It will," Tirdad said, not all that convinced and sounding it. He watched his blade as it devoured the light thrown by Chobin's torch, tearing it into the pearlescent waves that livened its surface. "If it doesn't, I'll do without. The sword will suffice."

"Your tales never involved many spells. Seems to me she got by on her knowledge," Chobin figured.

Tirdad gave a slight nod, and a nostalgic smile crept ever so faintly up his cheeks. "Oh, there was a great deal of luck involved. Bad and good. Bumbling, too. But she knew her craft and took pride in that. Hard-earned pride as far as I can tell."

The quiet that ensued did so in the pursuit of a question that had hung unspoken between the pair since Castle Dahag. Chobin, generally a man as frank as they came, harboured no small amount of sympathy and love for his friend. He wanted to broach the topic without accusation. "And how well is that?" he asked.

"Well."

"Hmm," grunted the marzban.

Tirdad pulled in a breath, inviting the brackish air to do its part in stirring long-dormant memories. He recalled giggling blithely as his brother gave chase, scrambling under branches and through brush, splashing across silver streams. With his illness weighing on him like a wet wool blanket, it didn't take long for his brother to catch up.

"Ashta," Gushnasp said, his tone both amused and admonishing.

"I—" He tried to say, but a wheezing fit doubled him over. "I won't—" The wheezing refused to relent. He felt as if he'd been beaten half to death, but at the same time as if it were routine. Gushnasp eased him to the forest floor, dry leaves complaining but bringing him closer to the earthy scent so at home in his life. "Won't sit around when we'll be separated soon," he finally managed to get out between wheezes. He followed with a weak half-chuckle, half-wheeze. "I'm dizzy."

"Of course you are."

"I like this," he said, digging his fingers into the earth.

"Of course you do."

He raised tired eyes to meet Gushnasp's, which were framed with the furrows of concern. A lump rose in his throat, unease in his chest.

His brother took a seat beside him, and began rubbing his back in the placating way he had since before he could walk. The hand that massaged him had grown powerful since. It pressed calmness into his soul.

"You will be fine," Gushnasp offered, reading him perfectly. "You are strong, and we will find time to see one another until you have finished your training."

"Strong," he said, dripping with sarcasm.

"You are," Gushnasp replied, his tone brooking no argument. His brother made a mess of his hair then, saying, "Here." Then he placed his other hand on his chest, warm and steady. "And here."

His heart leapt in his throat. He blushed furiously, and an utterly sincere smile claimed his cheeks so thoroughly they grew sore.

Tirdad forced the memory out, knowing full well what had next transpired on those noisy leaves. He glanced over at Chobin, who had a contemplative look turned his way. "Her memories are mine now," he explained. "Not to be referenced at will, but dredged up through necessity or outside forces. Just now, the scent of the sea showed me something I couldn't have known. Something intimate."

"Forgive me if I am skeptical," the marzban said, doing his utmost to convey sympathy in his criticism, "but this could all be your imagination fucking with you."

"It could. It isn't."

"Or the wine."

"Where'd you get this exactly?"

Chobin's only reply was to wink while wearing a sly smirk.

"The star-reckoner confirmed as much," Tirdad added with a shake of his head.

"Right before you killed it."

"Yeah," said the planet-reckoner. "I killed it. That's why you're having trouble coming to terms with this. That's the real issue here. And I don't fault you for it, not in the slightest." He eased his sword back into its sheath, guiding it with his thumb in what amounted to a good night, and his palm came to rest on its ram's head pommel. "It must've seemed like I'd gone mad at the time, but I killed it because it was right about her memories."

"So what the everliving fuck did it do?"

"Terrible things," Tirdad said, searching the darkness ahead. He spoke softly, but with an edge that'd been stropped to the point of hatred. "Things no one should have to endure."

He knew that wouldn't be enough, so he related in that deadly-soft tone all he'd seen and felt before putting an end to the star-reckoner. The conversation ended there. They navigated the plain in pensive silence, Chobin patently unable to put together a response because he was both ashamed and disgusted.

That suited Tirdad. He needed time to simmer. Relating meant remembering, and that meant reliving the experience in all its horrific detail. The reins creaked in his white-knuckled grasp. Would that the star-reckoner were still alive just so he could run it through a second time.

"So," Chobin began after a nightjar had darted by, ending their well-kept silence with its telltale trill. "How do you plan to achieve this 'planet-reckoner for good' angle?"

Tirdad shrugged. "To be honest, I don't know. I'd like to continue to root out divs for the good of the nation. Ashtadukht meant well in that, and Truth be revered I enjoyed it."

"You mean to travel as she did?"

"Yeah."

"And how the fuck do you mean to convince the star-reckoners, or the King of Kings for that matter?"

A sly smile of his own accompanied Tirdad's answer. "I don't."

"Hah!" Chobin punctuated the shout by slapping his thigh. "You fucker. Where has this Tirdad been all these years? I fucking love him!"

"I've been here by your side all along." The planet-reckoner gazed wistfully into the night. "But you had eyes for another."

The marzban burst out laughing. One gloved hand gave his thigh a series of emphatic slaps while the other offered the wine. "Take it," he insisted, giving the wineskin a shake as if it'd have the same allure as a topless dancer. "I want to hear more."

Tirdad needed no encouragement. He accepted, raising it in salute to his friend, and drank with gusto. Moderation, he decided, had gotten him nowhere enviable. It'd gotten him here.

• • • • •

With only a short rest before dawn, the pair reached the estate as the sun reached its zenith.

"Glad you cleaned the place up a bit," Chobin said as they traversed the forecourt, flanked by gardens in bloom, busy with bees and birdsong. He took a whiff and grunted his approval. "Almost drowns out the fucking stench of saltwater."

"I enjoy the smell," Tirdad evenly replied.

The marzban leaned over the head of his mount to inspect the path they followed. "Weeds could use some tending to. You sure you pulled them up before you left?"

"Yeah."

"Something bother—oh, hah! What are you now, fifty? Hangover must be brutal."

"Forty-five," said Tirdad. He dismounted, then went through the motions of tending to his horse and gathering his gear. When that was taken care of, he lumbered into the vestibule with the timeworn ram mural. "I'm going to sleep," he called over his shoulder, planting his hand on the plaster painting for support. Tirdad paused to consider it. His heart drummed painfully behind his eyes, but he wanted to take a moment to appreciate the image of the ram. Such a noble creature. And like the family it represented, it was fading from existence. He gave it a pat and moved on. "I'll see about getting you restored. You shouldn't suffer for our mistakes."

Merry with amusement, Chobin sounded off from the forecourt. "Drink some water!"

"I know," Tirdad grumbled, grimacing at the nausea that washed over him.

"Off to fetch something fresh!" Chobin cried.

Tirdad just groaned. Had the man never been hungover before? Why in the seven climes was he yelling? He passed into the courtyard with its modest three-sided dome and headed over to the bubbling fountain housed within. Tirdad splashed his face and drank generously—it was crisp and invigorating, and now justified his decision to unclog it during

50

his mourning period. There was a long list of repairs that needed taking care of, but he figured his ancestors' ingenious method of tunnelling into the mountain aquifer for irrigation should be given due regard.

With a newfound appreciation for his handiwork, he made for the living quarters. One of the first things he'd done after the estate had been cleansed was to clear out the carpet of eggshells, so he was in the middle of slipping off his boots when he stepped through the door.

And he stopped dead in his tracks. There stooped over a splintered table in the centre of the room a familiar div. While its exact physique was a mystery, the unhealthy coat of ashen fur could not obscure its bulging muscles. In one hand—large and strong enough to pop his head like a grape—it clutched a wooden spoon.

So that's why Ashtadukht had kept a random wooden spoon. He thought she'd left the phylactery with the old star-reckoner. Come to think of it, she'd probably killed him, too.

Wearing only the one boot, Tirdad drew his sword. It throbbed weakly in his grip, but with a palpable hunger, as if it sensed the prey in front of it. Cautiously, he took a few steps back until he was nearly around the corner. That's all he got.

The div turned on him a face like a mudslide. With inhuman speed it crashed through the wall in a spray of gypsum mortar, barrelling into him with its musclebound bust and taking him through the next wall. He careened end over end across the courtyard until he collided with the opposite side.

"Ugh," he groaned, pushing himself off the ground with one arm, which lit a fire in his chest and back. He'd felt a series of cracks along the way, and figured his ribs hadn't come out unscathed. What's more, his left shoulder had been dislocated. "Fuck," he spat.

Before he had time to consider his next move, the div was once again hurtling his way. This time, he managed to leap aside before it crashed through the mortar directly behind him, throwing up a cloud of dust and rubble. Coughing, Tirdad got to his feet.

"Chobin!" he cried out, hoping the marzban hadn't ventured out of earshot. "Chobin!"

He cast about for his sword, relieved to find it by the fountain he had so blithely left not a minute earlier. Too far, he knew, and the div would be the least of his worries. He scrambled over and snatched it up just as the div stepped through the new entrance it'd made.

One arm hanging limply, ribs in a bad way, Tirdad had his sword at the ready. He wouldn't be caught on his heels this time around. The div surged forward, bellowing as it did, with saliva flying like repulsive seafoam in every direction. It had its arms out, meaning to sweep him up again—surely to drive him through another wall.

Tirdad evaded by shuffling aside and ducking under a bicep that could probably take his head off if it tried. As he did, he brought his sword across the div's gut, and with only one arm behind it, the blade cut clean through with no resistance. As though the marrow, sinew, and entrails would rather come apart willingly than hazard the magpie-black.

Pivoting as it passed, Tirdad could hardly believe his eyes. He'd nearly hewn it in half, and surely would have if his blade were longer. Too busy trying to hold in its guts to control its charge, the div's momentum brought it head over heels onto its back, on which it skidded to a messy halt. Torso twisted backward, it did what it could to scoop its tangled organs back in, which was futile. Tirdad grimaced, but not due to his injuries. The div exuded the sort of stink that would make stone queasy. He summarily finished it off, then wiped his sword on its coat, but didn't sheath it. Better not risk staining the scabbard with its stench.

"What the everliving fuck?" Chobin strode in, sword and board hanging by his sides. "Heard your shouts. Came as quickly as I could. Why is there a div here?" Then, with an enthusiasm that suggested he'd breached protocol and forgotten the most important part, he gave Tirdad a slap on the back. "Hah! Took it down without me you fingernail-swallowing—"

Tirdad tensed, either unable or unwilling to speak over the splash of pain excited by the slap. So he groaned.

"—what?"

"I think . . ." The planet-reckoner exhaled through his teeth. "I think it cracked a few ribs."

The marzban whistled. "Sorry about that. Let's—"

A sudden blow sent Chobin soaring over the courtyard wall and out of sight. The div, fully healed but with its top and bottom halves reversed, had shot up within striking distance. A snarl was the only prelude to the cross it threw at Tirdad. He managed to bob and weave beneath the boulder of a fist, swinging his sword in an arc that severed the arm at the elbow as he came up.

Unlike fighting foes with conventional weapons, many divs were a matter of dodging and retaliating—parrying and blocking didn't quite do the trick. Tirdad had learned as much in his travels, but the blade ached for less dodging and more retaliating. The moment's hesitation cost him a dodge, and rewarded him with a blow to the abdomen.

It knocked the air from his lungs, and his blade rattled on the stone. He staggered back a step, but that was all he got before the div followed up with an uppercut to the chest, throwing him up and into the dome above the fountain. Before gravity could take hold, the div pinned him there, its palm pressed against his sternum.

He screamed.

Not one long, unbroken scream, but a string of cries limited to the paltry breaths he could suck in. The div would have crushed his ribcage like a walnut.

If a spear hadn't been thrust between its eyes.

Tirdad fell, bouncing off the div as he did and ending up on his back beside the fountain. With a wince that would stick around for weeks, Tirdad fought to sit up, but could only manage to post himself on one elbow. Turns out, he wasn't as close to the fountain as he'd thought. What he'd heard was an Eshm sister; more specifically, the squelching of her axe as she hacked at the div. She tossed the div's head, then started on its limbs.

"What're . . . what're you doing?" he asked.

"Chopping," the Eshm sister replied, patently irritated by the question. She stopped to indicate the half-severed limb with both hands the way a person does when your answer is right in front of you, you fucking dunce. A few more chops and an arm was flung aside. She was mumbling to herself between swings, but he couldn't make out what she was saying. He could hardly make her out as it was.

An attempt at a deep breath proved ill-advised when it stabbed at his lungs, but he needed to be sure Chobin was safe. "Chobin!" he yelled. "Chobin!" As he called, he inched his way toward his sword, which he hadn't even needed to search for. He could feel its presence now. By time he retrieved it, the Eshm sister was nearly finished. "Chobin!" he yelled again. "Chobin!" The planet-reckoner sidled up the nearest wall for support, and laid the blade across his lap. A hairy leg landed beside him.

The Eshm sister limped over, and it was only then that he got a good look at her. What he saw stole his breath away same as a knee to the gut had—more, even. The armor had thrown him off at first, but there was no doubt about it: this was Waray. She sported some gnarly new scars—most notably one that profaned her neck—but it was her. She seemed different somehow. Something about her carriage; something in her blood-red gaze as she approached.

"Howdy your damn self," she hissed at the wooden spoon she held between two fists, straining to snap it in half, and eventually succeeding. She tossed it at his feet. "Burn the šo-wretched phylactery. I think."

"Waray," he finally managed. "How did—"

"Shkarag."

He had questions, but the intensity of her stare drove them away. That stare continued, unblinking, until she asked what she'd traveled all this way to ask.

"Did you kill her?" She lowered her spear so the tip prodded his chest. She canted her head. "Did you?"

He smiled. The timing was abysmal, but he thought he'd seen the last of her idiosyncrasies. Yet here she was worse for wear but alive. Alive! He didn't care how. But the question remained, and she deserved the truth. "Yes," he said at length.

The spearhead pressed harder, then she jerked it back as if she would run him through. It clattered to the ground.

The high-pitched hiss she emitted defied any he'd ever heard. Any he'd hear as long as he lived. Lamentation poured out of her as if the thread of her soul unwound with it. As if she were coming undone.

Her knees buckled, but before they could commit, she staggered off, raking at her head. In his sorry state, Tirdad could only watch and await her judgment. With one hand clawing at the scar that ran from her temple and above a nipped ear, her other pulled out her bloodied axe to channel her emotions into feverish chops that found only air.

The dreadful hiss persisted without interruption as she paced away, then doubled back in a stalk that was unmistakably bloodthirsty, only to cock her head and turn back before she reached him. This went on for an indeterminate time. Long enough for Chobin to appear in the doorway, favouring one leg but ready to strike. Tirdad shook his head and raised his palm. The marzban furrowed his brow confusedly, but ultimately shrugged and took a seat.

Eventually, Shkarag stalked over less aggressively to stand before him, chest heaving. She swung her axe, though patently uncertain about it. "Who," she began, canting her head, "who decides, who says, who šo-fucking—" She dragged a hand contorted into a claw over her head, and swung her axe again. "Who kills someone they love?"

Tirdad frowned. He hadn't expected such a trenchant question, the very same he'd been flagellating himself with for the last few months.

"Who?!" she asked, screaming at the top of her lungs. "Who decides to? Who spends their šo-damned life with a person, not this person or that person or some other person but this one person, this one, then just, like some, like some—" She hissed. Another swing. "Turns their back on their love like some dastardly cliff face. And they're circling you and they don't understand why if you're a cliff face they can only see your back. Why, you pinecone-arsed Dourboat-sodomizing coward? Why would you betray your sist . . . er . . . ?"

The half-div gasped. Her lips moved, but whatever words they were forming were for her alone. She stared through him.

"I . . . made a mistake," Tirdad said, avoiding eye contact as he did. "A terrible mistake I'll surely regret for the rest of my life." He absently traced the edge of his blade. "At the time, I was too caught up in honour. But the truth is she was injured, Shkarag. And ready for it to be over."

"Sister," the half-div whispered. She gave her axe a lame look, canting her head away from him in shame. "Ashtadukht."

"Yeah," he said. Hoping the situation had been defused, he pulled himself to his feet. "About, uh—" He grimaced and rubbed his neck. "About killing you . . ."

"An accident," Shkarag said. "My fault." She glanced up at him, head tilted slightly. "You said some, said I was a hero."

"You were."

The tilt deepened. "Want to cleave your šo-double-crossing skull something fierce. All this pomegranate-red bullying like some overprotective sisters who tear you apart to make you stronger. But what about attrition?"

"I'd really rather you didn't."

"Want it, but . . ." She stepped closer, emanating the bloodlust he'd come to recognize and respect. "Maybe."

Tirdad gripped the hilt of his blade, though he knew he didn't stand a chance. Across the way, Chobin got to his feet.

"But . . ." She moved in, and in one swift movement, hugged him. "All I have left is some pinecone-arsed quack."

An audible sigh of relief escaped Tirdad. His ribs cried out at her attention, but far be it from him to deny her when the alternative was death.

"What a šo-wretched lot to draw," she said. "Šo-wretched. To end up with only a quack." She hugged harder. "The fish head or the egg you forgot in the bottom of your sack and come to find it's rotten and you wasted all that effort searching for it those months back. But it's all you have left."

"Thanks."

She nodded or canted her head. He couldn't tell.

"Could you let me go?"

Shkarag obliged, putting some space between them and stowing her axe. Having deprived them of its haft, her fingers flexed and loosened continuously. The dangerous glint had not left her eyes.

"Need to see this," she said, reaching behind her to pull out a roll of leather and paper. It creaked and bunched in her trembling grip. "Maybe."

Tirdad furrowed his brow. She'd offered him a blood-stained mess. "What's this?"

Her reply carried an uncommon gravitas. "Everything."

IV

E VERYTHING?" TIRDAD GRUMBLED. "I can't make heads or tails of this nonsense."

Shkarag stared at him from across the room where she sat, legs out straight, bathing in a pocket of sunlight. She canted her head, but offered no explanation.

He indicated the leaves of leather and parchment that were spread around him, wincing at the movement. "Rubbings, correspondences, seal impressions, maps . . . I don't know what I'm looking at, Shkarag."

"Everything." Her eyes flicked away briefly, and the accompanying nod seemed more for herself than him. She answered his exasperated stare with one of her own. "Maybe."

Their contest lingered for an uncomfortable stretch until Tirdad heaved a sigh, turning his attention back to the mess.

The trouble with rib injuries is that there isn't much to be done about them but rest. So after having Chobin set his arm he'd tried to do just that. Between the pain and this sudden turn of events, he couldn't sleep a wink. So he'd spent the last few hours going over the contents of the bloody bundle Shkarag had brought him. Only a fool would have expected something straightforward from the half-div.

Tirdad chuckled and shook his head. "I'm nothing if not a fool."

"Šo-foolish," she agreed.

"Well," he said, "fool or not, why won't you help? You handed these over as though I needed to see them, but all you've done since is sit around."

"Not won't." Shkarag finally looked away, wearing an enigmatic expression. "Can't." Her eyes roamed the wilds beyond the window.

Tirdad reclined, trying and failing to find a comfortable position. Relieved as he was to see her alive, he'd forgotten how irksome she could be where answers were concerned. So he waited.

"There's," she said at length. "There's—" Agitation plain, she held one hand in a claw by her head. "Ashtadukht explained. She preached like some . . . like some god declaring light is here, here is Everything. And she moved her hands like so." Shkarag swept her other hand as though spreading a map. "But I was . . ." Her hand flexed. "Overcast."

"I see," said Tirdad, and strangely enough, he did. "We shouldn't have introduced you to drugs. It's beneath you. I should've objected in earnest."

"Nothing's beneath me. And phylactery fixed the need." Shkarag got to her feet, sneering and muttering something unintelligible about phylacteries as she did. She limped over and picked a roll of parchment from the spread. "Need help?"

"No," he replied, deadpan.

"Oh." She dropped the parchment.

Tirdad tossed his hands, though they didn't get higher than his shoulders before his ribs denied him the gesture. "Of course I fucking need help. Why in the seven climes would you even have to ask?"

Shkarag cocked her head, but Tirdad was certain she wore an almost imperceptible smile. He'd missed her impishness.

"Chopped me to pieces with my own axe," she mused in a conversational manner as she unrolled the parchment.

If she was joking, it was unreadable. Her gaze flicked over the page either gainlessly or in a wondrous method of reading. "I'm not sure I follow," said Tirdad.

"Cleaved my legs and arm."

"What?"

"Clean off." Shkarag canted to consider, then went on conversationally. "No. Not clean. Šo-untidy cleaving. Poetic using my own axe, I think. Maybe."

A moment's speechlessness delayed his response while he watched her eyes dart erratically over the missive. When at last he managed to reply, it was thick with concern. "Poetic? That's terrible, Shkarag."

She stared straight at him. "A bit."

He blinked.

She stared.

He picked up a strip of leather, pointedly ignoring her crooked grin.

Patently satisfied with his reaction, Shkarag took a seat. The parchment crinkled in her hands. "They did," she said.

To Tirdad, her grim profile and the reality behind her joke made her seem almost human—as if those scales were a façade to be moulted away under the right conditions. He loathed that prejudice. Rare though they were, these moments should have enlightened him decades ago. It was never the case of her becoming less div, but of him becoming a better person.

Overcoming his reluctance, he reached out to rub her back. She straightened, inhaling sharply, but rather than her scales, he was pleased to see her tension slough away. Minutes passed, and there prevailed the whisper of a breeze adorned with birdsong.

Eventually, Tirdad broke the silence. "You've changed," he said, pondering the indiscriminate scars that befouled scale and flesh, the ear missing its tip. "You seem more sure of yourself . . . more here. Your carriage."

"Limp?"

"Well, not exactly. You're more confident, but more troubled."

Shkarag scratched at her neck. "Before the šo-wretched truths were—" She angled her head so that she was peering at him through the corner of her eye. "—at the edges."

"And now?"

The half-div turned, planting her hand on the plaster behind him and drawing so close he could smell the eggs on her breath. "Here."

Under different circumstances, it might've been provocative, and irresistibly so. The red in her eyes had been all but swallowed up by her dilated pupils. Her lips were parted enough for him to see the curve of her fangs. Her chest heaved. She trembled.

That image was sullied by what hung over her. It had no form or footprint, no indication it existed at all besides her composure, but it was incontrovertibly ugly.

Chobin cleared his throat from where he stood in the wrecked doorway, grinning widely. "So . . . should I leave?"

Their heads swiveled.

He lifted a sack in one hand, running his other through his fleece-like mop of hair. "Got the roots. Had I known you were the sort of friends who fuck I would've grabbed something for that. Still, should take something for the pain or you won't be much use to her."

"Oh, come off it," Tirdad said, shaking his head at his friend's casual crassness. "We're not up to anything untoward. She was—"

"Here," Shkarag finished, or thought she did, whipping face-to-face once more.

"—explaining in her weird way."

That had the effect of a slap to the face. She drew back, incredulous.

Chobin shrugged, walking over and favouring one leg. "If that's explaining, I can't imagine how she goes about seduction. Divs are weird indeed."

As he neared, Shkarag tensed like a bow being drawn. "Can't go . . . around . . ." Uncertain whether the perceived insult took priority over the perceived danger, she maneuvered to crawl over Tirdad while turning her back from the approaching marzban. "Calling a person a . . . šo-weird div when . . ." She transitioned to a defensive crouch and began her retreat as if she were sneaking away. "Who're . . . you to decide what's spicy . . ." She reached the wall. A sharp tilt of her head followed. It seemed she had forgotten about it, but couldn't risk throwing it the glower it deserved. "Or sour. Above your station, I think." She paused, narrowing her eyes. "Not a div, you šo-shifty sheep-haired sack of roots."

"Don't think she fancies me," said Chobin, finding some amusement in it. "Looks mighty div-like to me, though."

"Half div. Only half div," Shkarag hissed. "You half, you . . . what do you get when a man fucks a ewe?"

"Uh?" Marzban and planet-reckoner shared a look of confusion.

"You."

A smile cracked Tirdad's grimace.

Chobin caught on soon after, belting his approval and slapping his thigh. "Hah! Calling Pa a sheep fucker, huh?" Head inclined and pointing at her with bent forefinger, he acknowledged his defeat.

Never let it be said that Shkarag squandered the chance to strike a pose. She raised her fist, though none too happy about it, in the customary flourish of the victor. The flourish was hers. Flush as she was with the wall, its rich yellow stucco bordered in radiating petals and ornamented with confronted rams, and her in her sleek sanguine caftan, she could have been the focal point of a heroic mural.

All the while, she maintained her distance and wariness.

"Crude," said Chobin, "and formidable. You keep good company, my friend. Like her already."

"Yeah." Tirdad went to beckon her over, then thought the better of it. "Do you need him to go?"

Shkarag gave a quick tilt, adding a firm, "Maybe."

Tirdad drew his lips into a thin line, considering his options. From what he knew of them, Chobin would be the least likely to take offense, and Shkarag the least pliable. So he regarded the marzban, who was already doing the same. "She has trouble with . . . people," he tried to explain. "Rapport is hard-earned. I don't mean to come off as ungrateful, but—"

"You're too shy to fuck with me around," Chobin interjected.

"—she needs time." The jest came as a relief: it meant the marzban was on board. "Let her look after me awhile."

Chobin shrugged as if it were of no concern, but he had a pensive look trained on Shkarag.

"I trust her with my life," added Tirdad.

"I know. Just not sure I do," said Chobin. Another shrug, and he deposited the sack by the bed. "I'll head home and catch up. No doubt they're at one another's throats without me around to charm them."

"Surely."

The marzban gave Tirdad's shoulder a squeeze. "Get well, my friend." Then, more true to form, he winked. "Leave all the grinding to her."

Ignoring the vulgar comment, Tirdad bade him farewell, returning the gesture by grasping his forearm. "Safe travels."

Chobin gave the half-div one last wary glance before departing.

His absence brought another bout of calm owned by breeze-livened leaves and the birds that called them home. This one was threatened at its frontiers by charged breathing, but it persevered.

Dog-tired, Tirdad closed his eyes, content to wait while Shkarag found her bearing. There prevailed in her a latent danger, a need he could not hope to comprehend. A dreadful lineage that ran thick in her veins. Yet he trusted her all the same. If not her—this erratic, murderous, backwards half-div—then who? He couldn't help but grin at the absurdity of it.

"Don't grin," she censured, having silently made her way over. "Not going to grind like some pestle down on its luck, not discriminating between grains and herbs and—" She paused, listing toward him alongside her head. "Oh, I'd be the mortar."

"Sit," he bade her. "You look dizzy."

Oddly obedient, she did as instructed, facing him with her bum leg out straight. "Maybe," she said, and began to knead her thigh.

He observed her for a while, particularly the intense focus she'd bore through the spot where her hands worked, and how she'd list to one side whenever that intensity ebbed. Something was amiss. "I know you've issues with strangers, but I can't recall you ever reacting so strongly," he said. "You look unwell."

The glare she wore curtailed that conversation.

"Well," he went on after clearing his throat and avoiding the ire she'd trained on him, "you should know I'm relieved you're alive, and that we've been reunited. Ashta . . . she taught me to read the stars by finding one I could always recognize—the one light I could always rely on even when all the night was chaotic with war. 'Find that anchor, and the sky's yours,' she'd say. Ashta would, well, you know how she was. She'd brood after. I'd wager she thought she'd lost hers when she lost her brother. But I believe the three of us together were our one star. She's gone now, but—" He eased the blade free of its sheath, admiring it as he did, then continued. "We can still go on, you, me, and what's left of her."

The glare Shkarag had trained on him transitioned to a peculiar expression he couldn't quite place—almost as if she were baffled and unhappy about it. "Fuck," she said, angling her head away and averting her eyes.

After it became apparent she didn't mean to respond, he pressed on. "I suppose I should explain what I mean by what's left of her." He fully unsheathed the blade and lay it across his lap. "This sword—"

"Starling-black . . ." she said, eyeing it.

"I always thought it was more magpie-black."

She canted her head. "No."

"But I really think it looks more like—"

"No."

Tirdad sighed. He strongly subscribed to the magpie camp, but far be it from him to challenge her on such a topic. "Fine. Starling then. At any rate, this . . . starling-black coated the blade when I . . . when I put her out of her misery. It seems she had an imperfect phylactery, so what was left of her migrated to the sword, and uh, to me."

He glanced up from the blade. She was focused on it with that same peculiar expression. "Well," he continued, fingers running through his greasy hair, "in doing so it made me a planet-reckoner. I'm not sure how it works exactly, but that's what the star-reckoner told me before I ran the bastard through. Just don't—"

Shkarag grasped the blade.

"—touch it."

"Can feel my šo-lofty chum in here," she said, unusually grave. When she canted to look at him, it was with the same starling-black as the blade. "She's . . ." Shkarag trailed off, either searching for the words or unwilling to admit she'd found them. She relinquished the blade and turned her attention to a map. "Maybe," she said, plainly avoiding eye contact. She swept her hand over the topography as Ashtadukht had. "Should figure out the Everything."

Tirdad nodded, though he wasn't sure why she insisted on saying 'everything' with such gravity.

· · · · ·

After a month of poring through blood-spattered missives and unintelligible manifests, Tirdad was beginning to suspect this was all part of some elaborate prank. To Shkarag's credit, she was committed to the ruse: when she wasn't out and about, she'd be poring same as him.

Demonstrably, he'd just awoken to find the documents spread in a semi-circle, and her dozing on the floor with his sword hugged to her chest, a scroll bunched in one fist. She'd always manage to find a patch of sunlight, its warmth her bedspread and she a glutton for it. Somewhere down the line he'd forsaken his morning rituals to watch her sleep. A tranquility graced her features that she never carried while awake, and he found no small amount of solace in seeing her at peace.

An omelette waited by his side, surely just as cold as it was every morning. In all their years together he couldn't recall her having cooked a single meal. Not so much as a boiled egg. Occasionally, she'd indulge if invited for a feast; otherwise, she ate only raw eggs and the odd fruit. If the sizzling of her efforts hadn't roused him here and there in the middle of the night, he would've suspected she stole it from some luckless farmer come the break of dawn then rushed back.

Tirdad smiled at the omelette, then at her. It didn't stop there. She'd been industrious in taking care of him: gathering roots, helping with everyday chores, generally keeping him company. Like he was family.

"If only she'd make something other than omelettes," he said, taking a bite. "Least she makes a mean one."

Shkarag stirred at that. "Who calls," she grumbled, groggy and looking it with her bunched face and fatigued eyes. "Go prowl for eggs, tugging onions, lifting turmeric." She sat up with a grunt, and immediately set to massaging her thigh. "Because some quack, some šo-thankless mallard of a surgeon doesn't keep spices in the estate he lifted. Says it's mean. As if my omelette is some villain. Been serving him for weeks, but suddenly there's a change of heart, and—"

"Shkarag, please," Tirdad cut in. "That's not what I meant." He would have done so sooner, but speaking during a meal was rude, and the last thing he wanted to do was give her another reason to find offense.

Bristling, hurt, and nodding off, she fought to finish her wayward complaint, but her heart wasn't in it. Shkarag fell back, sending waves through the dustlight. "Does the recipe spoil, too? Maybe. Haven't cooked since . . . since . . ." The rest was little more than mumbling.

"It's delicious," said Tirdad. "And you're a good friend for looking after me. Don't get all bent out of shape. I was just thinking I'd like something other than eggs."

She craned so that he could see her disgust. "Added onions and turmeric."

"That's a pretty traditional omelette. What I meant was meat. Goat or lamb preferably."

"Don't scoff at tradition."

"I'm not."

She squinted.

"I'm not scoffing," said Tirdad. "Don't look at me like I'm some—" He caught himself on the cusp of an analogy that would've been more at home in her head. "I'm not."

Her squint tightened, then she eased her head back. "Won't promise mutton. But . . . will try to scoop up a lamb your šo-lecherous sheep fucker hasn't molested."

"You're kinder than you let on."

"You're a quack."

Tirdad reached for the glass goblet that'd been left with the meal, and took a pull of wine. He recognized it as a local harvest, notable because he hadn't stocked any since taking over the estate. "Thanks," he said as it warmed his chest. "You've no doubt been out all night. I'm sorry for waking you. Get some rest, Shkarag."

A glance told him she'd already succumbed to exhaustion. He hadn't the remotest clue what she did while he slept, but figured that was her business. There was no way she spent all that time gathering eggs; besides, they'd stay fresh for at least a week.

He knotted his brow at her, and a wine-widened smile brightened his features. That's when it hit him. "Oh, Shkarag," he whispered. "You're as clever as you are caring."

Quietly, and with the goblet in one hand, he collected the documents and began arranging them around the largest map. Now that he knew what to look for, it came to him almost immediately. The shipping manifests included eggs that made a regular trip between cities too far apart and too regular to make sense. The eggs would have spoiled in the time it took to cover the distance. He cross-referenced the manifests, and sure enough the ingredients were on every list. With omelettes being a staple, it wouldn't raise any eyebrows—it'd fooled him until now after all.

"They all originate in and return to the capital," he pondered aloud. "There must be some significance."

The breakthrough reinvigorated his drive to uncover the secrets hidden in that blood-stained bundle. Like a madman in search of his marbles, he rummaged.

"Seals?" he mused, sorting anything stamped from the pile. After laying them out, he counted many recurring seals, none of which he recognized. That wasn't unexpected with all the hands they passed through, especially coming from the capital. He drew his lips into a line and shook his head.

Mindful of his ribs, he twisted away slowly to retrieve a roll of parchment when one of the stamp impressions caught his eye. "A constellation," he said under his breath, still careful to avoid waking Shkarag. The stars were arranged in a configuration he wasn't familiar with. Closer inspection found five more seals, each unidentifiable. He fished in his sacred shirt for Ashtadukht's seal, which he kept around his neck at all times. As he suspected, it portrayed an unfamiliar constellation.

The same star pattern sealed every departure from the capital, with one of the five marking each destination. Arrayed before him was a method of covert communication between star-reckoners. Now confident in its significance, he canvassed the missives for anything that stood out.

Unfortunately, they weren't as forthcoming. Either some had been lost, or the paltry three were written in code. He'd trawled each countless times by now, and they all read as innocent letters to family.

Tirdad heaved a sigh that rang in his ribs, so he followed it with a long draw of wine. After laying the missives side by side, he stroked his beard and combed for anything out of the ordinary. Each had unique handwriting, for all that mattered in a world where scribes were easy to come by. If the letters had been written by star-reckoners, they were as unimaginative as they were secretive. The shipping manifests proved a better read.

Intoxication crept into his vision such that he had to concentrate on individual words as he went, which turned out to be a blessing: striking through that haze rewarded him with an unexplored perspective. Each mentioned death, but curiously so. The letter from the capital insisted that some woman had passed. One responded that she had passed too soon—that she would never be good enough. It urged caution almost sympathetically. The third agreed with the first, as if this woman's death were up for debate. Its author believed her passing would teach some party a valuable lesson in the dangers of meddling. None of this was said in so many words, but Tirdad could see it now as if it'd been obvious all along.

Another gulp of wine, this time for his heart. On the verge of tears, his back shook. Ashtadukht had tried so desperately to explain this when he caught her having murdered Mehr-farr, but he didn't want to hear it. The star-reckoners had conspired against her, knowing full well she was unprepared. This was her proof.

"Fuck!" he yelled, throwing his goblet across the room, where it dashed its contents and shattered over the stone. "Fuck!" He buried his face in calloused, weathered hands.

Tirdad had exiled the woman he loved, then he ended her life. Her sins were hers, and there was no getting around their breadth and severity. But this painted them with more telling strokes. A conspiracy by her superiors, her word against theirs? Surely, she knew accusing them would only show her hand. So she'd been careful, calculating, managing to convince them some phantom of a div was responsible for picking them off one by one. By Ohrmazd, the patience it must've required. The self-control. Until he'd gone and ruined it for her.

For the longest he'd seen it as misguided anger. Now, he wasn't so sure.

A shadow fell over him, lifting his reflection, and in turn his head. Canted and unreadable besides her fatigue, Shkarag stood with a pair of goblets. "Here," she said, offering one, and taking a seat once he'd accepted. She drank with gusto, then gingerly placed the empty cup beside her outstretched thigh, watching him as if to say this is how you handle a glass without breaking it.

He followed her example, then wiped his mouth on his sleeve. "Sorry for waking you a second time. I just . . ." He gestured at the documents. "I figured it out."

Shkarag probably cocked her head, but he took it as a nod.

"I should've listened," he rambled. "Should've . . . so much I should've done differently. Maybe we wouldn't be here right now. I'm thinking about how desperate she was to explain, for me to understand. It must've meant so much to her. She'd kept it to herself for decades. Can you imagine, Shkarag? Holding onto your purpose so resolutely, thinking all the while you can't trust anyone with the truth? Then, when the one person who should listen forces it out of you, you're unable to get through to them? They're deaf to your plight. And you're alone, exposed, and you were right all along in your distrust."

Shkarag's blank expression hadn't faltered.

Tirdad reached for his sword, eager for its comfort. He laid it across his lap, and absently stroked the scabbard. "What do I do?" he asked her, the wine loosening his lips. "She's gone, and I'm stuck with this guilt for which I can't hope to make amends."

She just stared, pupils expanding as a passing cloud cast its shadow over the estate.

"No long-winded analogy grasping at wisdom?" Tirdad pressed, unsettled by her inscrutable hush. "Not going to insult me?"

At that, she parted her lips. Surely, a thousand sinuous suitors crowded at the challenge, all vying to be the one to court her tongue. Shkarag disappointed them all when she deliberately closed her lips around her retort. Still blank.

Tirdad couldn't hide his astonishment. So accustomed to her pell-mell character, it was even more unsettling to see what might've been discretion. "Shkarag?" he asked.

She turned that expressionless stare on the sword, then got to her feet. Without a word, she took their goblets and left him alone in his room. Tirdad frowned at that. His thoughts were at the same time distressing and untamed, worried as he was over things he couldn't make out in his drunkenness.

After what seemed to him a lengthy absence, she returned laden. Shkarag placed a full goblet in front of him. Beside it, an assortment of eggs. She reclaimed her spot on the floor, and hooked her good leg around a rhyton filled to the brim with wine. All without breaking the silence or her composure. A quaff and she placed her goblet by her side, pointedly gentle. He followed suit, too muddled to do much else. She tilted the rhyton to refill his and only his cup, then picked a mint-coloured egg from the collection. Watching him as if to be certain he was doing the same, she lifted her chin and, looking down her nose, opened wide to give him a clear view of her fang as it uncurled then pierced the shell. A thin stream of yolk seeped into her mouth.

Tirdad considered the many-coloured clutch she'd given him. There were eggs belonging to eight or nine species, probably from her personal collection. With an expert right in front of him, he figured she'd know best, so he chose a mint-coloured one. Tirdad followed her example, tilting his head back and, because he had no fangs, cracking the egg over his mouth. The contents oozed over his tongue and down his throat, unexpectedly normal-tasting as far as yolk was concerned. What caused him to heave was the half-developed embryo that slid down with it. He drained his cup to wash it down and shot her a look of revulsion.

"That was fertilized," he said.

Still looking down at him with that faraway stare, she cracked open her egg so he could see that hers was as well. The shell joined it, which she chewed.

"Oh," said Tirdad. "Guess you use the unfertilized ones for omelettes, huh?" He let whim guide his hand to the next egg—spherical, and the pink of a sky over snow. "We're going to the capital," he told her. "I've some questions that need answering."

Shkarag refilled his goblet.

V

THREE MORE WEEKS OF WAITING and Tirdad's blood ran hot with desire. He wanted justice; he would demand it where she had not. Someday, he would demand it for his part in Ashtadukht's demise as well. For the time being his guilt would have to do—no one else was going to champion the truth in a society that claimed to live by it. He would have stormed off half-drawn if Shkarag weren't around to keep him level.

He wasn't too dense to see the tables had been turned, and it amused him to no end that he was being kept in line by a daughter of the hypostasis of discord. This dominated his thoughts as she stood before him, a thin silhouette at the vestibule's exit.

"My ribs have healed," he said. She cocked her head, which encouraged him to add, "Mostly."

Shkarag shifted her weight, rousing his suspicion that her leg bothered her more than she let on. She massaged it at every opportunity as it was.

"You should rest your leg," he suggested, not really expecting it to work. "Take a load off."

"Thigh's tickety-boo."

"Never mentioned your thigh."

She hissed at that. "Can't heal and travel. Can't do both. Think you're hefting two watermelons with one hand like some šo-strapping legend. But the legend isn't real, because it's a legend. It's a quack. You're a quack.

A šo-fucking quack. Not buying your piss water hair oil or tooth repair. Go to bed."

Tirdad blew out an irritated sigh. The amusement ended there. She was right, of course, and that only irritated him more. "The wait is eating at me, Shkarag. I can't sit around any longer. It's maddening."

"Wait is . . . wait is eating at . . ." She trailed off, but only because of the apparent rage that washed over her. Oftentimes, a person's voice can take an edge. Shkarag's skipped the edge altogether and dove off a precipice. She cocked her head the other way, fingers quaking and grasping at the air by her sides. "You don't know what it means to wait!" she yelled.

Tirdad took a step back. Perhaps, he admitted, he should just do as she says today.

"Never waited in your—" Shkarag braced herself on the doorway, fishing in her pouch for a handful of eggs, which she devoured. Her shoulders slumped, and the rancour fled her delivery. "Don't like waiting either," she garbled, mouth full and coming off as a confession. "Don't like it something fierce." She flexed a claw by her head, and the pitch that she ended on was one he'd come to recognize as an overture to something of import. Instead, she exhaled heavily and walked by, saying, "That's just as the crow flies. Hit the trail."

Tirdad followed her departure with concern. "Are you coming?"

"Maybe."

He prayed it was in the affirmative, because he had no intention of leaving her here, or anywhere for that matter. He'd convince her somehow. Fortunately for his nerves, he didn't have to wait long. Shkarag soon emerged in her armor with a full sack slung over her shoulder, spear on her back.

"We're walking," he told her. Palm on the ram's head hilt, he angled it to indicate her thigh. "Can you manage with your leg?"

She promptly dropped the sack and withdrew into the estate. Shortly after, she returned with a more travel-ready bag, and wordlessly transferred roots, onions, turmeric, and basic cookware from the sack. Shkarag pointedly looked up at him as she tossed aside a pinecone. "Made it this far like some gritted-teeth hero. Can walk just fine."

In no position to argue, Tirdad nodded and started for the treeline, determined to get to the bottom of the conspiracy, and if the planets favoured him, do some good on the path. A heady lungful of briny Mazandaran air breathed further life into his stride, with only a slight complaint from his ribs. Fond as he was of these journeys, he loved the smell of home, and missed it when away. The Gulf strove for a similar brackishness, but it was a poor imitation—too salty in its eagerness.

Shkarag trotted over and fell into step beside him. Finally, he thought, a chance to share the road with the half-div again; he'd yearned for it, but hadn't realized just how strongly until now.

"The more direct route is rough terrain," he said. "Mainly game trails to follow when there's a trail at all, but the views are worth it, and it'll bring us right alongside Mount Damavand."

Already using her height-and-a-half spear as a walking stick, Shkarag had her head canted, attention darting to sound after sound in the lively summer forest.

Tirdad regarded her in her half-sister's trappings, getting a good look for the first time. "The armour suits you," he said. "You look like someone seeking glory. I'd go as far as saying you look dignified in it."

Her stare roamed it appraisingly. "Maybe," she neither confirmed nor denied. "And the limp?"

"Well, you know, it's strange, but I think it ties the ensemble together. Adds experience to the image, and you are a veteran after all. Hardened suits you."

She stopped dead in her tracks, throwing him a furrowed brow, cant redoubled.

"What?"

". . ."

"Something wrong?"

". . . Maybe." Shkarag aimed one of her crooked grins at her bum leg. "I think."

At that, Tirdad grinned, too. That he hadn't the faintest clue why she was pleased didn't matter, just that she was. "Let's get moving," he said, waving her on. "Plenty of limping ahead of us."

The deeper they delved into the forest, the more the path narrowed until they were shoulder to shoulder, flanked by a thickening assembly of trees. Alongside the more mundane oaks and alders were the fluted trunks of hornbeam and silk trees flowering with pink tufts. Here and there, a date-palm would infringe on a patch of earth to lay claim to its share of sunlight. Tirdad relished it all. The forest was so verdant it glowed.

Before long, the path disappeared, forcing them to turn single file into a rut worn by the routine of game. There, woods transitioned to thicket. Low-hanging branches, ivy, and black-berried shrubs reached from all sides as if the pair were heroes advancing through an adoring crowd. They marched on without complaint up a gradual incline until dusk grew near.

Having happened upon a clearing, and with the sun so close to the horizon, they made camp. Tirdad recited his hymns as he did once during each of the five divisions of the day, then joined Shkarag where she leaned on her spear at the perimeter of the clearing. The treeline parted where a chunk of earth had fallen away, and the resultant vista afforded them a dazzling view.

Below, the setting sun streamed around the treetops of the plain, scoring swathes of shadows like a rising tide. Where the fleece-busy shore became the more relaxed waters of the Mazandaran Sea, its brassy ripples went on as far as the eye could see.

"Beautiful," said Tirdad, the distance of nostalgia leaking into his voice. "Though not by much, Ashta and I grew up farther east. Probably many of the same trees down there that we saw from our jaunts into the hills. I wish you could've known her back then. She was full of life, an explorer if I've ever seen one."

Shkarag surveyed the expanse, scrutiny lingering on select spots before moving on. "Oh," she said, distracted but not entirely uninterested. Tirdad averted his gaze when she moved to absently scratch the scar on her neck.

He unwrapped a piece of jellied meat and ate in silence while absorbing the image of what may as well have been his old stomping grounds. When he finished, he washed it down with a draught of wine. "You know, this sure is delicious, Shkarag. You're a great cook. It's a shame we went all that time none the wiser." Tirdad offered her a piece. "I won't ask where you found the goat, but I'm grateful all the same."

Her stare moved, but only to linger on another distant shadow.

"Shkarag."

". . ."

"Shkarag."

With that, she angled her head his way, eyes rolled high to train on him, paying the food no attention.

"Thank you for the jellied meat," he said.

"They say," she began, still scratching her scar, "they say you don't eat a goat until it's four. Don't get it. Checked for rings, and how do you tally age without? A real riddle until I quartered it."

"Clever."

Shkarag returned her attention to the waning sunset.

Tirdad figured he'd milk the moment for all it's worth. "I've been meaning to ask what gave you a limp. I'm sure you two had a great many adventures without me."

The half-div automatically rubbed her thigh. "Lion," she said. "Or ramparts. Or both. I think." She pursed her lips, then added, "Ramparts-lion."

"Ramparts-lion?"

"Maybe."

"I'd like to hear what happened," said Tirdad, taking a seat and hoping it'd encourage her to do the same. A dull ache had entered his ribs, but that was to be expected after a day's travel.

To his satisfaction, Shkarag followed suit, immediately seeing to her thigh. "Ashtadukht," she grunted, countenance drawn in a focused grimace. "That šo-dramatic planet-fucker, she . . ." The half-div went quiet for a bout of especially rough massaging. "I had that star-reckoner. So close. Close as slivers of bone right—" She squeezed, and Tirdad could've sworn he heard a stifled gasp. "There. Would've felled him something fierce, but she made the ramparts a lion, and only natural that a person ride a lion if it rears under you. But there's no šo-majestic mane to billow from, and you're riding it down, and you're thinking you'd rather not. But all those ramparts scatter and become ram parts."

Tirdad squinted, brow in furrows. "Did you just make light of the downfall of my family?"

". . ." She concentrated on her massage.

Since he had no confirmation, and because he wasn't sure whether he should take it as insulting or impressive, Tirdad let it pass. "Well," he said at length, "I'm going to get some shuteye. I suggest you do the same. Won't do to have you falling asleep on your feet come tomorrow morning."

He got up and started off in search of a comfortable plot when she surprised him with a question.

"What do you think of vegetables planted under fruit trees?" she asked soberly. "Living off the corpses of those heroic dates and limes that dare to hang on high?"

Tirdad looked back to find she'd ceased her kneading, and though he couldn't see her expression, her delivery spoke multitudes for her mood. "Heroes are only heroes with someone to depend on them," he answered without hesitation. "You strive to better the lives of others, especially those in need, and in death if you must."

The hush that followed endured, so Tirdad found a nearby plot of grass to lay down for the night. Worn out from the uphill hike, long sword by his side, he dozed off in no time. At the juncture of consciousness and dreams, he saw Shkarag standing before the cliff, claws by her head, lustrous in the moonlight and naked.

• • • • •

Tirdad awoke feeling like threshed grain. He emitted a groan, wondering whether this was how his cousin had felt every morning, and how she ever managed to get out of bed if so. With a wince accompanied by another groan, he sat up. Instinctively, he reached for his sword, to find only grass.

A sudden dread rose in his throat, which flushed out his grogginess like an ice-cold bath. Tirdad shot to his feet, spinning, head jerking in every direction. The clearing was empty. Dread became panic.

"Shkarag," he called out. "Shkarag!"

The woods stirred to his rear, and he spun on the sound to discover the half-div propped against a trunk with the sword clutched against her chest. Relief slackened his muscles, though he panted as if starved for air.

"Šo-noisy," she grumbled. "Can't shout a person awake if you want friends. Just won't do."

He stalked over and snatched the sword up, unsheathing it and trailing an admiring touch over its edge as he did, iridescence alive as ever.

"Doubly rude," Shkarag hissed.

Tirdad started to rebuke her, but decided that'd be unfair. "Forgive me," he said, scowl softening but still trained on the blade. "You didn't deserve that. I never did get around to explaining the danger. This sword is all that stands between me and annihilation. I'm not talking mere death here, Shkarag. I'm talking the end of my soul." He sheathed the blade inch by inch, watching the colors crawl across the starling-black as he did, then turned his gaze on her. "So please don't venture far with it."

"Right here," Shkarag said, clearly dissatisfied with his apology. "Didn't go venture like some, like some arms dealer posing as a merchant and—" She yawned, fangs flaring. "Mmn. And using some mighty unconvincing lines like, 'These fifty swords are sacred jewelry where I come from.'"

"Just do me a favour and promise to keep it near me at all times. Can you do that for me?"

Shkarag tilted her head. "Maybe."

Tirdad expelled a sigh and shook his head. "I pray that's a positive maybe, Shkarag. This is my existence we're talking about."

She got up with the help of her spear, looking ragged with sleep deprivation. "Maybe," she said with a lilt that suggested she might heed his words. She tilted further, considering the scabbard as he reattached it to his sword belt. "You're a—" she croaked.

"A what now?"

"I'm saying—" Another croak cut her off.

"I don't follow."

Shkarag released a hiss. She shrugged on her bag and started off like she knew the way, which she decidedly did not.

"Where are you going?" asked Tirdad.

She tossed a hand in the direction she was headed.

The planet-reckoner went to retrieve his gear—what little he had anyway—and stood at the opposite end of the clearing. "The path's over here," he called.

Shkarag threw a glare over her shoulder that swiftly transitioned to the uncomfortable realization a person gets when they've stormed off into a pantry. "Oh." She ambled over with an affectedly casual gait.

With her in tow, he ventured back into the woods on a course that rounded the side of the mountain they'd been ascending. The thicket soon gave way to an old cliffside path that, while overgrown, afforded a breathtaking view and more importantly a break from the cramped game trails.

Where the pair emerged, mountainsides with forests vibrant like colonies of moss sloped down to meet in a narrow valley. There, they thinned to patches surrounded by a carpet of flowers yellow as yolk. An osprey circled over one such patch, its excited yips carrying to every end of the valley. At the higher altitudes, the treeline prostrated before peaks that were bald, crimped, and powdered with snow.

"Not the worst scenery," Tirdad mused. "And there's an osprey soaring over there." He pointed, though he figured she had better sight than he. "Imagine you'll be out in search of its clutch."

". . ."

"No? I remember when I was young, I'd see them circl—"

"How does . . ." Shkarag cut in. She made a claw of her hand, jabbing her spear in the direction of the bird. "Kestrel isn't an osprey. Osprey are fishermen, you . . . you . . . how can you grow up not knowing a fisherman from a hunter?"

"I—"

"See water down there? A pond? So-stinking fish bazaar?"

Tirdad threw her a glare. "Stop fucking interrupting me. I was only trying to relate. Besides," he squinted at the plot of flowers below the kestrel, "there's a lake down there after all."

Shkarag followed his gaze, and he did his utmost to swallow a grin when after a few minutes of limping along she was still concentrating on that point.

"I suppose it could be an osprey after all," he said, beginning to think her eyesight wasn't nearly as sharp as he'd assumed, and deciding to have a joke at her expense. "Don't think we'd see a kestrel circling over a lake now would we?" He could tell from her expression that she was beginning to doubt herself.

"Making kestrel calls," she said, vehement in her insistence, but yielding to the possibility of being wrong in her body language. Shkarag cocked her ear toward the valley, wringing her spear with both hands. "Kestrel calls."

Tirdad continued without another word, letting her stew in her uncertainty awhile. A victory worth relishing. That's what she got for getting cranky with him over something so trivial as a misidentified bird. When at last their cliffside path disappeared into a forest, she drew to a halt to further puzzle over his lie.

"Strange that you'd make such a mistake," said Tirdad, threading some affected disappointment into his voice. He stood by her side, staring as she did at the kestrel. "You're named after a bird of prey after all. I'd always assumed you were an expert. Guess I was mistaken."

Evidently, he'd botched the act. Shkarag narrowed her eyes. "You quack," she said. "You šo-damned quack convincing me."

Some backlash was to be expected, which made the lopsided grin that stole her cheeks all the more striking. She lit up: first beaming at him, then at the bird. "A kestrel after all," she hummed. "A kestrel tried and true." Shkarag faced Tirdad again and hefted her axe. "Haft to fly off the handle you try your quackery again."

He backed away instinctively, but her playfulness was manifest in the double pun. "Try it and I'll cut you down in one fell swoop," he handily shot back.

Shkarag's response won the contest. She astonished him with a laugh—about as normal and honest as a laugh could be besides the suggestion of a hiss somewhere in its depths. It was neither drawn out nor boisterous, but it had the effect of a guffaw. If he'd heard her laugh in the past, he couldn't recall, and surely never so merrily.

She canted at him, further keeling that uneven grin. "Think you're not such a pinecone fucker after all. You grew up so quickly. I . . ." Her stare flicked away, darting over his shoulder for a moment before fluttering on him once again. "Think I like you better this way."

"I'm surprised you'd admit to liking me at all," said Tirdad, and he meant it. This came as an all too welcome surprise.

Shkarag nodded gravely, though her grin persisted. "Dark times."

She limped by at that. Tirdad followed in quiet rumination, giving pause to the relaxed laughter he'd just witnessed. In her relationships, what few he knew of, she'd come off as withdrawn and paranoid at best. Sure, he had eventually gained some rapport, but he was under no illusions when it came to the frailty of her trust. So that crooked grin and that comfortable laugh were achievements to be proud of.

Here, the forest took on a personality distinct and dreamlike. Ironwood, with its trunks of sinews ribboning just beneath the surface, ruled this place. Unlike the earlier thicket, the trees were spaced far enough apart that their lichen-choked branches could reach out freely to mingle with their neighbors. The canopy that resulted filtered all but the most resilient sunlight, most of it content to gild the higher leaves.

In that thick, refreshingly cool shade, the pair travelled side by side. Where undergrowth had hindered their progress before, they were now treated to a floor chiefly covered with dried leaves.

Still meditating, Tirdad reached an unexpected conclusion—one that marked a departure from the sorry path Ashtadukht had taken. He yet grieved for his cousin. He'd wake up in the middle of the night and come to the realization that she was gone and he powerless to do anything about it. Even so, Tirdad concluded that her death, while a tragedy he would undo if he had the power, had done some good.

He and Shkarag seemed closer now than ever; her passing had seeded their friendship. What's more, the half-div had improved. She was troubled, likely hopelessly so, but she had found something of herself where before he had seen her on the brink of falling apart.

A leisurely pace had them well within in the realm of the ironwood by sunset. Dimly lit by day, it became tenebrous by night. Tirdad couldn't see so much as a hand's breadth in front of him.

"Shkarag," he said. "Hold on a minute. I'm walking blind here."

The dead leaves ceased their crackling.

Tirdad reached out to where she'd been, but the leaves stirred and he caught only air. "Shkarag?"

". . ." The hush that answered did so with the carriage of an empty reply.

"All right, Shkarag. Quit fooling around. Where are you?"

Another rustle. ". . ."

"Are you screwing with me?" he asked.

". . ."

"Fine. Here's as good a place as any to spend the night."

"Maybe," she finally replied, breathing hoarse and heavy.

"Would you tell me why you always ign—" Tirdad began to lie down when he was interrupted.

"ترســـو."

"Huh?" said Tirdad.

"SHE RAN."

"A coward dies a thousand deaths."

"Lower-than-filth."

". . . and the eggs you once shared are centuries-rotten. The ties . . ."

"BETRAYAL BETRAYAL BETRAYAL."

"You-pissed-on-your-bond."

"take responsibility."

". . . carved out a place in this world. A place for the two of you to . . ."

"Unworthy of happiness."

"CAN'T HIDE ANYMORE."

"She ran and ran andranandranandranandranandran."

"Coward!"

"trembling again."

"ترســـو."

"There-is-no-escape."

"you ran!"

"DISGRACEFUL."

A din of voices bayed, coaxed, orated, and whispered from the darkness, each distinguishable from the next. Ugliness was their common thread.

"What in the seven climes is going on?" asked Tirdad. He brandished his sword, it drumming in his grip, and turned a circle. "Shkarag? What the fuck is this?"

A sickly glow like spoiled yogurt spilled around the trees just ahead, fainter than it should have been for all its aggression. Shkarag was on bended knee, spear and axe readied but visibly shaking. "D-don't," she stuttered. "No more. P-please d-d-d-don't."

"Shkarag?" Tirdad knelt beside her. Her eyes were wide, and though she pulled her head away, they never left the glow. "What's wrong?" he asked. "What's happening?"

She whimpered. "N-not in f-f-front of . . . I . . ."

He placed a hand on her shoulder and gave it a firm squeeze, though it elicited no response. Tirdad turned a worried frown on the glow. Whatever it was, it had her paralyzed with a terror unlike anything he'd ever seen in the half-div. Another squeeze and he inserted himself between her and what approached. "Don't worry," he said. "We'll get through this to—" His confidence and in turn his voice plummeted when the source showed itself. "—gether."

Out writhed a nightmare creature. A huge disembodied head effortlessly splintered branches as it passed between trees to bear down on them. Tirdad had seen a great many divs in his travels, but never something so horrific. It might've resembled Shkarag if she were beheaded and left for carrion to infest her flesh and scales, frowning fangs broken and awry, eye sockets like bottomless pits of starling-black that leaked the stuff generously—themselves faces twisted in horror. While at first it seemed to float, a colony of chittering scales hung from its head like imitation tresses to slither it closer.

The voices, which had persisted in their multifarious abuses, now spoke as one. "Kill yourself," they said.

Tirdad threatened it with the tip of his sword. He raised his chin as Ashtadukht had so often when invoking her title. "I'm a planet-reckoner," he said, projecting the same air of authority. "I've dispatched more divs than I can recall. So you'd best turn back before you're just another forgotten notch."

"I-I have," said Shkarag from his rear, speaking as if she were pleading for her life before a king's throne. "E-e-e-every—"

"Liar!" cried the voices. The face was quickly upon them, and as sickening as it looked from afar, it managed to be all the more hideous now that it towered uncomfortably close, branches snapping and creaking around it. Its proximity afforded him each burrowing grub that emerged from pores like a million faces in the throes of agony, their tiny feet wriggling to gain purchase on its pale surface, which gushed like wet paint around the streams of starling-black. "You will kill yourselves," the voices declared. "We will show you the way."

That was more than enough to convince Tirdad that this div meant them ill. He lashed out with a routine unpolished from lack of practice, but which nevertheless struck home. The thrusts scored three punctures in its hide, briefly revealing the starling-black beneath before closing as swiftly as he'd opened them. Tirdad made another attempt: this time with a series of sweeping slashes that rent long but equally temporary cuts. It watched impassively.

"Fuck," he said, shuffling back to stand immediately in front of Shkarag.

"We will show you the way," the voices repeated, harsh and clear within their ongoing abuse.

Tirdad cast over his shoulder to confirm that Shkarag was still frozen in place. "Fuck."

He concentrated on his visit to the cosmos, on Saturn, on the celestial theatre, on the clashing divs and yazatas, on the whole experience, and most of all on his sword. Surely, there had to be some way for him to invoke his planet-reckoning. All to no effect. He would have blundered further if the head hadn't surged forward.

Breathing a curse, he spun away and snatched up Shkarag, stumbling at the unexpected weight of her armor, but catching himself and fleeing at a sprint. Now that he'd left the div's disgusting glow, he ran blindly through the forest. Twice, he clipped a tree that nearly knocked him off his feet and would surely leave some mean bruises on Shkarag. The terror that paralyzed her seized him in his flight—all the trappings of a nightmare beading cold sweat on his brow. He ran until his lungs burned, the damning voices biting the fringes of his hearing. Who knows how long he went on, but the thought of that thing at his heels drove him well past his limits.

When finally he chanced a look back, the head had disappeared. Tirdad came to a halt and veritably dropped Shkarag. Even in the pitch black his sight was blurred and awash with those wretched stars. "What," he asked between breaths, "in the seven fucking climes was that?"

She panted so intensely it drowned him out. The thought came to him belatedly that she hadn't exerted herself at all. "You're hyperventilating," he said, as soothingly as he could manage while sucking in great gulps of air. "You need to calm down."

Only after did he figure telling someone to calm down had likely never actually had the effect since time immemorial. Tirdad scanned for the div, but couldn't make out even the faintest light. He prayed he'd lost it.

"Where are your eggs?" he asked. Only her runaway panting answered. Tirdad was hesitant to touch her like this, but he dare not light a torch. So he reached out, and to his relief he found only her arm. She shook uncontrollably. "Everything's going to be fine," he assured her. "You're safe. It's gone."

Last he recalled, she kept a few pouches along her belt. Supposing they were his best bet for finding her eggs, he began to feel his way down before pausing to warn her. "Listen, I'm going to—"

Her panting had ceased. The rings of her mail slid along his fingertips before moving out of reach. A curt rustle announced she'd fallen over.

"Shkarag?" Tirdad crawled to her side. "Are you all right?"

This time, the hush that answered was thin and meaningless.

He leaned over and turned his ear to listen for breathing; what he heard was smooth and relaxed. Tirdad inhaled so deeply it topped off his lungs and ached in his ribs, then released it in a measured stream. He repeated this seven times—he was counting—before the blood-curdling div reappeared directly in front of him.

Instinct stole his muscles, spent as they were. Tirdad hefted the half-div and put as much ground as he could between him and whatever manner of suicide the abomination had planned for them. To his dismay, the sickly glow followed. At the same time illuminating his escape and demonstrating its futility, it buoyed his heart in his throat.

"Dizzy," said Shkarag, in the second of consciousness before horror reclaimed her.

"You fainted," Tirdad heaved between breaths. A bed of fallen leaves rushed beneath him as he wove between ironwood—their sinews now seeming as if they were extensions of the creature shooting up to impede him just beyond the reach of the glow. "It's right behind us," he said. "How do we defeat it?"

"Wants me. Throw me to the hounds."

"Wh—" A second of bewilderment distracted him from an oncoming trunk, which he collided with directly. Shkarag was thrown from his arms, and he knocked flat on his back. "Ugh," he groaned, vision swimming.

The voices returned in a mad deluge, with every current ending at, "We will show you the way." The div entered his vision, staring down with those portentous sockets that somehow gave the impression this beast had been normal until it'd been shown the way—that he'd continue the legacy. Its frowning maw parted, forcing grubs out of their burrows and . . .

It dispersed in a plume of smoke.

"What?" He sat up with a groan, and what Shkarag had said at the outset came to him with clarity: can't travel and heal at the same time. He clutched his chest. "Nngh."

"Hope you learned your lesson," said a voice sweet as a child's but stern as a mother's. "Bringing a div to this sacred place. Even going as far as sorcery. You are better than this, Tirdad."

"How do you? Who?" Tirdad faced the source, and it occurred to him then that the nature of the glow had changed: it had been purified. A humanoid the size of an adolescent and assembled from dead leaves stood hands on hips between a pair of ironwood. Light emanated from within its chest like the sun through treetops.

"Figures," it replied, cheeky but agitated. "You stomp all over me, even hear me cry underfoot, but never bother getting to know me. And here

I have gotten to know you well, what with you and your kin frolicking through me for generations."

"I don't under—" It hit him, and his jaw went slack. A yazata.

"Pick up your chin," it said with a hint of humour. "Surely this form cannot be that tantalizing. All crackling and dry and pah, pah, pah."

A yazata. He planted his forehead on the ground, praying he hadn't seriously offended it. Unlike divs, the champions of Truth and order were few and far between. Powerful as they were, yazatas were outnumbered one million to one in the realm of mortals. They could cut swathes through a div host, but losing even one would be a severe blow. So they generally avoided the light, working instead from the shadows, ironic as that was.

"Zam, by the way. Not that your family has cared to ask even with all its tramping. Well," it paused to consider, "a part of Zam. Cannot rightly fit all the planet into one incarnation. But you may call me Zam. And do stop prostrating. Dagnabbit."

Tirdad lifted his head obediently, but stayed on his knees and kept silent. His tongue was dry as the Lut, and even if it weren't he was deathly afraid of saying the wrong thing. Yazatas were as just as just gets, but this one did not seem pleased with him.

Shkarag charged by, or would have if a tangle of roots didn't catch her mid-stride, winding around her so completely only her head was visible. "I'll wipe my shit with your face, you šo-crunching bird sympathizer!" she hissed. "I'll start a forest fire!" Shkarag gnashed at the air, fangs flared and whipping back and forth, slinging a spray of what he mistook for saliva until it landed just short of his hand to sizzle through the ground.

Venom. At that, he backed away, giving her a wide berth. In all his years with her she'd never so much as hinted at having venom.

"I'll piss in your mulch!" she seethed.

"This is the company you keep," said Zam. "This is a div. I cannot fathom what it did to coerce you into trusting it, but this is their true nature. Its sorcery would have ended you then and there had I not intervened. Then and there."

Tirdad furrowed his brow. "Sorcery? I've never known her to use sorcery. She was terrified."

"An act, surely. Have you forgotten the wiles of divs, Tirdad?" Zam wagged a leafy finger. "Tsk, tsk. I promise you it was her doing. How well do you think you know something that has existed longer than the dynasty you have pledged allegiance to?"

"I'll fill your hollows with honey!" cried Shkarag.

The planet-reckoner shook his head. He may not know her past, but he knew her. "She befriended me, even took care of me when I was ill."

If Zam had facial expressions, its disappointment would have been plain. "I have known you since you were a fledgling, Tirdad. Your soul has always impressed me with its resilience, so pah, pah, pah, I forgive you. But you need to look. Really look at it."

Tirdad obeyed. Shkarag snapped with what was surely unchecked bloodlust at the yazata, at the roots, at existing, at nothing in particular. Streamers of smoke unfurled from the earth directly beneath her chin, where her venom had eaten a hole in the ground.

"When you strip away all the lies, the manipulation, the play at humanity, the . . ." Zam's tone took a knowing turn. "The attraction . . . this is a div. Hate. Destruction. Chaos. Pah, pah, pah. Recently, this one led a company of divs in felling one of my forests for no other reason than to upset my master, Amurdad. Just to deal a meagre blow to the grand guardian of plants and good health."

"I didn't—"

"Dagnabbit. Of course you did not know. Just as with the sorcery. Divs deceive. That I need to remind you of this at all . . . How many lives has it ruined? How much discord has it sown? All without your knowing or before you sprung from your father's loins."

"I'll masturbate with your šo-wretched sap!"

Tirdad turned a crestfallen stare on his hands, which he wrung nervously.

"Good," said Zam. "Never been fond of disciplining. Makes execution less of a hassle, too."

"Execution?" asked Tirdad. "You don't mean . . ." The light that had cosseted the forest hardened, retracting its touch and gathering like squalls into a glowing spear with eddies at its head. He sprung to his feet, palm reluctantly finding the ram's head pommel. "Don't," he begged. "Please! She's half human! She's my dearest friend!"

Zam brought its arm level with its shoulder, and the spear came to hover by its open palm. "All the more reason to be rid of her."

Until recently Tirdad had been a man of honour—a man who lived by it. Ethics vary by upbringing, personality, society, so it is only natural that forsaking honour would be an experience unique to the individual. Tirdad hadn't reached that impasse until now.

He drew his sword.

Jupiter, mightiest of the planets with its bands of thousand-year storms, ransacked the Bull constellation. The seven stars of Pleiades flashed across the heavens to intercept, trailing bright blue streaks. They were too late. Jupiter turned the most fearsome of its storms on their approach, and from that Great Red Spot flashed the evil eye. The stars it charmed turned on the others; the chaos began.

This time Tirdad watched from the fringes of the conflict. A confidence coursed through him—a newfound intimacy with the celestial theatre—and with it the many calculations of a planet-reckoner drawing a lot.

He knew at once that Jupiter was the only planet above the horizon, and therefore his only ally. Constellations, conjunctions, exaltations, falls, detriments, oppositions, dominions, elements, aspects: it all raced through his mind. Equations and star charts came to him as if they'd been branded onto his psyche. Most of it was superfluous, as planets below the horizon were out of reach, which rendered aspects and conjunctions null. Jupiter didn't occupy any windows of the sky with notable reactions, and its predilection for corrupting life meant it'd do well with any element. The Bull was a patron of earth, so he had some manifestation of crumbling, heaviness, sensuality, crops, or black bile to hope for.

Tallying the factors, he determined that his odds of success were a cosmic coin flip. All things considered, he respected Ashtadukht's boldness. To have cast so many lots when such risks were involved.

"Jupiter stands victorious bestride the Bull," Tirdad breathed, strangely silvery as he disrobed his sword. The die of earth rode the furrows of his mind, its six faces caressing wherever they touched, until it settled comfortably into one such furrow. His lot had been favoured.

Arousal washed over him, graced his soul. Every conceivable fetish was laid bare and him turned on by the whole display. Then it was gone as abruptly as it'd come. He wouldn't know the outcome until it reared its lascivious head, so he gripped his long sword in both hands and aimed the starling-black blade at Zam. "You won't hurt her," he growled. "I won't allow it."

The yazata lifted its palms defensively, backing away. "Woah, woah, woah, woah, woah. Put that away, you stupid, stupid boy. You cannot fathom the . . . you cannot fathom that blade."

"You first," said Tirdad, matching its steps by marching forward. "Give me your word you won't harm her."

"Dagnabbit! Can you not see how unreasonable you're being?" Zam looked from one to the other as if considering his offer. "Really putting me between a div and a hard place here. Annoying. I guess my only option is to—" Zam shoved a palm toward Tirdad, which commanded the blindingly bright spear to dart in his direction. "—be rid of you both!"

Tirdad shifted his blade a fraction of an inch to the left, and miraculously, it caught the spearhead square on the tip. His muscles bunched, he roared like a lion, and it was all he could do to halt its progress. The eddies took on iridescent currents wherever they touched the blade; starling-black sparks cold as winter littered his face. Across the way, Zam had its palm out, only marginally invested in the struggle. The yazata was winning, and they both knew it.

"In way over your head," said Zam. "Pah, pah, give up, pah, pah."

The planet-reckoner set his jaw. Surrender was not an option as long as the threat to Shkarag's life remained. He side-stepped, and the spear rocketed past, trunks exploding behind him until they were too far off to hear. "I'll defend her to the death," he said. "So please just fucking let us go."

"Tsk, tsk. No can do," Zam replied, sounding genuinely sorry. Three more eddy-tipped spears materialized, this time drawing from the light in its chest. The yazata flicked a hand, and one after another they queued to fire at Tirdad.

He made for a desperate parry when his planet-reckoning finally bore fruit. The sensuality of earth had beguiled the yazata's roots; now, they served Tirdad. They encircled him entirely, and where his reflexes would have failed, the roots maneuvered him around the spears with inhuman dexterity.

Zam snarled, or what passed for a snarl in leaf vernacular—it rustled, but aggressively. Then it abandoned its nonchalance in favour of throwing its arms wildly.

Spears flew at Tirdad as if an army were behind them, so bright and numerous that he could no longer see the yazata. Thanks to his planet-reckoning, they all passed harmlessly by, the root system coordinating a veritable dance through the volley.

The light grew more and more intense, until it seemed as if he were wading through a star. The whir of spearheads had become constant. An iridescent afterimage trailed his blade where it gorged on the eddies and squalls. When he was beginning to wonder whether he was covering any ground at all, he emerged directly in front of the yazata. The roots withdrew, leaving the rest to him.

Tirdad stepped in just behind a swing, and before the yazata could retaliate, he thrust his sword into its core. The tip clinked against resistance, but it had the desired effect. The spears winked out of existence. Zam slumped to its knees.

It looked up at him, twitching. "Please d-d-donnnnnnnnnnnn—" Zam's failed plea stretched in search of its remainder, and likely would have continued its feeble droning had Shkarag not collided with the yazata, plunging her fangs into its crown even as she bowled it over.

Tirdad watched, not entirely sure what to feel. A flick of her head, and the half-div tore off what would've been its face. The spray of leaves sizzled on its way down, and the body seized violently. Shkarag was too far gone to stop at that. She bit with ravenous abandon, the acrid stench of her venom mingling with burning leaves and underscored by her hisses, the sound of tearing parchment, and breathing like a saw over wood.

Having shredded the head beyond recognition, she moved to its chest. There, Shkarag rent and clawed, no longer seeking to mutilate but to get at the shining core. Once she'd opened a large enough cavity, she posted on its torso, squatting and taking purchase on the core. It took only a single tug to dislodge the thing.

"What're you doing?" asked Tirdad, which elicited a warning hiss. He swallowed hard at the image of her bared fangs, caustic venom still dribbling generously from their points. He'd only witnessed that unhinged, predatory glint once, but once was enough. "Never mind," he said, giving her some space.

Yazatas and divs were natural enemies in the cosmic theatre, so he supposed it was fanciful to have hoped for a peaceful outcome. At least this div had prevailed. The single div who mattered. It occurred to him just how sacrilegious this was: his thoughts, the scene, his part in it—all of it.

But looking on as Shkarag compressed the pearly core between her claws, fissures spreading through the light and over its surface, the one thing he did not feel was wrong.

A strained creaking arose in the core, ominous and disquieting as if he were hearing it on a frozen lake. The fissures approached a breaking point, and the glow all but vanished, leaving only a dimly lit, glassy sphere. Shkarag stopped there.

She turned an inquisitive stare on him, free of that pernicious glint. Her arms dropped by her sides, and her scrutiny flitted over their surroundings, ending where it started. "Don't know sorcery," she said, retracting her fangs but coming off as defensive. "Don't know it one bit. It . . . she hounds me because . . ." Shkarag lifted the core beside her head, meaning for it to be a claw. She canted at it, eyeing it curiously, then glanced sidelong at Tirdad. A faint whine of a hiss bled through her lips.

He saw her fear and uncertainty plain as day—not of him, but of what this meant for their friendship. What the yazata's accusations meant. What their slaying it meant. He didn't need the paltry light thrown by the core to see as much. Even so, the half of her face that wasn't lost to darkness was fraught with the harsh basins of worry.

Tirdad put his blade away, taking care to apply a gentle touch in doing so, which recalled her condescending lesson in the proper handling of glass. He started over, wearing a disarming smile, and drew up in front of her. With that gentleness in mind, he had intended to hug Shkarag, but reconsidered. Instead, he chose a more light-hearted approach.

"Can you hear the sea?" he asked.

She blinked.

He nodded to the core. "You're listening, aren't you?"

"The . . . sea?" Her eyes darted to the orb and back. "Don't . . . the sea?"

His disarming smile became more genuine. "Isn't that what you listen for? Although, I suppose we're in the forest, so you'd be listening for a lake instead."

Shkarag tilted her head by only a few degrees. "Not a shell. A yazata's . . . I just . . . in front of you like some pearl diver with the find of a lifetime that won't stud the bravest brocade. Not a shell. Can't hear the sea. Can't hear a lake."

"Oh," said Tirdad. "Thought you might be listening since you sure as fuck can't see them."

It took a moment of contemplative silence for it to register, but once it did, a small grin tempered her features, and more importantly, flushed the worry away. A bout of further quiet followed before she responded. "Thank you," she said with earnest sincerity. "For . . ." She appeared to be concentrating on her stare, making sure it didn't falter, which spoke for how difficult this was for her.

"Don't mention it," he said, saving her the trouble. "I'd never betray you." Tirdad only glimpsed the shift in her expression before she lowered the core—not long enough to make anything of it.

"To fell a yazata," she awed. "To fell it something fierce. Planet-reckoning's out of this world."

"Yeah."

"Out of this world," Shkarag said again, more insistent this time.

"Yeah," Tirdad repeated, all too aware. Even now, the celestial theatre hummed at the furthest reaches of his senses.

Once awakened, it never slept. He'd become a planet-reckoner.

VI

EVERYTHING WAS DEAD. THE MOUNTAINS wore the bone-dry still of an ossuary where a stale air prevailed. The ironwood were pale; most were shattered. Not even a breeze creaked through the aftermath. It was as if winter had rushed in overnight, as if the sun had forsaken this one valley, though it still blazed high on the ecliptic. Tirdad turned a slow circle, gaping as he did at the desolation. "What happened?" he asked, rubbing the drowsiness from his eyes.

". . ." said Shkarag.

He faced her where she sat beside a campfire, one leg out and focused on the pan in which she fried an omelette. "You made a fire," he said, disbelief plain.

". . ."

Somehow it hadn't occurred to him until now that she'd been using fire to cook his meals all along. Divs were extraordinarily weak to fire, turned by it if not killed outright. This was why the divine glory of the sun had such a profound effect on them. Indeed, he'd noticed she was weakened during the day, but never forced into the underworld like most of her ilk.

"Although I really wish you wouldn't use green wood for it. You must know that's profane." He gestured at it. "Does it not hurt? The fire?"

Shkarag shot the pan a glare. "Wood is wood. Don't go out to gather morning wood like some arborist all sniffing bark and asking if they're

92

virgins or underage, squinting and trying to count their rings without looking up their skirt. Šo-itchy wood is šo-itchy wood."

Tirdad gave her a knowing look. Of course it hurt. He cleared his throat, eyeing the omelette and breathing in its pleasant aroma. "Everything's dead," he half observed, half asked.

"Not us," she answered, maintaining her focus. She canted. "I think."

"Yeah," said Tirdad. He had a sinking feeling he knew the cause, but he needed to hear it from her. "Why?"

At that, she looked up at him without moving her head, which had the all too appropriate effect of rolling her eyes. "Can't just fell a yazata and . . ." Her attention darted back to her cooking, which she bored into with a creased brow. She tried again, notably mild this time around. "Can't just fell a yazata without complaint," she said. "Fell the heart and you fell the dell. More effective than some tree-hugging lumberjack who . . ." Shkarag trailed off, her maundering replaced by the hiss of the omelette as she flipped it to fry the other side.

Just as he suspected. Tirdad blew out a sigh, and took in the breadth of the valley. It seemed as if a forest fire had swept through overnight, sparing nothing and devouring all colour. The few trees that weren't snapped in half had withered to thin lines so black they appeared to be cracks in the scenery.

"This is my doing," he declared. "Rarely are the consequences of your actions laid out with such brutal clarity." He directed his gaze back to the half-div, who had taken the omelette off the fire and dropped the pan by his boots. "It bothers you, doesn't it?"

". . ." Shkarag kneaded her thigh, wearing the same strained countenance as usual.

Tirdad took a seat in front of the pan, but refrained from eating just yet. "I meant what I said last night," he added. "I would've said more if I weren't so spent after, well, all that happened. As much as I deplore what I've done, I don't regret it. Honestly, you're the only one in all—"

"Eat," said Shkarag, head cocked and avoiding eye contact. "Just eat your šo-damned eggs." She gripped her thigh as if it were her anxiety, and she strangling the life out of it.

Taking the hint, Tirdad did just that. A few bites in, and he was enjoying it as if he weren't surrounded by what must've been his greatest sin. Maybe it was the wood; maybe she'd lifted a new clutch; maybe it was all in his head. Whatever the case, this meal was a different sort of delicious—the sort you only get from returning home after time abroad, your mother and grandmother eager to cook your favourite meals. He savoured every bite.

"Won't be the last," Shkarag spoke up when he'd finished it off. She still wouldn't look at him. "Been lucky. Maybe. Always saw them first. Found somewhere to hide. We—" She scratched the scales behind her ear. "Divs are stronger now. I—" That same hand became a claw. "The pull is lopsided like . . . like the world, and you're a real daydreamer when it comes to imagining all the ways you could—" Shkarag inhaled sharply. She clenched her thigh so tightly her muscles bulged in the fitted sleeves of her caftan. Her lips parted enough to reveal her lowering fangs. Tirdad paid special attention to the pouch she reached into to retrieve a handful of eggs, which she crammed into her mouth.

Without a word, she began packing her things. Tirdad watched her stiff movements, and a quiver of questions lined up to loose before he discarded them all and followed suit. The sooner they put this place behind them, the better.

They traversed the splintered, greasy trunks and scores of branches, as if slogging through a detritus-choked riverbank. Each concentrated on their boots, at the same time crestfallen and careful of their footing. Not a word was shared for the duration of the trek through the thicket's remains.

The magnitude of his actions weighed heavily on Tirdad. To anyone who knew him or his creed, the reason was obvious. It's an awfully, perhaps unjustly, insignificant thing to kill. Less so, to consider the far-reaching effects, and more intimately, that you have snuffed out a spirit with dreams of its own. Even in defending oneself, even in peacefully living off the toils of others, a tacit scale pits one life against another.

And Tirdad figured he'd put a real strain on the scale with this one. Maybe he'd tipped it forever in her favour. He'd gone as far as striking down a being of pure good, a paragon of Truth and order, and in doing so weakening both. Odds were the true extent of the damage would elude him. What could possibly hope to compete?

That considered, the more he thought about it, the more he felt a welling pride in what he'd done. An unusual, conflicted pride, but pride all the same. Tirdad glanced at Shkarag, who had a pensive frown trained on the branches that creaked and popped beneath her boots. Before she'd curtailed him earlier, he'd meant to tell her that she's the only one in all the world for whom he'd go to such lengths. Perhaps she'd seen it coming.

She was smarter than she let on. More empathetic. But her eccentric nature and mental unrest did an exceptional job of masking it—when they weren't disrupting it entirely. What he wanted to know was why she'd cut him off at all. One thing she had never been was forthcoming.

At the tail end of the thread, it occurred to him that his thoughts lingered on her more often of late than they had in any of their many adventures. More often and in earnest.

Tirdad was mulling over the meaning of this when at last their clogged path thinned out to a gentle slope carpeted in tussocks, wildflowers, and huddled shrubs. Ahead, the hills were mantled with all the accoutrements of a thriving forest. Now and then, the uneven treeline parted for outcrops or clearings, much like the one they occupied.

"Well, this is a relief," said Tirdad, peering now at the turquoise lake hemmed in by the hills. "And here I was worried that sorry sight would go on for farsangs." He indicated the lake with the pommel of his sword, where more and more his palm had come to rest when idle. "Don't write that osprey off just yet."

Shkarag followed his gaze, hugging her spear and yielding her weight to it. Her eyes described the lakeshore before she muttered an unenthusiastic "Oh."

Tirdad swallowed the urge to pry, extending a palm instead. "Mind sharing one of those eggs of yours?"

After drifting for a time over the surface, she regarded him with an enigmatic cant. He noticed, however, that she wouldn't look squarely at him. Rather, she described his outline much as she had the lake.

"A single egg?" he asked. "It needn't be a rare one. I don't have your refined tastes after all." Truth be revered, his stomach turned at the request;

it was a wonder he'd kept them down the day he'd sampled her collection. So if it turned out she had her misgivings, all the better.

The half-div either inclined or cocked her head, a distinction that he'd never get down, and adjusted her grip on the spear to free a hand. With marked deliberation, she unbuckled the pouch on her hip and took her time feeling around until she pulled out an egg. Not bothering to confirm the accuracy of her touch, she placed it in his palm, scales ridged yet smooth.

"There," she said. "Glossy ibis because . . . because plumage could festoon your sword." Her eyes flicked over something in the distance. "If not for starlings. Maybe."

The pale blue egg almost matched the sheen of the lake. He accepted it with a smile he hoped she noticed, and summarily cracked it open over his tongue, fighting the urge to gag as the undeveloped chick oozed down his throat. "Thanks," he said, tossing the shell aside. Then, with another tilt of his pommel toward the water, "Shall we? Wouldn't mind some fish, and a bath would be nice."

Shkarag assented by limping down the slope.

Tirdad leveled a frown on the ossuary-still forest to his rear. A long road lay ahead, but he prayed the worst of it was now behind them—though they'd be hard-pressed to find something more formidable than a yazata. Heaving a sigh, he tore his stare away and joined Shkarag on her way toward the shore.

It turned out there wasn't much of one. The hills met the water at an incline that was less navigable than it let on from afar, all stone and scree plunging straight in. Still, they were determined now that they were here.

Shkarag disrobed without so much as a warning, unstrapping her blood-red cuirass and pulling off her mail.

"What're you—" Tirdad about-faced. "Have you no modesty?"

"No," Shkarag flatly replied. "I'm half div. And haven't molted since I—" She grew quiet, though he could hear her peeling off her caftan. "Nothing you haven't gawked at in my dreams," she said, followed by the murmur of water.

He supposed she was right. Those statues of hers had spared no detail. He turned around to find her huddled on the shore and submerged to her neck, staring blankly across the lake. She looked utterly despondent—the sort to be wading to the bottom, or entertaining the idea if not.

"Hurts," she said. "Hurts. They say—" She held up a claw, which afforded him the cruel scar where her arm had been severed, and the rippling sinews beneath. "They say words are all so much wind. And you think that's just as the crow flies."

Tirdad replied with the same meaningful hush that she so often resorted to. Given her empty stare and recent behaviour, the threat of her mood coming to a head was all too real. So her willingness to open up came as a welcome relief. All ears, he took a seat.

For a long while, she only stared—straight ahead, gaze neither darting nor drifting. Unlike the blank stare he'd witnessed earlier, she wore the intense focus of a struggle. Venturing a guess, he supposed her guarded nature was objecting to the even the slightest admission.

Shkarag finally broke the silence with a barely audible, "Maybe." Louder then, "Never the words that smart, but the truth they carry. Like some, like some šo-famished osprey with its talons in your belly, and you're shouting that having scales doesn't mean you're a pike or carp or whatever they eat, and it's just flapping away without a care because finally a meal." She let out a low hiss. "Truth smarts something fierce."

Another bout of quiet struggle passed before she continued. "That—" She raked a claw over her scalp. "That bird-sympathizing heap said some truths. Been around long enough to see empires crumble. Helped." She cocked her head. "A bit. I think.

"Remember the trumpet of elephants as the Conqueror led the charge that would end your ancestors." She paused to reflect, seeming nostalgic, if dismally so. "Watched an eruption . . . a two-thousand-year-old boom that rattled my bones and drowned the sun. More memories than nests to stow them in. Most have been forgotten. So afraid hers will be lost again in the—"

Shkarag clammed up, and though it was only for a moment, what followed was patently forced. "Been around," she said. "Blood's—" She flexed her fingers. "Blood's scorching. But it's not enough. Have to spill it. Discord's scorching. But have to sow it. Instinct. Rewards overwhelming pleasure."

Tirdad had been listening with an alertness he hadn't used since the studies of his youth, so the shift in her speech was abundantly clear. While it remained soft, the delivery had grown stunted. He eyed her egg pouch.

"Truth smarts," she went on, as if the syllables had to be stropped across her cords one at a time. "Smarts when a friend hears. Spilled so much. Sowed so much. Countless. But . . ." Shkarag trailed off, then splashed her face with water. "Not with you. Afraid you don't see. Want it something fierce. But not with you. Fight the pomegranate-red always."

So that was it. She'd been distant and depressed since their reunion, but their encounter with the yazata had been the straw that broke the camel's back. He'd feel similarly if his secret sins were laid bare against his will—before a friend, no less.

Shkarag closed her eyes and entered another of her lulls, which could probably be likened to coming up for air. The stretch lingered until he thought she'd fallen asleep, and was nodding off himself by time she spoke up. "The water makes everything sluggish, makes me sleepy," she said, lending credence to her claims with a yawn. "But it helps to control." She glanced back, and her gaze found his for the first time since the incident, searching and anxious. "Yazata said some truths. A few. Maybe. Whispering in your ear like some—"

She caught herself. "True that you know me less than you think. Guess I only look half human anymore. Swear I'm not manipulating you. All I want is your company. That's the truth. The truth like some—"

She couldn't hold back any longer. "Like some šo-stupid div saying a thing that makes her skin crawl, like some maggots having a grand time in her throat, and they're all dancing merrily so fucking proud of themselves like some, like some campfire that bites something fierce. And who to bite but that same šo-stupid div?" She ended with that, eyes trained on his.

Tirdad matched her stare—really looked this time, giving her sanguine gaze the consideration it craved, though it flitted around in its usual way. What he saw there was ancient, weary, and above all else, sincere. The real significance of what she'd shared, and surely the driving force behind her desperation, came to him then: what she hadn't shared. Those thousands of years weren't spent in solitude. Until a few centuries ago, she'd been with her sister. Then all of a sudden, alone. What's more, she hadn't just shared, she had confided.

He made certain to tread lightly, maintaining eye contact for as long as she wished it. "That toenail-swallowing yazata could've said you were the Stinking Spirit himself for all I care. Like I told it, you're my dearest friend, and nothing, I mean absolutely nothing will get in the way of that from now on."

Shkarag averted her gaze at that. "You loved Ashtadukht."

Trenchant as ever. Perhaps treading lightly had to be thrown to the wind. For a time, anyway. "You loved your sister."

The hiss she loosed was quick to deflate. "Maybe," she conceded.

"Yeah. We've both made a host of terrible decisions. Difference is you've been at it for thousands of years. So, if it's something you need to hear, I don't hold your past against you any more than you hold mine against me. You wouldn't be here if you did."

"Maybe," she conceded.

"You want to be here. I want you here. It really is that simple, Shkarag."

"Maybe," she conceded.

"Then it's settled. We're stuck with one another."

"Maybe," she conceded.

Tirdad got to his feet, brushing the dust off his poppy-red tunic and resting his palm on the ram's head pommel. "It must've been hard for you to get all that out, but I'm glad you chose to. Has it put your fears to rest?"

Shkarag canted away. "Maybe."

"Give me a clear reply, won't you?"

"Thank you," she said. Then, after dunking her head, she stood, which prompted Tirdad to turn around.

"Please warn me," he said. "For my sake if not yours."

The millennia-old half-div dressed, but didn't bother equipping her armor. Instead, she packed her mail into a pillow, and pulled out a cloak to bundle under. By time Tirdad turned back around, she was already sound asleep. She hadn't even washed.

"Well," mused Tirdad, "I've got to hand it to you. That was a creative approach to regulating your bloodlust." He knelt to adjust the cloak to better cover her, frowning as he did at the scars he'd thought he'd known for decades. Turns out they could've been inflicted by a bronze sword in some civilization lost to even the most learned historian.

His frown transitioned to a tempered smile as he stood. "Of all those civilizations, I can't imagine there's no statue or legend of The One Most Slithered. Stands to reason someone out there would've wanted to immortalize your . . . well, I'm sure you've done a great many things worth immortalizing."

With that, he set to bathing and washing his clothes, sword always nearby, and wondering how a div survives for so long, phylactery or not.

• • • • •

"Bandits," said Shkarag, jabbing her spear in their direction and tilting her head. "Circling something fierce, like that kestrel you think is an osprey, because of course some noble-born runt wouldn't learn fishing from hunting."

Tirdad peered down the dry, tussock-bare slope where they stood, to the activity below. A dozen or so horsemen were circling a lone rider, laughing and kicking up dust. "Seems so," he said. Then, refusing to let her insult go unchallenged, he added, "Every noble is trained in the hunt—it's tradition. Even Ashtadukht, weak as she was, knew how to draw a bow. A man who neither hunts nor fights is worthless."

"Must be trained in hiding worth, too," said Shkarag, which drew a sneer.

The last few days of travel over and around increasingly tanned ridges had crossed them into the arid domain of the Iranian plateau, and evidently, onto the east-west road home to merchants and their predators.

Planet-reckoner and half-div exchanged a glance, which the former affirmed with a nod. Time to do some good, thought one; time for bloodshed, thought the other. Tirdad began by removing his bow from its case, and rather than securing the quiver to his sword belt, he chose three arrows from the lot and sat it on the ground. He strung the recurve's stiff ears and furrowed his brow at the leisurely pace with which Shkarag limped down the hillock.

"Get moving," he said, nocking one arrow and stowing the other two in his drawing hand.

Tirdad lifted the bow and drew with practiced finesse that bunched the muscles in his back. Rather than follow the targets, he chose a spot in the circle to lead them by, and let loose the first shot. It whizzed unerringly over Shkarag's head to find the flank of an unsuspecting bandit, which fell from his saddle. One down. The riderless horse reared, which disrupted the ring as riders swerved to avoid collision.

Not a breath after that initial twang, he was advancing at a jog. Tirdad shifted a second arrow down to line up with the bowstring, and it wasn't until he nocked, closing swiftly on the half-div, that she surged forward.

She'd been an uncharacteristically pleasant travelling companion given just how hot it'd grown the nearer they got to the plateau—only the lethargic swings of her axe gave any clue as to just how much it nettled her. But it came as no surprise that when she finally had cause to burst into action, it was delayed by fatigue. Once in motion, however, she barreled down the hillock so fast it seemed she'd tumble head over heels.

A savage hiss announced her charge, anticipated a crest in its rising volume. It wasn't until she'd nearly reached the bottom that it reached that crest, but it did so with her trademark flourish. Shkarag planted the butt of her spear in the dirt. At her speed, she was vaulted over in a wild spin that had her careening toward the crowd. Taken aback by the display, they were even less prepared when she loosed the spear, its velocity amplified by her spin, to spit three—head, chest, and abdomen—leaving the third pinned to the horse of a fourth. Less impressive was her crash.

Her bouncing, skidding tumble threw up a veil of dust, and her and the bandits into chaos. Tirdad trusted she'd thrive there if anywhere, so he put her out of mind, focusing instead on the riders who were yelling and turning circles. Aiming to capitalize on her distraction, he quickly loosed his last two arrows, each of which found their mark in the chests of two confused bandits, and drew his long sword.

A vulgar throbbing greeted him. It tugged on his arm, urging him into the fray. He answered the call by running through the first bandit he came upon, who was too busy shouting and pointing to notice until he shuddered and collapsed at the biting cold in his gut. Tirdad climbed into the saddle and turned the horse about, getting a lay of the skirmish. The bandits' prey, an elderly merchant, was standing beside his camel—neither of whom seemed all that concerned about the clamour surrounding them. Nearby, a trio of horsemen fenced in what could only be Shkarag, though the din and dust made it impossible to tell how she was faring besides that she wasn't dead.

Tirdad readied his sword and roused his steed into a gallop. He drew up beside the nearest horseman, and would've cleaved his head from his shoulders if another hadn't emerged on his left with the same in mind. Tirdad fell back flat just in time for the blade to arc overhead. This afforded the bandit to his right time to respond with a thrust intended to skewer him while down, but a timely flick of his wrist turned it just shy of its mark to pass harmlessly through his tunic. Tirdad sat up abruptly, which snagged the bandit's blade long enough for a starling-black rebuttal that plunged bitter cold into his heart.

The horseman on the left had circled back around, but without the benefit of surprise. And without that, the confidence to swing with abandon faltered. Tirdad easily matched the first strike, then turned aside the backstroke, taking advantage of the opening it created to further sate the starling-black with another frozen heart on which to feed. With the immediate threats dispatched, he finally caught a glimpse of Shkarag.

By Ohrmazd, her routine was spellbinding. He'd forgotten after all these years just how gracefully she handled an axe—and would've never believed it if he hadn't seen it for himself. She'd dispatched a bandit of her own, which had her one on one with the last of the crew. Shkarag whirled like leaves in a breeze, at the same time erratic and lissome. A single parry by the bandit would give off a series of whines as it caught the bit of her rapidly whirling axe. Then, in unwinding, she'd slip in like a boxer and whirl again from another angle, which would force the horseman to sidle his mount away and draw another string of whines.

True to her character, the next whirl broke rhythm with a technique he'd learned to use with maces, but never thought to apply to an axe—though it suited her brilliantly. She slipped forward again, but rose this time with the axe primed on her shoulder, ready to lash out like a snake. When with a shrug of a shoulder she did, the bandit didn't stand a chance. Her unnatural strength paired with the leverage of the attack made parrying impossible. The blow rung on the bandit's blade then bit clean through his shin, rousing a cry from the bandit. Shkarag whooped and shuffled back a step. She paused, canting. Then she whirled back in, and it occurred to Tirdad that she was doing precisely what the Eshm sisters had done to him: she was toying with the bandit. The man must've realized as much, or at least that he didn't stand a chance, because it was then that he disengaged and tore off at a mad gallop.

Shkarag gave chase, though it became apparent she couldn't keep pace much less close the gap. "Goat-courting . . . fuck!" she hissed, stomping. "Ruining a šo-welling orgasm all pomegranate-red and frothing higher and higher and there's the peak, but no, let's not finish our expedition the risk is too steep." She shivered, bared her fangs, and expelled another agitated hiss, raising her axe for a throw, but coming to terms with the bandit being too far away.

"What a shame," said Tirdad. "I'm more than willing to help you fin—" He snapped his teeth around the tail end of the comment, grin plummeting to a confused frown. Thankfully, she was too caught up in her frustration to notice. He watched as she bristled over to the dead horse her spear had impaled, and the struggling bandit it'd pinned. She'd found an outlet. With a heft of her axe, she started chopping. Tirdad turned his attention to the merchant. It wasn't that he was squeamish; he just didn't take pleasure in needless violence.

More bushy brows than eyes, the merchant had them trained on her display. Tirdad urged his mount over to greet the man with a raised palm. Closer inspection afforded the merchant's ancient countenance—leathery lips sunken and constantly chewing, ears and nose almost comically large. That considered, he seemed hale for any age old enough to look as such, straight-backed and alert.

"Are you injured?" he asked, sheathing his blade after a quick wipe.

The merchant gave a curt grunt. "Going to take more than some toenail-swallowing bandits to do me in." Another nod toward Shkarag. "Some company you keep," he said, punctuated by squelching in the background. "Not many who consort with divs so openly."

"No," agreed Tirdad.

"Suppose I should be grateful," the merchant said with a harrumph. He folded his arms. "Suppose."

"I suppose so," said Tirdad, taking a stern, disapproving tone. "Div or not, she risked her life for yours."

"Suppose." Another harrumph. "What you youngsters see in them is beyond me. But unlike my peers, I remember senile old men thinking the same of me in my youth." He chewed for a moment while slapping at the dust that clung to his white robes before reaching out a timeworn hand. "Well, hard to come by honest folk. Would say these days, but that has always been the case. So I count anyone willing to save this merchant's hide a rare blessing. Call me Adur-mah."

Tirdad shook his hand. "Tirdad."

Those bushy eyebrows lifted an inch. "Of the Eighth, uh, late Eighth House?"

"The same." The planet-reckoner withdrew his grasp, made uncomfortable by the fact. So he shifted the subject. "What's a merchant doing alone on the route—" Tirdad glanced at the camel. "—with bolts of silk no less?"

"Like to call it enterprising. Truth be told I was growing restless." He gestured to the east. "With all the tariffs and customs posts en route to Hrom, decided to finance some consignment in the other direction— frontier permits favouring our own and all. Then that cousin of yours causes a row, so I was worried about my investments." Adur-mah gave the silk a pat. "Turns out she did me a favour. Slew the sorry lot I invested in, but hadn't the time to spend my profits. Thinking maybe I should keep to the shipping lanes originating in the Gulf from now on." He mulled over the thought, chewing as he did.

Having found her release, Shkarag limped over, sprayed with blood— though her attire did a fine job of hiding it.

"Let me introduce my companion," said Tirdad, only after taking thorough stock of her body language to ensure she'd settled down. He indicated her with his pommel. "Adur-mah, this is Shkarag."

A curt nod by the merchant was all she'd get, and all things considered, fairly polite as far as greeting a div went.

Shkarag either didn't notice or didn't care. She set to rifling through the bodies and saddlebags without so much as a pause for consideration.

"We're heading to Ray," he said to the merchant, though his scrutiny lingered on the half-div. "Then Ecbatana after that. I'd prefer you join us rather than risk another attack, and I won't ask for payment."

"Am also heading to Ecbatana," said Adur-mah. "No payment for an escort, you say?"

"What use are we if we can't share the road with our countrymen, especially if it means a safe journey?"

Another curt nod. "You are a rare one, Tirdad. Befriending divs yet honourable all the same. A rare one indeed. I would welcome your company."

Tirdad flinched inwardly at the mention of honour. It crossed his mind that perhaps he should leave this foolish merchant to his fate. Then it occurred to him that the merchant may be able to weigh in on his quest. They'd travel together. For the time being.

The dust had begun to settle, which revealed more and more of their handiwork. The bandits' faces, twisted in pain or fear but never serenity, cut deep. Bandits preyed on the weak, but Tirdad always made a point of remembering that brigands were people whose children needed feeding or who had themselves fallen victim to circumstance. Desperation could bring out the worst in the best of us, and judging the desperate came too easy to those who weren't. He'd find a priest to perform the rites once they reached Ray.

Their horses had scattered, but only just. Most loitered nearby amid the parchment-dry tussocks and half-buried boulders, with one or two having galloped off, and one dead. He squinted at a nearby copse, one of the paltry clusters of trees that endeavoured to throw shade on one another in the suffocating heat. Might be a good place to rest until the sun wanes.

He faced Shkarag, who was elbow deep in a saddlebag. "Would you help gather the horses? We may as well see what we can get for them in the city."

She pulled her arm free, and with it a pair of gloves, which she slipped on. "Maybe," she replied, flexing her fingers experimentally, and appraising them as she did. "Always said looting was her favourite pastime. A hobby that changes with the eras—never know what they'll think up next. Liked the surprise, because you stick your arm in, not looking because that'd ruin the mystery of the great beyond where the cosmos is all shifting dunes that only chooses its shape when you reel in your reward. Then you violate that sack or those pockets, and could be a scorpion pricks you. Could be you find a toy prick." Shkarag set her head awry. "Looting is an antiquarian's game."

"Never thought of it that way," mused Adur-mah, patently intrigued by her rambling, and now following her as she rounded up the horses. "Antiquarian's game, you say? A novel take if I have ever heard one! What better place to discover cultures than in their closest belongings? What does a bandit keep close to heart?"

"Great," said Tirdad. "Another one. Why can't one person I travel with just act normal?" He looked on as Shkarag went from horse to horse, threading each into a train while the merchant yammered on about her fascinating take on social and cultural discovery, the half-div ignoring him all the while. Tirdad chuckled at the sight.

"Think she might've met her match already," he said to the camel, camels being at the same time the creature you feel the most compelled to talk to and the creature who cared the least about anything you had to say. "Have you ever noticed that those ornery old folks always walk in pairs, one acting as if the other should hurry up and die already?"

The camel grunted, irritably most likely.

"Yeah," said Tirdad. He turned his attention to the scattered corpses, where a radiant lemon-yellow caught his eye. Closer inspection found a scarf, which he unwrapped and held out to get a better look at its pattern. Lemon-yellow diced with a sparse diamond pattern that hadn't kept its colour well. Dirty and worn, with a rip that spanned half its length, it would do. Shkarag couldn't just stroll into a city after all, and its daring if faded colour suited her—perhaps more so because the diamonds had faded.

Rather than stand around gainlessly, he did some rummaging of his own. Although, contrary to Shkarag's magical rambling, there wasn't much of interest. A small sum of coins, water, an apricot wrapped in fig leaves, and a canteen with what remained of—he took a swig to check—a passable liquor distilled from dates.

"What I wouldn't do for a yogurt right about now," he said, wiping the sweat from his brow and stowing his loot. Now that the adrenaline had subsided, his ribs were beginning to object to all the exertion, so he brought the liquor out for another swig. By then, Shkarag was returning with the horses. Some of them anyway. Tirdad indicated the stragglers with his canteen. "You left a few."

Shkarag curled her upper lip. "Maybe." A tilt, which she swayed into. "Going to tie them to the ankles of this šo-swindling merchant and see how he likes it shelling out tariffs on three borders at once. Don't know what trousers he's trying to coax me into, but not buying them."

On cue, Adur-mah crossed between horses. He drew up beside his camel to check on his goods, chewing all the while. "I have four limbs, you know."

"Everyone knows no tithes in the southwest," Shkarag hissed. "Shouldn't let merchants out of bazaars. Shouldn't. Just shouldn't." She flexed her fingers. "At least the no-good cheats can only gesture and mutter there like some namby-pamby milksops so afraid a curse will dribble out, all so much soggy bread."

"Lass sure knows a lot about merchants for someone who despises them," the old man pondered merrily. "And here I really thought she was onto something with that antiquarian looting theory. Ah, well."

Shkarag's fangs unfurled. "Really beginning to—"

"Never mind that," said Tirdad, dismounting and inserting himself between the two. "I found something on the bandits."

The half-div cocked her head. "Already checked."

He brought out the scarf, then wound it loosely around her head and neck, leaving only her reptilian irises and sanguine eye colour as any real indication of her lineage, and not all that damning at a glance. "Thought you'd prefer it to a veil," he said, a tapered smile alongside. "Really suits you, too. Brings out your eyes and complements your gear." And it did.

Shkarag's enigmatic stare lingered on the scarf before finding something below to dart to. She cocked her head further, swaying. His trousers were roughly the same colour, a thought that only came to him now.

"How is it?" he asked.

"Suppose it does match your trousers," said the merchant.

"No one asked you," said Tirdad.

"Maybe," Shkarag muttered at length, unreadable. "Maybe," she repeated, then limped off toward the shade of the copse.

She hadn't outright objected to the scarf, so it seemed a favourable enough reaction. Tirdad followed her departure for a moment before turning to the merchant. Here he was on a quest to get to the bottom of what seemed to him a conspiracy against his late cousin, and as luck would have it, a man of commerce had fallen into his lap. This wasn't lost on him either. His offer to escort the merchant hadn't been entirely altruistic. As in trade, a deal needn't be plainspoken to be fair—the most happy, and oftentimes the most successful merchants, are those circumspect few who know how to play the market while making a great many friends along the road. Not quite so crafty, Tirdad nevertheless hoped to make use of the old man's experience.

"Find the legends rarely ever stack up to reality," said Adur-mah, thoughtfully trained on her departure. "But I suppose they would not be legends otherwise. Not always a bad thing either."

"Huh?"

"Ah, just thinking you and your div friend have been wildly exaggerated."

"I have a legend?" asked Tirdad. "Well, that's the first I'm hearing of it." He reached for the reins of the lead horse in the train and started for the trees.

The merchant drew up alongside, camel in tow. "Not all that flattering, if I am being honest," he said. "Overheard some of the boys in the Nishabhur garrison carrying on about you. About as flavourful as you would expect. Something about the only thing more flaccid than your shaft being your sword. Oh!" Adur-mah piped up as if he'd recalled a beloved childhood memory. "Told a tale of your duel come to think of it, all hollering and carrying-on. But the gist, from what I could tell, was that you only won because you went ass up for the champion, and she was pounding your shitter with abandon. So hard she choked to death on her tongue."

Tirdad nearly choked on his saliva. "That's—" He let out a whooping cough. "That's—" There was no helping it. A coughing fit seized him, doubled over the planet-reckoner and had him clutching his ribs. Even after it'd passed, he waited hands on knees, red-faced and gasping, for the pain to recede. Once it'd returned to the same nagging soreness he'd had since setting out, he straightened and addressed Adur-mah. "That's no legend. That's an everyday insult. Figures they'd besmirch my name at every turn. Although," he took a pull of liquor to soothe his ribs, "if we're being honest, it isn't that far off. She was downright wasted during that duel, and even then she had me on my heels. That I killed her at all was an accident."

"Might be best you keep to their story," advised the merchant.

"Yeah."

They'd reached the line of trees by then, a narrow tract of green only a few wide that kept well away from the slopes that flanked it. Tirdad secured two of the horses to neighboring trunks and left the rest to graze. "Well," he said, stooping to remove his boots, "this legend needs some time out of the heat. Let's rest until dusk approaches."

Shkarag had laid claim to a juniper far removed, reclined against its trunk and panting, but not so far off he missed the drowsy, unfocused stare she watched him with. He offered another tapered smile.

"Stay here," he bade the merchant, and made for her refuge. What he mistook for a stare was more vacant than the distance had let on. He knelt to offer his waterskin, which she paid no heed. That drew a worried frown. "Shkarag?"

Her eyes met his, though sluggishly, and she accepted the water after a few failed attempts at grabbing it. Even dizzy as she looked, she had enough wherewithal to nurse it slowly.

Tirdad stood, beetle-browed. "You really should take care out here, Shkarag. There's no shame in minding your body temperature. How about we refrain from travelling while the sun's high?"

Shkarag just panted between sips.

"Well," he said, "I'll make certain that old swindler doesn't give you any trouble. In the meantime, relax." With that, he left her to her private plot, making a mental note to check on her regularly. Tirdad was well aware she could take care of herself, but if her industrious caretaking had demonstrated anything, it's that they were better off looking out for one another.

"The heat?" inquired Adur-mah upon his return, which was confirmed with a nod. "Trying enough for cold-blooded creatures in this blasted weather without exerting themselves to save a rickety merchant, eh?"

"She'll manage," said Tirdad, unintentionally cold. Then, in seeking to pursue some answers, he took a seat across from the man, whose camel had seen to squeezing in beside him. He traced the contours of the ram's head pommel. "Tell me," he began, finding common ground and projecting a cheer he did not feel, "what has you headed to Ecbatana? I've travelled for the better part of my years, but always seemed to get pulled away if I ever got too close. Now that the two of us are, well, I guess we're retired, I figure now's the time."

The merchant bobbed his head, his lazy chewing now wholehearted. "Enjoy it while you can—I see those grey hairs of yours. They have a way of sneaking up on you. Let me tell you, I used to seek out those faraway places where the locals find you exotic and the other way around." He raised those bushy eyebrows, and it was as if a pair of bouncing silkworm cocoons were stuck to his face. "Ah, but before you know it, you are resting your back or relieving yourself every hour, and that throws sand in your pants if you know what I mean."

"Yet here you are," said Tirdad, spreading his hands. "And you seem to be faring well enough, all things considered. Would that I had such brio in my later years. I wake up ready to rest as is."

Adur-mah grunted at that. "Only goes downhill from there."

"So, about Ecbatana?"

"Oh, yes, Ecbatana. Simple enough, really. It is home, and has been my base of operations for longer than most have been in the trade."

Tirdad inclined his head. "I've heard it's a fair place to call home. You'll have to show me around."

"I will do more than show you around, friend. Once you have shared the road with a person, a traveler's bond is tied. My house is your house."

To be expected, as it was customary to offer lodging and food to even the newest of acquaintances. "I'll take you up on that offer," said Tirdad.

Then, as if it'd just come to him, "Oh, it's actually something of a co-incidence you're a merchant. My friend and I," he gestured to Shkarag, which reminded him to check on her condition. The half-div was staring in their direction, probably eavesdropping, and seemed to have gotten her breathing under control. He offered yet another tapered smile. "Anyway," he went on, "my friend and I tend to pass the time discussing our ad-ventures, and we've been butting heads over one in particular. You see, we were charged with unravelling the mystery around this merchant's missing shipments, because he was convinced divs were involved. Turned out as mundane as you might expect: his consignees were smuggling the goods away and running off with the profit."

The merchant smacked his lips disapprovingly. "Whatever happened to honour?"

"Yeah," said Tirdad, pressing through the unwelcome tide that came with the mention of honour. "What baffled us about those shipments was why he even bothered with some of them. I mean, why would a person ship clutches and clutches of eggs such a distance that they'll be rotten and fly-riddled by time they arrive?" He took a swig of liquor, and offered it to Adur-mah, who accepted with a salute. "She thinks it's on account of your peers being fools one and all—a mistake at best. I don't believe it.

"Much as he was getting played for a fool, I'd wager there's more to it than that," said Tirdad. "The market must have its secrets, even if I don't know them." He folded his arms and reclined against a tree. "You're the expert here, so do you mind settling the bet once and for all?"

The merchant took enough contemplative draws from the canteen to drain it, then peered inside and gave it a shake. "Some theories you have there," he replied. "And reckon either could be true. But here is what I think." Adur-mah leaned in, glancing left and right as he did and sidling closer. "I think this merchant of yours was craftier than he let on. If you would have had the stomach to dig through all those rotten eggs, you might have found hidden missives." He tapped his temple and wagged his eyebrows. "Stumbled upon some clandestine network backed by the Stinking Spirit himself, and you were none the wiser."

Tirdad caught a breath in his throat. He regarded the old merchant through narrowed eyes. "What?"

He waited, holding onto that breath and expecting a grin to break Adur-mah's grave countenance. The permanent squint that had obscured the merchant's eyes parted enough for Tirdad to see them clearly; they were grey, mirthless as drought. Without another word, Adur-mah settled in for a nap.

Tirdad remembered to breathe, rationalizing that it was probably the fancies of a senile old man too long in the sun and shaken by brigands, but he couldn't ignore the feeling that there had been an ominous undercurrent.

VII

A RIDGE INCISED THE SKY LIKE a crocodile skulking beneath the surface, its plates a tacit warning. Barren and crimped, its slope shored up a fortress city that girded the lower reaches. Mudbrick ramparts, honeyed by the setting sun and bordered in a luxuriant pattern, extended from the mountain. Ray was all angles—its stern façade upset only by the squat towers that flanked a vaulted gate, and the rounded parapets too merry for their imposing height.

From beyond its walls, Tirdad turned around to peer through a crowd of faces, behind which a lone castle interrupted the horizon as if it awaited a duel with the citadel commander. It brought Chobin to mind. His family manned that castle, and was responsible for the defense of the entire province. He hoped the marzban fared well.

Pressed close by the crowd, there hung the lemon-yellow of Shkarag's scarfed head. To her side, a pair of bushy eyebrows. "Figures we arrive during Tirgan," he said, leaning in and raising his voice to be heard over the clamour. "The festival will do us some good, though I would've liked to rest first."

"By time we are through the gate it will have passed," said Adur-mah. "Never seen them so spooked as to keep it within the walls. Your—uh, that Ashtadukht really put the fear of divs in them."

Tirdad appreciated his discretion. The last thing they needed was for all these people to turn on him. This brought his attention to the half-div at his fore. While her nearness permitted him only the top of her head,

113

the death grip she'd applied to her spear told him everything he needed to know about her mood.

He frowned at that faded scarf. During the scorching two-day walk it took to arrive, they'd spoken less than usual. Hardly at all, actually. He'd wager it was a mix of the heat and brooking an unwanted travelling companion, but she'd only half-heartedly bemoaned the merchant's presence, likely because she grasped his part in their quest.

As they'd drawn near to Ray, farms, trees and the shade they threw grew abundant—thanks chiefly to the qanats that had been tunneled into the water table to irrigate otherwise unproductive fields. With that came civilization. More concerned with getting rid of the horses than playing the market, they'd pawned them off for a bargain and wine—all of it profit at any rate.

"Oh," he said, taking out his wineskin and edging back a bit to offer it to the half-div. "This might help."

The scarf first tilted, then canted. Shkarag pried one hand from her spear, which surely creaked in relief, and grabbed the wineskin. She tucked it under her scarf to down it all in one long series of gulps, then handed it back. If she said anything, it was drowned out by the noise.

A rider approached from the direction of the castle, visible only because everyone had been made to leave their mounts outside the city for the duration of the festival. When the lone rider neared, Tirdad's mood was lifted. Chobin, sporting a regional tunic whose straps were decorated with plum and magenta circles, and a brooding frown besides, broke into the crowd.

A head taller than most everyone there, Chobin spotted him soon after, and brought his horse over. "Hah!" he exclaimed, grinning and extending a hand. "Knew you'd come crawling back to me sooner or later. Where's your lover? Leave the goat fucker already?"

Tirdad shook his head, indulging in a grin of his own and clasping the marzban's forearm. "I don't know how you manage to be so casually jovial and insulting, but you do it well. As for Shkarag, she's here." He inclined his head toward her, where she stood a bit less stiffly, eyeing her boots. Giving the horse an affectionate pat, he went on. "I guess the rules don't apply to you, huh?"

"Not here," Chobin confirmed. "To your benefit I might add. Let's go."

With that, he continued through the crowd, the three following in the wake of his horse and through the low, vaulted arch of the gate. More and more, the sounds of the festival took shape. Carefree laughter joined the spirited santur, the strum of the lyre, the hand drum's subtle appeal to the rhythm of the heart, the shouting and carrying-on that rose and fell as merrymakers all thrived on a melody both sweet and rousing.

Tirdad glowed. By Ohrmazd, he loved festivals. The gateway opened to the wide main thoroughfare, framed by mudbrick buildings accented with an ecstatic display of many-coloured plaster murals and stucco reliefs, their entrances a line of vaults that wafted a host of smells as diverse as a nightingale's song. Regularly, a dome would surface to grace the skyline like hillocks rolling over a plain.

Ropes bisected the thoroughfare at intervals to allow rope-dancers to spin overhead, entertaining the children with a feigned wobble now and then. Tirdad grabbed the first wine ewer he came across, choosing to forego both moderation and a proper drinking vessel. He downed it gustily, which had his head craned back and directed his gaze to one such dancer. She swayed and undulated, her four plaits fanning and swinging with every movement, and sprightly though she was in her flowing gauzy dress, she still dredged up sour memories of his cousin. Looking away, he took a few more draughts of wine.

"Shkarag?" he said, only just noticing her absence. Fortunately, he had no trouble finding her scarf. She'd stopped in front of a crimson tent to leer at it suspiciously. "Running off already?" he asked. "And to a tent like that no less. You know the so-called sorcery they practice in there is just for entertainment? All gears, illusions, and banging on metal. Oh, and obtuse answers. I'm told that's an important part."

She canted her head, but offered no reply.

"Well, obtuse answers do seem to suit you." He stared as she did, and only then did he notice a small bird perched atop the tent. "Ah, a snowfinch is it? So that's what's got your attention."

Shkarag's eyes darted up and down. She faced him, inclining her spear as he so often did with his pommel. "Won't run off. Your goat fucker is."

She threw one last wary glance at the bird before limping off toward the horse.

Tirdad knotted his brow, and though his thoughts were hampered, it came to him that there'd been a snowfinch in her illusion, and years before that, a bickering snowfinch and magpie. She'd described their dispute as marital then, sweeping her hand over the ground in doing so. No surprise then that it unsettled her.

"Wonder where the magpie's gone?" he pondered. Tirdad shrugged and caught up with Chobin, who had turned around in his saddle to train bemusement on the planet-reckoner.

"Fuck are you doing staring at a bird?" asked the marzban.

Tirdad offered the ewer. "Shkarag had paused to look at it," he explained as if it were obvious.

Chobin took a long draw of wine, went to wipe his mouth on his sleeve, but stopped just shy of staining it. "Thought that was her thing," he said. "Disappearing, absurdity, generally being a nuisance."

"Never called her a nuisance."

"Didn't have to. Listen to one of your tales and it's mighty obvious that skink-slicker is a nuisance. And that's treading lightly."

Tirdad turned to address her, but drew up short of it. She had an inquisitive stare trained on him, and her cant was decidedly less sharp than usual. It listed ever so slightly.

"Skink-slicker," she said, the nebulous list swaying. "What's a . . . skinks should just decide. Just—" She waved her spear, and it was a good thing the street wasn't nearly as packed as the gate. "Sit down and have the . . . take the vote like some, like some . . ." She trailed off, nodding sharply. She glared at Chobin. "Skinks should stop straddling the fence. Either you're a šo-lizard skittering . . . šo-skittering lizard, or a šo-slithering snake. Pick a side. Hayk can't play the field forever, cozying up to Hrom then Iran then Hrom then Iran. Someday skinks will find themselves staring down the spear of a snake—" She punctuated the eventuality by thumping the ground with the butt of her spear. "And either they get rid of those measly arms or they take up arms."

Tirdad looked down. She hadn't bothered with a ewer. Instead, she was dragging around one of the large glazed jars used to transport and store wine. He rubbed his face, more amused than exasperated.

"Skink-slicker," she mouthed. "Skink-slicker. What's a skink-slick— oh." She redoubled her glare. "Never fingered a skink. Never had those too-tiny toes curling while I—" Shkarag heaved as if to vomit.

"We've only just arrived and you've drunk yourself sick," said Tirdad.

"Learn some moderation," Chobin censured light-heartedly. "Not like you're a div or anything."

Her grimace was plain behind the scarf. "Not the wine. To slick a—" She heaved again.

"Hah!" belted Chobin. "Would you look at that. Never thought I'd see the day when one of her ilk is disgusted."

"Rare indeed," said Tirdad, scanning the area as he did. The jar didn't seem to be drawing any undue attention, which could change when she next hefted it for a drink. He wasn't worried about her taking it—wine ran freely during festivals. What he didn't want was a display of her strength in broad daylight.

Naturally, that was when she strained to lift it. Tirdad hurried to put on a show by slipping his shoulder under the jar. As he stood there watching her drink, it came to him that if anything, her display only helped them to blend in. They probably appeared a regular pair of partygoers to those around them.

She drained it summarily, then sat it down, giving him a funny look as she did. "Can heft fine without you."

"And I can do much without you. Doesn't mean your help isn't welcome."

"So," said Chobin, "much as I'd like to watch while the two of you buzz around one another just shy of threshing, I must tend to the family." He directed his attention to Tirdad. "Don't drink too much. We're hosting an impromptu wrestling tournament, because no one told me they wanted one until I left the castle. Should compete."

Tirdad shook his head, patently disappointed. "I'm afraid not. Ribs aren't fully healed, and we had a couple rows on the way."

Chobin lifted his brows. "A couple rows, huh? Go figure. Here I've been cooped up with the folks. Speaking of, weren't you travelling with Adur-mah?"

"Yeah. Must've lost him in the crowd. You know him?"

"Done the city a few favours. Frankly, I'm surprised to find you travelling with another star-reckoner so soon."

"He was waylaid by bandits, so Shkarag and I intervened and offered an escort." Tirdad smiled at a passing festival-goer, an exceptionally ordinary-looking young woman who he recognized but didn't know why. He made to greet her when it hit him. "Wait. What'd you call Adur-mah?"

"Star-reckoner?" The marzban dismounted, relinquishing his horse to an attendant. He straightened his tunic, checking the sleeves for wine. "Hear he's more of a merchant these days, not that I keep up with his affairs."

Beetle-browed, Tirdad cast over his shoulder as if the star-reckoner would be right behind him. He wasn't, of course. Only Shkarag, listing against her spear, and the crowd besides.

The missives. He swallowed; his chest and throat grew tight; his mind raced. The missives. He thought he was being clever coaxing something out of the old man, but he'd been a blundering fool. The missives. The planets loomed closer, as if they could sense his rising panic and were poised to take advantage.

"Tirdad." It was Shkarag. She'd clasped his forearm, and trained a knowing gaze on his. For a time, its flitting was confined to searching. For what, he didn't know. But she must've found what she was looking for, because she soon listed once more into her spear as if nothing had happened, watching the crowd but wearing the unfocused stare of inebriation.

"Coming?" asked Chobin.

"Yeah." Tirdad said as much, but he lingered a moment to concentrate on the celestial theatre. What little he could sense was a mirage well beyond the horizon, distorted much like the setting sun in its final window. That mirage carried the tempered whine of steel too guarded to ring. The planets were nowhere to be found. "Yeah," he said again, finally falling in step with Chobin.

"Well, I am due for a beating," said the marzban. He gestured to the stump-like citadel, which occupied a slate further up the mountainside. There, it crested another mudbrick wall of rounded parapets, as if leering down at all the strangers come to its city. "Care to join?"

"No."

Chobin flashed a full-toothed grin. "Escort me then? Haven't seen your sturgeon-kissing mug in months."

Indulging his friend, Tirdad waved the marzban forward. "Escort only. I want nothing to do with your family's affairs."

At that, Chobin's grin grew more toothsome. Tirdad accompanied him up a flight of stairs that'd been carved into the side of the slate, which were hemmed in by the sheer-walled citadel to his left and an increasing grade to his right.

While he had a wealth of material, Tirdad didn't have time to strike up a conversation before they reached the height of the stairs. The gate, vaulted and squat like its outer cousin, sat ajar. In it stood a man who bore a striking resemblance to Chobin, but older than Tirdad by a few years. The planet-reckoner lowered his head and put his hands over his chest deferentially—even when he had belonged to a House it had paled in comparison to this noble family.

"Father," said Chobin.

He knelt to kiss the man's feet and hands as etiquette bade, before his father embraced his head. The intimacy of their greeting made what followed all the more striking. Before Chobin could fully put his feet beneath him, his father snatched a staff that'd been propped against the gate and began whaling on the marzban.

Tirdad glanced up enough to see Chobin taking his beating with a grin plastered on his face, then back down again. This is what he'd wanted to avoid.

Fathers all had their unique approaches to instilling in their children the traits they valued, but this was unorthodox at best. Tirdad assumed as much, anyway. His father had died young, which placed him under the wing of the head of the House. As such, Ashtadukht's father had raised him as his own, and he had been among the gentlest of men.

"Satisfactory," said the man once the beating had concluded. "A flinch or two can be forgiven. Remember, son, the fate of our House will soon rest on your shoulders. Our people will look to you for guidance, our soldiers for courage. You must be their pillar."

"Yes, Father."

"Tirdad," hailed the man, which gave him leave to lift his head. Chobin had his bowed, but didn't seem all that worse for wear.

"Bahram," replied Tirdad. He remembered Shkarag, and a glance told him that while she hadn't bothered with a show of respect, she was otherwise sedate.

"It warms my heart to see you in good health, not to mention here in my city during Tirgan. How fares your family?" Bahram grimaced, likely realizing too late what he'd asked, and no doubt aware that Tirdad's part in his House's downfall had fashioned him an outcast.

Tirdad fought off a grimace of his own, instead carving a smile that had no place in the conversation. "As well as can be expected. And yours?"

"Well enough. You've ensured as much where my son is concerned, and for that I am grateful. It does him good to spend his time with a veteran rather than those his age. Too impulsive, and no experience to impart. Would that you'd visit more often. For what it's worth, I'd welcome you into our family."

Tirdad inclined his head. "I do what I can."

"Friend of yours?" asked Bahram, facing Shkarag and offering his hand.

She backed away, assuming a guarded posture with one claw hovering over her axe. Her attention darted between the two of them.

"Strangers make her uncomfortable," Tirdad was quick to explain. "Doesn't mean anything by it. She's ill."

Bahram retracted his hand with swift but measured grace. "All the same, it's a pleasure to meet you," he said. Then to Tirdad, "I'd invite you in, but we are using the citadel as a staging area for the festival. Will I see you in the wrestling tournament?"

"I'm afraid not."

"Is that so? Chobin gave the impression you'd make a worthy contender. A real shame to have you here without a show of your prowess."

Having emerged from his subservience, the marzban cut in. "His ribs, father."

That drew a nod from Bahram. "Ah, my apologies. With the festival in full swing there's a great deal to keep track of. Still, it's a shame."

Tirdad shared in his disappointment. "Would that I were in better shape. Festivals and wrestling were the passions of my youth, though I've never had anything you'd call prowess."

"Indulge your youth as often as you can," said Bahram. "Or run the risk of forgetting how." He waved at the busy citadel to his rear. "Well, as you can see I have my hands full. To be frank, some of the more prickly citizens decried the cancellation of the tournament this year. We haven't the space, but fuck me with a fishing rod if they care. So I sent my son out to gather contestants, and turns out some of our regular lot rode east days ago and haven't returned. Won't be much of a tournament if we come up short."

"I'll do it," said Shkarag.

Tirdad turned confusion on the half-div. "Do what?"

". . ."

"Shkarag?"

". . ." She canted, shooting the ground a dirty look.

He blew out an exasperated sigh, and was about to address Bahram when she finally spoke up.

"Wrestle. I'll do the—" Where she would have made a claw of her fingers, she wrung her spear instead. Her back straightened, and she trained determination on Tirdad. "I'll do the šo-damned thing from your glory days. And you can . . . your fall from grace and your old age will be cast away like some . . ." She wrung in earnest, white-knuckled now, and listing unsteadily but only just. "Molting. You'll be the cuckold. Watching and vicarious."

Puzzled, Tirdad drew his face into a grin that joined a host of other creases. He'd grown comfortable with her overelaborate, metaphorical, oftentimes vague speech and thought patterns, then this phylactery of hers went and revived her. For that, he was more and more grateful with each passing day. But the lucidity she had gained made her speech a challenge to follow—a change that brought up the question of whether it was her unclouded mind laid bare or if she had trouble translating her train of thought to words. He would ask later.

She drove the butt of her spear into the ground. "Fate, all those crabby stars and cranky planets, all swirling and making your decisions for you. Like some host waving you in, a cold meal primed, but he's asking you what you want for dinner and you're getting gruel and calling it that. This is their hallmark. Must wrestle."

"You want to compete?" asked Bahram, able to pick out the word or two that mattered. "You're ill, are you not?"

Shkarag finally had cause to contort a claw over her head. "Only here."

"Only there?"

The half-div cocked her head, finding something in the city below to focus on. ". . ."

Tirdad pondered the back of her scarf, and chose to let her response stand on its own rather than risk coming off as unsympathetic or undermining her will.

Bahram, a military man himself, took stock of her as he hadn't when they were introduced. "Caftans can be misleading," he said at length, and approvingly. "A lean person comes off as thin and unassuming. Had me fooled. You're—" Someone called to him from within the citadel, which drew a frown. He looked back and expelled a sigh. "Looks like we're needed. We'll see you at the tournament. I expect your lady friend to throw cinnamon on the fire."

With that, father and son grasped Tirdad's forearm, then left to tend to House affairs.

"You all right?" he asked Shkarag.

A cant. "Maybe."

He ran his fingers through his hair, sweaty and unkempt, thinking he could do with a bath and she could do with a reprieve. "We can avoid the crowd for a time if you need a break," he said. "Grab something to eat and find some shade away from the bustle."

Shkarag responded with a hiss. Though she faced the city, her agitation was made plain by the tautness that gripped her. Most telling, the hiss prevailed. "Not an incorrect . . . an invalid. Don't need your šo-righteous pity."

122

Tirdad eyed her blood-red caftan, her muscles straining against its confines as she strangled her spear. There, in the still between city and citadel, hedged by the arch of the gate, he waited. It occurred to him that he still hadn't learned to navigate her eggshells, that she'd returned uncharted, as if a cyclone had wreaked havoc on the half-div he'd grown fond of, leaving the lay the same but the scenery out of sorts. So he waited.

It seemed like longer than it was—only a few minutes—but when her caftan lost its tension, it threatened to move to his tunic. She made for the stairs, and he for her.

"I'm sorry," he said, leaving room for her to walk by if she pleased, but drawing close enough to get her attention. "I meant nothing by it."

She passed by as if to ignore him, and perhaps she had meant to at first, but upon reaching the first step she about-faced. "Why?" she asked, curt as a deathblow.

Tirdad parted his lips to reply, then closed them. He had an explanation, but she'd caught him off guard. He'd expected her to ignore him when he continued without offering a response. He should've known better. After getting his thoughts in order, he tried again.

"For making you feel pitied. I only meant to be considerate. You've recovered a part of yourself—for the better, I think. That much is certain. But your illness, it seems to hound you more where before you took it in stride." He lifted his hand as if to stop her from leaving, though she made no move to do so. "What you said to him just now caught me by surprise." Tirdad mimicked her hand-turned-claw. "You said, 'Only here.'"

Shkarag set her head askew, but only that, so he went on.

"I don't think it really hit me until then that you're aware of it—of its nature. I . . ." He trailed off, snorting and shaking his head at his foolishness. "I should've known. I should've been more sympathetic. If nothing else, I should've asked."

". . ." The look she gave him was as inscrutable as ever, but it was a meaningful look all the same. She shifted to favour her thigh, which threw the glare of the sun on her face and narrowed her pupils to slits. "Why'd you mean nothing by it?" she asked.

Leave it to her to take issue with the unexpected.

"Well . . ." His hand found the comfort of the ram's head pommel. So perplexed by the question, he never got around to racking his brain for an answer. What could she possibly be asking, and was the risk worth venturing a guess? More eggshells and uncharted waters. By contrast, pranks had been a walk in the hunting park, pheasants the quarry. These eccentricities of hers were the lions and tigers.

She remained unreadable. "We should go," he said, hoping she'd drop it. "I'm starving, and Tirgan only comes once a year."

When he made to leave, she stepped aside, that stare of hers trained on him as he passed, and likely kept there as they covered the way down. They'd nearly reached the bottom when she posed a more mundane question.

"You grappled?" she asked. "You wrestled?"

Tirdad paused to aim a furrowed brow at her. The stare had persisted. Coming from the half-div, mundane was more eccentric than eccentric. Still, no change. He started forward again, and figured at least this one was clear enough to answer. "I did," he said, imagining the thrill of the competition, the calculating give and take that would be lost on outsiders, the testing of defenses for the slightest lapse, the camaraderie. "Truthfully, I was never good at it. I wrestled for sport. I wrestled because I enjoyed it. I wrestled because tradition should be observed. Wrestling develops character."

The stairs emptied them into the main thoroughfare, which still wore the trappings of the festival: smiles, music, and food. From ahead, the metre of poetry joined in.

"Sholezard," Tirdad thought aloud. "I haven't had it in ages." He faced Shkarag, whose eyes darted suspiciously over the bustle. "Do you see any?"

". . ." More darting.

"Well, let's look then."

The bulk of the festival was traditionally held outside the walls, and for good reason. For all its energy, Ray was far from sprawling. With that in mind, Tirdad snatched up the first wine ewer and sholezard he came across, then abandoned the main thoroughfare for the side streets. Other festival-goers had the same idea, but the closer he got to the residential area, the fewer there were. He set a course for the wall, where a sentry let him pass without a second glance. The nearest tower threw ample shade, so he figured its shadow was as favourable a spot as any.

Shkarag was quick to claim a patch, sitting leg out and alternating between a ewer of her own and a fistful of sweetmeats. "Who'd you pantomime?" she asked, mouth full.

"Don't—" Tirdad shook his head and took a seat by her side. Half div, and his elder by magnitudes. Who was he to tell her not to talk while eating? It made him cringe to recall all the times he'd took it upon himself to remonstrate her. "Pantomime?"

Tirdad ate in respectful silence, savouring the saffron that gave sholezard its yellow colour and honey-hay aroma. Meanwhile, Shkarag explained.

"Who'd you pantomime?" she reiterated as if it were obvious. "Who had his arms crossed? Who went through the motions like some . . . like the spark when it dwindles, like a life without your—" She ceased her chewing, and spat out her sweetmeat as if disgusted by it. Her chin puckered so briefly Tirdad would've missed it if he weren't watching. She sucked in a breath as shaky as it was steadying, and continued as if nothing had happened. "And you're doing your utmost, really doing your utmost to fill in the hollows with the flair they deserve. Because you think . . . you think those šo-sweaty sweeps and throws and grapples should remember the theatrics they once loved. And you're not unkind. Even if everyone thinks you are. Even if all creation conspires to inter you like some—"

"I get it," Tirdad interrupted before her explanation could turn into a tale of recursion. "Ashtadukht's father taught me. He could've hired a tutor, but he strove for a close relationship with his children, and though he was my uncle, he treated me like his own."

"Oh."

"And who'd you pantomime? I assume you did since you volunteered."

Shkarag shrugged, then set to massaging her thigh. "Wrestling belongs to cubs. Being edged is frustrating something fierce. Would rather—" She stopped massaging long enough to shoot him a glance. "I won't." She turned her attention back to her thigh. "Maybe."

More kneading followed before she resumed. "Learned on an island. Before the sea swallowed it up. Dourboat might've been behind it. The vizier behind the boom."

Tirdad took a pull from his ewer, and the pair shared a silence limned by the distant festival until the shadow cast by their tower stretched well over the wall. They would've stayed like that until the tournament if a familiar voice hadn't risen from below.

"All right, all right," said Adur-mah. "You young ones are like baby goats with all your hopping and carrying-on. Maybe I should shear your hair and put it on this head of mine."

"No!" a chorus of children cried. "Do not shear us!"

"Tell us a story!"

"A story!"

"You are the story-reckoner!"

"Only if you keep quiet," said Adur-mah. "One interruption and you will spend the next few months in mystery, because I will stop right there. Now gather round and get comfortable, because have I got a tale for you."

Tirdad approached the parapets and looked down to see the children, still soaked from their water games, following instructions and fidgeting in doing so, but generally well-mannered in respecting their elders—and in feeding their curiosity.

The star-reckoner turned merchant shielded his eyebrows to look up at him, then waved him down. "Ah, Tirdad!" he called, waving, which caused the children to all pivot at once. "Come, come!"

Tirdad set his jaw. Should he interrogate the old man now? Would he have what it takes to subdue him? What impressive lots could such an experienced star-reckoner draw? He gave the ram's head pommel a squeeze, drawing confidence from its place on his hip.

"Don't drape the lion over your horse before you've slain it," Shkarag advised from his side. She pulled the scarf down to cover her face. "Cubs and daylight. Wait."

Checked again by the half-div. He offered her a tapered smile, grabbed his ewer, and proceeded down to the gathering. "Don't mind us," he said, sitting against the wall and noting that the sentry had left his post. Shkarag followed suit.

Adur-mah gave them a nod, then directed his attention back to the children, chewing all the while. "Now, I was ready to regale you little goats with the tale of Erash and his mythical arrow shot. A fine tale, a fine tale indeed. But I believe you are ready for . . . no, you are too young." He crossed his arms and shook his head. "Maybe in a few years."

The children responded exactly as goaded, shaking their heads vehemently while holding true to their quiet.

The star-reckoner harrumphed. "I see all these heads a-shaking. Some strange little goats I have. Hmm." He chewed thoughtfully. "Maybe you are ready."

Energetic nodding followed.

"I tell you what," he said, leaning forward and putting his hands on his knees. "How about something special this year? Something you can only hear from old Adur-mah?" He wagged his bushy eyebrows for effect. "The tale behind the tale."

The children somehow managed to nod more energetically.

Adur-mah swept his gaze over them, ending it on Tirdad. When he next spoke, it was with the warp and weft of a storyteller. "From the darkest, dustiest, long-forgotten annals of legend, known only to a privileged few in my order, sworn to secrecy on punishment of death—unless of course you are entertaining precocious children like yourselves—I bring you 'The Wrath of Erash'."

He chewed a moment, looking from child to child, and in so doing fanned their anticipation. "You all know of Erash, heroic and selfless, who scaled the treacherous summit of Mount Damavand. How with bow and arrow blessed by Spandarmad, imbued with the wisdom and will of the planet itself, he strained—"

Adur-mah acted as if he were pulling a bowstring and having a hard time of it. "—he strained sliver by sliver to draw that mighty bow and loose the single most important, the most spectacular shot in all history." He pretended to release the arrow, then turned a countenance severe with mourning on his audience. "For the good of his countrymen, in service to Truth, Erash threaded his soul into the fletching, to be unraveled as it soared over Iran and into Turan. When, after days of flight, it finally lodged in a walnut tree, it would mark the border between rival nations, secure peace, and put an end to a terrible drought. All in a single shot."

The star-reckoner lifted a glass of wine and took his time drinking, looking over the lip as he did at the restless children, and stringing them along all the more.

"The Wrath of Erash," he began again after they were sufficiently teased, "is a misleading title, and cause to ban star-reckoners from naming their tales. You see, Erash wanted only to do his duty, but there were those who would use war and drought for gain. Those greedy men cared not for others, and had strayed so far into the Lie that their souls were rotten and corrupt. You hear of Erash, of his climb, of his archery, of his legend, but never of his pursuers, or of the unlikely heroes who would save him.

"These merchants and warmongers, they would stop at nothing to slay Erash. For they knew that arrow would bring their ill-begotten profits and power to a swift end. So they hired mercenaries; they enlisted divs. They sent all so much death."

Adur-mah blew out a sigh, shaking his head somberly, and Tirdad could imagine each and every child had the same question bouncing on the tip of their tongues.

"What did he do?" Adur-mah asked. "Well, with the mercenary bands and slavering divs approaching Damavand like a storm cloud, he knew his only chance was to climb. To climb and hope beyond all hope that he would reach the summit in time. As he did, death closed on him in the valley below, biting at his heels like rabid wolves. Word had gotten out of the treachery, and indeed, heroes aplenty had answered the call for good, but none would reach him in time. Erash had hardly begun his ascent when he was confronted by two half-divs.

"Now, these were no ordinary divs. His pursuers paled in comparison—as you will soon come to learn. Erash saw in them the vile blood of Eshm, and he knew it in his bones that his quest had come to an end. For Eshm is the messenger of Ahriman, the embodiment of wrath itself. So zealous is his wrath that he slaughters divs and men alike. Woe betide any man who crosses paths with Eshm or his offspring. Erash was doomed."

A pause for effect. "Or he would have been. See, my little goats, Erash had inspired more than heroes. It just so happened that these sisters were in the area, and upon learning of his plight, even their half-div hearts had been moved to action. They said as much in a roundabout way, and the archer of the two expressed her respect for Erash's mastery, then they bade him good luck and promised to hold off his pursuers. Erash thanked them for their uncommon bravery, and asked them their names. 'Waray,' said one. 'Shkarag', said the other."

Tirdad glanced to his side. Shkarag was staring in the direction of the star-reckoner, but she wore the faraway gaze of reminiscence, and had never looked as old as she did then.

"With that, Erash proceeded to the peak without interruption, and secured his place in legend. Meanwhile, the sisters chose a pass better suited to defense. There, they waited. The host of divs and mercenaries filed into that pass, confident that they were the only force in range, and so eager to catch their quarry that they would have taken the direct path regardless. Their blood boiled, and they all argued over who would be the one to make the killing blow. That was until the sisters blocked the way. At first, whispers arose."

Adur-mah cast left to right confusedly, shrugging and making faces that drew giggles from the children. "The warriors quarreled. Some scoffed at the display—surely a bluff. Others suspected a trap. The ranks grew more unsettled when it became clear what they were up against. Even the divs were having second thoughts. All signs had pointed to them catching Erash without incident, so their morale was sorely unprepared for this development. Even the fiercest of hearts are frightened by Eshm's bloodline. Rightfully so, too.

"Perhaps they would have turned back, but a lone warrior charged from the line, sword raised and naively thinking he would steal the glory while the others squabbled. Well, they could not have that now could they? The host swarmed forward—" Adur-mah threw his hands out toward his audience. "—to bring a swift end to the sisters."

He tapped his chin, chewing as he did. "Come to think of it, maybe you are too young for this after all." He got up as if to leave, dusting off his rear and patting his robe.

The children were all leaning forward by now. Even Tirdad was engrossed in the story, though he was getting irritated by the display much as he appreciated the effort Adur-mah was putting into it.

"Please tell us," blurted a boy, unable to hold it back any longer.

"Please!" said another. "We have been good!" Soon enough, they were all pleading.

Adur-mah lifted his hands to quiet the children. "Shush now. I will finish the tale on one condition: that you keep it from your parents. I have had my fill of earfuls."

Full of enthusiasm, the children nodded.

"Ah, I suppose I can break the rules just this once. Told your parents stories when they were your age. Who are they to tell me which I can and cannot tell?" Adur-mah reclaimed his seat and cleared his throat, returning once again to the scene and his storyteller tone.

"The swarm advanced with shouts and shrieks, shoulder to shoulder in the narrow pass and clambering to reach their prey. Meanwhile, the sisters watched, still as can be—unshaken in the face of death. And just when the swarm was upon them, swords and spears reaching out for first blood, it collapsed.

Clever as they were brave, the sisters had rushed to dig a ditch and lined it with spikes, on which the swarm was gored. More and more fell in, unable to stop or shoved from behind, until it was full of bodies. Only then could the swarm cross. And cross it did."

Adur-mah threw his hands in the air. "Oh, what a sight! In a flash, Shkarag set her axes to whirling—" He spun his finger to demonstrate. "—like an angry dust tornado, winding and unwinding, and between those lethal spins she would throw off her attackers with one of the many techniques she'd learned in her travels. Those she fell upon, and those who fell upon her, they were all cut down.

"What of Waray, the half-div archer who had been so inspired by Erash? Well, any archer worth the skin on a buck's back would have taken the high ground, but not this one. Not Waray. She inserted herself into her sister's routine as if they were snakes coiling around one another. Where Shkarag left an opening, Waray would plug it with an arrow. As quickly as the horde could advance, they would fall to axe or bow.

These half-div sisters had spent lifetimes together, and together they had survived by coming to know their weaknesses. So, one complementing the other, Shkarag and Waray continued their display, gradually giving ground so that Waray could snatch up the quivers they had stowed along the pass."

The star-reckoner took a gulp of wine to soothe his throat then went on. "They fought and fought, drenched in sweat and fangs bared, while high above Erash struggled to draw his bow.

"Now, it is no secret that an Eshm sister is worth thirty men. Their numbers may be few, but their battlefield presence is unmatched by any but a yazata or forty-armed div. This was different. Eshm sisters cooperate. Shkarag and Waray fought as one. In that, they were worth thirty Eshm sisters. Even so, eventually they tire.

"After dealing with a quarter of the host, Shkarag's exhaustion finally got the best of her. Her valour faded, and with it came one too many holes for her sister to plug. So a spear did instead." Adur-mah doubled over and clutched his stomach. "Oh, it got her good. Went clean through."

At that, the shoulders in his audience slumped as one. They had all been rooting for these mysterious sisters despite their lineage. "No one really knows whose spear caught her in the gut," he said. "The chaos made it impossible to tell."

Daggers shot up Tirdad's forearm from where Shkarag had applied an iron grip. Any tighter and it'd fracture. He gritted his teeth through the pain, once again drawn to her thousand-yard stare. "Should I ask him to stop?" he whispered. Shkarag gave a brisk shake of her head, and retracted her grip.

"That, my little goats, was the last anyone saw of the sisters. For that would be the spear that would unleash the full extent her bloodlust. An injured Eshm sister . . . well, they are formidable and throw caution to the wind. Shkarag answered by snapping the spear and disappearing into the host. What followed was not recorded, or has been lost to time, but we do know Erash fired his arrow without incident all thanks to those sisters."

Adur-mah yawned and sat back. "And that is the tale of 'The Wrath of Erash'. You should take it to heart, because there is much to learn from those unsung heroes. Waray and Shkarag were a shining example of your freedom to choose your fate, to serve good or evil, the Truth or the Lie. Recall that they were half div, which meant they were also half human—a distinction most would rather not acknowledge, because in that duality they might see themselves. Whether they chose to follow the sway of Eshm or their human mother, they would be making the same decisions you and I make every day. At the end of the tale you were each and every one of you rooting for them, because Shkarag and Waray had walked the path of justice. See to it that you take heed. Because if they could fight the pull of their lineage, you have no excuse for falling into the clutches of the Lie."

Adur-mah waved his audience off. "Now, go spend Tirgan with your parents. I am not as young as I used to be. Need some rest."

The children surrounded him for a parting hug, all thanking him for the tale, some curious about one detail or another, before they went on their way. In parting, they were already re-enacting the story, and many claims were made for the role of a sister.

Tirdad watched Shkarag as she followed their departure with interest. He'd learned more about her in the last few months than in all their many years together. To think she had a role in one of the most ubiquitous legends of his culture. He would have found it far-fetched at best if he hadn't been around to witness the effect it had on her.

Adur-mah approached, chewing as usual, his brows trained on Shkarag as she got to her feet. "Tried to keep to the record," he said. "Time in the archives was not kind to it, so I had to fill in some of the blanks."

"I've never heard or read anything of that before," said Tirdad. "Not in any of the frahangestan lessons, or in my travels."

The star-reckoner's eyebrows shrugged alongside his shoulders. "Those schools for nobles are grand for culture, but it is a dictated culture. Measured. No one wants a legend painting divs in a positive light, and I cannot say I blame them. When the sun has set and we must take up arms, divs are still the enemy." He turned his brows on Shkarag. "Most are. How close were the records to the truth?"

"Enough," she muttered, weary enough to have been there. "I think. Going to . . ." She looked around as if she were still half in the past. Glossy-eyed and dazed, Shkarag left for the stairs that led up the wall.

"Bad form?" asked Adur-mah. "Thought I would recount the legend as thanks for what you did for me back there. Really is forbidden to repeat outside the archives, you know."

Tirdad tore his gaze from the half-div and leveled it on the star-reckoner. "She wanted to hear it," he said. "Seemed to take her back."

Star-reckoner. That's right. Heading to Ecbatana, a merchant, and that ominous explanation for the egg ruse: Adur-mah could very well have been the star-reckoner he'd been seeking all along. Tirdad's palm, steadied by wine but tense with alarm, came to rest on the ram's head pommel. He entertained the idea of running him through, but he needed Adur-mah alive. Well, alive long enough to get some answers. No, that wouldn't do. Simply being a star-reckoner wasn't enough to justify such treatment. Tirdad would not become Ashtadukht. He would get his answers without resorting to violence if circumstance allowed it.

He'd intended to strike up a conversation to that end when Shkarag's footsteps signaled her return. She ambled over, ewer in hand, took a swallow, then offered it to Adur-mah. "Here," she said, shaking it to the sound of sloshing. The gloss in her eyes was all but gone, driven out by granite. "For the . . ." Shkarag squinted at the ewer, giving it another slosh. "For the overturned memory."

Adur-mah accepted with a toothless grin. "Sharing wine with a div," he mused. "Even at my age there are firsts to be had. Never fails to surprise." He summarily downed the wine, ending with a smack of his lips. "You know, almost tastes unalloyed coming from such an uncommon hand. One of legend no less. Ah!" He slapped his thigh. "Do an old man a favour and tell me how you escaped the horde. Been eating at me."

Shkarag cocked her head. She stepped back. Her stare flashed back and forth. "Don't know. The pomegranate-red was . . . I was in its possession like some, like some—" She cocked the other way, and took another step back. "Like the pollen on a bumblebee, along for the ride. All bobbing about, fanned by its fluttering wings, thinking this isn't so bad while you're connecting the stars, arms tucked behind your head. The buzzing irks you something fierce. Blood splashing your face. There's—" She cast sidelong at Tirdad. "Wrestling soon."

"Oh," said Tirdad. "It'd nearly slipped my mind. Wouldn't want to miss your matches—either a chance to see you embarrassed or a chance to see you triumph. Either outcome is a victory for me."

Shkarag canted so sharply she nearly capsized. Her expression was surprisingly soft, almost amused. "Maybe," she said.

"Be a shame to miss," agreed Adur-mah. "You two go ahead. Joining me on the road to Ecbatana tomorrow?"

"You can bet your life on it," said Tirdad, hoping it didn't come to that.

VIII

Y EAH!" TIRDAD SHOUTED AS SHKARAG swept her opponent off his feet, throwing up a cloud of dust and claiming yet
another victory. Next, the semi-finals. Tirdad shared a full-toothed
grin with Chobin, who had been generous enough to grant Tirdad a seat
to his right—a gesture of true substance that named the planet-reckoner
his closest companion in trust and status.

"Hah!" Chobin belted a too-loud laugh and stopped short of slapping
Tirdad on the back. "That skink-slicker is a wrestler worth her weight in
gold. Wasn't expecting much, and her style is foreign, but fuck can she
wrestle." His grin became a sly smirk. "Bet you know that already."

"Oh, give it a rest," said Tirdad as the half-div strolled over. "You're
going to make her get the wrong impression if you keep at it."

"Is it the wrong impression?" asked Chobin.

While her veil, secured by beaded ropes, obscured her frown, it was
plain in her delivery. "Wrong impression?" Shkarag asked. She bent to rub
her leg. "Not impressed?"

"All right," conceded Tirdad. "The first few matches might've been
flukes, but you've convinced me. That was an impressive throw." He
leaned forward, and she canted to stare at him through the veil. "And the
sweep, you moved as if you were lighter than air, like brocade in a breeze."

Chobin grunted. "A poet now. You aren't even trying to hide it anymore."

Tirdad shot him a glare that didn't reach his smile. "Don't be jealous. When you wrestle as well as her I'll send for the King of Kings himself to compliment you."

"Better," grumbled Chobin, playing cross. "Besides, if we learn to wrestle before we pick up a weapon because it's the foundation of everything that follows, how's it work for someone like her who learned after the fact?"

Shkarag cocked her head, though it was still trained on Tirdad.

"Your guess is as good as mine," said the planet-reckoner. "Maybe it's just like learning from the end of the curriculum."

"Maybe," agreed Shkarag. She took a seat in front of him, which was a heinous breach of protocol, but no one seemed to mind or be paying her any attention. All eyes were on the next semi-finals bout. "What if I win?" she asked.

Tirdad was already engrossed in the match. A skilled warrior under Chobin's command was pitted against the other newcomer, a pale middle-aged man with knobby joints who looked as if he couldn't wrestle himself out of a whore's embrace. They circled, the warrior plainly disturbed by his opponent having made it this far, and the knobby one moving as if only one joint could bend at a time.

"Who is this guy?" asked Tirdad, leaning toward Chobin.

"Must be a traveler. I've never seen him around. But he volunteered, and far be it from me to turn him away when we're short on contestants."

"What if I win?" Shkarag piped up, a hint of a hiss in her tone—likely at being ignored.

"There's a prize," answered Chobin. "But it's only symbolic. Hope you weren't expecting gold."

Shkarag leaned back on one elbow to crane at Tirdad. "Wasn't asking the goat-fucker. What'll you bestow if I win?"

Tirdad pried his attention from the bout long enough to say, "Whatever you want," only affording her a glance before the match was underway. The warrior moved in for a clinch, which the knobby one returned. They circled head to head, exchanging attempts to steer the other but neither willing to make too bold a move just yet. After a few revolutions, they broke the clinch, each sizing the other up from a safe distance. Tirdad had expected the warrior to be more aggressive given his opponent.

Instead, they continued their circling, each shuffling in and out to feign a takedown. The third such takedown belonged to the warrior, who burst forward at the tail end of a feint in an attempt to sweep the knobby one's leg. He countered by sprawling on top of the warrior, digging his twig-like forearm into the warrior's neck, and using the leverage to counter by coming around his side and flinging the warrior overhead and out of bounds. Claiming his victory with an upraised fist, he threw Tirdad a smile that, while outwardly friendly, made the planet-reckoner's hair stand on end.

"Well, he wrestles better than his build lets on," said Tirdad, probing his mind for any memory that'd explain the smile or the goosebumps.

"What build?" grunted Chobin. "He's all branches and knots. Technique doesn't explain it."

"Doesn't add up," Shkarag declared, sounding as if she'd made the observation. "Think your manifest is all reconciled, really šo-balanced inventory, and you've tallied with the finger calculations." She demonstrated by flashing the gesture for ten thousand (and homage to kings and gods) by tapping the tip of her index against the tip of her thumb so that the nails were parallel. "Even pulled out the abacus because something isn't right." She cocked her head. "Something isn't right."

"Yeah," said Tirdad. He toyed with his sword where it lay in his lap, departing from his usual ministrations to trace his fingers thoughtfully over the feathers of its gilded scabbard. "It seems like I know him, too. But I can't recall us ever meeting." He leaned in so that he could speak into Shkarag's ear. "Whatever the case, you're up. I'm rooting for you, so give us a victory and take the tournament."

"Maybe," said Shkarag. She limped back into the arena, which had braziers situated in a diamond, generously stoked to ward off the night and all its dangers, and to liven the crowd by casting the wrestlers in billowing sheets of bronze.

Tirdad soaked in the whole of that image. Shkarag flanked by flames, casually favouring one thigh, never bothering to hunker down into the ready stance of a wrestler. She just waited. Confidence, apathy, boredom—he couldn't pin a name on it. She wore it well all the same. Framed as she was in the haze of dust and smoke between matches, he could scarcely believe she had no love for the tradition. This improvised tournament in the dead centre of the main thoroughfare, children watching from the rooftops, the chanting and drums that gave the wrestlers their tempo, the utter lack of pomp found in the capital—this was wrestling, a scene that suited a rock relief or silver plate. When the match was called to a start and Shkarag started limping to her left, he gripped his sword in both hands, utterly invested in her triumph.

She and her knobby-limbed opponent mirrored one another, orbiting the centre in suspicious circles. It was nothing like Shkarag's previous matches, which she'd wrapped up immediately with successful takedowns. He noted how she made claws of her hands; if he didn't know better, he'd think she were nervous. At least a dozen more agonizingly tense circles and the crowd was growing restless. The suspense had to break. Shkarag must've felt the same, because she finally darted in.

Her takedown reached for his ankle, meaning to use momentum and her shoulder to pluck it from under him, but her speed failed her. The takedown would've been punished had she not rebounded so nimbly to the side. Shkarag was hardly on her feet again when her knobby opponent was on her. He moved effortlessly, and though his size hadn't changed, something about him gave the impression of being much larger than when the fight began. She sidestepped his takedown, went for a throw, was rebuffed by an escape, escaped his counter, and the two ended up in a clinch.

Now, Tirdad was certain something was off. Shkarag fought so hard she trembled. She gave ground step after step, bad leg almost buckling when under the weight of the clinch. Her veil turned his way, and it was then he knew she had lost.

His disappointment was short-lived. Only because what came next was so much worse.

The knobby-jointed wrestler emitted a hoarse laugh, and stepped to the side, which flung her forward and off-balance. He caught her mid-stumble with a sweep that threw her into the ground, immediately jamming a knee in her back. With that same hair-raising grin aimed at

Tirdad, he took her by the chin and, with a nauseating crackle, snapped her neck as effortlessly as a stick of cinnamon.

The braziers popped. A heavy speechlessness endured.

"I win," clucked the knobby man. He stood on her corpse, and though he didn't tower, his presence made it seem as if he unfurled in doing so. He tilted his head. "Time to claim my prize. I'll have what she was having."

Tirdad was blind. He couldn't see for the sanguine haze that stole his vision. Looking into it obliquely, he could hear Shkarag say 'pomegranate-red'. The ring of the planets played a counter-melody to her words, the starling-black a silent observer.

Shkarag. She had a phylactery. She had said as much, said it restored her. A truth he had not forgotten; trouble was, he couldn't get to it. Just then, all he knew was loss. Supreme and eternal. The thing about loss was that there was no beating it. Deny it, distract it, shape it, avoid it—never fight it. Any defense was untenable, any offense unsustainable. Tirdad had brought this upon himself, had invited loss into his life as destructively as an enemy into his home. He'd killed them both.

The sting of that truth cut through the red. Like a true leader, Chobin charged by, bellowing the call to attack. "To arms! Everyone else to safety!"

The screaming in his ears soon took form as his own. It wasn't until Chobin's hide shield buckled in fending off a blow meant for Tirdad that his senses fully converged on his body. He'd charged just behind Chobin, blade eager as ever, adrenaline amplified like never before—fire in his veins and a forge in his muscles. His scream went on, rattled in his ears but never broke, joining the sharp chorus of shrieks left by fleeing civilians.

He ducked a left elbow that passed overhead with such force it made his ears pop, weaved in and around a straight knee that would have obliterated his torso. Tirdad retaliated by plunging his blade into the man's side, and dragged it down and out. The starling-black sliced with whetted impunity.

Staying in melee range of such a powerful foe was ill-advised, but something uncanny pushed Tirdad to maintain the offensive. Not once did he so much as entertain a withdrawal. The knobby man cackled hoarsely, breath reeking of cadaver in summer, and lunged forward to try for a grab. Tirdad bobbed under, and he would have been punished with a rising knee fierce enough to tear his head from his shoulders. Lucky for him, the man wasn't as heavy as he was strong. Chobin intercepted with a charge that sent him hurtling.

"Fucker's a div?" asked the marzban.

The question registered, but the part of him it registered to had been shoved aside. It wasn't needed. His response was an ear-piercing scream. He bent his knees, muscles bunching, and leapt forward with a ferocity that would have matched that of the half-div, scream following close behind.

For all its might, and for all its bluster, the div recovered in time for fear to flash across its features. Then, its ragged baying challenged Tirdad, and the two met in a hail of metal and flesh. Tirdad crouched and pivoted beneath the kick meant for his jaw, severing the div's other leg at the knee as he passed under. It laughed, cartwheeled forward, and by the time it had, the leg had already regenerated.

"You can't kill me, Tirdad!" It let out a whooping laugh. "She molded me for your demise. Your fate was sealed before you ever joined your cousin."

Again, the words fell on deaf ears. Another scream, and Tirdad rushed in. A clean thrust into its undefended sternum followed by a twist, and he pulled his sword up and straight through its head, which looked much like it smelled. The blade's unnatural sharpness allowed for maneuvers that wouldn't have suited it otherwise.

The div's skull split in half for a heartbeat before it was whole again, and wearing a shit-eating grin.

What finally reached Tirdad was the frustration of his sword, its obscene throbbing returning his grasp and urging him to kill the div as if Ashtadukht were there tugging on his hand. With it, the understanding that this div was after him, and that he couldn't defeat it by normal means.

He opened his mouth to intone the lines to a lot, reached out to the part of him that now belonged to the celestial theatre . . . and stopped short. Chobin was there, onlookers crowded around corners, a few brave children peeked from rooftops. If he failed, who knows what would befall all the innocents gathered around him.

"Fuck," he swore, and tore off into the nearest alley. If it was after him, it'd have to catch him first. And maybe he could lure it far enough away that drawing a lot didn't pose such a threat to others.

Tirdad turned corner after corner, stumbling over shapes in the night, crashing through some, with hoarse laughing in pursuit all the while. His eyes would flash up every few turns to maintain a course toward the ridge. Porcelain shattered around his boots as he barreled through the section of the bazaar dedicated to pot makers and into an adjoining alley. More crashes sounded behind him, and though he would have liked to blame it on a delayed fall, he could hear the div's stride, its summer-stink growing more offensive by the second.

His next glance at the ridge demanded a double take. Someone was up there, outlined in the gauzy cast of the moon. He felt their gaze follow him even after he looked away, and it came to Tirdad just as the alley emptied him in front of an unassuming flight of stairs that he would have been better off leading the div beyond the city walls.

A cackle behind him curtailed that thought, spurring him up the stairs and into the pitch-black tunnel that burrowed higher up the ridge. Tirdad didn't slow down; instead, he relied on instinct to guide him through, following the incline and the walls as best he could at a near sprint.

When at last he reached the exit, he nearly missed it. The moon had vanished. Only the constellations and a pair of sorely outnumbered planets sneered at him from the heavens. His mind burned where a caustic die had left sizzling clefts. Tirdad felt as if he'd been rolled up in a carpet and flung down a mountain. He braced himself against the exit, wheezing for air, and a braid slipped over his shoulder to smear the sweat of his cheek and blood across his chin.

"Now Ashta," remonstrated a voice smooth as leather but rank as a tannery.

"Don't you fucking call me that!" he screamed. Or tried to. It emerged as little more than an electrified rasp. Rage rose in his throat, quelled by the bile that joined it and splattered his boots. Screw Venus, and screw the Crab for its elemental phlegm. Somewhere in the back of his mind, he realized he'd been drawn into another of Ashtadukht's memories.

"Mmn. I admit that was uncalled for, but you really should take better care of yourself. Can't we just discuss this over something warm like we usually do?"

He made to wipe his mouth on his sleeve, but another wave of vomit spewed forth. Now he felt light-headed in addition to everything else. "You went too far, Niyaz. I can't look the other way any longer."

"I meant nothing by it."

"You always mean something by it!" He coughed, his throat raw from all the stomach acid. A dry heave doubled him over even as he straightened, which drew a frustrated growl. "The rules were clear," he said. "Peddle all you like, but no contracts with children."

"Can you blame me for trying to pull a fast one on you? I'm a div after all."

Having finally gotten his retching under control, Tirdad straightened to face his quarry. She was a shadow against a backdrop of shadows, but he knew that had the moon not scurried away from the theatre, her only outstanding feature would have been how she managed to be so ordinary. She had been pleasant company, her tea a welcome respite. So it made him all the more irritated that she refused follow one simple rule. She'd forced his hand one time too many.

"Turn back, Ashtadukht. I heard you utter the rites to two lots. You and I both know a star-reckoner's third tends to be her last. Can't imagine the failed ones are treating you very well either. So what's your angle here? Neither of us are fighters."

"Menstrual-bathing . . . fuck," he cursed under his breath. So much for his bluff. Louder then, "I can't just let you go."

"Let me? You're spent. Your family will cut you down before you catch me."

"I . . . huh? I'm not one of your addle-brained clients you can spook with some cryptic reading of squirrel guts or the flights of birds."

"You aren't," agreed Niyaz. "But self-fulfilling prophecies aren't unheard of, and it doesn't hurt to try."

He sneered and turned to leave. "If it comes to that," he said, "they'll end you when they're done with me." With that, he returned from whence he came, eager to put the whole affair behind him, but dragging his feet under the weight of his illness and failed lots. He'd liked Niyaz; she was one of the better ones. Back in the city, he lurched through streets all but dead—with the exception of a young couple out for a tryst. Tirdad passed by without a second glance, his course set for the gate where he knew a star-reckoner's stamp seal would grant him passage, even at this hour.

A ways off from the couple he passed another youth, this one kneeling behind a stall and gazing longingly down the thoroughfare. He glanced over his shoulder, then back at the boy. He knew that look. On any other night, he wouldn't have cared. But this boy, so lanky as to be knobby, compelled him to walk over. "Won't get anywhere like that," he said. Naturally, the boy was startled, but that only froze him in place. "There's a woman at the overlook. You know it? See her, ask for what you desire, agree to the contract. If she isn't there, look for a red tent tomorrow evening."

Moonlight returned as if from behind a cloud, gleaming where the night had been impenetrable, though the sky was crisp and clear. With it came the realization that Ashtadukht's memory had released him.

Ahead, standing at the vantage that pored over Ray, there waited a woman. No, he realized, a div. Even the flattering ivory moonlight couldn't surmount her ordinary appearance. She wore it like armour. It kept her out of mind.

"Niyaz," he said, tone even.

She inclined her head. "You killed her, and now you're here for me. When I heard . . ." She blew out a sigh. "Haven't had tea since. Ashtadukht was so hard-headed. We both were. I'm not above admitting it was my doing."

"You're a div after all," Tirdad stated. "Like you said back then."

That drew a long pause, during which Niyaz contemplated his sword. "I took precautions," she warned at length. "That same night some love-struck fool devoted himself to me, and I made the most of it. How long can you outrun him? He will prevail."

143

Tirdad couldn't contain his laugh. "You—" He sucked in a breath and nearly choked on another. "You played into your own prophecy."

Another pause, and the confidence in her posture waned as she eyed his sword. "Would you like some tea?" she asked.

He nearly blurted out a yes. And when a knobby limb reached up and over the lip of the vantage, Tirdad gave it serious but brief consideration. He brandished his sword. "You shouldn't have done that to Shkarag. I might've let you go otherwise. Even taken you up on that tea."

"Mmn. Well, if I knew what was good for me I wouldn't try to turn self-fulfilling prophecies into weapons either."

Tirdad swallowed hard. The unpredictability of planet-reckoning was fresh in his mind after the flashback. He could still taste the vomit on his tongue, still feel the burning in his throat. But what really worried him was that he was still in the city—a failure might mean more than just vomit for him and its citizens.

The knobby human made it over the ledge, which drew a frown. It brought to mind that oblivious boy from Ashtadukht's past. Had she sent him intentionally, was it a whim, or maybe her playing into the prophecy? It could have been all three. He'd never know. At least he had her memories, which is more than he could have said for her of her brother, or Shkarag of her sister.

"Kill him," commanded Niyaz. "But don't toss him over. I want that sword."

"My pleasure," rasped the man, cracking joints so swollen they disrupted his silhouette. His stalk had only just begun when it was cut short by an axe that chopped clean through his ankle. Even with his regeneration, it was enough to throw off his balance, and all the hissing shape that leapt up the ledge needed to drag him over the side.

Tirdad and Niyaz shared a bout of silence as each watched the lip, as if expecting one of the two to come climbing back up at any minute.

"Shkarag has a phylactery," noted Niyaz. She wrung her hands, head bowed. "That comes as a surprise, especially with how her sister died. How they managed all that time without one is beyond me." She shook her head. "Should've sensed it when I passed you during the festival.

That's Eshm's stock for you. To regenerate so quickly . . . she must've died a great many times for her phylactery to know her so well."

"You sure love to talk," said Tirdad, drawing up beside her, and wondering why she reminded him of Ashtadukht. He saw his cousin's traits, or what he thought were her traits, everywhere now.

Niyaz emitted a nervous chuckle, eyeing his blade out of the corner of her eye. "I'm stalling, of course. Hoping to string you along until he returns. Your cousin related her travels to me every now and then. I could regale you. I'm not very good at regaling."

"You're terrible at this."

"Pleading for my life? Probably."

"No phylactery?"

"Oh, I have more than I can remember. Soul is vouchsafed across the world."

Tirdad inclined his head. "You aren't a fighter, so you work with what you have."

"Reminds you of her, doesn't it?"

It did. "No."

"Doesn't matter," she lamented. "That blade . . . it'll eat through them all." Niyaz lifted her head to meet his eyes, and only then did he realize she was tying her hair into plaits. "Would you like some tea?" she asked.

The plaits were a bad move. They infuriated him. Without pretense, he plunged his blade between her ribs, and the satisfied heartbeat it poured into his palm and up his arm felt as if someone were reaching from beyond the bridge of souls.

Niyaz did not die well. She grasped the blade in trembling hands, trying futilely to pull it out or back off—even trying to turn away in her desperation. Niyaz spoke so fast it all blurred together. "What's itwhat'sit doing?What'sit?Wait. Wait.Tirdad, please.What's this? Thisissomuch worse than I th—what'sthiswhat'sthiswhat's this? What's—"

Then, she collapsed.

Tirdad trained curious remorse on the fallen div. He knew he only felt it because of who he saw in her, but he felt it all the same. He would have welcomed that warm tea, and over it tales of Ashtadukht's past during her solitary missions as a star-reckoner. Or just some anecdotes.

He knelt to wipe his sword on her dress, it thrumming contentedly in his grip. Tirdad gingerly traced its blade from guard to point, the iridescence more vivid in moonlight than during the day. Briefly, he got caught up wondering whether it felt his touch, which would have led to a whole slew of questions if more pressing matters weren't at hand.

Shkarag. He approached the edge, but peering over only granted him a view of scores of shadows steeled against the glow of the theatre. He hoped she'd survived. Tirdad gave Niyaz one last look before heading back down through the tunnel. It was more difficult to navigate now that he wasn't barrelling through it, but he eventually made it down to ground level.

Shouts rose throughout the city, where patrols and their bobbing torchlight scoured the causeways and alleys, searching building after building. Tirdad didn't give them a second thought. Instead, he took a right and paced to the area directly below the overlook.

The knobby-limbed man lay flat on his back, limbs out to his sides as if he'd just fallen over for a night of stargazing. Tirdad blew out a sigh. He didn't care to contemplate what had transpired between the div and her bodyguard—what kind of pact that boy had made decades ago that it'd come to this.

"Shkarag?" he called. "Shkarag?"

No answer. Not even a meaningful silence.

Canvassing the area turned up nothing, which had him worried. He believed in her phylactery—had witnessed it for the second time when she dragged the poor soul over the cliff—but he worried all the same. All eyes had been on her when her neck snapped, so her reappearance would raise the sort of questions that even Chobin's charisma couldn't smooth over.

"Shkarag?" he called again, much louder this time. That earned him a croak. Tirdad craned up just in time for blood to splash his face. "Fuck!" he swore, clearing his eyes and jumping back.

This afforded him a clear view of a thin stream that was already petering out, but caught the light enough on its way down for him to trace it to the parapets overhead. Tirdad was eager to bolt off, but he suppressed the urge. He wasn't sure how to reach her.

It was then that Chobin came rushing out from the city, nearly tripping over the body, and curling his lip at it. "What the everliving fuck?" he exclaimed, panting. "Are you all right? What is going on here? I've been searching all over for you."

"I'm fine." Tirdad indicated the parapet with his pommel. "But Shkarag is up there, and she's hurt. I need to get to her."

Chobin bolted off without another word. He was always roused to action with such surety it was a wonder he still had his head. Tirdad hurried to follow, not exactly sure what he was rushing for, but rushing all the same. Maybe he just felt she shouldn't have to die alone, even if it was temporary.

He followed Chobin down the lane, turned into another, took the steps to the citadel two at a time, fell when he tried to cut a sharp corner, then after scrambling to his feet, finally found himself at the parapets. Chobin came to an abrupt halt, uttering a curse and pressing his back to the cliff face to let him by.

Tirdad had mourned her death in his own way back when he slit her throat. He felt it in his heart when her neck had snapped. But as he approached the half-div, torchlight illuminating the streak of blood from where she must have impacted the parapet and slid down, dread gripped him, irrational and suffocating. Like it was Ashtadukhr all over again. He had to keep repeating the word phylactery in his head just to avoid losing it.

She was curled in a gap in the battlements, head hanging loosely over one edge, boot and bootless foot over the other. Her hands, drawn into claws, scrabbled aimlessly at the puddle of blood she lay in.

"Shkarag," he said, gentle and low. "I'm here. You aren't alone." He knelt in the puddle, removing her glove and taking her finely-scaled hand in his. "You're going to be just fine. You have a phylactery, remember?" Mid-way through the question he realized he was asking for himself. She gave his hand what scarcely amounted to a squeeze, not even tightening when she hacked up a river of blood. It would be her last.

The silenced that crept in was short-lived. "She's gone," said Chobin.

"Yeah."

147

"So, is she going to, I mean . . ." Chobin shifted uncomfortably, scratching at his head and wearing a grimace. "Haven't lost her, have we?"

Tirdad searched her gaze. Her pupils were dilated like the day she had drawn close in order to explain the change in her condition, hovering only a breath away. He'd found the terrible, insuperable yet indescribable weight that hung over her ugly then. It wasn't the weight that was ugly, after all; it was what it did to her. A steeper breed of ugly. To suggest otherwise would have been romanticizing something that oppressed. The key was so simple yet so hard to come by. All he had to do was see the person behind it.

"She saved my life," he said, grave and at length. "Again."

Chobin grunted from behind. "You're accruing quite the debt. Everything taken care of with the div?"

"Yeah." Tirdad waited for minutes that seemed like hours, keeping constant watch for her spark. He deliberated the implications of a phylactery, what it meant to trivialize your own death. There had to be ramifications; everything comes at a cost. Especially for someone who had escaped death for millennia.

A flicker. Her pupils narrowed in the torchlight. They darted to him, her hand, and back again. She pulled herself up, looking around as if disoriented, and the scene slowly returning to her. Half her head glistened with fresh blood, favouring the mounting scars as outlets over which to gather and run—especially the short one that bifurcated her forehead and nose at an angle slight as her touch when she retracted her hand.

"Shkarag?" he asked. "Have you recovered?"

She canted away, but glanced at him obliquely. ". . ."

"Shkarag?"

"Phylactery did the mending. Must've—" Her gaze flitted about, finally coming to rest on her lost boot. "River shifted, so the road cuts through town again. Business is booming. I think."

Chobin cleared his throat. "Glad to have the skink-slicker back. Wasn't around when she came to, but someone was bound to have seen it."

"What do you suggest?" asked Tirdad. He hadn't once broken his stare, still transfixed on the half-div. "It's your city after all."

"Suppose it is," agreed Chobin. "Just lie low here while I check on things." With a convenient excuse to leave, he did just that.

Shkarag pulled her boot back on. She then reached into her egg pouch, which elicited a sneer—likely all broken from the fall. That was the last Tirdad could see of her before the light cast by Chobin's torch was out of range.

"You gave your life for mine," he said. "That . . . well, whatever it was, it would have been the end of me if you hadn't been there."

The half-div murmured something too indistinct to make out, then stood to the squelch of her own blood. Tirdad took her by the hand before she could leave, glad and more than a little relieved when she didn't object. The firmness of her grip was all the more welcome after how weak it'd been earlier; that it was slick didn't bother him in the slightest.

"I wouldn't have gotten this far without you," he said, wanting to say so much more, but unsure where to start or even if he should. "You need to know that."

She canted, made evident only by the shine of her head. "Don't need to convince me like some, like—" She caught both her wandering and her temper; he could make out a claw raking at her head. What came next was as soft as he'd ever heard her speak. "Long as you need me, I'll be here."

She stood staring at the cliff face as if she had more to say, and while she usually had a slew of tales eager to devour their own tails, he suspected she was holding back more than that. "Until you die," she added with a tilt. "Maybe."

Shkarag punctuated it by tightening her grip, then wandering off into the night. He was about to call for her when the familiar sound of her spear clacking on stone signaled her return.

A decisive clack that either laid claim to the plot of stone or demanded his attention had her leaning into the spear before him. "Didn't win," she confessed as if he weren't there to witness it. "Gave it my all, really swallowed the urge to kill something fierce, but the šo-branched—" She clacked the stone again, agitation seeping into her delivery. "His roots were sturdier than mine. Must've been gilded because they had more purchase."

Tirdad smiled a tired smile. His chest ached. Although, if he were being honest with himself, it was more than just his ribs. He was coming back around to honesty, but wasn't there quite yet—it hadn't served him well in the past.

"Well," he said, getting to his feet and bending backward to work the kink out his back, "I'm exhausted. How about we find somewhere to settle in for the night, then see what we can get out of that Adur-mah tomorrow morning?"

". . ." Shkarag shifted uneasily.

"You're right. It'd be best to confront him at night. But I'd rather not draw a lot in the city. I'd rather not draw one at all. Let's do it after we're on the road."

". . ." More meaningful silence, which he took as tacit consent since he had nothing else to go by.

Eventually, he resigned to the kink going nowhere and figured he had no room to complain after the bone-deep ache he'd experienced in Ashtadukht's memory. He started back the way he'd come, a regular clacking to his rear.

The pair returned from whence they came, but drew up short of entering the city proper. Tirdad mulled over how best to tackle the issue of what may very well have been her compromised disguise. Divs weren't universally hated, but they were distrusted, and distrust is only a scapegoat or misstep away from hate. He turned to her to find she'd already drawn her scarf around her head. He didn't need to see her eyes to know she had trained that expectant look of hers his way. There was something about her poise, the calculated silence that hinted at a withheld remark—like a parent entertaining a child. Maybe he was a child to her. That's what he made of it anyway; wasn't like she was ever so forthcoming as to explain the nuances of the many things she left unsaid.

"What do you suggest we do?" he inquired. "I don't want a mob to descend on us."

Shkarag cocked her head. "Hide."

"That's it?"

"Hide. Lie in wait for the goat-fucker. Like snakes in the—" She emitted a hiss. "Lie in wait."

Tirdad nodded to himself. Drawn taut as a bowstring over all that'd transpired, he'd forgotten about waiting for Chobin to return. He pointed toward the tunnel he'd taken in his flight and before confronting Niyaz. "There's a natural spring up a ways. I know it isn't my place to order you around, but you're a mess, and being covered in blood isn't going to do us any favours with the locals." He paused, furrowing his brow and speaking his mind before he realized what he was asking. "Do you get off on your own blood? Or just others'?"

"Both," she stated matter-of-factly. She canted his way. "Only fresh. Only free-range."

Tirdad tangled his fingers in his hair, which had managed to grow even more greasy than before, and grimaced at his crassness. He supposed throwing in with someone as ribald as Chobin was bound to rub off on him sooner or later. "Sorry. I asked that without thinking."

Shkarag started off, spear thumping on dirt, before coming to a halt a few thumps away. "They say," she began, "they say you make decisions here and there. Here, with wine. There, without. Here, th—"

Her speech dropped off sharply, as if taking a dive into something frigid and paralyzing. She'd left the dim light that strived against the shadows at the edge of the city, so his only indication that she was still around was that he hadn't heard any thumping. Shortly after, she picked up where she left off.

"—the wine dislodges things. There, you consider the things you shook free. You're always too worried about being there. Makes you forget here. Here is . . ." Shkarag trailed off to the sound of thumping. "Ask more without thinking," she insisted.

Tirdad loitered in place, tracing his thumb over the horns of his ram's head pommel and reflecting as he did. This late in his life, he'd be hard-pressed to experience another festival as eventful as this one. He'd have been hard-pressed at any point in his life. So embroiled in the events of the day, he'd nearly forgotten why he was here at all. The answers were close; that star-reckoner had to know more than he let on. With what he'd said when they first met, Tirdad was all but convinced. He would untangle this mystery, and do right by Ashtadukht. He owed her that much.

A yawn escaped, the day's exertion swiftly catching up to him. Already, his lids were drooping. Tirdad walked to the nearest mud brick building and sat against the wall. He unsheathed his sword and laid it across his lap, one hand on the hilt, the other gingerly hugging the blade. He had just nodded off when the approach of footsteps stirred him from his much-needed rest, which made him feel twice as exhausted as he had minutes earlier.

"Chobin," he grumbled as the marzban passed by without so much as a glance. "Chobin."

He spun on Tirdad, sword blazoned and eyes wide, which transitioned to a strained smile upon recognizing the planet-reckoner. "What're you sneaking up on me for?" he asked, slipping his sword into its sheath. "Ahriman's musty testes, what're you down here for at all? Really need to talk to you about making the most of these intimate moments. You're, what, fifty years older than me? Shouldn't have to tell you this."

Tirdad blew out a sigh. He was too worn out to argue. "How's it look?"

"Couldn't find anyone who actually saw what happened, which is either a miracle or a lie. Most had run for cover, and according to the few in the area, one moment she was there, the next she had vanished."

"But they did witness her death," Tirdad reasoned. "It doesn't matter whether they saw her run off or not. What matters is what they're going to think when they see her alive and well."

Chobin flashed an embarrassed grin. "If I'm being honest, I hadn't thought of that. Could we just get her a change of clothes? Not like anyone saw her face."

"Let's do that, assuming she agrees." Tirdad gestured to the west. "I left the div's body on the overlook, and her thrall is below if you didn't catch it earlier."

"I'll have them disposed of. Thank you, friend. My city owes you a debt. If not for the two of you, who knows how many more lives would have been lost. You're turning out to be quite the planet-reckoner."

"Don't mention it," said Tirdad. He strained to put his feet beneath him, accepting Chobin's outstretched hand in doing so, and thankful for his casual kindness. Trying again in vain to get the kink out of his back, he considered what the marzban had said—namely, what stood out. "Do you mean to say someone died?" he asked. "Other than Shkarag?"

Chobin's grin faded at that. "Yeah. Seems the div got old Adur-mah before you put it down."

Tirdad froze in his stretch. "Huh?"

"Yeah, it's a damn shame. Many of the folks here grew up on his stories, and the same can be said for their children—not that I ever numbered among them."

Astonishment wrestled rage and dejection for supremacy in Tirdad's mind; ultimately, it was a stalemate. So he just slid back down the wall, head in hands. "You've got to be kidding me," he said. "How? How does a star-reckoner like him—just how?"

"Can't say for certain, but seems to me he was poisoned. All signs point to it, but I'm as lost as a fat man's penis when it comes to divs. Besides," he went on, and the shift in his tone told Tirdad he was beaming, "since when do you care about star-reckoners? He charm the grudge out of you?"

Tirdad sat there for a moment, damning his luck to the sibilance of Chobin's torch, wondering if this was what he had to look forward to until at last what was left of his soul crossed the bridge of judgement. When he finally spoke up, it was thick with resignation. "Remember those documents Shkarag brought? Well, we spent countless hours trying to make sense of them. When at last I found the right vantage to view the details, a plot against Ashtadukht was laid bare before me. Or a plot with her underfoot at any rate, and by her peers. The whole time, she had known and told no one, because who would believe her? And if they had, what could they have done?"

"Took it into her own hands then," Chobin observed with a grunt.

"Yeah. That's why I'm out and about so soon. I need to investigate, to get to the bottom of this shit-clogged qanat."

"Here I thought you missed me."

"I did." Tirdad raked his fingers over his scalp and blew out his exasperation. "To think a chance encounter would have me befriend the star-reckoner who could have been the key to it all, only for him to die before I could get any answers." He craned to look at the marzban. "Adur-mah had answers, Chobin. He made that much clear. And now he's gone, his secrets scattered like so much wind."

"So, what now? Move on? Can't bring him back from the dead, now can—what's that look? Don't like that look one bit."

Ashtadukht had done just that. She'd resurrected two star-reckoners long enough for them aid in her clash with the forty-armed div. Trouble was, he hadn't the faintest clue how she'd done it; worse, neither did she. While he couldn't reference her memories at will, they'd imparted enough about planet-reckoning to know she hardly ever got exactly what she asked for—if she were lucky, it was only a world away in the same stellar neighborhood. She just asked. The more precise you were the less likely you would get what you wanted. A sort of fortune-telling for one-self. Surely, she'd considered all the portents, the planets, constellations, and elements at her disposal, chose which skirmish to project her soul into, weighed the risks of it backfiring. But it never mattered how much she calculated. It always came to a roll of the die. And she was an expert. There's no way he could pull it off.

"Yeah, I suppose you're right," said Tirdad. "I'll see if I can find his home in Ecbatana. Could be that he left some clues behind. Does he have somewhere here he usually stays?"

Chobin shrugged. "You'll have to ask around. Have enough to worry about without keeping track of some geezer who's got it in his head that he should bounce between cities on the regular." He scratched at his di-sheveled hair, looking as dirty as Tirdad felt, and cast about his surroundings. "Say, where's the skink-slicker?"

Tirdad waved a listless hand at the direction she'd gone. "Sent her to the spring to clean up. Suggested it anyway."

"You sent a half-div to rinse the blood of Eshm in our spring?"

"Well, when you put it that way, I guess I should've joined her and contaminated it in earnest."

The marzban slapped his thigh, his trademark full-toothed grin crack-ing for a bellowed, "Hah! Pollute it all you please if it means you get yourself some—" His brow creased. "Would they be quarter-div? Wonder how that works."

"Haven't thought that far ahead."

Chobin needn't say a thing to that; he just beamed.

Tirdad sighed. He didn't know whether to laugh or cry, but he was too spent to do either. So he surrendered to the complaints of his aging body and aching ribs, and fell asleep.

IX

TIRDAD AWOKE TO A MANY-LAYERED murmuring. Nearest, subdued speech conversed with the rippling of water; further, the multifarious sounds of the city became a steady susurrus; and at the furthest reaches, the metallic whine of the celestial theatre went on, heedless to his world.

He opened his eyes and was greeted by dirt-stained trousers and the scaled hand that kneaded them. Tirdad lay there in a daze, staring blankly at the individual scales and picking out their golden speckles. She seized every opportunity to massage the injury, which made him wonder if it had any effect at all, and why her phylactery hadn't healed it. It wasn't until he'd finished going over the scales on her knuckles that she ceased her massaging.

". . ." The measured quiet.

With a groan that didn't do the ache in his bones justice, he pushed himself off the ground, drawing his face into a grimace and rubbing his lower back where the stone had given him its worst. "Why am I up here?" he asked, shielding his eyes against the sun and peering out over the city.

"That šo-toothy goat-fucker told me to hide. Told him I'd hide my spear in his arse like some squirrely quartermaster stocking up for a harsh winter. Don't like his teeth; too showy."

"Yeah, it takes some getting used to. Did he tell you what happened to Adur-mah?"

156

A nudge turned his attention to the half-div, who had a bowl in each hand. One was heaped with mint-dashed yogurt, the other full to the rim with spinach soup. He'd been hankering for yogurt for a while now, and had mentioned it several times. Spinach soup was a staple during Tirgan. She'd brought both.

"You know," he said, accepting the bowls with a drowsy smile, "you can be mighty thoughtful for a daughter of Eshm. Never ceases to amaze me."

Though her blank expression showed no change, the way her eyes flicked away without returning was enough to alert him to the oafishness of his statement. "Sorry," he mouthed through a yawn. "I didn't, well, I spoke without thinking. I'm still half asleep is all. You were kind to remember the yogurt, and to think of the soup."

Her eyes flicked back for a passing glance, then seemed to train on something in the distance, though he had seen that look, and knew enough that she was farther off than any horizon. She parted her lips, but only just.

Tirdad began with the yogurt, which was still cool, and signified an inspired care on her part. The bowl was wet; this gave credence to his suspicion that she'd been using the spring to keep it cool until he came to. Curious, he gave the soup a taste: delicious, and still warm. The slate he'd been sleeping on could've achieved as much.

That cheered him up enough to consider the road ahead while he ate. True, Adur-mah's death had been a serious setback, but that didn't mean he couldn't pick up the trail again. Tirdad decided he'd head to Ecbatana before coming to any hasty conclusions, and if that didn't turn up any leads, he'd set a course for one of the routes taken by the merchants in his documents. He nodded to himself. Belatedly and bothered by it, he figured he'd discuss it with Shkarag to see if she would weigh in. Perhaps she'd seen something he hadn't. Chobin, too.

After he'd finished his meal and recited his morning prayer, he went to rinse his hands in the spring, frowning at his reflection.

"Tonight," Shkarag piped up. "Not until toni—" She canted to her right where he'd been sleeping, then to the left where she flashed him a leer that shifted to something more contemplative. "You devoured the twins both. Left them all concave like those upturned bowls under the threshold, thinking they ward against us like some, like some star-reckoner who thinks squinting and craning makes a person, makes a person immune to—" She canted away, though her eyes stayed put. "You devoured them."

Tirdad shot the bowls a glance. "What else was I supposed to do with them?"

"That," she confirmed, wearing a smile so guarded he wouldn't have noticed it if he weren't so accustomed to her otherwise deadpan or inscrutable expressions. "Maybe." Her countenance twisted, then ironed itself out just as abruptly. "Oh, the shit-eating one who courts goats, he said something . . ." She trailed off, staring at him intensely for a bout of quiet before continuing. "Insisted something fierce you come along for the war with Hrom. Said we had rank without the file, šo-yammering about telling you the moment the sun strikes your brow."

Tirdad checked the sky; the sun hung around noon, probably an hour or so earlier than. "Sun's pretty high," he observed.

"Had you in the shade." Shkarag cocked her head. "And yogurt was elusive."

"Well, be that as it may, we need to discuss the reason we're here in the first place before we even begin to entertain his offer." He sat beside her, drawing his sword so he could marvel at its rippling hues. "Adur-mah was our only real lead. I won't let his demise bring our quest to an end. It's only our first setback, after all. But I'm not above admitting I'm now back to grasping, so if you have any advice or thoughts on our next move, you're welcome to share."

At that, she grew a different sort of distant. Where she'd returned to her regular kneading, she now strangled; she fumed as plainly as the hiss that leaked through a curled upper lip. Shkarag bore her weight upon her thigh, countenance drawn in a crooked scowl, and twitching.

"Uh, Shkarag?"

Her breathing took on a sawing growl, and she promptly dunked her head into the spring water. Tirdad waited, wearing a disconcerted frown that grew more concerned the longer she stayed under. About the time he began to worry she had no plans of emerging, she shot up, gasping for breath. Once she'd gotten her breathing under control, she returned to her kneading. "Don't go chasing mirages," she warned, staring daggers at her thigh. "Don't—" A wince curtailed her ministrations, so she lay back on the stone. "Mirages are there, out there šo-tantalizing, and you're thinking you'd like a row or a tumble, so you think maybe this one, this is one of those magical mirages with hidden treasures or lost cities. You always chase the mirage, thinking that's just as the crow flies—" Her gaze darted to meet his. "—diverting your eyes from the rest—" And darted away. "Never find a thing. Maybe. Or turns out you find it. You find it and you wish, you wish you hadn't chased it at all. Mirages only take; mirages are misers."

Tirdad had a sigh brewing the longer she went on, and he was finally given leave to release it now that she'd finished. It seemed she wasn't going to be of any help. Maybe Chobin would have some advice. He slid his sword into its scabbard, thumb along the flat of the blade, and gathered the bowls to rinse in the spring. After he'd finished the first, she spoke up.

"War means star-reckoners," she said as if in resignation and already securing her weapon belt beneath her lapis lazuli girdle. She grabbed her spear and leaned into it, looking at him blankly but with an expectant slouch that suggested she knew exactly how he'd respond.

"You're right," he said. "But if you're against it, you don't have to—" Her fangs were unfurling. "Right," he hurried to correct himself. "You aren't going anywhere, because you think I need you."

Her attention jumped from one thing to another as he approached, though her deadpan expression persisted. Tirdad reached out, hesitating when she flinched, and only proceeded to grasp her shoulder once she'd relaxed. "Of course I need you," he assured her. "How about we go see what that goat-fucker wants from us?"

". . ."

· · · · ·

"Hayk betrayed us, not that it comes as a surprise," Chobin dictated in the authoritative voice he adopted whenever acting as marzban. "Turns

159

out Hrom has been throwing cinnamon on the flames of rebellion. Again, not that it comes as a surprise."

He planted his hands on a leather map, drawing one finger from their location in Ray along a path to Dvin. "The rebels have already dethroned our representative in Dvin, which means we need to retake the city and establish a firm presence before Hrom sweeps in, which is bound to happen since they're behind the unrest. I've been summoned to lead a cavalry force in the army of the King of Kings, may he live forever." He looked up from the map. "So?"

"That's great news," said Tirdad, breaking a smile. "Well, not the war, but that you're being placed in a command position alongside the King of Kings. You've earned it."

Chobin shook his head. "Don't know that I have. Marzban's one thing, but Hayk and Hrom in the west? That's a lot of lives in my hands. Lives I need to do right by."

"You will," encouraged Tirdad. He moved around the map to sling an arm over his friend's shoulder, who was smiling even in his anxiety. "You led well against my cousin. You care for those serving under you, and they know as much, each and every one. Remember, I spent years in their midst after you invited me into the fold. They look to you for leadership because you're a natural. Because you care enough to want to do right by them."

Chobin stared at the map. Tirdad figured the lack of a reply meant he was getting through to him. Across the room, leaning against one of its mud brick walls, Shkarag broke the silence by biting into an egg.

Marzban and planet-reckoner lifted their heads in unison. She just stared, unmoving, with a thread of yolk escaping from the corner of her mouth. Shkarag slowly tilted her head back, focused on the pair as a sliver of yolk drained from where her fang had penetrated the shell.

"Why's she do that?" asked Chobin. "The staring. It's fucking unsettling."

"Yeah," agreed Tirdad, turning his attention back to the map. "So where do we come in?"

"Simple, really. It'd put my mind at ease to have you there with me, and you're an accomplished swordsman besides."

"Accomplished?"

"I'm sure we could make something up. Point is, I want you around, and I wouldn't ask you to come without her. So, I'm offering you both rank befitting your—" He turned a broad yet patently uncertain grin on Shkarag. "Your worth."

"What does your father have to say about this?"

"He suggested it. Not that it'd matter. I'm leading this contingent, not him."

Tirdad nodded. "I'll support you as best I can, but you should know I intend to investigate the star-reckoners stationed there."

"The skink-slicker suggested as much last night . . . I think she did anyhow. Communicates like a tangled net. I won't get in your way. Just don't let it end up like last time."

Tirdad trained a knotted brow on the half-div. She conveniently found something else worth her fitful gaze. What had she been getting at this morning, if she had already determined he'd want to go the night before? He shook his head. No sense asking; he'd just get another meandering non-answer, or one of her stuffed silences.

"There's more," Chobin went on. "Been putting this off because I don't know how to bring it up." He turned his grimace of a smile away and scratched the back of his neck. "Know your uncle went above and beyond for you. Did right by us, too. Don't want to presume to, uh . . ." He trailed off.

"What is it?" Tirdad stroked the ram's head pommel. Seeing Chobin like this made him nervous.

The marzban cleared his throat. "Want to, uh, formally offer you a place in our family." He still wouldn't look at Tirdad, boring into the map instead. "Yours means a great deal to you, and for good reason. But what Ashtadukht did . . . even if you can somehow prove beyond a doubt she had been conspired against, it won't erase her actions. There's no going back. Don't like it, but it's the truth, and you need to hear it."

Tirdad knew that better than anyone else. He was the one who had been disowned; he was the one who had shared her path; he was the one who carried the burden of ending it. Everything seemed to remind him of it, not the least of which being his own guilt, so he sure as fuck didn't need to hear it. Tirdad clenched both his jaw and the hilt of his long sword. Out of the corner of his eye, he noticed Shkarag push herself off the wall. Chobin furrowed his brow.

Heaving a sigh, Tirdad deflated. The marzban was only trying to be a good friend, and he wouldn't raise his sword against him for something so trivial besides. "I'm well aware," he said, unable to swallow his agitation. "Don't talk to me as if I'm not."

Chobin inclined his head. "Didn't mean anything by it."

Tirdad directed his attention to the half-empty glass of wine Chobin had deposited beside the map when he first arrived, and the ewer beside it. "Do you mind?" he asked.

"Help yourself."

Tirdad did just that. He finished off the wine, refilled it, finished that off, and continued until the ewer was empty. It warmed his chest, and more importantly, smoothed the edges of his thoughts. By time he sat it back down, his hand was steady, the celestial theatre too distorted to make out. He spotted the concern in Chobin's smile as an uneven slant, as if it sought to copy Shkarag's crookedness but hadn't the cant. The man's smiles had more nuances than his body language and voice combined. That irritated him more, but it didn't stick thanks to the wine.

"I'm sorry," he slurred. "Here you are inviting me into your House, and I'm being more of an ass than an angry onager."

"You said it, not me." Chobin's concern shifted to amusement, which showed the white of his teeth. "So, what do you say?"

"I'm torn," said Tirdad. "This is my family we're talking about. Banished or not, I'm one of them. But you've been good to me, treated me as family. Give me time to think on it?"

Chobin nodded.

"Thanks. When do we leave?"

The marzban eyed the map, though he'd surely done as much dozens of times since the messenger arrived with a call to arms. "We can't just deploy as we are. Our—my House stuck around to bolster the frontier defenses after your cousin's invasion." Chobin paused, probably damning himself for the mention before going on. "That is our charge, after all. I've sent to have them withdraw from the marches. The timing is terrible for us. Those menstrual-gargling fuckers in Hrom were right to seize the opportunity. Can't fault them for a sound strategy."

"Nishabhur is a good two months out," Tirdad observed. "Maybe less if they push themselves, but not by much—not in the height of summer and over the plateau, or with a baggage train."

"We'll have the current regiment and supplies rendezvous with the main force. For what little it's worth. But I think it'll do us some good to have a lighter load, and them to have what paltry fucking support we can provide in the meantime."

Tirdad tried to concentrate on the map to no avail. He blinked hard and slow. Quality vintage. The cheap swill you get on the road just makes you sick if you overdrink. "Agreed," he replied at length.

"So we're sitting on our hands while either Hrom captures Dvin, or another commander claims all the glory in defending or recapturing it."

"There will be plenty of glory to go around," said Tirdad. Of that he had no doubt. Hrom was a worthy rival and wouldn't back down without a fight. A fight or coup, anyway. "In the meantime, I should hone my technique. I'm feeling more than a little out of practice after all that time being bedridden. Nearly had my head chopped off by brigands."

Chobin straightened, wearing a pensive grin. "Honestly, thought you'd accept. Had a horse and gear ready for you. I tell you what, consider it a gift, but promise you'll think on my offer between now and setting out?"

Tirdad nodded. "I will."

"Your rank is . . . I don't know what your rank is. Find some epaulettes and make something up. Point, is you sit to my right; I trust you above anyone else. Know logistics aren't your thing, but I'll be relying on you."

The marzban directed his grin to Shkarag. "And you, skink-slicker. Don't cause any trouble in my city. Only reason you're here at all is because of Tirdad, and because of what you did last night. Don't mean to sound ungrateful, but Ray and its people are my top priority, and can't speak for how they'll react to a div stirring up trouble, good deeds or not."

Shkarag bared her fangs, but offered no rebuttal. She seemed reasonably uncomfortable around Chobin, but whatever had gripped her upon their first meeting seemed to have passed for the time being.

Chobin waved the two of them out. "Now go on. You'll be sick of these tortoise-sodomizing meetings before you know it. Besides, your gift awaits, and I'm dying to see your reaction."

Tirdad exited with Shkarag and Chobin in tow, the guards at the entrance parting to let him through, each lowering his head respectfully until the three passed.

"It's just behind the citadel," said Chobin, directing them through an arch and between the pomegranate and pistachio trees that populated a modest orchard. "The symbols all belong to my House," he explained with an unreserved guffaw. "Got ahead of myself there. But you'll be fighting in our ranks, so you may as well fit in."

Just beyond the reach of the meadow, favouring the shade thrown by the citadel, there waited a horse with a coat like fresh snow and ears like tufts of wheat. A carpet dyed plum and embellished with remarkable detail hung over its back, and on that a quality saddle with a high cantle in the back and a knob up front.

"Shouldn't be travelling on foot," said Chobin. "Know you switched horses often because of the nature of your—of a star-reckoner's life. But you're a noble, damn what everyone says, and you need a horse to mourn your passing." The marzban let out a laugh. "Won't be long either! You look half in the ossuary already."

Tirdad hardly registered the jab.

From an early age, he had been raised alongside horses—by them, from some angles. Learning to ride was only the beginning, a gateway to time-honoured traditions. Horse archery, jousting, polo, hunting and fighting on horseback: all of it had been ingrained in his spirit, weaved so intimately that riding came more naturally than walking.

As such, a noble was supposed to be inseparable from his mount. Traveling long distances by foot was plain disrespectful. Tirdad had weathered the resultant dishonour because the greater honour lay in es-corting Ashtadukht. Afterward, his family had turned their collective backs on him—not that he held that against them. But it meant he hadn't led the life of a noble for years, so why bother keeping to its tenets?

Against his will, he'd cast off the only life he knew. From there, apathy had been quick to swoop in. And here, in the form of a beautiful charger, his dear friend was offering him his life back as casually and selflessly as everything he did. Arranged on a nearby slab were all the accoutrements of a Savaran, neat and bearing the insignia of Chobin's House.

"All yours," the marzban inserted into the lengthy silence. He took Tirdad by the scruff, pressing his forehead against Tirdad's grey-banded hair. "It's been a long time coming. You deserve this, family or not. You never should've lost it."

It took a moment for Tirdad to collect himself. He didn't deserve this. Not after what he'd done. Nevertheless, he'd been given a second chance. Knowing the nature of the gift and seeing it were worlds apart; seeing it gave it substance, pulled it into reality as if drawing a lot.

Tirdad broke the huddle and wiped the tears from his eyes, drawing in a breath so deep his ribs complained. "I thought . . . thought that life had ended."

He felt as if he were in a slow-moving dream, which could be traced back in part to the wine. He clasped Chobin's shoulder, and tried his best to sound sincere. "You won't regret this," he said.

The marzban's already indefatigable smile gained a second wind. "Surprise me," he said, slapping his back and matching the flinch it engendered. "Oh, right. Sorry."

Tirdad gradually broke out of his flinch, not all that eager to see how upset his ribs were. To his relief, they'd taken it pretty well.

"I should get back to it," said Chobin, indicating the way they'd come. "Do me a favour and take the time you need. I know it's been a busy few days for you what with the bandits and divs and festival and fucking half-divs." The marzban ended on that and a smirk as he made for his command center.

"Thank you," Tirdad called, to which the marzban just threw a hand over his shoulder to wave it away. Tirdad turned to Shkarag where she leaned into her spear; she'd been characteristically mum. "See? Chobin's a good man."

The half-div aimed a cant square at him and said, "So were you." She looked away. "I think."

He didn't need that translated. Neither did he disagree with the sentiment. "Yeah."

Tirdad approached the charger, which had its head down and one hoof rested on the tip. Its wheat-coloured ears pivoted his way as he approached. He matched its calmness in reaching up to stroke its neck. "I'm Tirdad," he said, low and soft. "I promise to do my utmost in taking care of you."

Motion to his left caught his attention, which turned it on Shkarag. She was standing over his accoutrements, swinging an axe while trained on its head. The first swings were listless, patently experimental. A couple more and she set it to a spin, running through a short routine before returning to the listless swinging.

He patted the horse's neck and joined the half-div by his gear. "What's the verdict?" he asked. "Does it suit you?"

". . ." She turned it over in her hand, drawing her fingers over the ornamental flourishes carved into the wood and engraved into the head, across the golden floral overlay that bordered the blade. "Maybe," she said at length.

"A bit?"

She sniggered at that. "An axe is an axe. Either it swings with gusto—" Demonstrably, she chopped the air. "—or it's a branch crowned with ore, wearing a too-big tunic and doing a šo-lousy impersonation of an axe. A pretender."

"Sounds to me like you're going out of your way to avoid saying you do have an opinion."

"An axe is an axe," Shkarag reiterated.

Tirdad eyed the one that hung from a loop on her hip. It had quality ornamentation of its own. He recalled her having two axes during their duel, and supposed she'd only recovered the one because it'd been used to chop her apart. "It's yours," he said.

Shkarag hadn't looked up until now. She cocked her head and stared as if waiting for him to explain what he actually meant, likely because his giving it away so soon if at all was absurd, even to her.

"Take it," he insisted. "It's yours."

Her eyes darted down and back. "That goat-fucker gifted it. Just now like some, like some overeager dowry."

Tirdad waited. She stared. "Oh," he finally replied. "That was strangely concise. Throws me off when you're always so long-winded once you get into it."

". . ."

"Well," he said, blinking against the fog that suffused the edges of his vision, "I'd like you to have it. I can't bring along both axe and mace at the same time, and you'd put it to better use than I ever could. Besides, I always went with the mace. It'd collect dust otherwise."

Shkarag held the axe up to better appraise it. She let her spear clatter to the stone so that she could apply a two-handed grip to the haft. Evidently, she approved, because she slid it into the empty loop on her weapon belt.

". . ." Shkarag further evinced her approval by turning a crooked smile his way.

She had the lemon-yellow scarf around her neck, which laid bare the scales that dominated her head, the scars that imposed upon them, and her enlarged pupils. The crisp lapis lazuli scales suited her—as striking as her personality. The scars spoke to her experience, gave further credence to her legend. She'd probably faced and overcome more trials than she could recount. Her eyes, though; her eyes were a thin band as bright as poppies growing around utter darkness—a line easily drawn between the div in her, or in a different light, her illness.

These were all important characteristics because they were borne of her lineage. What gave them their importance at the moment was how thoroughly captivating he found them.

He realized he was drunk. He also said this aloud.

"Maybe," she agreed, uneven smile vanishing as completely as a crescent moon dipping below the horizon. Her eyes darted away, instead finding the mail-and-iron spangenhelm amidst his gear. He picked it up and rolled it end over end in his hands.

"Never did like all the armor," he said. "It's sweltering at best, though the mail breathes better than lamellar, laminated, or scale. Doesn't do much good when you're wearing it over a surcoat with metal plates sewn in."

Tirdad glanced up from the helmet, and her abruptly down at it. He found it pleasantly surprising that she was paying attention at all—even if she was only entertaining him—so he went on.

"You still have to deal with the laminated thigh guards and gauntlets, which can work up a sweat in no time." He placed the conical helmet where he'd gotten it, and let his attention roam the arrangement until it landed on a tunic.

"Plum," he said, noting the colour and indicating it with a tilt of his pommel. "The whole of the empire would be plum if his family had their way. What do you think of it?"

No response.

"Well," he continued, accustomed to her non-replies, "they're outfitting me, so I don't suppose I'm in a position to complain." He swept his gaze over the gear, naming it as he did. "Breastplate, mail, girdle, helm, strips of metal on leather—it's mighty effective, but you won't find me wearing it all at once unless I'm made to be shock cavalry. I'm telling you, it's a veritable oven. Can't even mount your horse on your own."

Tirdad chanced another glimpse of the half-div. She was gone. He turned a circle, squinting in his inebriation as he did. "Shkarag?"

Hush.

"Shkarag?" he called.

Hush, ragged and meaningless.

He would've scowled at it if he could have; instead, he just scowled. "Shkarag?"

Hush, thinned to background noise, deprived of the unspoken currents that coursed a hair's breadth from the surface.

"Fuck." His palm shot to the ram's head pommel as if to check if it too had left him. He hadn't overlooked the fact that she'd spent her time by his side for what amounted to his every waking moment. Since she'd thrown in with him, she hadn't found a single reason to disappear. That is what troubled him the most about the hush. It didn't belong.

Without a second glance, he left the gifts behind and went in search of Shkarag. Her footprints led him back through the orchard, and into the traffic of the citadel, which warranted another scowl. "Great," he said. The trail had been trampled away.

Tirdad spent the better part of the day searching for her. He asked around, but wasn't all that surprised when he couldn't find a single soul who had seen her scarf or cuirass. She'd always been able to vanish without a trace.

When evening rolled around and the waning sun once again smeared honey over the mudbrick city, he called it a day. Shkarag was more than capable of handling herself. But that'd never been the problem.

Tirdad took the stairs leading to the spring, figuring he'd spend the night away from Chobin's mirth and all that entailed. He conceded that he was depressed without the half-div around; he'd grown used to her company, had crossed the city many times over in seeking it out.

He'd grown adept at blaming himself since exiling Ashtadukht—self-loathing came to him naturally by now. At no point did he consider that perhaps she only needed time alone. Too caught up in his mistakes and deathly afraid of losing the scraps that remained of his life, he assumed the worst. She couldn't die, but she could walk out of his life same as Ashtadukht had.

So that's where he ended the night. He'd pushed her away, same as he had his cousin. In doing so, he'd lost to the same fate that had damned him from birth. As he lay there beneath the planets he now belonged to, sword throbbing where he clutched it to his chest, he returned to a ritual abandoned upon Shkarag's return. He replayed their adventures together until he fell asleep, and any semblance of happiness ran away from his face, his life an empty stage where his companions once were. He always thought she'd come back, always hoped. And when she finally did, she left him with no choice. If he but reached—and only lethargy prevented him—he could have visited those lonely nights during which Ashtadukht contemplated suicide.

· · · · ·

Eggs. Rotten, rancid, and like sulfurous steam wafting over his flesh. It was the strangest thing, because within the stench there mingled the savoury smell of breakfast, of the omelettes that had become a cornerstone of his morning routine.

For the second day in a row, he awoke to an odd scene—though decidedly more striking. Shkarag lay close enough that her steady breathing tickled his face, and explained the stench. He curled his lip, but only as long as it took him to become acclimated to the smell.

Tirdad lay there for a moment, watching the slight movements of her lips that betrayed an inner dialogue, the tips of her fangs where they curled back into her mouth. In other circumstances, he would have either wondered what she was up to, or written it off as her natural eccentricities. For the time being, he was just happy to see her.

Sober and in a better mood, it came to him how much he'd overreacted the night before. He felt silly and embarrassed, but acknowledged the authenticity of it all. The saying that one should consider a decision first while drunk, second while sober rang true as ever, and now that it was on his mind, Shkarag had advised him to do the former more often.

He sat up, meaning to speak with her, but her gaze didn't follow him or flicker as it should have.

"Oh," he said. He figured she had entered one of her faraway stares, and wondered whether it'd be inappropriate for him to ask her what exactly went on during those unresponsive stretches.

He entertained the possibility of them being a state of absolute quiet—an escape from the reality that caused her so much grief. Perhaps it was a time for revisiting what was no doubt a storied past, turning over those nests beneath which she so often stowed memories. Maybe she simply thought better without distractions.

Tirdad went about his morning ritual: praying, tying his sacred girdle, and cleansing in the spring. He devoured the omelette, which to his dismay had gotten cold. When he'd finished and she still showed no signs of having sobered, he frowned, but thought nothing of it—reeking as it was, he'd awoken to her breathing, after all.

It wasn't until he went to retrieve his sword, which she had clutched in one hand between them, that he noticed the grape leaf bunched between her palm and its golden scabbard.

He took a knee and leaned in to further inspect it. Food was commonly wrapped in leaves, so it was only out of the ordinary because she didn't make a habit of bothering with conventional meals. But the festival had only just passed; he figured she had likely scavenged something from the sweetmeats that remained.

Putting it out of mind, and careful to avoid stirring her, he eased his blade from its scabbard. The usual greeting was warm in his grasp. A heartbeat that had once been repulsive now soothed him. Transfixed on its nacreous sheen, he pondered its nature.

With it, he had slain star-reckoner, yazata, div, and man alike. Come to think of it, a star-reckoner had been the first to fall to the blade, and neither yazata nor div had matched the utter satisfaction it'd communicated through its hilt. Not by a long shot. It was almost as if some of Ashtadukht's will remained. Tirdad, no longer hopeful but willing to entertain a fancy here and there, liked to think a part of her personality had been preserved.

There was more to it than that, of course. More to the blade. Twice now, he'd been given further insight. The yazata had warned him, said he didn't know what he was dealing with, though it hadn't been forthcoming with the details. Niyaz had looked at it with a fear that ran deeper than that of a mundane weapon. She had spoken of its power to destroy her many phylacteries, had wanted it for herself.

This still left Tirdad in the dark. That no one bothered to explain themselves irritated him to no end. Speak in riddles all you like, but if you're going to be ominous, speak straight. Otherwise, you're just drawing a person's nerves taut as a bowstring, and giving them no outlet through which to loose.

He tilted the blade, scowling at the thought, and watching the iridescence run as if it were paint clamouring to dribble over the edges.

Beyond it, the grape leaf caught his eye once more. Tirdad shifted his focus to the fine black residue that clung to one of its folds. He squinted, blinking and trying to remember where he'd seen it before. His memory wasn't as reliable as it used to be, but damned if he hadn't—he dropped the sword. "Fuck."

Tirdad threw caution to the wind, prying her fingers from the scabbard one by one so he could get at the leaf. Once he had it in his hand, all it took was a sniff for him to confirm his suspicion. The very same drug Ashtadukht had taken and administered.

He let the leaf fall free. A chill like Saturn's icy glare gripped his spine. This path was all too familiar, as if he were doomed to relive the same dreadful journey over and over.

He sat. Because he didn't trust himself to stand, and because he was already resigned to waiting. Tirdad alternated between staring at his sword where it'd clattered to the stone, and checking for signs of the drug subsiding. Eventually, he made a circuit of it by adding the city below.

When at last she groaned, he was ready to berate her for being such a toenail-swallowing fool. It never came to that. He had the wherewithal to catch his tongue, which was more than he could say for her.

"I'm a . . . coward," she intoned. Where her attention would have darted, it floated like leaves on a lazy creek. "I'm . . ." Her voice moved much the same.

She tried to get up, but it was obvious her limbs wouldn't listen. All she managed was to roll herself onto her back.

"ترســــو."

she spat.

"ترســــوترســــوترســــوترســــو."

The language she spoke was entirely foreign; all he could make out was that she was repeating something. He knelt beside her, turning a frown on the way her head would list from side to side.

"Shkarag?" he asked, making an effort to wring the tension out of his tone and keep it low. Ashtadukht had admonished him plenty for speaking too sharply or loudly when she was coming down from her highs.

She canted toward him, but not directly. Her eyes roamed the sky, only oscillating over him as a matter of their wayward course.

"ترســــو."

Tirdad sighed. Whatever she was saying, her carriage of its intonations seemed appropriate, as if she were more than fluent, native even. It must've had some special meaning. He doubted she'd have any recollection of having repeated it once lucid; he'd inquire all the same.

He hung his head and expelled another sigh. He loathed his helplessness. Celestial theatre at his fingertips, planets at his behest—might enough to fell a yazata. And some good that did him. Here he was kneeling before a dear friend who teetered on the cusp of a dangerous spiral, and he hadn't the remotest clue what to do about it. If his failure to save his cousin had taught him anything, it's that he was unprepared to do anything for Shkarag.

She saved him the trouble.

One minute Shkarag was muttering in her foreign tongue, the next she was posted on one arm, elbow trembling under the load, her rotten-egg breath as subdued as her mind where it tickled his nose and cheek. Her gaze still followed its vagrant path from nowhere to nowhere, but it now did so directly in front of him. She lifted a hand, unsteady and likely meant to be a claw if the asynchronous curling and uncurling of digits was any indication. It stopped short of her head, hovering instead at shoulder level.

"ترســـو.."

she said.

"Shkarag, I can't under—"

Her daze was swept away as if by a sudden flood, and it was all he could do to brace himself as she bared her fangs and lashed out. She bowled him over, taking him into the bank of the spring with a splash.

"Wait!" he cried, as she pinned him to the ground, rearing back enough for him to see her wild-eyed and fangs flared to strike. "Shkarag! It's me, Tir—"

She seized the opportunity, and, one claw snaking into his waterlogged hair to take purchase on his scalp, she came in for the kill.

Tirdad could have fought back. Overpowering her was out of the question, but he did have a dagger on his thigh. He wouldn't even entertain the option. If she wanted him dead, so be it. He accepted his fate.

So it came as a shock when, instead of sinking her teeth into his face, she kissed him with all the abandon of her bloodline.

She was ravenous. Greedy, sloppy, tongue roving as if she needed to taste all of him at once, and leaving an aftertaste of rotten eggs wherever it went. Her nails bit at his scalp; she tugged at his hair so roughly he thought she'd yank it free.

Briefly, he was too taken aback to return her fervour. Her kiss had stolen his tongue twofold. Had roused teeth and gums, tugged and split his lips, smeared his cheek and chin with saliva and blood. Her sawing breaths urged him to do the same.

Tirdad began to consider how to react when he recalled the image of her limping away, spear thumping, and bringing a clear end to her wine analogy. Don't think.

He sat up. Doing his best to match her enthusiasm, he found her fangs where they were tucked away near the roof of her mouth, indulging a newly-discovered desire to tease the points with his tongue, which drew an approving hiss. It petered out between their lips, escaped in earnest, and vibrated in her throat following their charged give and take.

She locked her legs around his waist; he secured hers with one arm, using his other hand to scrape at the scales and scars of her head same as she always did. That drew another hiss, though this one was cut short.

She went limp, and would have fallen back to crack her head against the stone if he hadn't caught her. Tirdad eased her the rest of the way down, following with his ear to her lips to listen for breathing.

When a breath roused more than just his ear, he blew out a sigh, and pulled away. She lay there as if she were all but unstrung, head lolling once again.

Tirdad stared at her. Where the din of excitement had once drowned it out, thinking hurried back in.

"What in the seven climes just happened?" he asked himself. He smacked his lips, and passing concern darkened his features. He could still taste her.

Tirdad was not a dense man, but he had been through a lot of late. He couldn't have been honest with himself, not entirely. And she was even more of a puzzle than she had been before their parting. Reading her meant considering both her nature as a div and her illness—not making the mistake of misinterpreting her eccentricities. She'd seen to clearing all that up for him.

So he sat there with her legs over his, and gave her the time she needed. Staring at the half-div and still more than a little nonplussed, he couldn't help but laugh.

One thing he knew for certain: eggs would never taste the same again.

X

WHEN SHKARAG DID COME TO, she carried on as if nothing had happened. This made Tirdad doubt the integrity of her actions made while under the influence, and in turn crushed his confidence. Not to mention making him feel guilty for indulging her. So, striving to respect her illness, and more than a little embarrassed, he made no mention of it. There was something that needed addressing, though.

"Shkarag."

She looked up from rummaging through her pack. ". . ."

Looking at her felt strange now. Like that cyclone had returned to once again rearrange her scenery. He'd been with women of pleasure many times, especially after throwing his lot in with Chobin. Where there were soldiers, whores weren't far behind.

This was different. It wasn't as if he'd fucked her there in that spring, but it was enough to force his feelings to surface. She'd wrung it out of him with that display. Shkarag was more than a friend. By Ohrmazd, he loved a fucking div!

During his introspection, she'd returned her attention to her pack.

"Shkarag."

". . ." She looked up a second time, eyes narrowed yet inquisitive.

"Why'd you do that?" he asked.

She cocked her head.

"You were on the drug again."

Her eyes darted here and there. She pursed her lips. "Brings in the clouds, and you're, you're under cover. The—" Shkarag successfully made a claw by her head this time. "The noise goes silent. Background runs off. You forget."

Tirdad nodded. He'd always understood the allure. The desire for escape was an easy enough concept to grasp. "But why now?"

She reached back to pluck an egg from her pouch—evidently having renewed her supply overnight—and crunched into it as if in deliberation. As she did, she aimed an inscrutable stare at him, flitting only marginally. "Needed it," she said at length, popping the rest of the shell into her mouth and swallowing it.

"Is there some way I can convince you to stop? Or something you can replace it with?"

". . ."

"Shkarag?"

"Why?"

Tirdad matched her stare, and mulled over a response as he did. The last time she posed such a question, he hadn't handled it well. Less thinking, he told himself.

"I care about your wellbeing, Shkarag. You resort to drugs again and no path you take is going to end well."

At that, she broke eye contact. "Everything is . . ." She trailed off, raking her nails over her scalp as she did. "And . . ." Her scrutiny flashed over him and back to her pack. "Bothers you?" she asked. "Something fierce? Like some, like some worrywart of a wife, some šo-wistful mistress stationed on a promontory, peering and thinking, 'If he never returns, all I've left of him is his smell.' And she's got, she's got his old trousers bunched in her fists, taking whiffs, really flaring her nostrils, and never washing them." She canted, raking as she did. "The trousers."

Tirdad couldn't help but crack a grin at her rambling.

She canted further, leering out of the corner of her eye. "For you," she said. "Maybe."

"For me?"

"For—" She bared her fangs, voice sharpened to a point. "You asked like some, stuck your nose in there and—"

"Thank you," he cut in. "If you need anything, absolutely anything, you come to me first."

Her cant deepened; with it, her expression softened. "Maybe," she muttered. She retrieved a second egg, pale yellow like sun-bleached stone. She offered it to him.

Tirdad accepted, wearing a smile he hoped she noticed. With a crack, he spared no effort in putting on a show of enjoying it, even as its repulsive contents oozed down his throat, all slime and underdeveloped feathers.

"It's kind of you to share," he said, which inspired an enigmatic look that strained her features.

"It's . . ." Shkarag sucked in a hefty lungful of air, and swept her darting scrutiny over the spring and down the steps that led up to it. "Always feels like, like everything is . . ." She exhaled, slow and steady. "Even you. All out to get me. Conspiring. But . . ." Her wandering scrutiny stopped where the stairs disappeared.

He followed her lead, inspecting the same spot from afar. That she was suspicious of others came as no surprise. Her actions often suggested as much, though he wished he didn't number among them.

An extended silence intervened before she pressed on. "But . . . I argue, and have rows. Tell myself you'd only ever skewer my chest. Never my back. Try to remember the šo-crunching yazata." She set her head askew. "I think."

It was strange. More than anything else, Tirdad felt accomplished. There were satellite feelings that orbited, revolved in their own way, but a sense of accomplishment was chief among them. "You're right to trust me," he said.

"Maybe." She craned up at him. "You're out of practice."

"Maybe," he agreed, or didn't.

"I'll give you a beating."

• • • • •

Later that night, she approached him, spear thumping on earth, to draw to a halt by his side. He glanced up from the table where he and Chobin were in the middle of a game of nard. Removed from the citadel, secluded by the orchard, and lit by a single brazier, it was a much-needed respite for the marzban.

"It's time," she said, canting.

He creased his brow. "Time?"

" . . ."

"Shkarag?"

Her gaze darted over the board dozens of times as if she were playing the game in her head. Eventually, it ceased. Having won her imaginary match, she said, "You're out of practice."

Tirdad took a pull of wine, and turned his confusion on Chobin, whose only reply was a shrug. "What're you getting at, Shkarag? I've been playing nard with Chobin regularly."

"Not that." She pulled out the axe he'd given her, training a deadpan expression on him, and tilted it such that the bit glowed in the firelight.

"Oh," he said. "You want to train?"

"You're out of practice," she repeated. "Don't want your—" She gave the axe another tilt so that the glow played at its golden inlays. "Don't want you to lose your head."

Well, she wasn't wrong. Tirdad looked to Chobin again, who offered another shrug.

"Wouldn't mind watching you two go at it," said the marzban, flashing a toothsome grin. "Plenty of time for nard. And she's right. Said it yourself, you're out of practice."

Tirdad returned his attention to Shkarag. "Here?"

She turned a circle to soak in her surroundings. "Maybe."

"Not very well lit."

"Not always going to be," Chobin countered.

"Yeah." Tirdad stood and dusted off his plum-coloured tunic, thinking belatedly that it'd be worse off after sparring. He went for his sword, and the pommel encouraged him to set it free, but he stopped short. That wouldn't do. "Mind if I use your sword?" he asked Chobin.

The marzban gave him a bewildered half-smile before eyeing the ram's head pommel, which was enough to remind him.

"Oh." He unsheathed his sword, which was identical to Tirdad's in style, and flipped it over to offer the hilt. "All yours."

The planet-reckoner accepted, then faced Shkarag where she'd limped further into the clearing. All things considered, it was a pleasant enough location to practice.

The orchard afforded privacy, but not so much as to obscure the moonlight-rimmed parapets that overlooked its grounds, or the ridge that loomed black against the heavens, only highlighted here and there where light graced rock at the right angle.

Shkarag dropped a ewer, and began draining the one in her other hand. "Fucking skink-slicker took our wine."

"She'll need it," replied Tirdad. "She doesn't want to kill us." He threw a grin of his own at the marzban. "Well, me."

"Hah!" Chobin slapped the table, which threw nard pieces in the air and ruined their game. He had been winning, so Tirdad made no complaint. "Let her try!"

To his side, the sound of Shkarag's spear dropping beckoned him over. ". . ."

Tirdad took the hint and strolled opposite where she stood, the dim light of the brazier gilding her in exaggerated contours, with the northwestern reaches of Ray a sprawling backdrop—busy with roofs, domes, and the suggestion of brightly-coloured accents. She wore a cant, axes in hand.

"Well," he asked, "should we take a moment to warm up?"

Shkarag canted further. She listed slightly, which made the abruptness with which she set into motion all the more jarring.

Shkarag casually tossed her axe as if hefting it, and within the adrenaline-second it hung at the top of its arc, a flick of her boot lifted her spear into the air, which she snagged and flung at him in one swift motion.

Tirdad side-stepped the spear, but it hit the ground early, never meant to endanger him to begin with. It did, however, put him immediately on his heels. Having recovered her axe the instant the spear was airborne, Shkarag dashed in behind. She spun like mad, blades glinting as she did to render a ring of orange in their wake.

Tirdad shuffled out of range, which kept him on his heels, and realized too late that was exactly what she wanted. She leapt—axes high, fangs bared, and eyes alight. He responded in kind, setting his jaw and punishing her leap with a shoulder slam that connected square with her cuirass. Only as she fell back did he realize why he'd done it.

Brazen as her leap was, the opening had been obvious, but he only risked a counter where most would not because it came to him that it was an opening her sister would have plugged—and he was right. She still fought as if she weren't alone.

She crashed with a hiss and the rattle of metal.

"Hah!" Chobin bellowed from behind, laughing from his gut.

Tirdad leveled sword and smile on Shkarag. She was gasping for the wind that'd been knocked out of her. "I'm not so out of practice am—"

An axe flew end over end by his ear.

"What the everliving fuck?" shouted Chobin into his other ear.

Between the axe and the marzban, Tirdad was distracted enough for her to bat aside his blade and spring up behind it. Shkarag drove the haft of her axe into his ribcage, and her weight behind it.

His ribs flared where she ground into them with force enough to have him backpedalling. He cried out, braced his forearm on her neck, and—was rammed into the trunk of a pomegranate tree. A flash of white swamped his vision, ribs all the more livid.

When it passed, he found her waiting a few steps back, cuirass rising and falling, an uneven smile trained on him as if to challenge him to try again.

"Fucker chucked her axe at your head," said Chobin. "Could've killed you."

"Yeah," said Tirdad. He returned her smile in kind, and brandished his blade. What a thrill! This was nothing like their duel, and he was more excited for an honest bout than he'd thought.

Following her example, he burst into action. A step-thrust at her chest incited the expected parry, so—a blade stopped a hair's breadth from his neck. She'd recovered her second axe during his disorientation.

"You're out of practice," she said matter-of-factly.

"Didn't see you'd retrieved your axe."

"Enemy won't stop and regale you like some, like some—" Her eyes darted away, and he could now hear the sawing in her chest over the popping of the brazier. She'd distracted herself. Tirdad capitalized by bobbing under and past her axe, meaning to bring his sword across her abdomen, but she wasn't quite as distracted as he thought.

Instead, it whined over the inlay where she parried as he passed, and threw her other axe in a backhand that naturally transitioned into one of her whirls. This time, she didn't let up. It was all he could do to pivot on his heel and intercept her axes as they shrieked along his blade in quick succession. Shriek, shriek, shriek, reverse; shriek, shriek, shriek, reverse.

It wasn't just that, though. She rose and fell, winding and unwinding so that he had to change the angle of his block with every whirl. After the fifth round of shrieks, she shifted to a style he was more accustomed to dealing with—perhaps in seeing that he was only defending, or as part of her normally unpredictable style. Whatever the case, he preferred it.

She spun an axe in one hand and brought it in an overhand chop that he intercepted, only for her to bring her other axe up and around, clapping against his blade and trapping it by the bit.

Shkarag followed with her now-freed overhand axe for another strike, which he denied by unsheathing his short sword with his off-hand, catching the axe in its downward stroke, and retaliating with one of his own. She responded in kind, and with that they found their rhythm.

They fell into a routine for hours, Shkarag sometimes throwing him off by inserting a random technique or whirl, but always returning to the more traditional method of axe-fighting. At some point Chobin had turned in, but Tirdad was too engrossed to notice. He'd trained for his entire life, but it had never felt like this. Every parry, every strike: they all fell into place as if by instinct. Reflex, not reaction.

He could tell she was holding back; she could have killed him every other stroke. Shkarag was his better by leaps and bounds, but he was content with that. It made him feel young again, exuberant. Sadly, he wasn't, which was most apparent in the increasing protests of his body.

Shkarag must have noticed he was getting sloppy, because she ended it by slipping in under his downward stroke to throw him off his feet and flat on his back. His ribs would not be happy come morning.

Breathing through his mouth, new tunic soaked with sweat and sticking to his skin, he lay with his arms spread, basking in the afterglow of their duel, adrenaline still coursing through his veins.

Nearby, there came a thump. The rattle of cuirass. The slink of mail. The rustle of fabric. Tirdad rolled his head in time to catch a glimpse of his sword falling from her grasp. He swallowed. Shkarag lifted a blood-soaked hand from her side, which revealed a stab wound, and smeared the blood over her nose and mouth as if starved for it. She let her hand fall, brushing a broken line of flame-kissed blood over her torso as it did. Her chest rose and fell in great heaves.

She limped—no, stalked over, wearing only her caftan, which hung loose and undone. As she did, his attention was drawn to that tantalizing streak of blood down her torso, over her heaving chest made all the more alluring by what her caftan hid, along the ridges of her warrior's abdomen, to the trickle of blood that pooled around the nasty scar where her leg had been severed, to finally roll over and between the sinews writhing in her thigh. The brazier glinted on her lapis lazuli scales, shimmering as she neared like mail in the sun, bronzing her already golden-brown flesh.

That she was half-div didn't so much as register; neither did any of the things that might've been seen as ugly. To Tirdad, she was beautiful.

Shkarag straddled him without pretense, but with a carnal grace, as if swooping down like a raptor in flight. He reached out to stroke her thigh for the first time, trailing scar and blood where she so often kneaded. Her stare, sanguine and intense, darted to his touch. She laid one hand on his and squeezed so hard he could feel a sliver of bone beneath the surface. She bared her fangs, but didn't let up. Instead, she bent at the waist to press her lips to his, other palm coming to rest against his cheek.

Strange. It was short-lived, affectionate. When she pulled back, the look she gave him was anything but inscrutable; it mirrored the kiss. That didn't last.

She gathered more of her blood, fresh and hot, and smeared it over her mouth, then his. Tirdad breathed it in, tinny and, perhaps because he saw it in her, arousing. Shkarag shivered in his lap, and next thing he knew she was kissing him with the same wanton abandon as she had while drugged.

All the while, Tirdad felt as if he were in a dream—as if this turn of events were nothing shy of impossible. He took her lead, teasing her fangs as he had before to the same approving hiss, indulging in the stench of eggs that clung to her breath, abiding by her will even when she took him by the hand to plug her wound with his thumb. It was more than mere lust; it was the closeness of it all, the immense leap of faith it must take for someone like her to do something so intimate.

A sizzling rose between them, which broke Tirdad away to find her untying his sacred girdle, hands burning all the while. "Let me," he offered, moving to help.

She bared her fangs, patently embarrassed, and kept at it until the girdle fell away. Shkarag didn't fight when he took her palms, grimacing at the burns and gingerly pressing his lips to each, though she did avert her gaze.

Her embarrassment was quick to fall to the scent of fresh blood that hung in the air. She took his lapel in her fists and pulled him up into a sitting position, peeling his tunic over his shoulders and heaving rotten-egg breaths into his face. She looked crazed, wild. Straddling the thin line between lust and bloodlust. He loved how true she was to herself.

Once she had his arms free, Tirdad plugged her wound again, which elicited a delighted hiss and further encouraged her grinding. That in turn emboldened him to take purchase on her ass with his free hand.

She froze.

"Shkarag?" He pulled his head back to get a good look at her. She was boring into his chest. A glance was all he needed: Ashtadukht's stamp seal. Fuck. It hadn't even occurred to him—he never took it off.

She reached up hesitantly, fingers in a claw above it, and somewhere in her heaving, trembling pomegranate-red, she was asking permission. Tirdad nodded, too caught up in the moment and his newfound love for her to argue.

Shkarag tore it from his neck and flung it into the city below. With the stamp seal gone, all that remained was an untrammeled desire, an unlikely pair, and a night made increasingly sinful as only a daughter of Eshm could. Until she died.

• • • • •

What followed was two months described by routine. The wait was made pleasant by Shkarag's company, not to mention their incendiary relationship. While Tirdad still had his reservations, he knew they'd crossed a line—one they often revisited after training sessions. Waking up beside her would take some getting used to. This was the same half-div whose pranks had been endless, who couldn't recall the past without clamming up. But death had changed that. The phylactery that brought her closer to who she used to be also dismantled the wall she'd erected against her struggles. Remembrance is a double-edged blade. Tirdad doubted she'd ever get over her paranoia or withdrawn nature, but that was Shkarag, and it made the care she did show all the more meaningful.

He reflected on that as they travelled the long road to Dvin. She rode beside him, resting against the mane of her charger, scarf spread over her to provide shade. The more the garrison had witnessed their evening training, the more he and Shkarag walked the streets of Ray, the more comfortable the citizens were with her presence, until the scarf was only ever worn around her neck. Tirdad liked that she still wore it. From beneath her cover, she returned his stare as she was wont to do: darting and inscrutable.

"Messenger's here," said Chobin from his left. "Wonder what it is now?"

Tirdad looked up in time to see the messenger raise his right hand in salute, which both he and Chobin returned.

"What news do you have for us?" asked Chobin. Burdened with anxiety over his command, he'd been less jovial the further along they were, though he was careful to wear a smile when around his subordinates.

"The King of Kings, may he live forever, commands you to turn for Nisibis. Dvin is ours for the time being, and Nisibis is under siege."

"Goat-fucking—" Chobin screwed up his face before ironing a grin back on. "Thank you. Get some rest. You've no doubt been riding hard."

Once the messenger departed, he turned a strained grin on Tirdad. "What'd I fucking tell you? They retook the sturgeon-kissing city, and here I am empty-handed with neither glory nor loot."

Tirdad opened his mouth only to be cut off.

"And don't tell me there's glory to be had elsewhere. This is my first meaningful command besides what your cousin forced on me." Chobin deflated at his misstep, removing his conical cap to run his fingers through his hair. "Sorry. Damn insensitive of me."

Tirdad waved the apology away. "You don't need to mince words. It won't change what she did. But take it from someone who spent the last decade wallowing over what he should've done: it won't get you anywhere. Nowhere enviable anyway."

"Hah!" Chobin slapped his back, spirits so effortlessly lifted. "Ah, but it got you here with me. A world where we aren't comrades isn't one I'd like to entertain. Not to mention you're threshing a daughter of Eshm to boot!"

The marzban leaned in. "I confess to peeping once or twice. Thought some of the pleasure women I've been with were inventive. Turns out they were amateurs. I'm not one to judge, but something is fucking off with the two of you."

Tirdad turned a knotted brow on Chobin. "You watch?"

The marzban shrugged, grin growing by the second. "What do you expect when you're going at it in my backyard? Figured the show was part of the deed. Sure as fuck wasn't the only one to get tight in the trousers over your displays."

Head shaking yet unable to stifle a chuckle, Tirdad turned to Shkarag, feeling more embarrassed than he let on. "Hear that?" he asked. "The goat-fucker's been getting off on us."

". . ." She flicked her eyes from one to the other, lips parted and arm limp by her horse's side. "Only see," she replied at length, voice hoarse. "Only see the pomegranate-red when—" She coughed. "—only see it and—" Another dry cough.

Tirdad put his waterskin to her lips, from which she took a gulp and finished her thought.

"Only see the pomegranate-red and . . . and you." Her attention found somewhere in the distance to flee to. "Maybe."

He offered her one of the regular smiles he hoped she saw. "Come to think of it, I guess I should be grateful you haven't revisited that insult of my being pinecone-arsed, trying to make it a reality."

185

Still trained elsewhere, her lips grew marginally more crooked—not a smile, but it'd do.

"Something is definitely fucking off with the two of you," said Chobin, amusement plain. "All right. Let's change course for Nisibis. We'll make Hrom rue the day it went rabble-rousing."

Tirdad signalled one of his subordinates over, relaying the order and feeling out of sorts in doing so. He'd never actually held a position of authority, and likely never would have even if his family hadn't been disbanded. "What's the plan?" he asked once the subordinate was off to further relay the order.

"Something they'll remember," said Chobin. "Want them to have second thoughts about besieging our cities and conspiring against us in the future." He flashed a full-toothed grin. "Don't know how yet, but now my blood's boiling for it. You and me, Tirdad, we're going to rout them and gain the favour of the King of Kings."

"Not sure what I'd do with that," said Tirdad. "Besides, power is like a bird, jumping from branch to branch. I'd rather be the tree than try and please the bird."

"What would the tree be?"

"Uh," Tirdad scratched his head. "Ironwood? That isn't the point. You struggle to gain the favour of one king only to have him replaced by another. Or your House dissolved."

"Birds shit on trees," Shkarag countered. "Paint them whites and greens and blacks. Do you . . . saying you want me to shit on you? Not against it. Might just work. I think."

Tirdad bunched his nose at her. "No."

"Oh."

"I'm telling you something is fucking off," said Chobin.

• • • • •

They kept the Iranian plateau to their right, Drafsh regiment of one-thousand cavalry to their back, and plotted a course northwest until they reached the escarpments of Hayk—sheer and tenable—upon which they veered further west. This deposited them into the fertile plain known as the Land of Rivers. To one side a limestone range engraved a deformed boundary into the sky. Reminiscent of Shkarag's grin, its crimped, snowy ridges were livened into plumes of powder by a constant gust. Where its incline leveled to plain, vast swathes of farmland stretched as far as the eye could see, their golden-brown harvests dominating the southern horizon except where incised by a wide river.

Moving as a force, loaded with gear, combat imminent: resting their horses every few days was made all the more necessary. One such break had them camping in a gap in the ridge for cover.

Tirdad had been waiting for the chance to strike out into the pastures and forests harboured by the mountain chain, and while fortune had favoured him with an encampment on its threshold, it sought to balance his good luck with torrential rain and an untimely chill. Still, he was determined. Chobin in tow, he scoured a grove of oaks not far from camp.

"So," asked Chobin, pulling back his hood now that they were sheltered by the canopy, "what now?"

"Your guess is as good as mine," said Tirdad. He squinted up into the broad-leafed oaks, rain pattering against leaves and crowding his eyes, the crisp scent of a nearby fir companion to the earthy aroma of rain. "There have to be some eggs around here somewhere."

"Have to say, searching after sundown and during heavy rain is not the brightest idea you've ever had."

"Sound reasoning, but the opportunity hasn't presented itself. Between marching during the day, her always being around, and the scarcity of forests on the plain, this is the only chance I've been given."

Chobin craned to join him in squinting. "See anything?"

"Nothing," said Tirdad. He pressed further into the grove, searching branch after branch for a nest. "Oh, there's something I've been meaning to ask. She's always gone at night. I don't want to pry, but can't help but wonder if your scouts have brought you any reports?"

"Truth be told, I sent a few out whose only orders were to track her."

Tirdad broke his search to scowl at the marzban. "What? What in the seven fucking climes are you doing that for?"

Chobin lifted his hands, palms out, and put on his most disarming grin. "Didn't you just take a roundabout approach to asking me if I'd done just that?"

Tirdad expelled a frosty sigh. "Yeah."

"Can't blame a person for wanting to know where the div you're harbouring is disappearing to at night. Not that anything came of it. Skink-slicker outpaces my best trackers. Guess it's true the night embraces them."

Tirdad could blame him, and he did. "You don't trust her."

Chobin's grin strained. He found somewhere else to look. "Well, no."

His palm snapped to his ram's head pommel. It urged him to act. His frosty breaths grew intense, became plumes. Deep red tinged with purple bled into his vision. A heat like mad desire swept over his skin, making his hair stand on end as it passed. Her voice came to him, quiet and understanding, laced with an accent he never could place, with a gentle hiss insinuated in its depths. She said his name. He remembered her in the busy thoroughfare, searching his eyes for something she recognized—something she knew intimately.

He had his sword brandished, its starling-black menacing and aimed at Chobin.

"Tirdad?" the marzban asked as if it weren't the first time, smile gone, and having gripped the hilt of his own sword.

Cold rushed in, quenching the fire that'd spread over Tirdad's skin. It freed his mind. Whatever had him under its thrall retreated. Tirdad blinked. He cast from his blade to Chobin and back again. To its dismay, he sheathed it. He glanced from trunk to trunk, feeling out of sorts as if he'd left and instead of returning found another world. This one was like his, but not his. Not the same. Disturbing as it was, it passed as swiftly as it'd come.

"Tirdad?"

He blinked hard and shook his head. "Sorry."

Chobin visibly relaxed, a smile softening his features. His sword hand hung loose by his side. "What the ever—what happened there?"

Tirdad shook his head again. "I don't know."

He didn't, and that troubled him. Perhaps Shkarag could tell him. She seemed to know more than she was letting on, though he didn't believe for a moment she withheld it out of malice if so.

"Really had me worried there," said Chobin, trying to sound amused but failing to smother his concern. "You looked ready to cut me down. Didn't like my odds after all the training you've been doing."

"Let's just finish what we're here for," said Tirdad. Chobin prying would only make him all the more frustrated by his not knowing. He crossed further into the grove where it ran along a cliff, watching the treetops as he did. "You need to trust her," he said after they were well into the forest. "She deserves as much. If not for me, then for what she did for your city."

"I know," Chobin eventually replied from behind. "I know all too well. She saved our sturgeon-kissing asses back at your estate, too. But, Tirdad, have you forgotten that mere months ago she was the right hand of another half-div who brought so much death and destruction to the lands under my protection? To my people? Try as I might, I can't just forget that." He paused long enough to draw up beside Tirdad.

"You love her," he stated. "That much is evident, has been since before you were threshing. And that's why I've went as far as I have in tolerating her. Because I respect you, and because you deserve to be happy even if it's with a half-div. But I must keep the well-being of my people in mind. That means keeping tabs on her." The marzban let out a self-deprecating laugh. "Not that I've had any success."

Tirdad couldn't logically argue the assertion. Chobin was acting duly as marzban and protector, and with good reason. He knew as much. But it still irritated him, because even as he told himself it was irrational, the truth remained that people didn't operate rationally. The wedge she drove between them deepened, if only marginally.

"Good," he said, now more interested in her eluding Chobin's scouts than knowing what she did while out. He returned to his search, scanning everything overhead. "I'm not sure what's in season. Think we'll have better luck with the trees or the cliffs?"

"Your guess is as good as mine. I'm only here as an extra pair of eyes. Eyes that can't see worth copper in the dark, but eyes."

"You have moonlight," replied Tirdad.

"What moonlight? It's pouring."

"All right. I admit this was an awful idea. She cooks for me every morning, so I thought it'd be nice to return the gesture."

Chobin laid a hand on his shoulder. "Your heart is in the right place, my friend, but your mind leaves much to be desired." Tirdad cracked a smile, tempered by his wish to be upset with the man. He was just too damn charismatic, too friendly.

The clouds parted, throwing light on the grove and adjoining cliff as if the moon had overheard their conversation and refused to let its honour go undefended. Initially, the only difference it made was that his abortive search was now illuminated. Further drawing his scrutiny over the rock face, it glistening with the silvery sheen of rainwater, he made out the shadow of a recess. In that, a nest.

"There," he said, pointing. "My mind's keen as ever."

"Clouds literally parted they felt so sorry for you," Chobin mock-grumbled, squinting and following his finger. "Hard to tell, but could be a nest. How do you propose we reach it?"

Tirdad deliberated the question, stroking the ram's head pommel as he did. "The rock's going to be slick, not that I'd be all that confident climbing even if it weren't. Think the trees will support us?"

"Us?"

"Me."

"Maybe," said Chobin, as if with a shrug.

"Well," Tirdad reckoned, "we're wasting moonlight. Better try before it decides to slink back behind the clouds." He approached the oak nearest the nest, went to remove his sword belt, realized how much of a mistake that'd be, then set to climbing. The oak bore him well, its wet branches not much of a hindrance. Tirdad scaled its trunk without trouble until he was level with the recess and the nest it held, relieved to find his eyes hadn't deceived him. There were a pair of birds in the nest, obscured by shadow but with silhouettes that didn't belong to a raptor. An important distinction to anyone looking to steal their eggs.

He hadn't actually considered how he should go about the task if the parents were around; he'd never really entertained the fine details of the act. Shkarag seemed to get along well enough, but how did she manage without being pecked and mauled?

"So, is there a nest or not?" called Chobin from below. The silhouettes canted toward his voice.

Figuring it as good a time as any, Tirdad threw caution to the wind and lunged for the eggs, unintentionally punching one of the birds as he did. Having caught them off-guard, Tirdad had time to snatch half the clutch and slip it into a pouch before one of the two birds was on him, flapping, pecking, and squawking. He swatted at it, cursing as he did and trying to make his way back down. After a few branches and more than a few pecks, one such swat batted it into the cliff face, after which it tumbled to the ground below.

When he reached the bottom, Chobin was waiting, hands on hips. "Didn't have to kill it," he said.

Tirdad turned a frown on the bird. "I only meant to—" Movement in the distance interrupted him, where high atop a faraway cliff there stood a figure cast in the diffuse glow of the moon. Chobin had caught on, and now shared in the spectacle.

"What the everliving fuck?" he asked. The figure spread its arms. "Why's there a—" It jumped.

That marzban and planet-reckoner were stunned was evinced by their still silence. It lasted only a few short breaths before Tirdad was off to help, though he knew the odds of surviving such a fall were slim. Cold rain biting at his face, he ran out of the grove, charged across the wild-flower-laden field that measured most of the distance, splashed through the swollen creek that fed it, and stumbled into another grove. Branches whipped his face, roots wrenched his ankles, once throwing him into a mud puddle. Ragged from his mad dash, he made it to the clearing where the body lay.

To say the sound that greeted him made him wince would have been accurate if woefully understated. It creaked like wood in winter, cracked as if splintering; it grated like stone dragged over unpolished stone. The figure lay at the opposite end of the clearing, but faint as the sounds were, their repulsiveness carried clear.

Tirdad squinted against the night. The clouds had once again renewed their downpour, and smothered the moon as a result. He plodded over, sobered by the dreadful sound, which only got worse the better he could hear it—the individual splinters, the mortar digging into pestle. As he drew near, he could make out the silhouette of a person in the darkness, contorting in ways no silhouette should. Not only did it grow louder, but somehow more intense, as if rising to a peak, and begging the question of what sort of peak broken bone could hope to achieve.

"Are you alive?" he asked, stopping a few steps away. More of the terrible sound answered.

Chobin burst out of the forest, winded and stumbling. "You—" He doubled over, hands on knees, and waved a hand in Tirdad's direction. "Really—" He couldn't get it out.

Meanwhile, Tirdad kept an eye on the figure, which was rapidly beginning to take on a less disgusting silhouette. He furrowed his brow at its slender frame, at the faintest hint of glossy colour that would surface now and then.

"Training really—" Another heaved breath. "Training did a number on your stamina," Chobin half-breathed, half-laughed. "Either the threshing or the training."

"Shkarag?" asked Tirdad.

"Who the fuck else?" blurted Chobin.

Tirdad kneeled, and as the bones quieted to crinkling, trusted his instinct: he reached out to stroke the figure's head. Scales, smooth and semi-keeled, scored with what could only be scars. "Shkarag?" he asked again.

" . . . "

He recognized that measured quiet. Now that he'd learned what she was up to during her nightly romps, he felt sorely unprepared to so much as entertain it. What in the seven climes was she doing? Jumping off cliffs the entire time? More importantly, why?

Her head canted beneath his touch, and though he could hardly make her out, he knew she hadn't the same trouble when looking up at him.

"Are you injured?" he asked.

" . . . "

"Sorry. I never meant to intrude on your privacy. I was out searching for, well, here." He retrieved one of the eggs and offered it to her. "I'll leave if you want."

". . ." She transitioned to a sitting position, one leg out as usual. Only then, as the dim reflection roved her scales, did he realize she wasn't wearing anything.

"I'll go," he said, moving to do just that when she caught him by the forearm. Gingerly, she accepted the egg. A crunch followed, underscored by a low hum, to be replaced by the measured quiet. Tirdad waited for her to release him, but her grip didn't relent. He took that as a firm enough sign to stay, so he sat in front of her, drenched and now sitting in a puddle of mud.

Whatever ritual he had interrupted, he gathered she must've been made to feel awkward or at least uncomfortable if she'd gone out of her way to do it in secret. Anxiety burned like bile in his throat and chin. The last time he interrupted a ritual, it had been Ashtadukht's, and he had mishandled that to catastrophic effect.

The dread of making the same mistake kept him from speaking, from asking the many questions begged by the scenario. Perhaps, he thought, it'd be better if he did. Shkarag wasn't the greatest at expressing herself. Then again, maybe no communication was best.

For a time, the chorus of a downpour spoke for them, and removed the need to fill an uncomfortable silence. Thunder soon stormed in to liven the steady conversation of rain. Lightning preceded the rumble, a stark flash that caught a still of her hugging one knee, eyes fierce and trained on him, as if preserved in rock relief.

That's right, he thought, she must be freezing—her viper blood all the more vulnerable to the chill. He unclasped his cloak and swung it around her, lifting the hood to cover her head and securing it as best he could to fend off the rain. "Where are your clothes?" he asked. "You're going to die again if you aren't careful."

He took her hand, which trembled in his grasp, and leveled concern where the flash had last illuminated her face.

"ترســـو."

"Fuck," he cursed under his breath.

- AN ILL-FATED SKY

"ترســــوترســـوترســـو.„

"She Was Your Sister."

"she's trembling."

"you ran!"

The next lightning strike did so with prejudice, such that its spoiled-yo-gurt glow only spilled over a distant figure. Another strike followed immediately after, bringing the figure considerably closer, canted and every bit as horrific as Tirdad remembered from their forest nightmare. "Shkarag?" he asked, the yazata's warning fresh in his mind. This sorcery belonged to her. For all its hatred of divs, the yazata would not have lied to him. That would have strode counter to its nature.

The lightning picked up pace, flickering and giving the disfigured face leave to advance in a series of unholy cants.

"What the everliving fuck is that?" yelled Chobin. "Tirdad! Look out! It's coming right at you!"

Tirdad fought to tear his gaze away from its starling-black sockets and the terror they promised. In doing so, he discovered that he could move his head, but his eyes refused to budge; he couldn't look away. He reached out, finding Shkarag and feeling his way up to her face, where her hastened breaths soothed his rain-chilled fingers. He cradled her cheeks, using them as a guide to find and caress the scales of her scalp, paying special attention to the furrows disfigured by bit and blade.

"Shkarag," he said, calm as he could manage with his heart in the grip of the oncoming nightmare. "Relax. Let it go, Shkarag." He kept up his ministrations. "Relax."

At his words, the flashes of lightning rapidly lost their tempo, which brought the terrible, stuttering advance to a crawl. The face twisted as if in recognition of its defeat, becoming more repulsive as its broken fangs sagged, as its soul-empty sockets bent into a scowl. Like a mirage meeting its end, the image warped and ran. It vanished. So too did the storm, flushed away and replaced by a starry sky.

Now that the celestial theatre had reclaimed the night, it cast them in a lustrous sheen. With the constant reminder of its true nature warring at the fringes of his soul, Tirdad knew better. Lustrous was too gentle a term; it implied beauty, grace.

"Would someone tell me what in Ahriman's unwashed scrotum just happened?" Chobin shouted from behind. "I'm not even wet!"

"Now you have something in common with your women," Tirdad called over his shoulder. Then, to her, "How're you feeling?"

". . ."

"Better?"

She cocked her head. Veiled as she was by the hood of his cloak, she came off as more distant than usual. Shkarag reached into the hood, making a claw over his hand.

"I won't judge you," he said. "And I won't bring this up again if that's your will."

She cocked further.

A shadow fell over them. "What's she—oh, fuck, where are your clothes?"

"Chobin," Tirdad growled, thinking it was impossible to be this dense.

"Sorry. I'll, uh, I'll, yeah." The shadow retreated.

Shkarag let her claw fall by her side, and Tirdad withdrew his touch, surprised by the slickness of her cheeks as he did.

"Father forbids us," she started, "forbids . . . phylacteries. Vouchsafing blunts our, what makes us, dilutes the pomegranate-red and—" Shkarag bunched her fingers into fists. "She didn't have one. She just, like some . . . I should've, too. Should be dead. They say, they say a coward dies a thousand deaths. I'm due a dune's ransom in sand." A sob shook her, and it took all his self-control not to embrace the half-div. If this was her penance, the last thing she wanted was to be consoled.

"You do this every night?" he asked.

". . ." Her cant intensified.

Tirdad contemplated her fists, the signs coming to him with the benefit of hindsight: the night he'd thought he dreamt of her standing naked before a cliff, the div's comment on how many deaths she must've endured to have such an impressive rate of regeneration. He'd been waking up to omelettes, oblivious to the truth behind her apparent sleep deprivation. He'd written it off as her div half trying to adapt to a more human sleep schedule. During their earlier travels, before they split up, she would rarely if ever go an entire day without an extended nap, even if it was on the back of a horse. Not now.

"Can I help you do this from now on?" he asked, astounded at himself for offering, and uncertain whether or not he should be ashamed.

She lifted her head enough for him to see beneath the rim of the hood. There, her expression was patently perplexed. She parted her lips, canted forward, and screwed up her face.

"I'll do the deed for you," he said with conviction. "However you like, as much as you like." Much as he hated that she spent her nights ending her life, it wasn't his place to lecture her on it. Better she didn't do it by her lonesome.

Shkarag offered him one of her uneven smiles. "No," she replied, flat and direct.

"Maybe?" he asked.

"No." Her gaze darted over his shoulder, and her lips formed an unspoken 'maybe'.

Tirdad sighed but left it at that. He retrieved the other egg and held it out. "For you," he said. "Where are your clothes?"

She plucked the egg as if choosing it from an assortment and reached back to stow it in her pouch, trying several times to find its flap before coming to the realization that it wasn't there. Shkarag brought the egg back around and turned it end over end between index and thumb, tacitly contemplating its texture.

"I don't have your eye for eggs, or even know where to begin," Tirdad said, wondering whether he'd foraged a worthy one. "But I'm willing to learn."

Shkarag set her hood further askew. Still occupying her hands by turning his gift end over end, she tucked her outstretched leg under so that she could lean in and express her gratitude with a kiss—fleeting, with a whiff of egg, but heartfelt.

"You try," she began, sitting back and briefly heedful to some faraway distraction. Shkarag bundled in her cloak to stave off the chill, shivering underneath but pressing on. "No one has ever tried. You're a . . . a trailblazer. You hack and hack, like some, like some quack of an explorer in uncharted territory, and you don't have a map because that's the, that's uncharted territory, but you don't care. You try. You keep your head down in blizzards and sandstorms, and when you stumble upon, when there's a ruin, you ponder it. You see an antiquity site, and you're no historian—historians turn up their noses at you, their šo-wretched collective noses. But while they're off curating or snorting potsherds, you try. You . . ."

She trailed off, shivering and made drowsy by the cold. Slowly, she brought a claw up by her head. "You try to get ahold of, try to capture, try to grasp my . . . you try even if you never can understand. Never. I think."

"You're the first to try, to . . ." She transitioned from the faraway distraction to dedicating her stare to him. "Šo-damned everyday things smart something fierce, but you just, you just explore and don't leer down that kestrel's nose."

Her stare darted to the egg she still tumbled just outside a gap in the cloak. "You try, and take care not to disturb those antiquity sites. So . . ."

She deliberately placed the egg in the palm of one hand, and held it out for him to take. Her eyes, already dedicated, didn't so much as waver. "We share. Like . . ." An inward turn sloughed the focus from her pupils such that she looked through him, and left as abruptly as it'd come. "Time for you to go," she stated.

Tirdad accepted the egg, but only after clasping her hands in what he hoped was a comforting gesture. "I'll keep the bed warm," he said. Tirdad held the egg between thumb and forefinger, blemished like the spotted flycatcher it belonged to, and allowed a smile to ease his worry-strained features. "But this doesn't mean I won't be expecting an omelette tomorrow morning."

"Maybe," she said.

"Maybe," Tirdad agreed, and her eyes, having rekindled their habitual darting, did so with what he took to be mirth. Without so much as a goodbye, she wandered off into the trees. The night embraced her such that even her limping came off as effortless.

Tirdad knotted his brow at the egg, turning it over as she had and replaying the conversation in his mind. She'd shown genuine appreciation. So why couldn't he get over the sinking feeling of knowing she was off to commit suicide—who knows how many times and in who knows how many ways?

"Skink-slicker told you it was time for you to go then went and left herself," said Chobin. "That's a div for you."

Tirdad glanced up at the marzban, who was watching the spot where Shkarag had disappeared into the darkness. "I appreciate your backing off," he said.

Chobin shook his head, scratching it as he did. "Sometimes I speak without thinking. All the discipline father beat into me, and I can't break the habit."

Tirdad returned the egg to its pouch on his belt, and groaned as he stood, knees none too happy about how long he was kneeling. "This is worse than expected," he said.

"Hmm?"

"You heard her."

Chobin nodded. "Won't claim to know her better than you do, so I'm not equipped to weigh in. Especially not after all she said." He drew his face into a grimace and rubbed the back of his neck. "Admit I might've been too caught up in my perception of her based on what she is and what she's done."

"Yeah." Having achieved what he set out to, though not nearly as he'd expected, Tirdad made for the encampment. The weight of what he'd learned exhausted him. He just wanted to sleep.

"Something is seriously off with her," Chobin said, falling into step by his side.

Tirdad shot him a glare, which the marzban either didn't see or didn't acknowledge.

"I don't mean that as a joke," Chobin went on. "There is. It's fucking obvious to anyone who spends a bit of time in her presence. But that's easy to come by. What she . . . expressed back there? As your friend, I need to be certain you got the meaning."

"I believe I did," said Tirdad. "But I welcome your perspective so long as it isn't an insult."

Chobin grunted, still rubbing the back of his neck. "You don't just see that she's fucking off. You don't even see that—not like the rest of us. You see her as someone who struggles with something beyond her control, do your utmost to come to understand her without judging, and she knows it."

The marzban slung an arm over Tirdad's shoulder, which did nothing to help his exhaustion. "Way I see it, she isn't used to that."

"That's about what I took away from it," said Tirdad. "Although I worry I don't try nearly as much as she thinks."

"Only makes it all the more sincere."

"Maybe."

"Well, no matter." Chobin slapped his back, grin brightening effortlessly. "Soon we'll be too busy claiming our glory for you to worry! If you're half as improved your sessions let on, I'm eager to see the two of you in battle. And that isn't even considering the training you do beforehand!"

Tirdad's sigh was drowned out by a boisterous laugh.

XI

TIRDAD WANTED TO SCREAM. FROM his saddle, where he lay in wait in the shadow of a trough between hills, he could see the enemy. And they were tantalizing. Their lanterns, bobbing on their way across the river, were beacons that signalled a checked thrill, inspired the steady pooling of adrenaline. The reins creaked in his fist. Soon.

Second to that, Shkarag had his abdomen in a vice that bunched the mail he now wore beneath his plum-coloured tunic, and for which the mail did nothing. Her sawing breaths vibrated against his back, as clear a sign as any that she was drunk with bloodlust. However infuriating his anticipation, it no doubt paled in comparison. She wasn't holding on to avoid falling; she held on to avoid letting go.

It poured into him, amplified his own eagerness. Their sessions had made sure of it. Those warriors nearest fed on it same as they would the minstrels during hunts. The bloodlust that vibrated and heaved her cuirass threaded its way into their adrenaline. When unleashed, her lineage had an almost visible battlefield presence; it spoke to those around her in certain terms. It emboldened her allies; it struck fear into her foes.

Of course, she had been outfitted with a charger, so she needn't necessarily share his horse. But they'd reasoned it was better left behind. Shkarag hadn't the expertise for fighting on horseback, and together they would fare better.

The legionnaires were disembarking now. Not yet, Tirdad told himself. Chobin's command was vastly outnumbered, but with the cover of night, and by striking the bank as the legionnaires disembarked, they just might gain the upper hand.

A new star smoldered into life, streaking across the windows of the sky, and flaring up at the height of its arc. The signal. Tirdad let out the battle cry that'd been struggling for release, and spurred his charger into a gallop.

Under a cloudless sky, crisp and clear, a thunder arose that caused hearts to skip a beat. The accompanying cries made it all the more harrowing. Tirdad charged at the head of his company, lowering his pike as he bore down upon the legionnaires, who were scrambling into formation. Across the river, the same thunder rumbled, but it may as well have been a world away. Tirdad had relinquished control to the spirit of battle.

Pomegranate-red didn't swamp his vision, but it did tinge the edges, bleeding in such that it augmented the senses he'd honed since childhood. To his sides, his company followed his example, each choosing a target to level their pike on. He screamed, urging his charger into a burst of speed that threw off the huddle of legionnaires he'd been riding for, and without pretense, gored two on his way through. That tore his pike from his grip, but it was enough to scatter the group. Combined with similar efforts by the other riders, his side of the river descended into chaos.

Everything seemed to move in slow motion from there. Fires from discarded lanterns danced between combatants, making the clash all the more stilted by delineating movements in a flickering cadence. He brought his horse around and called it into another charge, brandishing his starling-black sword as he did and, with a downward stroke, scored a mortal blow on the nearest legionnaire.

Ahead, a pair of legionnaires had mounted and, likely marking him as an officer due to his epaulettes, charged. The vice released. He grinned, gleaning no small amount of pleasure from their connection, and paid no heed to the advancing cavalry. Instead, he hacked at those locked in combat to his flank, blade gleefully running through one of two warriors who were on the verge of gutting one of his comrades. The throbbing in his palm intensified.

Embers flitted about like the snowflakes of war; smoke obscured skirmishes and filled lungs; metal rang, whined, and clashed to the many screams and shouts that made up the din of battle. Invigorating was the word. He felt invigorated.

Just then, as he peered beneath his helmet and through the mess of hair that had fallen free, the cavalry closed on him. He only bothered to glance up after dispatching his second target by summarily running that one through as well.

It was just in time to catch Shkarag's rebuttal. She planted one boot firmly on his shoulder, and with a nimbleness that defied her heavy armour, sprang over his charger's mane. She'd never been one for convention, so while her display was nothing short of spectacle, it was expected.

She hurled her spear as she bounded from his shoulder, aiming for the rider on the left, who was closer by a wide enough margin that what followed transpired as if orchestrated for theatre.

Her spear lodged in the flank of the horse, butt protruding at an angle which Shkarag had the dexterity and timing to land on with one foot, squatting and sweeping an axe as if casually reaching down to run her hand through the waters of a stream, and in so doing cleaving clean through the legionnaire's face. That smooth motion went on, becoming an off-kilter whirl that unwound on the butt of her spear. The second rider passed by right as she finished uncoiling for Shkarag to spring straight into her, fangs bared and axes primed. The collision tore her from her saddle, and meant certain death for the woman. An unceremonious chop to the brow saw to that.

Shkarag broke away from straddling the soldier's torso just in time to dodge a spear thrust at her chest. Hissing, she holstered her axes. When the next thrust reached for her abdomen, she nimbly stepped aside, and caught it in a fist. The legionnaire yanked at it, but her grip didn't so much as budge. She'd found another spear. Shkarag snatched it out of his hands without an inkling of effort. This caused the legionnaire to stumble forward, which made it all the more smooth when she flipped the spear over to skewer him through the gut. Shkarag stomped one boot forward, hissing over the din as she did, to shove the spear further and come up flush with the man. Like a viper lashing out, she seized his throat with her fangs, then stomped back with a jerk that rent flesh and withdrew most of her spear. Before he had time to clutch his neck, she leveraged her spear to fling him overhead as if discarding an empty egg shell. For Tirdad, that meant riding beneath a rain of blood.

"For fuck's sake, Shkarag!" He yelled over his shoulder, but she had already bowled into the fray.

Tirdad brought his charger around, watching her out of the corner of his eye while surveying the battle. Harried as they were, the Hrom battalion was too out of sorts to mount a proper defense. Some were stuck on the river, unsure which bank to turn to, or taking cover from arrows loosed from either side.

He took heart at that, content in the knowledge that they would wreak further havoc. Heartened, and high on adrenaline, Tirdad stabbed his sword at the heavens, a part of him wishing he could do just that, and bellowed a battle cry. All along the bank, similar cries took shape.

Tirdad urged his horse into action, his sights on the crowd Shkarag had amassed. She had her axes spinning in either hand and could have been mistaken for a fire-juggler with the way they gleamed, their afterimages vibrant brushstrokes against the night.

He imitated her display with a flourish of his long sword, a twirl that ate the light instead of reflecting it, and which preluded a jab straight through the neck of the first soldier he passed. As that one fell, so too did another. Shkarag stepped to and fro in long flowing movements, footwork light and smooth in its gradual transition from heel to toe and back again. She'd grown accustomed to her less daring, yet equally wicked, axe-fighting as a result of their sessions. Leaning back and bringing an arm overhead, as if sweeping a cape over her shoulders, she chopped clean through the wrist of a man directly behind her. Then, emitting a hiss that crackled with energy, she interrupted her routine by slamming her shoulder into a legionnaire who had no way of anticipating the sudden change in tempo and direction. Her play at grace collapsed, and as he stumbled back she snatched him by the helmet, which exposed his throat for her to tear open with her fangs.

The spray of blood was the last Tirdad caught of it, though her hisses and serrated breaths were unmistakable—each emboldened him, as if right by his ear. In the battle-seconds it took for her routine to command his attention, he'd passed through the crowd, having trampled at least one assailant under the hooves of his charger.

Over the course of an hour or more, he shadowed her mayhem. Where she thrived in chaos, he rode nearby, using his vantage to support her with sword and arrow while taking stock of which way the scales of the larger battle tipped. He knew she could have managed alone, but it was fulfilling to work as partners. Besides, the fighting was fiercest wherever she went, and he had to be ready to sound orders if things turned sour.

After all that time moving from one skirmish to another, he'd only just now lost sight of her. Tirdad squinted through a curtain of smoke, eyes burning. Sweat caked his face, matted hair to flesh, collected blood and soot. He wiped the tears from his eyes.

"Fuck," he cursed. The fires weren't really blazing to anyone's benefit at this point. Tirdad pulled his scarf up over his nose and galloped through, emerging from the other side where the fighting was thickest. That being the case, he didn't slow down. Instead, he spurred his charger through the horde, throwing his blade in downward strokes with abandon. Having spotted her at its centre, he fell into orbit around Shkarag's circle of mayhem, scattering half of it on the way there. The legionnaires were quick to regroup.

Rather than circling around for another charge, Tirdad brought his horse about and began hacking and stabbing at those who accosted the half-div. Between the two of them, the legionnaires' attention was divided and unorganized.

Tirdad batted aside one spatha, turned another, and riposted by interring his blade into the heart of a Hrom soldier. That the man wore cuirass didn't matter; his starling-black blade pierced it without effort. The hilt gave an abrupt throb, and Tirdad withdrew it before the legionnaire could fall. By then, the remaining legionnaires had their shields up, having fallen back into a tight circle. Without his pike, Tirdad wasn't going to have much luck penetrating their shield wall, so he pulled back to assess the situation.

Pockets of Hrom units were banding together, forming larger groups. The banging of Shkarag's axes sounded off as she vented against their shields. Hisses accompanied. Soon, enough groups would be united to mount a serious counter-offensive. That was fine; the strike was meant to be incisive, opportunistic. Never had an outright routing been part of the plan. He reached for his horn where it hung from his weapon belt and gave it a drawn out blow. The signal carried, clarion and well over the river to Chobin's command. It told everyone to fall back.

That was a crucial distinction to be revisited in later celebration. You could fall back in victory, but the same could not be said for retreat.

"Shkarag!" Tirdad called, riding straight for her, heedless to the legionnaires who leapt aside to avoid being trampled. Wild-eyed and fangs bared, she had her axes spinning, scraping over and clanging against shields. Her assault didn't relent until just before Tirdad neared, arm out and ready to extract her. With a snarl of a hiss, she holstered her axes and snapped a claw out to grip his forearm, which swung her up and onto his charger.

Together, they joined the ranks in racing away at full gallop. Triumphant shouts roused the air around them like the drums of war. What a thrill! Tirdad belted a whoop of his own.

Behind him, Shkarag sat backwards on the plum-coloured rug that was slung under the saddle, cuirass flush with his back. Although he couldn't see her, he could sense her smoldering bloodlust. It was mesmerizing. Beautiful. He wanted to embrace her, to share an intimate moment between the carnage of combat and the excitement of a victory well-earned. For a spell, he concentrated instead on putting distance between them and the all too real threat of a counter-strike.

"Fuck it," he soon said. Reins in one hand, Tirdad leaned back and turned in his saddle, slipping an arm under hers, which encouraged her to do the same to face him, though her focus didn't leave the battlefield to their rear. Her fangs were still lowered; her eyes darted over the fires in the distance.

"I've never seen you in action before," he said. "Not like this. Not in war. You were a presence, a wonder. Like all the theatre revolved around you. You—"

Why in the seven climes was he talking to her? Tirdad towed himself closer by her lower back. That her fangs were primed didn't stop him—on the contrary, he paid them extra attention, even stained as they were with blood. He kissed her with a flame stoked by adrenaline. He treated her fangs to the majority of his passion, sensitive as he'd come to learn they were. The hiss it elicited was low, dangerous but not displeased. Absorbed as she was in the pocket of chaos from which they fled, Shkarag nevertheless had the wherewithal to return his kiss in kind.

Where had this been all his life, and why had he squandered all those years oblivious to what they could have shared?

• • • • •

Unchallenged in their withdrawal, they regrouped in the relative safety of a gorge hemmed in by the nearest ridge. Those who had been on his side of the river sung Tirdad's praises—a far cry from the so-called legend he'd earned mere months earlier for his part in thwarting his cousin. Likewise, those who had witnessed Shkarag's prowess, and those who had thrived on her aura (though none as much as his bond afforded), were generous with their salutes. As uncomfortable as the attention made her, she made no attempt to turn away the date- and raisin-distilled liquors it won her.

As regrettable, as destructive as all wars were, even having forsaken the honour to be gleaned and glory to be honed in the crucible, this easy camaraderie always struck Tirdad as a righteousness to be found in the midst of so much death. That he felt the call of the war drum in his heart was not the same—it was visceral.

People from all walks of life could be crowded into a battlefield, be forced to face their demise head on, and come out of it with an appreciation for those who had shared in that struggle despite their many differences.

"Fuckers will remember that pounding next time they're rubbing on the olive oil," said Chobin, which drew Tirdad out of his introspection. "Heard they put up less of a fight on your end."

"Could've been much worse," Tirdad agreed. He tore his attention from the half-div, who was sitting backwards on her charger and going through distillate after distillate, swept it over the clan bannermen where they milled about tending to the wounded and their horses, to finally stop on the marzban. "All things considered, I think we got off easy. They could have swarmed us if they had pooled their numbers."

Chobin tapped his temple, grinning from ear to ear. "They didn't. We kept them on their heels. General was on our bank, though, so there were a few times I was afraid he'd mount a counterattack."

He took a generous swig from his wineskin, and laid a hand on Tirdad's shoulder. "Feels strange being your superior. Officially and all. But I want you to know you've earned these epaulettes."

"Thanks." Tirdad didn't care, if he were being honest with himself. He only wore them as a favour for a friend. Chobin didn't need to know as much.

"This'll surely turn that nasty legend of yours on its head," added the marzban.

". . ." Tirdad turned a deadpan expression on the marzban.

"What? Think I haven't heard it? It's amusing as all get out. Something about you going ass up for Shkarag in your duel? Hah!"

Tirdad sighed. "I can't catch a break."

"Ah, but you're on the other end of things now, so that legend hasn't made much sense lately."

"Lately?"

"Yeah."

Another sigh. Tirdad shook his head in exasperation. "Well, what's our next move?"

Chobin scratched the side of his head, where his woolen hair was disheveled and greasy. "Wait on the King of Kings. He isn't far off, and we'll need the bulk of the army if we hope to lay siege to Dara."

"Oh?"

"Messenger arrived just now. King of Kings probably wants to make them regret besieging Nisibis. Can't say it's a sentiment I disagree with."

Tirdad nodded. Giving them their just deserts was all well and good, but it helped that Dara was a frontier fortress crucial to Hrom's defense. Taking it would be as severe a blow to them as losing Nisibis would have been to Iran.

"In the meantime," said Chobin, "let's find something to eat. All that fighting worked up an appetite."

"Joy," said Tirdad, dismounting. "Rations."

· · · · ·

Having hastened their march to reach Dara before the garrison could call in supplies and aid from the surrounding area, the army of the King of Kings was able to unite with Chobin's contingent the next evening.

Tirdad, despite being raised in part by a talented general, never had a mind for strategy—or an interest in it besides. So he was relieved when, because he had no official rank to go by, he never received a summons to the pavilion where discussion of the sort took place. No poring over maps and arguing tactics for him. Most of all, no coming face to face with the very same King of Kings who had dissolved his House.

This is what crossed his mind when, well before sunup, he was rudely awoken in his modest pavilion. His hand shot to his sword where it lay beside him. The royal guard who had used his pomegranate-headed mace to prod Tirdad awake was already on his way out, standing aside deferentially and holding the tent flap open so that another man could enter, ducking as he did.

"Tirdad." The voice was aged, wise, and in that wisdom, clement. "I hope you will excuse the rude awakening. There is something I would ask of you." The figure glanced at his guard, who left without the need for an order. "Get dressed if you would."

Tirdad blinked. Having been disturbed during a state of deep sleep, he was still out of sorts. "Uh."

The hand on his chest stirred, preceded a drowsy grumble. "Šo-rude crown-baster. Just fell asleep, too."

"Crown . . . what?" Tirdad turned his attention to the man. Outlined in the glow of the camp, it was easy to miss the more subtle divine blessing that brightened his features. "Oh." He clapped a hand over his mouth and hurried to prostrate, but was interrupted by an upraised palm.

"Your diligence is noted, but that is not necessary," said the King of Kings, hands now behind his back. "We are at war, and alone besides. There is something we must discuss, but not here."

Tirdad gave a quick nod and hurried to get some clothes on. Languidly and with a drawn out yawn, Shkarag did the same. The King of Kings led them out without a word, having the courtesy to hold the flap open as they exited. They wound through the encampment where it capped one of the rolling hills that surrounded Dara. Across a dip between their hill and the next, Tirdad could make out the stone-hewn walls of the fortress city where tiny patches of torchlight patrolled.

The three made their way down a calm gradient, passing between quiet pavilions and startled soldiers who were quick to prostrate, the King of Kings with his hands clasped behind his back, Shkarag limping into a spear she'd lifted a few minutes earlier, and Tirdad wondering why he'd been singled out. He had no desire to become a puppet of this man, even if he was, by and large, a just ruler. Tirdad had his own plans.

When the King of Kings ushered them out of the camp on foot, rather than retrieving their mounts from the keeper of horses, Tirdad couldn't help but wonder what he had in mind. They stopped about an arrow's distance out—not an accurate shot, but one belonging to a salvo—and the King of Kings turned to address them. The moonlight was dim at best, but his divine blessing helped Tirdad to see the calm countenance he wore.

"You must hate me," he began. "I would. It pained me to do what I did to your family. I still lose sleep over it. Of all the Houses, yours was far and above the most loyal. Sadly, matters are never so simple, and your cousin forced my hand. I was fond of her, you know. She was one of a kind. Troubled as she was, it made me respect her all the more keenly."

Tirdad said nothing. It wasn't that there weren't a thousand responses all ready to cut. It was that they were all ready to cut; none were kind. Instead, he fidgeted with the ram's head pommel.

The King of Kings leveled his gaze on Shkarag. "Are we the only ones you see in the vicinity?"

" . . ."

"Do you see anyone besides us around?" asked Tirdad.

"Maybe."

"Who?"

Shkarag indicated the King of Kings with a tip of her spear and a subdued hiss.

"It's just us," said Tirdad.

The King of Kings inclined his head. "Many thanks, Shkarag." He stroked his beard thoughtfully before continuing. "You have been busy these last few months, Tirdad. I have had a hard time balancing your actions, but I know you to be an honourable man."

Demonstrably, he turned his back to the pair. "You were the one to put your cousin's war path to an end. Then you cut down a rogue star-reckoner, a div, a yazata, saved Ray by killing another div. And today I discover you are enamoured with an infamous half-div. In all honesty, I cannot see any rhyme or reason to your actions."

That drew a grunt from Tirdad.

The King of Kings shook his head, and turned back around. "That being the case, I have brought you here to offer a chance to make your motives clear. What do you say to that?"

"Well . . ." Tirdad glanced to his side. Shkarag wasn't bristling, but her temper had flared. "Truth be told," he said, "I'm only here at the request of a friend. Otherwise, my motivations aren't as complicated as they may seem. I'm travelling with my companion, who happens to be half human. Making up for lost time."

"Hmm." The King of Kings looked between them in the direction of Dara. "The night before your forces rendezvoused with mine, my royal star-reckoners were found dead. All of them. Poisoned. I assume Hrom wanted to blunt my ability to lay siege to their fortress. They succeeded."

Shkarag had leaned into Tirdad the moment star-reckoners were mentioned. Ostensibly, she favoured her leg. But before the news hit him she'd already begun to rub placation into his back. He did his utmost to keep a straight face, to control his breathing. He was beginning to suspect the stars were actively working against him—that his pursuit of an unseemly truth mattered more than their favoured few. He gave the pommel a white-knuckled squeeze.

"You need not worry," said the King of Kings, seeing through him. "Hrom does not have the resources I do. Not in this. They would have no way of knowing what you have become."

While Tirdad did visibly relax, and while that seemed to convince the King of Kings, it was because the man did not suspect him. The news was disheartening, to say the least. How many star-reckoners were left? Ashtadukht had dispatched a great many in her time after all. The King of Kings answered that for him.

"Only a few star-reckoners remain, and it will take them weeks to arrive. So I ask this of you, Tirdad: show me your loyalty, use your planet-reckoning for the good of the realm."

Tirdad stared at the ground. It was thanks to Shkarag's timely ministrations that he was only crestfallen. She read him well. He would have been worse off without her around. Setback after setback, he thought. All he wanted was the truth. To know with certainty whether his cousin been a pawn in their plan—one that had backfired on them to devastating effect.

Now, here he was with another setback, and an offer he literally could not refuse. You simply did not say no to the King of Kings. To make matters worse, he was not in a position to bargain. Someone had been feeding the man information on his whereabouts and all he'd been up to. "I guess I don't have much of a choice," said Tirdad. "I'll do what I can, but to be honest, my lots are . . . unpredictable at best. I try to avoid using them. It's all very new to me."

"While I appreciate your honesty, I have been made aware of your limitations. All I ask is that you try. Dara must fall. We cannot let Hrom think they can walk away from this relatively unscathed. A message must be sent."

Tirdad nodded his subservience. "As you wish."

"Shkarag," addressed the King of Kings. Tirdad looked up at that, cursing himself for thinking she could travel unchallenged in such prestigious company. "You are a menace."

". . ." Though she ceased her rubbing, she gave no other indication of having acknowledged what he said.

"You are fortunate, then, that I have no star-reckoners to deal with you. I would have you put down by normal means, but how many would you take with you? That is operating under the assumption that we could find and deal with your phylactery. As a consequence, I would be faced with an angered planet-reckoner." The King of Kings shook his head, though it was becoming more and more apparent that he was being coy: that he was grateful circumstances stayed his hand. "I suppose I have no choice but to endure your presence." He looked at Tirdad. "See me tomorrow at dusk. No later." Then he walked past and toward the camp, and would have kept walking if Shkarag didn't speak up.

"You wear, you put on—" She drove the butt of her spear into the ground and pivoted to face him. "You šo-wretched kings slip into your airs as if they're more than garments, and you don't know, you're none the wiser that you were swindled in. You're making fools of—" She parted her lips, and though her fangs lowered, they weren't quite bared. A hiss escaped between them. "Embarrassing yourselves sauntering around huffing like some, like some šo-draughty cavern, but the most anyone will ever think of you is why won't someone do something about that breeze before we catch a chill."

Tirdad laid a hand on her shoulder, but it was already relaxed. Knowing her, she seemed remarkably controlled given how pissed she sounded. Maybe that was the point.

The King of Kings opened his mouth. "Shk—"

That she'd berated him wasn't enough. Shkarag had to interrupt him, too. Tirdad was growing more worried by the second, but he dare not do the same to her. "I've seen kings shit their trousers. Cleaved them like so many draughts. Cracked empires. Ride on their rickety litters and pretend, say they're—" She drew a claw over her scalp. "Think they're conquerors or chosen or . . . All you ever become is some statue to be toppled or coin to be flipped.

"I'm worthless. I'm worthless. I'm worthless, but all those, all you, you fucking kings who think you aren't, you're more delusional than I am. Could bury my axe in your skull and the world wouldn't care."

The King of Kings smiled. "You speak the truth. About all of it." He started off again. "You could, but I know you will not."

Only once the man had disappeared into the night did Tirdad stop holding his breath. "What in the—" He sucked in a few gulps of air before continuing. "What were you thinking?"

"   . . .   "

"Shkarag?"

". . ." This time, the silence was anything but measured. She trembled beneath his touch. A hiss was gathering somewhere in her throat and chest, one that was soon expelled as she snapped her spear in half. She threw it to the ground, still shaking.

"What's gotten into you?"

"Don't like them," she said, almost too softly for him to make out. "They're the reason why . . ." She trailed off, a hiss seeping between her lips. "Because of them she's . . ." Shkarag turned to him, and pulled her scarf over her head. "I want to leave. You do this šo-damned task, then we leave."

Tirdad nodded. "As you wish."

• • • • •

"Think the skink-slicker will pull it off?" asked Chobin.

Tirdad pondered the way she'd left. He wasn't sure whether his lack of anxiety was due to her phylactery or a confidence in her being capable of doing what she set out to. "She will."

"Been two nights," said Chobin. "She promised one. Those grates are sturdy, meant to stave off intruders. She isn't the first person to think to enter via the water supply."

Tirdad eyed the fortress city where it herded three hills into its walls, an artificial terrace sharing their intersection, and the shadow that rose behind it. There, a river cut through a ravine, and had been dammed to bring water to the city. Being early autumn, the river was likely beginning to swell. "I believe in her," he said.

Chobin rubbed his neck, cracking an uncomfortable smile. "So, uh, be that as it may. Either you do this now and at least make it look like I have some authority over you, or wait for the King of Kings to stroll over to make us both lick his boots."

Tirdad set his jaw. He had no desire to embarrass Chobin, and while he may not have cared what the King of Kings thought, the marzban's future relied on currying favour. So, his palm came to rest on the ram's head pommel, and he drew a lot.

The words to the lot spilled over his lips, rote memorization that was at the same time his and not. A childhood of lessons hardened or invalidated by a lifetime of experience chose the phrases for him. Tirdad found himself once more on the fringe of the celestial theatre, the terrible dragon Gochihr on a collision course that acted as a rippling curtain above the cosmic battlefield.

He trained what little remained of his soul on the expanse, first confirming what his mind had suggested: that Mercury revolved out of sight, obscured as it was by Earth. Too far removed to make out more than a glimmer, Jupiter came to blows with the Bull constellation. Formidable as the planet was, a more favourable theatre thundered a rallying call. It quaked like a thousand planets being torn asunder. It was vehement; it reached out to him with an uncommon enmity.

Tirdad focused his soul on the constellation of the Ear of Grain, a misleading title if there ever was one. If the cosmos quaked, the Ear of Grain was the crust it threw into loathing. Embattled in the thick of those fissures, novae their eruptions, were Saturn, Venus, and Mars. The latter two, having united in a conjunction, faced off against stalwart Spica, the defender of the constellation. Venus was at a disadvantage astronomically, but not elementally; Mars was an even match. Both were weakened by the sun's presence in a different constellation of the same element.

Tirdad considered this in a flash. The lay of the theatre came to him as naturally as breathing. Given the factors at play, the battle would have been about even if it weren't for the wild card, the liability in a craft in which risk was already inherent. Saturn.

While the luminaries were locked in combat, Saturn wore the same glacier-patient scowl he remembered from their first encounter. Though it had no countenance to scowl with, the planet had a soul of its own, and what Tirdad sensed there could be fashioned a scowl, cold and calculating. It watched, storms whirring, curling into eddies in which its legions bided their time. Once the opportunity presented itself, Saturn would turn the tide.

The six-sided die that ricocheted across the reaches of his mind did so with something runaway. Something unhinged. As with his first lot, the feeling went as quickly as it came, but during that tumble, it was as if his senses were overloaded to such extremes that it made him want to end his life just to be rid of it. The pommel tickled his palm.

"Mercury loiters out of sight. Jupiter sets upon the Bull. Venus and Mars are at odds with the Ear of Grain, while Saturn orchestrates its demise. The lot has been drawn."

Tirdad exhaled, uneasy over the visit and what he'd felt upon returning. His lot had been favoured, that much was certain. He'd been lucky so far, but he had to fail eventually. Ashtadukht had failed so much her mind had scars, her soul unravelling here and there like well-worn silk. That unsettled him. Because the implications were a mystery, and not knowing made it so much worse.

A shriek pierced the night. Not a scream—a shriek. The distinction was harrowing, as if a scream had been whetted with secrets no mortal should know before it was stropped to keenness. Another. A laugh, stropped same as the scream, to become a cackle. A host of outbursts sounded from behind the walls of Dara.

"What did you do?" asked the King of Kings, having drawn up beside him.

Tirdad shook his head. "I haven't the slightest."

"Sure sounds nasty," Chobin said. The host had become a din; the din, unintelligible noise.

The King of Kings pulled in a deep breath, which exited as consternation. He swept his gaze over his camp and back to the fortress city. "Whatever it is, it seems it is not getting us in. Draw another, if you would."

Tirdad was preparing to oblige when the gates were flung open. Out scattered a mix of the garrison, the Hrom legion, and the city's population. Some were aflame, lighting up the night as they tore off screaming. Others were attacking their countrymen with abandon. Yet others were rolling on the ground, clutching their sides and cackling uncontrollably. The worst of it was the shrieks, which passed through flesh and bone as if imbued with horror, and were only silenced once their owners had dashed their own skulls over the nearest wall.

The King of Kings raised a hand ridden with trepidation. His disgust was plain. Tirdad took some satisfaction in that, even as he balked at what he'd wrought.

"You drove them mad," observed Chobin. "They're fucking sturgeon-loving mad. Look at them down there."

The King of Kings finished his gesture by extending his hand, which signalled the attack. Horns sounded to either side, and a stampede teeming with standards and pikes spilled down the hill, throwing up chunks of earth in its wake. Tirdad made to join when an outstretched palm halted his advance. He tried to hide his frustration with the King of Kings as Chobin rode off at the head of a charge, cavalry thundering behind and close enough to upset Tirdad's tunic.

He waited, staring straight ahead and doing his utmost to control his temper. Below, the Iranian forces converged on the gate, and the massacre began. The screams of the dying were somehow less disconcerting than those of the mad. Only those Hrom legionnaires who were already on a killing spree fought back, and while they fought like rabid dogs, they were put down all the same.

"This is not what I expected," said the King of Kings. His tone was one of introspection, not accusation. He lowered his hand, but did not grant permission to leave. "I should not have resorted to such means, and I apologize for ordering you to do something so heinous. You are right to avoid lots that draw upon the planets, and would do well to stay that course." The King of Kings fished around in his tunic before retrieving a small pouch, which he offered. "A token of my gratitude. It is no brocade or belt, but those are honours you have not earned."

Tirdad accepted with a respectful nod, the contents explained by a slight jingle.

"You have done as I asked, so you have my blessing. See to it that it stays that way, Tirdad. Do not tangle with star-reckoners, keep your div on a short leash, and do what you can to enjoy what years you have left. If that involves throwing your lot in with Chobin, so be it, but you will need to make yourself scarce in the company of star-reckoners. The same goes for your half-div."

With that, the King of Kings turned his mount about and returned to his retinue, many of whom belonged to the great Houses of the land. More than a few scowls were aimed Tirdad's way. He mocked them with a smile; their approval meant nothing to him. He slipped the pouch into his tunic and was off, charger galloping down the slope to join the fray, already heady with the thrill of battle and seeking out a cuirass through which to run his pike. Sadly, the opportunity had come and gone. It was an absolute slaughter. His planet-reckoning had seen to that.

Tirdad wanted to think it meant fewer lives lost, but as he eased his charger to a walk, there was no mistaking the reality of it. Civilians outnumbered combatants by a wide margin. As he led his horse under the low gate, it was forced to pick a path through the host of bodies that had fallen there in seeking to escape the city. He grimaced as he passed, tears welling in his eyes at what he'd been forced to do. This was his doing, all of it.

Tirdad advanced through the sobering city, past buildings cut from stone and the gore that befouled them. The blood-curdling shrieks and cries of those in thrall to his lot broke out in pockets between hills, to be summarily truncated. He did happen upon a few who were alive, their eyes the same breed of wild he'd seen in Shkarag, but rather than end their suffering, he urged his charger to hurry by. He hadn't the stomach to do more harm.

With nothing to plot a course for, he followed the thoroughfare that squeezed between two of the three hills that marked the corners of Dara's triangular plan. The sounds of discord still rang out from all around of the city, but they were never joined by the sounds of war. There was no battle to be had, only lives to end. The King of Kings would have leashed his forces, limited them to pillaging so that the citizens could be deported to the mainland where they would settle, bringing with them their crafts and the economic boon that came with an increase in population. Planet-reckoning had seen to ruining that option.

Tirdad passed more storefronts, more homes carved into the stone at the foot of the hills. These, too, were dashed with gore. It's a wonder how zealous humans become when you amplify their emotions to cosmic proportions. How effective at savagery. There was, he mused, an analogue to be found there between humans and divs. Perhaps divs were all that remained of humans once you stripped away pretenses and civilization. It was, he thought, at the same time heretical yet not without a morsel of truth. Heresies oftentimes operated as such.

Soon the small valley opened to an intersection of hills, which housed a central terrace lined with steps and laden with the uneven shadows of corpses. The terrace, functional as it was, would not have been worth mentioning if not for the pyre that engulfed its main building—curling around pillars and licking at eaves. The shadows all stretched as if their souls were writhing in the heat of its light, saddled even in death by an eternal madness.

"..."

Strange. Tirdad could have sworn he heard a laboured quiet within the roar of flames. He turned his horse about, it obliging with awkward steps that avoided stumbling over the scores of bodies. Empty. The cavalry was no doubt doing a circuit of the city, so it could have been—

"..."

Shkarag was directly in front of him. He'd missed her for two reasons: the steps leading up to the terrace had her level with and hidden by his charger's neck. Also, she sat amidst the corpses as if she belonged there. With the way her silhouette moved, she must've been kneading her splinters. The thought of it made his skin crawl.

"Here you are," he said.

"Here," she agreed, casting about. "I think."

"Where were you?"

She canted at that. "You just . . . like some—"

"Here?" he cut in.

"Maybe."

"What happen—" Tirdad caught himself. He really wasn't in the right frame of mind for enduring her vagaries. "Why didn't you open the gate then? You said you were off to do as much."

"Sluice gate trapped me something fierce," she muttered. "Know I deserve it, but don't like drowning over and over and over and over again, especially not in a sluice gate."

"Oh." Tirdad looked away, uneasy despite the fact that he couldn't see more than the impression of her figure.

"Then I felled the general." She held up what must have been a head. "A trophy," she explained, patently pleased with herself. "Šo-wretched crown-basting King of Kings doesn't deserve a trophy. So I beat him to the, flogged him in the, beat him to the execution. Didn't put up much of a fight, but that's just as the crow flies."

"When was this?" asked Tirdad.

"Before . . ." She trailed off, and in her moment of deliberation dropped the head so that she could return to kneading. "After making an omelette. Maybe. Oh. Your breakfast is . . . around."

"And after that?"

"Waited for you."

"All day?"

". . ."

Tirdad pinched the bridge of his nose, and tried to smother his anger. She'd caused this. And now she just kneaded as if she were oblivious. "Shkarag?" Try as he might to dampen it, his tone had taken an edge.

". . ."

"The least you could—"

"I know."

Tirdad screwed up his face. That was unexpected. "You know?"

"Never intended to open the gate. You were, you were, would've drawn a lot to find me. If I open the gate, a div opened the gate, and no one cares because I'm just some, just some waterlogged, can't be a hero. If you do it, you're loyal. Crown-baster forgives you, so you're happy. Display of power also makes them think twice about crossing you like some, like some dozy river that needs fording, and it used to be this dozy river, and you know, like in the capital, the course swerves over time, drowns the metropolis, so now it's a, it's a dozy river with crocodiles." She lowered her voice to mutter. "And I really want to leave."

Tirdad shifted uncomfortably. He didn't like the implications of what she'd said. Not in the slightest. "You manipulated me."

". . ."

"Why would you do that?"

"Maybe," she belatedly replied. Then to his more immediate question, "We take care of one another."

Rage pounded against the back of his ribs, eager to burst from its cage. He hadn't reached the point of shouting, but he was damn near to it, and angry enough that he spoke without thinking. "Don't you fucking play innocent with me, Shkarag. Look around you. You think this is taking care of me? Putting all these deaths on my hands when you could've just opened the fucking gates? If you're as clever as this lets on, why in the seven fucking climes would you think it'd make me happy? How often have you manipulated me in some attempt at . . . whatever you aimed to get out of this, but sure as fuck not in trying to make me happy."

Shkarag got to her feet. With a hiss, she flung the head at his chest, which it struck square before tumbling to join the rest of the bodies. "You think—you—that I—you think—" She raked her claws over her head, hissing as she did, and sucking in great gulps of air like the teeth of a saw biting at lumber. "Ashtadukht never cared!" Shkarag shouted, shoulders heaving where the firelight glanced off her cuirass, a sharp hiss bristling in its depths. "Always about her! Not you or me or anyone! Too busy with the dead! Never did anything for us! We weren't friends, we were tools! And you just, you take your šo-damned blade and you stroke it! You're tender with it, but you . . ." As abruptly as it flared, her temper faded. "I care, and I . . . try. And you just think . . . like some . . ."

She bent over to retrieve her spear. "Didn't think about this part," she confessed. "Just that you'd, you'd do it, and they'd call you a hero." She ground the butt of her spear against a step, wringing the shaft between her fists as she did. "So I thought that's just as the crow flies. Didn't think about the—" Her head jerked toward the farthest hilltop. "What'd happen when you drew a lot. Because I knock things out of place like some, like some sentinel watching from the ramparts. And there's an orchard out there as orchards are wont to be, congregating and carrying-on, and you see them every day, those trees all lined up šo-orderly, and you're thinking, you're thinking to yourself that their keeper is really putting in work transplanting them every morning. Must be the soil, you say. Rich soil with all the nutrients and things. But once they're at the foot of the wall and you're peering down, and there's a gnarled eye peering back, you discover you'd missed the, the pomegranates for the trees and the trees for the pomegranates and the pomegranates for the trees and the tree for the pomegranates and the pomegranates for the trees and the trees for the pomegranates—"

She droned on, and her breathing quickened to a runaway pace, hands flexing and unflexing such that her spear clattered down the steps. "—for the trees and the trees for the pomegranates and the pomegranates for the trees and the trees for the pomegranates and the pomegranates for the trees and the trees for the pomegranates and the pomegranates for the trees and the trees for the pomegranates and the pomegranates for the trees and the pomegranate trees for the trees trees the pomegranates for the the the the the the the th—"

"تَرسِــــو —"

She collapsed, going the way of her spear down the steps.

"Fuck," spat Tirdad, dismounting too late to prevent her from hitting the landing head over heels. He knelt beside her, first confirming that she was breathing, then scanning the darkness for any signs of the telltale spoiled yogurt glow. Nothing as of yet.

Tirdad blew out a defeated sigh saddled by regret. His harsh words had been unwarranted. She could not have known how horrifically his lot would resolve any more than he could have. Shkarag had just assumed he'd succeed. She had admitted to manipulating him, but how was that any different than using what you know of a person in doing them a boon? It wasn't, he decided.

He lifted her, cursing his lower back as he did, and eased her over the back of his charger. What she'd said about Ashtadukht was true to an extent. He knew as much; he'd known from the outset of their journey. She had trouble forming new connections because she could not get over the one she'd lost. However, that didn't mean she didn't care. Tirdad firmly believed Ashtadukht cared. She'd shown as much over the years. But it was oftentimes overpowered by her grief. She was not to blame for that. The star-reckoners were.

Tirdad placed a kiss on Shkarag's head. She'd hyperventilated herself unconscious for the second time now. He worried about her more and more. While that cyclone ravaged landscape that followed her shift in personality had grown familiar in their time together, there was still much to learn. And the more he learned, the more afraid it made him.

With a grunt, he retrieved the severed head, not really knowing what she expected him to do with it. Probably wanted to flaunt it in front of the King of Kings, pacing back and forth atop her steed, head literally held high, triumphant like one of her statues.

". . ." She'd returned.

He greeted her by applying a tender touch to her scalp. She stayed draped over the horse, only moving to reach up and return the favour.

"Sorry," she said.

"Yeah. Me, too." He lifted the trophy. "Sorry for losing my head."

Gaze fluttering about the pyre, Shkarag emitted one of her rare laughs—subdued, fleeting, and all but normal were it not for the subtle hiss it provoked. It faded to a slight, crooked smile.

With a smile of his own, he secured her spear, and hopped into the saddle. "Are you going to ride like that?" he asked, looking back at her.

"Maybe."

"Can you at least hold the head?"

"Generally against it."

XII

WITH CHOBIN'S BLESSING, TIRDAD AND Shkarag headed east from Dara. What transpired on the front would not concern them until Chobin came calling: that was the promise Tirdad had made to the marzban in leaving and to the half-div in asking. With that in mind, and in the pursuit of a break, they followed the swift river that led south to and eventually bifurcated the capital of the empire. Being the capital, and a metropolis besides, Tirdad had decided against bringing his quest there quite yet. The teeming streets would hardly be a break for Shkarag. But the river made for good scenery and promised easy access to civilization.

It wasn't long before Tirdad had grown accustomed to its carved river-bank, to the winking waters that, while lacking the scent of brine, lent to a certain nostalgia. He could imagine splashing in the shallows. Memories of two childhoods blurred together, each too carefree to belong in any reality. On the opposite bank there rose a wall of dirt like a miniature escarpment, which made crossing all but impossible. He made a habit of searching its precipice, though he hadn't the slightest what he hoped to find. Occasionally, passersby would wave from their boat or raft.

Only nine days had come and gone since they set out, but the road had already proven itself a boon. Shkarag seemed to be in higher spirits, and that in turn uplifted Tirdad. He took pleasure in knowing he'd done her some good. What's more, the path breathed life into him; it harkened to a past in which they had shared many such journeys.

He turned his attention from the river to the half-div. She rode her horse backwards, as she often did, and was casually popping berries into her mouth. "What're those?" he asked, unaccustomed to her snacking on something without a shell.

She glanced his way, piercing one with her fang as she did. She canted. ". . ."

"The berries," he specified.

"Deadly," she mouthed against it. Her pupils, drawn to slits in the midday sun, flicked away and back. "I think."

He squinted at her, briefly taken aback before recalling her immunity to poisons and toxins. Curious how she'd respond, and looking to toy with her besides, he extended a hand. "Mind sharing?"

Meaning to oblige, Shkarag leaned forward and reached into her saddlebag, where she stopped elbow deep and threw a cant at his upturned palm. It was her turn to squint. "Deadly," she insisted.

Tirdad beckoned. "Come on. I can handle it."

Shkarag sat back up, now staring daggers at the berries in her hand. "Seems like a šo-nasty way to go," she said. "Saw them squirming and writhing like some, like some snake pinned by the tail, all throwing a fit and hissing and there's venom all over the place. But if you, if you want it done, I'll . . ." She trailed off, and hefted an axe in her other hand. The look she gave him was utterly resigned, as if nothing in all the cosmos mattered. "I'll make it snappy."

"I was only joking," he hurriedly clarified. For someone so prone to turns of phrase, she had a knack for taking the wrong things literally. "I've no desire to end my life." He chose not to tell her that he had inherited Ashtadukht's desire to do as much, and that while only ever fleeting, it would return with those memories that had taken place after Gushnasp passed.

"Not a thing to guffaw and hold your paunch over," she said. The resignation sloughed away, leaving something inscrutable. "Not at all amusing when the person you, you—" What had just shifted to impenetrable parted briefly so that fear could surface, wide-eyed and darting, before it, too, was overtaken. She turned that deadpan expression on him and opened her mouth as if to speak. Her stare darted around uncertainly, or what he took as uncertainly, until it came to rest nowhere, falling instead into a faraway state.

Heaving a sigh, Tirdad brought his horse closer so he could take hold of her waist, mooring her to the saddle for the duration. It wasn't long before she returned, heralded by her regular silence, and signalling him to give her some space.

". . ." She ate another berry.

"You know," he started, coming to the realization that he'd yet to express how much he treasured what they had and not wanting it to go unsaid. For a moment, he clammed up, unsure how to convey it without stumbling. Then, once again, her lesson in wine gave him the direction he needed. Don't overthink it. He spoke as it came to him.

"We are each of us a lone rider, the horizon our end, where we'll stand before the bridge of judgment, and us with no choice but to push forward." He paused and had to force himself to go on without thinking too much on what came next. "So on those rare occasions when our path converges with someone whose company we truly enjoy, we should be careful not to lose sight of that. I once made the mistake of being too obsessed with honour, with the sum of my deeds, but I don't care about that horizon anymore, Shkarag. What comes, comes. I just want to share the path with you."

Downcast, countenance drawn in a grimace, Shkarag reached up to feel the uneven scar that divided her brow. Her touch roamed the other scars in turn, as if reliving their experiences, and none too happy about it. When she'd traced the last of them, she exhaled. That only seemed to burden her further. Her hand became a claw, which raked down the scales of her scalp, stopping to hover over her ear. Shkarag turned her grimace on him. She canted.

With only her body language to go by, Tirdad ventured a question, hoping she'd grace him with an actual answer this time around. "Does that make you upset?" he asked.

Her eyes jerked away. She shook her head.

He reached out to stroke the disfigured scales above her ear, but hesitated, thinking the better of it. "Something about it bothered you," he reasoned. "Of that I'm certain."

"Maybe," she agreed, or didn't. She looked up, once again wearing her guarded expression. "I want . . ." She trailed off, only to pick up again almost immediately, and the remainder came out in a hurry. "Want that too."

Tirdad was well aware she was holding something back, but that was Shkarag: cagey, and anything but forthcoming, even in her admissions. What might've agitated him in the past only endeared him to her all the more. She was so withdrawn, so ancient, that knowing everything there was to know about her was impossible; in that, he felt privileged for those fleeting moments when she mustered the strength to open up. And that privilege was further shored up by the allure of mystery. The unknown.

He grinned at that, thinking back to their return from Dara, and to the small mark he'd left on a life that could fill annals. "Oh, the look on his face when the King of Kings spotted you with the general's head high for all to see, riding through his army like the hero of the whole sturgeon-fucking campaign. He looked ready rupture a testicle!"

That drew a crooked smile, though it scarcely pressed into her cheeks and could not have aspired to her eyes, which leered at him as if in suspicion. Shkarag pulled her cloak around her shoulders, her scarf over her head.

Tirdad frowned, but left her to her refuge. They continued along the river without sharing a word, following farmland demarcated by its bends, oftentimes sharp enough the river nearly doubled back on itself. With dusk nearing, and the autumn chill creeping in, they happened upon a farming city not a quarter the size of Ray. Tirdad figured a warm bed would be a welcome respite, so he veered their horses into its narrow causeways. Flanked by high adobe walls, he ventured deeper, through arched tunnels, beneath a roofscape trimmed in luxurious stucco and the copper of dusk.

The streets were as calm as he'd expect in a small city at the end of the day: vendors closing shop, children returning home, and here and there someone rushing to finish a chore put off until the last minute. He drew to a stop by a vendor, knowing they had nothing better to do while waiting for customers than to keep their ear to the ground.

A middle-aged man looked up from the scarves he'd nearly finished stowing, hiding exasperation behind what was clearly a manufactured smile. "Bit late for business, but far be it from me to turn away a customer. What can I do you for?"

"A scarf," Tirdad answered. "I meant to ask for directions, but come to think of it, I could use a new one. Something yellow. As bright and bold as you can get." He fished in his tunic for the pouch of coins the King of Kings had rewarded him with, which had been further padded by Chobin. "And I'd like a place to stay. Know where I can find one, or if your fine city is in need of a star-reckoner?"

Before Tirdad could finish talking, the man had a scarf spread over his hands. "Silk," he said. "And would you look at that there motif? Pearl roundels embellished with peacocks and—"

"Thank you, but I can see it just fine," Tirdad interrupted. "I'll take it. As for my other question?"

The man flashed the cost in the sign language of merchants, which Tirdad agreed to with a nod. He handed over a little more than was asked for, though considerably less than he would have a decade earlier. The assets that once belonged to his House had been redistributed. Ashtadukht's estate was his only because no one wanted anything to do with the place. He had to be frugal, though he had it easier than his relatives. He'd been living off of Chobin's generosity since around the time his savings had run dry.

The middle-aged man grunted, handing over the scarf and screwing up his face in thought. "Suppose I know a few places might be open to you staying for free. Empty bed in my place come to think of it, but—" He glanced at Shkarag, who was still bundled in her cloak and scarf, and his face screwed up further. "Your friend's facing the wrong way."

"She does that," Tirdad replied without looking back at her.

"Oh." The man eyed her for a moment before continuing. "Strange. You say you're a star-reckoner?"

Tirdad inclined his head.

"Slipped my mind, but come to think of it, Rakhsh, he's been—oh, Rakhsh runs the bazaar here—he's been throwing a fit on account of our star-reckoner. Late to return from the capital, and it's got Rakhsh rearing to wrestle an onager."

"Why?"

"On account of our star-reckoner taking his damn time I suppose. Try to keep up."

Tirdad sighed, hoping he hadn't run into another Shkarag—one was a handful. "Can you introduce me to this Rakhsh?"

"Ah, sure. You were kind enough to pad your payment, though I suppose you were thinking it would encourage me to say exactly that, eh?"

Tirdad cleared his throat. "Well, yes."

The vendor tapped his head. "More coin to count, less time to fuss. All the better, I say, and not just because I'm the one counting." He started down the corridor, and waved Tirdad along. "No justice in being insulted when someone on in their years puts all that experience to work. Hope I'm savvy as you are when the grey's got me in its clutches."

Tirdad ran his fingers through his hair, feeling his age and unhappy with it. "Yeah."

He followed the man through more corridors lined with high walls whose shade cooled the residents during the day, under low archways that did the same and more. In the event of a sandstorm, refuge could be found in their depths. They passed stalls closed for the evening and the two-story mudbrick residences that rose behind them, faces accented with floral stucco. Here and there, an ibex or lion motif would further liven the decoration. Unlike Ray, this city hadn't bothered with maintaining its colour, but the stucco reliefs alone were effective enough.

Eventually, the vendor came to a stop before a building that was larger than the rest, if only by a small margin. "Here we are," he said. "Guild headquarters. May come off as strange, but I live here—even this humble bazaar demands vigilance. And work's right at my doorstep. Oh, you can call me Rakhsh." The man extended his hand.

Tirdad stared. That was it then, he was convinced. All his life he had been fairly average, never really excelling but getting by on honour and hard work. He'd come to terms with that reality long ago. Turns out he was special: he had a penchant for attracting the weird ones. They flocked to him. Whatever sky he was born under, it had been a mischievous one.

"Tirdad," he flatly replied, reaching down to clasp the merchant's forearm.

Rakhsh perked up at that, grin anything but manufactured now, which better demonstrated the spryness of youth. Tirdad had mistaken him for middle-aged the way he carried himself, but he couldn't have seen much more than two decades. "Oh, your name was mighty popular in the bazaar couple weeks ago. You the same Tirdad what gave that div a beating in Ray?"

"One and the same." The longer it went without explanation, the more Tirdad suspected the merchant had no intention of addressing his, well, whatever had just happened. A prank?

"Then that means . . ." Rakhsh looked past Tirdad, and it was evident where his attention came to rest. "Is that?"

"Seems word travels fast," said Tirdad. "You mentioned being in need of a star-reckoner?"

"Is she really a, uh, one of . . . thought the tale had, you know how they are, going and getting a life of their own." Rakhsh turned his attention back to Tirdad, as if he needed to see the truth in his eyes. "She's a daughter of Eshm?"

That drew a frown.

"Oh, she is!" Rakhsh laughed. "Well, rob my wife and fuck my coffers it's true! That is great news if I have ever heard it. Those forty divs don't stand a chance against the likes of you."

Tirdad knotted his brow. Surely he'd misheard. "Forty what now?"

$$\bullet \bullet \bullet \bullet \bullet$$

"Forty divs."

Tirdad glanced at Shkarag, who was still bundled—probably against both the encroaching chill and the merchant's ongoing interest in her existence. They'd been led through the bazaar administrative building, back to the room where this man, scarcely old enough to own a stall, much less run a bazaar, had settled behind a desk cluttered with seals, rolls of leather, and scrolls of parchment. He lit an oil lamp and, with an exasperated huff, made room to place it on the desk with a sweep of his arm. It didn't do much to light the room, but it was enough to illuminate the immediate area.

"There," he said. "Now, suppose you are wanting an explanation before signing the contract? I would."

"Contract?"

"Terms and conditions, binding, no lack of words to scratch your head over."

"I know how contracts work, but in so many years I've never signed a single contract. Star-reckoner's aren't contractual. This isn't a trade."

"Huh." Rakhsh leaned back, ostensibly perplexed by the idea. "Always seemed like the thing to do. Anything else is plain slapdash, running into a deal belt half notched."

Tirdad furrowed his brow. This man had some odd illusions about the process. That or Ashtadukht had done things differently, which wasn't all that far-fetched, now that he considered it.

"Oh, that's a thought. Only around come harvest through winter, and he never was one for cleanliness, but his home is vacant. Hardly call it a home, considering. Residence then. You assume his responsibilities, and the star-reckoner's residence is yours till either you leave or he gets it in his head to fulfill his contract." Not bothering to wait for a response, Rakhsh set to amending the terms, mumbling to himself like an old curmudgeon as he did.

Initial impressions aside, the man seemed to take his responsibility seriously—an observation Tirdad could respect. If you were capable, willing, and committed yourself, age was not an issue. And the merchant was offering up a prime opportunity to search the star-reckoner's records, or lie in wait besides. Something did seem off, though. "Why're you doing this instead of someone who runs the city?"

Rakhsh didn't look up from his writing. "Speaking."

"Oh."

"Tale's all so much death," Rakhsh added. "You're thinking it's unorthodox, and can't fault you for that. By Ohrmazd, I never asked for the burden, but it fell on my shoulders all the same. Shrug it off and I'm no better than those good-for-nothing divs who brought it about." He paused, throwing an embarrassed glance at Shkarag. "No offense."

" . . . "

Likely taking the silence for the everyday breed, Rakhsh turned the contract to face Tirdad, who searched for his stamp seal where it should have hung around his neck, wearing consternation the more he failed to find it.

"Well," he said, realizing Shkarag must have flung it along with Ashtadukht's, "I'd like to discuss these forty divs before I stamp anything binding."

"Ah, the sort of man to bite a coin. I suppose any star-reckoner worth his salt would want the lay of his quarry." Rakhsh fished a ewer from under the desk, along with three goblets, and filled each half-way. The cloudy, faceted glass caught the flame of the oil lamp, which struck out across the surface of the wine, granting it the comfortable appearance of a hearth in winter. Or, more simply, blood in firelight.

"I'd gamble they're no match for a star-reckoner and a daughter of Eshm. Would that you'd yank them up by the roots this time. That there star-reckoner, he does a mighty golden job of scaring them off, but he's never of a mind to send them packing for good."

Joined by a scaled hand looking to do the same, Tirdad took a goblet, raising it with an appreciative nod to Rakhsh before taking a few swallows. It wouldn't win any awards. "You still haven't told me what exactly these divs are doing," he said. The questions that followed did so rapidly, and Tirdad without a clue to their significance.

"What's their nature? What do you know of their mannerisms? What are their defining features? Do they speak? Are they known to come out before dusk? Have they ever entered a house? A warded house? Have they called you by name? Have they ever spoken a truth? Do they appear before you, or do you only see the aftermath? Have they been known to transform? Practice sorcery? Have you experienced an increase in any mental or physical maladies since their appearance? Has anyone thrown flour dough at them? Have—"

"Woah, rein it in," interrupted Rakhsh. "I didn't catch a lick of that, what with you yammering like mad."

"I . . . uh, never mind." Tirdad remembered a salvo of questions, but their contents were as lost to him as a memory on the tip of his tongue. "Would you just explain the situation?" he asked.

The merchant leaned forward, though not with a storyteller's carriage. Rather, with the intent of pouring more wine. "Been around forever, the reed-loving scoundrels. Far as I know, they are old as this city. Used to come around every winter on the same day to wreak havoc, slaughtering and causing so much grief, this band of divs." He took a swig, and squinted. "Know you're thinking brigands, but this ain't no superstitious cover. We wised up—well, my ancestors did. Cozied up to star-reckoners, and convinced them to winter with us. Now the divs just cause minor trouble. Dead livestock, pranks, painting the city some disagreeable colour overnight. If they get it in their heads to do more, the star-reckoner yells at them." He finished off his goblet and sat back. "Not above admitting I am afraid of what they'd do without someone around to keep them cowering. Happened once, and, well . . ." Rakhsh grimaced, and averted his eyes. "Now I run things."

"How long until they arrive?"

"Forty-one days."

"That's precise."

"In this, they are orderly. If only to deliver chaos upon us."

Tirdad drew his lips taut, giving the contract due consideration. Somewhere, he had the knowledge to thwart this band of divs. Of that much, he was certain. And accepting meant gaining access to a star-reckoner's lodging, which could prove insightful in his quest for the truth. In the event that the star-reckoner returned, all the better; he'd get it from the horse's mouth. If the contract proved to be more than he could handle, they could run. He had forty-one days to figure out the details. Best to get Shkarag's opinion before committing, he thought. Tirdad turned to her and asked, foolishly, "What're you thinking?"

Still withdrawn into the cover of her scarf and cloak, Shkarag had the former lifted enough to get at the wine. She paused between gulps to cock her head at him, staring from behind her hood as if she could see through it. Rather than lowering the goblet, she spoke into the rim.

"Wondering if the swindler wants to betray us, or if you want to betray me, or if the scarf is really silk. Thinking it might be nice to have a gift. Want to tell you about the sword. If the stars are watching, plotting something fierce to make creation revolve against me, it means she's watching, too. This wine tastes like marsh water. What would I do with two scarves? Need to die like a šo-wretched coward. Can't tell. I'm doing it for you. I'd keep them. So afraid of you. Teetering like some, like some beached Dourboat, with its too-slack gullet and its šo-barnacled hull, and it slept in the cape looking for solace after death, only to awake on a lone pillar, the tide absconding and not looking back, and all it takes is a shift in the wind and she wants to—" Her delivery lit up as if a war raged around her, fires and all. "Dismember everyone in this pitiful city, bathe in their smoldering—" Her goblet clattered to the floor, and she snatched the ewer from the desk, taking swallow after swallow until she'd finished it off. Hands around its neck as if strangling it, she eased the ewer to her lap. Tirdad glanced at the merchant; he was as spooked as a horse in a thunderstorm.

After a few steadying breaths, Shkarag pressed on. "Think we can be victors together," she said. "Maybe." It warmed his heart to see the confidence she wore upon drawing back her scarf and hood, the vigor in her eyes. She'd won—for now. "I want, I want to be partners," she said. "I'll stamp the šo-jargoned thing, too."

Rakhsh cleared his throat, a shiver visibly claiming his spine. "Well, uh, that, uh . . ." He trailed off and wrung his hands.

"She won't bathe in the smoldering gore of your citizens," Tirdad consoled. "Right, Shkarag?"

"Maybe," she said with a cant.

"See?"

"She, uh, doesn't seem to have made up her mind," said Rakhsh.

"Sure she has. She gave us a maybe, after all."

"Uh."

"Never mind that," said Tirdad, waving away his worry as if she hadn't said what she had, and with that predatory tone. "We've agreed to take on the task. Trouble is, I left my seal back in—" Shkarag held out a fist. "Huh?"

"Your seal," she said.

Tirdad accepted it with a smile, knowing she'd gone out of her way to scour the city for it after their first night together. "Well, no objections then?" he asked the merchant. "We'll enter the contract and protect your city."

That called for another cleared throat. "Enthused to have you here, don't get me wrong, but ain't ever heard tale of a div putting stamp to contract, much less abiding by it. Goes against your nature, doesn't it?"

". . ." Shkarag just stared at him, deadpan and flickering.

"She's only half div," Tirdad explained. Why he thought that made a difference was beyond him. "Besides, we're partners. There's no way I could do this without her."

Rakhsh sighed, and pulled a second ewer from beneath his desk. "Given my position, I both should and should not protest. Leaning towards having a star-reckoner, though." Shkarag took the ewer. Rakhsh retrieved yet another. "Keep a few ready for guests," he explained, though no one had asked. "Anyhow, the benefits outweigh the risks. The two of you give me your seal and I'll agree to a joint undertaking."

Tirdad did just that. He went to hand his seal to Shkarag, only to find her rummaging beneath her cloak. When at last she found what she was searching for, she stamped her seal alongside his, slightly overlapping, which left the impression of a coiled snake.

"Oh, you have a stamp seal," he observed. "This is my first time seeing you use it."

It vanished beneath her cloak, and she set once more to rummaging. "We all make one," she said when, after some trouble, she'd finished stowing the seal. "Carve it out of bone like some, like some arts and crafts session all huddled around a dead one and squabbling over choice cuts like some, like some vultures who've—"

"I get it," said Tirdad. Then to the merchant, "Would you show us to our lodging? I'm exhausted."

Rakhsh gave the contract another once over, nodded to himself, and disappeared into a back room, presumably an archive. "Let's be off then," he said upon returning. "Bit of a hike, and I'm about ready to nod off myself. Wine saw to hurrying that along."

"Lead the way," said Tirdad.

Shkarag emptied her ewer, and together they followed Rakhsh through more high-walled corridors, now thick with shadows, to the muffled sounds of a city turning in for the night. They passed between a pair of domed cisterns that housed the city's water supply, through which air was vented and cooled during summer, and to the lone residence tucked behind.

"Beats me why it's out here like a dog what refused to chase off the Nasu," said Rakhsh. "Been used by star-reckoners for who knows how long. Well, I'll leave you to it. Time for me to sleep this wine off. You know where to find me." With a wave, he started back the way they'd come.

"Friendly fellow," said Tirdad. He faced their new residence—secluded, but two stories and adobe like much of the town—and figured it'd be pleasant to live again as they had in the estate. Just the two of them. Only now, he needn't worry about the mystery of Ashtadukht's past eating at him. Either he'd find answers here, or he would get them from the star-reckoner. Tirdad rested his palm on the ram's head pommel, confident that, whatever the outcome, he would find justice.

The pommel hardly had time to welcome him before Shkarag snatched his hand away, half-dragging half-leading him through the night and into the house where it was black as frostbite. "What's the hurry?" he asked. "Shkarag, I can't see a fucking thing." She began unbuckling his weapon belt. "Oh, you're hankering, huh?" He reached out to stroke her head. "I can't say I haven't been. Sleep can wai—what are you doing?"

Shkarag had hefted him as if he were a doe, effortlessly moving through the residence and up a flight of stairs. She was oftentimes aggressive in her lust, which wasn't remotely surprising given her lineage. And while he indulged all her obscene desires—in time, he himself had come to enjoy even the most heinous—Tirdad drew the line at being carried around. He was on the cusp of voicing as much when she laid him down.

"Go to sleep," she ordered.

Tirdad's agitation was plain. After she'd provoked him, the last thing he wanted to do is sleep. "What in the seven climes, Shkarag? I thought you wanted to fuck?"

". . ." The meaningful silence made it seem as if she were entertaining the notion. That it hadn't occurred to her at all. "Maybe," she said, with anything but conviction. Something hit the floor, probably his weapon belt, and the silence lost its meaning. She'd left.

"Shkarag," he called. "Come back why don't you? I'll open a wound, and let you wallow in my blood until you're satisfied. Whatever you like." He waited, but the silence remained woefully untended. Heaving a sigh, frustrated above all else, he closed his eyes. Surely, she had a reason for doing that out of nowhere; the trouble lay in unearthing the reason. There was no way he was going to fall asleep in his condition.

"Fuck," he breathed and lowered his trousers.

• • • • •

They were out early the following morning to stock up on essentials. The city was a lazy one, acting mainly as a hub for farmers from the many neighboring villages or a rest stop for travellers on their way to the capital. On a normal day, the residents might have gone on with their routine as if Tirdad were just another stranger passing through. Shkarag had other plans. She'd fashioned them a spectacle.

She wore her cloak and scarf, but brazenly: hood down and silk scarf—which he'd given her before setting out—loose around her neck. For his part, Tirdad had only objected once and respected her silent refusal to conceal her identity. Whispers arose as they passed, which came as a surprise to Tirdad because they carried more than the well-deserved fear of a daughter of Eshm. More than once he heard mention of the star-reckoner who saved Ray, and of his div companion who had died for the city. He knew she had died for him at best, but plausibly only as a result of her reckless bloodlust. They didn't have to know that. Besides, she'd come to the aid of the legendary archer Erash and saw none of the prestige she was owed. Who knows how many other feats had gone unappreciated.

Thinking on that injustice left Tirdad rankled, which distracted him enough that he nearly bumped into her. He drew up short, beetle-browed and matching her stare where she leaned into her spear and craned up at him. "What?" he asked.

". . ." She directed her attention somewhere over his shoulder.

"Out with it, Shkarag." He glanced past her. "Oh, looks like we found the bazaar."

At that, she hissed. "Said you need to lift, to steal, to abduct, to—"

"Buy?"

Another hiss. "—to buy apricots. Forty apricots, all shriveled and sun-dried, to count the days."

"Huh?" Tirdad turned his attention back to her. "That seems mighty unnecessary. Why count with dried apricots when I can just count, well . . . most any other way seems better."

Shkarag sharply angled her head, throwing one arm wide, which rolled her spear on its butt to jab at the bazaar behind her, nearly impaling a passerby in doing so. "Are you going to, going to count the šo-damned stars like some planet-reckoner slipping into the trousers of a star-reckoner, shoving one leg in and losing your balance, all making a fuss about how you're a true bona fide star-reckoner and don't want to fuck a planet until it's—"

Tirdad clapped a hand over her mouth. "Shkarag!" he breathed. She just stared. "You win. I'll get the apricots. Just drop the whole roving explanation."

"Maybe," she said when he removed his hand, retracting her spear as if she were a royal guard permitting him entry. "I think."

He offered her a smile and headed into the same square they'd visited the night before, though it was markedly busier. Rather than being separated according to an artisan's craft, stalls were arranged in two concentric circles, where sundries were on display beneath canvases beaming with primary colors. Lively as it was, the bazaar was small and had a subdued atmosphere that always seemed to gloss these small cities, whose residents took pride in their work. The bustle of the capital and other sprawling urban areas drained everyone involved. Leisure. That was the key, he figured. A person could find leisure here.

Shkarag's spear thumped as she approached a stall. He joined her, where she glared at a pile of sun-dried apricots. Every few seconds, her gaze would flick up at the vendor. She sucked in several heavy breaths before pulling herself straight by her spear. She donned her hood. "Forty apricots," she said, now darting between the wares and anything but the vendor. "Dried in the, in the šo-wretched sun."

"Come to think of it," mused Tirdad, "we used to eat these often on the road. Between all the dried fruit, I'm surprised I'm not sick of them by now. Actually, been having something of a craving for them lately." He reached out to pluck one from the pile, and when his fingers came into contact with its leathery skin, he was abruptly shunted into a memory.

"Date," he said in Ashtadukht's voice, palm extended and watching himself expectantly. His bones ached terribly; it burned just to breathe. Worse than his stubborn body was the weight of the past. He wanted to die. More than that, he yearned for it. All that kept him afloat was the promise of the festival—his annual rites. So he stared from that precipice daily as if to say, "Soon."

There was more to it than that, an undercurrent focused on himself: chiefly resentment at being escorted, but somewhere in there the leanings of gratitude. With the date placed in his palm, the memory dispersed, and Tirdad was back in the bazaar, sun-dried apricot in hand, sun hot on his neck. He bore into it, blurry and unfocused. In passing, the memory hadn't been so complaisant as to take its emotions.

"Why're you crying?" asked a voice accented and somehow managing to hiss words that could not be hissed. That broke the spell of the past, and he looked up to see a hood aimed his way, off-kilter as it was wont to be. Shkarag reached up to smear his cheek with an uncommon tenderness. The same hand disappeared beneath her hood. "Salty," she confirmed. "Why?"

Embarrassed, Tirdad used his sleeve to finish what she started. "I . . ." He trailed off. By Ohrmazd, Ashtadukht had been so much stronger than him. He almost felt as if she deserved to finish what she'd started. He respected her tenacity when faced with such suffocating baggage. Tirdad couldn't tell Shkarag as much; he wagered she'd take it the wrong way. "It was only a memory," he replied at length. "Only that."

"Memories are . . . memories smart," Shkarag agreed, turning back to face the stall, and angling her hood away from the vendor. "Forty sun-dried apricots," she said. "Not more, not less, and I want, I want them yesterday."

The vendor, a jowled man with his better years behind him, had not spoken a word. He hadn't even moved, and were the bazaar not in swing, the sound of swallowing would have filled the silence. Tirdad gathered as much from his salt-white complexion and the beads that pooled on his forehead despite sitting in the shade on a cool day. He extended a hand, chiselling onto his face the same smile he'd wear when forced to take a pillow near the door in court—farthest from the King of Kings, thus furthest from his favour. Not that his lowly House would ever again be invited to sit on the fringes.

"I'm Tirdad," he said. "Your new star-reckoner."

The vendor gave him a look that was plainly dumbfounded—as if he'd appeared out of thin air.

"Rakhsh hired us," Tirdad added.

"Rakhsh . . ." the man muttered. He blinked and rubbed his eyes. "Rakhsh . . . right," he got out at length, finally managing to grasp Tirdad's forearm. "That is a . . ."

"This is my partner," Tirdad explained. He couldn't fault the man for his reaction, especially after the recent invasion. "She won't hurt you as long as you don't give her a reason to. Haven't you heard what we did for Ray? We're here to do the same for your city, so you'd do well to get used to us. Now—" He held out the apricot. "I need forty of these. Sometime today if you would."

Now more afraid he'd lose his throat if he didn't oblige, the vendor hurried to fulfill their request. "Forty," he said, looking a little less pale.

"Thirty-nine," countered Shkarag. "Don't like merchants. Always trying to swindle you into more trousers or fewer apricots." Her spear creaked in her grip. "Forty," she hissed, "or I'll fucking—" She snatched them away once he'd added another, fury having overcome anxiety. "Forty," she said, spear thumping to her departure.

Tirdad gave him an apologetic smile-turned-grimace and left the vendor to remember how to breathe. The remainder of their trip was decidedly less confrontational, now that Shkarag had accomplished what she set out to and subsequently retreated into her cloak and scarf. Loaded with supplies, they headed back. With Ashtadukht's memory fresh in his mind, he was eager to run the star-reckoner's residence through a sieve. Or run through a star-reckoner. He had to find something incriminating.

Upon returning, he immediately set to the search. Rakhsh hadn't exaggerated the state of the place: with all the dirt and strewn belongings, it looked as if a sandstorm had swept through, with an army galloping behind. Tirdad took the time to explore the building, and as far as he could tell, every room served as haphazard storage. So, without a clear direction, he began his search on the second floor, aiming to go from the top down.

Shkarag joined him in rummaging through the mess, which was about as multifarious as a mess could be excluding outright garbage, and piled high enough to curtain the faded hunt murals that decorated the walls.

At a glance, sheafs of old scrolls were bunched beneath jars replete with contents too warped to make out, above which barsom twigs shared space with vulture feathers and rolls of leather—all of it littered with astrolabes, armillary spheres, and various apparatuses only of use to star-reckoners, mariners, and select other professions. From the rise of the nearest heap, an elaborate bronze astrarium emerged, its mechanisms green with patina and representative of the luminaries, which it could predict more accurately than any star-reckoner.

In searching, Tirdad rifled through manifests, recipes, star charts, missives, everyday bookkeeping—he scoured it all. Having found the thread's beginning in trade manifests, he refused to part with even the most mundane entries. This made the search painstakingly slow. Eventually, he struck up conversation to pass the time.

"That was . . . different, what you did last night," he said. "It's unlike you to carry me around, or run off in the middle of it—neither of which I appreciated by the way. What were you on about?"

Shkarag was picking through her pile as if plucking choice eggs from the clutch of a lifetime. She cocked her head, still facing her charge but casting at him from the corner of her eye. She went on searching, and the silence that followed was unsettling in its emptiness.

"You can talk to me, you know." Tirdad reunited the latest in a series of aged astrolabes with the others he'd found. He tinkered with its plates, which were uncannily familiar. "I don't know how challenging it is for you to share, only that it is. Not your driftwood tales—to really share. How you vacillate between being a thrall to one thing or another. But I can't help but worry."

"Can't," Shkarag blurted.

"Huh? Can't what?"

"Can't—" She hissed, and flung a jar across the room. Rather than her usual claw or raking, she clutched her skull. She opened her mouth as if to speak, but all that emerged was a drawn out croak.

Tirdad ceased his tinkering to come over, meaning to rub her back, but she flinched away. "Don't answer," he said. "Not if it's causing you this much grief." He'd seen her all sorts of distressed, but never like this.

In labouring to look at him, her movements were stilted. What's more, her eyes bulged, and a prominent vein crossed her temple to join the furrows of her forehead. Again, she croaked, and it went on until at last it formed a broken, "—ay—be."

Tirdad didn't know what to make of it. Only that she was straining to get something out—straining like he'd only ever seen in mortally wounded warriors clinging to the last vestiges of life. She trembled, and so too did her voice.

"Swor—d, can't . . . str—ron—" Briefly, it seemed her eyes would roll into her head, but she steeled herself. "Stro—n . . . ves—sail—sailor . . . you're can't." A claw jerked from her head, stilted in finding the ram's head pommel, and missing it four times before taking ahold of it. "Plea—se don't," she croaked as if it took everything she had just to get the words out. A line of blood trickled from one nostril, and her pupils went from slits to saucers, unwavering and trained on him. She lurched forward, baring her fangs and shoving the pommel of his sword as she did.

Tirdad was more than a little nonplused. "Stop," he bade her. "I'm telling you to stop. Whatever you're doing, just stop."

"D—on't." She gave the ram's head another shove, his weapon belt creaking at her strength, which nearly brought him to his knees. "Don—'t an—y any an—y a—ny—" A second trickle joined the first, and a convulsion had her doubled over, wheezing and hissing and clutching her head.

Tirdad grimaced, wanting to console her but uncertain if he should. Just what was she doing to herself, and why in the seven climes would she go to such lengths to speak? Or need to for that matter?

Suddenly, she collapsed, hitting the floor with a hiss. He reached out to help her, but thought the better of it when her hiss went on until she'd sidled up against the nearest heap. "Smarts," she said, licking the blood from her lips, and staring ahead as if in a daze. "Something fierce. Not enough blood to, to . . ." She brought a claw up by her ear, then let it fall to her side. "Smarts."

Tirdad joined her, feeling awkward and unsure of himself. "You look like you're in a bad way."

"Maybe." She rolled her head toward him. "Need to rest. I think."

He raised his hand so she could see his intention before reaching down to hold hers. He squeezed, which she returned weakly. "Want to tell me what happened there?"

"Maybe."

"Is that a 'yes' maybe or a 'no' maybe?"

"Want to, but . . . I tried. Really need to—" When next she parted her lips, she emitted a croak that became a hiss. "Need to," she said, patently furious but too drained to do anything about it.

"Want to, but you can't?" Tirdad ventured. "Can you not say it? Can you write it? Can I help at all?" She only stared. He made to press further, and would have liked to, but that would be both unkind and futile. Whatever she needed to tell him, she'd fought tooth and nail to get out sputtered gibberish. "Promise me you're hale?" he asked.

"Maybe," she said in the affirmative, reassuring him with another weak squeeze before closing her eyes and going limp against the heap. That unnerved him for a moment, because as much as she killed herself, even in the odd times it'd happen during sex, he never could stomach it. So it was comforting that her chest still rose and fell.

To avoid stirring her, he moved his search downstairs for the time being, trying to make sense of what she'd said as he did. Sword, don't, sailor: those were the only whole words he could recall. And they made even less sense than she was prone to. When, after hours of trawling, dusk rolled around, he remembered the dried apricots, and figured he may as well use them if only to please Shkarag.

Tirdad took one from the lot, and in doing so said, "Well, that's one down the hatch."

As he swallowed, he was alerted to a thud followed by the sounds of scuffling just outside the house. He had his sword out in a flash, heart beating in his throat, chest heaving, and adrenaline honing his senses to a keen edge. He stood fastened in place for a moment, debating whether he should go out or let it come to him. Ultimately, adrenaline and a dash of pomegranate-red had him flinging the door open so hard it clapped against plaster. Chin held high, sword brandished, Tirdad stepped out, feeling every bit the redoubtable planet-reckoner she had been—and he was not.

He swept his sight over the cisterns, the stretch of dirt between them, the autumn-coloured sky, and when that turned up nothing, spun on the adobe, checking first above, then taking the time to skulk around back to the nook between it and the wall. All he found were the leaves and debris that'd accumulated over years of neglect. Surely, nothing could have—something tickled his neck. He spun around, ready to strike.

He saw nothing. "Just the wind," he said, scowling at the thought that had wormed into his mind. Whatever happened to those terrible divs that'd—no, never mind that. Tirdad tried not to think about it. The last thing he wanted to do right then was yawn.

"Fuck," he mouthed as he did just that. He swung his sword wildly, slashing at the air around him like a madman until he felt confident he'd dispatched any invisible divs, which would not have been comforting if he'd stopped to think about it. "Footprints," he said and set to inspecting the surrounding area, which turned up only his own. Empty-handed, he paced a circuit out and around the cisterns, if only to calm his nerves before retreating back inside.

Once in, he started stringing up noisemakers throughout the place, thinking himself clever for those he hid with tripwires. With that done, Tirdad was too unsettled to do more rummaging. Besides, the sun had set, and that meant making himself a beacon by lighting an oil lamp. He kept telling himself he was overreacting, but something in him had responded to the noise—like a conjunction, or an animal catching wind of another in its territory. Heaving a sigh, Tirdad headed up to join Shkarag. He had thirty-nine more days to pick through the place. May as well enjoy the luxury of sleeping under a solid roof while it lasted.

Shkarag hadn't moved an inch since he left her. He laid beside her, resting his head on her good thigh, and repeating the same three words in his mind. Sailor, sword, don't. Don't, sword, sailor. Sailor, don't, sword. Sword, sailor, don't.

XIII

THE DAYS THAT FOLLOWED WERE occupied from dawn til dusk with investigating the hoard strewn throughout the house. Within five days, Tirdad had amassed an archive's worth of documents to pore over and was beginning to come to terms with the fact that he'd need months, maybe years, to study it all—and that was only about half the hoard sorted.

"Well, that's six down the hatch," he said after eating another apricot. As with the days before, scuffling followed. He'd went out to check every time, always to no avail, and always with that uncanny feeling in his gut. Tirdad figured today would be equally fruitless, so he didn't bother. He pivoted to get back to work, only to find that Shkarag had drawn up beside him and was watching the door with a blank face. "So you hear it, too?" he asked.

". . ." She canted his way.

"The scuffling." He indicated the door with the hilt of his sword, which his palm had found instinctively, like those troubled souls who, so accustomed to its grip, flock to misery. "You're looking right at it."

". . ." She canted further, attention split between him and the door. "Why aren't you with your family?" she asked, limping back to a pile of scrolls to resume her search. "Family is important."

Tirdad eyed her back, watching the caftan as it bunched and shifted alongside her movements. Dodging questions came as no surprise with

Shkarag; asking them did. The normal ones anyway. They were as rare and as powerful as a five-planet conjunction.

When he didn't reply, Shkarag cast over her shoulder and said, "Don't have to answer."

"It's all right," he said, and she returned to her task. In truth, it was a sore topic, and she likely knew as much. But she'd asked, so he would answer. "I'm . . ." He ran his fingers through his hair and screwed up his face at the memory of them turning him away. "You're right. Family is important. That's why I volunteered to become Ashtadukht's guardian all those years ago. If it wasn't me, someone less accommodating would have—and it was the honourable thing to do besides. Back when I was fucking stupid and thought of honour as this be-all and end-all. My part in her travels, namely in not putting a stop to her downward spiral, led to the fall of my family's House. Our standing, our name, our assets, our history—everything."

". . ." Shkarag kept her quiet but for the crinkling of scrolls.

"Now, well, I suppose I do miss them, especially the deepened sense of belonging during festivals. It's more the . . ." He trailed off, still watching her back, and tried to find the words. "It's the guilt that eats at me. That I might've done something to prevent their fate."

". . ."

"That aside, I'm with my family. I'm with you. I've spent the better part of my life by your side. What are we if not family? They were never unkind to me, and Ashtadukht's father was caring beyond reason. But as far as I'm concerned, you're more my family than any of them." When she kept sorting without the hint of a response, he drew up beside her. "Shkarag?" he asked. "You know that, right?"

". . ." She unrolled a length of leather, and her scrutiny flicked from top to bottom. Her lips belied the thoughts behind words, but she squirrelled them away before they could take shape.

"You come before anyone, including myself," he told her. "Part of you knows that, even if the other part thinks I'm out to get you."

She opened her mouth, glancing his way and seeming as if she'd actually reply this time, when there interrupted a hurried rapping at the door.

"Who the fuck is that?" Tirdad grumbled.

"Star-reckoner!" a hoarse yet homely voiced called when he didn't immediately answer. "Star-reckoner! Get yer arse out here!"

Tirdad groaned, recalling the occasions when Ashtadukht would have them stop off in a town or city during those months-long breaks between missions. There was always someone who needed a star-reckoner—or more often someone who thought they needed a star-reckoner. He sucked in a steadying breath to prepare for whatever absurd request or complaint was coming and opened the door.

"Took ya long enough," said the woman on the other side of the door. With her shawl over her head, straight back, and slouched shoulders, she seemed ancient—a stubborn sort of ancient, like an ironwood that refused to bend. "What're ya waiting fer?" she asked, waving and starting off without him, grousing all the while. "Fucking young'uns are lazy as all get out. If it was ole Valash what did the reckoning, he'd a showed up of his own volition. Got an old woman going across town when it's cold and dark as Jeh's cunt. Fingernail-swallowing . . ." Her grousing became unintelligible when she passed between the cisterns.

"I guess I should probably follow," Tirdad said with a groan of a sigh. He stepped out and turned to face Shkarag. "Coming? She could have me divining with horse shit for all I know."

Shkarag disappeared into the house and returned soon after with her spear. She passed in silence, limping and leaning into it, and he followed close behind.

"Get yer arses moving," snapped the old woman once they'd passed between the cisterns. She waved them on with her torch. "Come on, come on. I'll light a fire under you if you don't get a move on."

"What's the hurry?" asked Tirdad.

"Not fer digging around in guts, are you?" she asked. "Always seemed messy that divination, but yer forebears did it, and that got them to the task."

Tirdad hadn't the slightest clue what she was going on about, and she never bothered actually answering his question—just more grousing.

"Got three what knows the blade," she said upon drawing to a stop before a house. "Got a fire stoked, too. You do yer part, and we been around long enough to know the rest."

Childbirth. She was describing the protective rites of childbirth that warded off divs due to the proximity of death and puerile fever, and the divination that followed. Tirdad didn't need his cousin's memory to know as much; he'd joined her for this routine task dozens of times. He drew his starling-black blade and turned to Shkarag. "Let's get to it then."

She followed him through the door, past the shadow-still entry room where the darkness felt thicker than normal, and toward the warm glow of fire. A brazier burned in the centre of a common room, and at the far end, a woman who hardly looked old enough to claim the term had been made comfortable on the floor. She stared at him, wide-eyed and with a sheen of sweat, when he entered. He offered her the most disarming smile he could manage. "I'm Tirdad," he said. "We'll get you through this."

She jerked her head in a nod, plainly frightened. He signalled to the three men who loitered to one side, and they all moved to surround her. None of them looked like they knew how to use the swords they were carrying.

"Hurry yer arses," shouted the old woman as she entered. "Baby is due yesterday!"

Tirdad found Shkarag waiting just outside the ingress, scales polished with firelight. "Are you staying out here?" he asked. "You know it isn't safe."

". . ." She canted at him, then at his waist. She touched his sacred girdle, which elicited a hiss from both her and her fingers, and leveled them on the common room. "Worse," she said simply.

Tirdad nodded. Come to think of it, she'd never been around for these in the past. He tested the waters by lifting a hand just shy of the side of her neck. When it was clear she wouldn't object, he placed it just below her ear where scale met flesh and gave her a brief kiss. Her breath reeked of eggs, but he revelled in it all the same. More than that, he was happy to see the almost indistinguishable slant her lips wore just beneath the rim of her hood. She covered his hand with her own, lips parting to the cadence of some unspoken thoughts.

"Four directions," she said at length. "Four directions and three, three šo-burning nights."

Tirdad gave her another nod. He remembered the ritual well enough, but that she cared to remind him was a welcome gesture all the same. "I'm afraid you'll have to eat those apricots yourself until I'm done here," he said.

"Maybe," she replied.

With that, Tirdad returned to his duty. By reaching out to the celestial theatre he was able to position the three sword-bearers around the pregnant woman such that their blades, directed at her stomach, faced east, west, and south. Tirdad took up his position in the empty spot, completing the ward by pointing his sword northward.

"Now, we wait," he said to everyone in the room. "Keep your swords where they are, and keep the fire stoked." The old woman shouldered her way into the circle where she knelt beside the mother to be. With everyone else having left the house, he figured she was the midwife.

Hours would pass before the delivery, during which Tirdad and his assistants stood mostly motionless—besides some fidgeting that drew rebukes from both star-reckoner and midwife. For the duration, Tirdad felt an oppressive weight, as if the darkness outside the room were pressing in on it, and in turn, the room compressed him. It reminded him of the first few weeks following his broken ribs, when he often found himself having to focus on breathing, and the frustration that came with being unable pull in that last bit of air that would top off his lungs. Always feeling as if what he did get was somehow inadequate.

So, with the newborn delivered, he sucked in a hefty lungful, revelling in that comfortable pressure before easing it through his lips. "All right," he said to the men who had joined him. "You can go now. The rest is up to me." Two left without complaint, but the third stuck around to join the woman and her bawling newborn. The pair shared a smile, each of them exhausted and doused in sweat, and doting over the infant.

That made him think of Shkarag. He glanced at the exit, but saw no signs of her. She'd likely left for her twilight penitence. Tirdad frowned at the thought, and again at the newborn. He wondered if she wanted to have children with him. If she could. They hadn't been in the relationship long, but he was old enough to know this was serious. And, well, he was old. With that on his mind, he sheathed his sword and leaned against the wall, sliding down until he sat facing the fire.

"Three nights," he whispered to himself, staring blankly into the flames and wondering if it'd be wrong of him to bring a child into a world in which his House had been dismantled. Or one in which its lineage was universally feared.

With a heavy sigh, he closed his eyes. The next three days would have him confined to the room with the family, and while the riskiest step was behind them, there still remained the threat of attack by opportunistic divs. More often than not, it wouldn't come to that. The monotony would make him wish it had. Tirdad completed his charge without incident, spending the days that followed sitting by the fire, isolated with the parents and their child. This gave him time to reflect, which was the last thing he needed. So when Shkarag invariably dropped by to insist he ate the day's sun-dried apricot, it was a welcome reprieve.

When at last the third night had passed, he had one final task to wrap together the ritual. He would read the skies to divine the destiny of the newborn. That it was day was of no consequence: planet-reckoners could read the sky just fine while the sun was out. Calling to the theatre, on the other hand, was impossible.

Tirdad exhaled, and with it, reached out. Three planets were in the Ear of Grain; another wasn't far off. Come dusk, they would wreak havoc on the constellation, and the only solace to be had in that configuration was that Jupiter would be isolated on the opposite end of the celestial theatre. Their combined efforts meant a lousy life for the child, but not one beyond redemption. Tirdad had his doubts when it came to fate. The word inspired as much good as it did evil. When used carelessly it had the power to ruin lives. As far as he was concerned, people put too much stock in readings and prophecies. That came as no surprise given the abysmal lot he'd drawn—according to the star-reckoner who'd overseen his birth anyway. Looking back, he saw, or thought he saw, a pattern in the way his parents and uncle had treated him. Not negatively, especially not in the case of Ashtadukht's father. Just different.

With that in mind, he approached the mother. Her colour had been fully restored during his stay, which made her youth all the more apparent. He fashioned an affected smile. "You can rest easy. The young one is favoured by the Ear of Grain, unaccosted by the planets, and his years will come and pass as the harvest: a challenge with the promise of reward."

A circumspect answer that stopped just short of a lie. The challenge would surely appear, only to have sown a crop ruined by flood or insect.

The woman gave him a smile brightened by ignorance. Tirdad found some comfort in that, and in the hope she turned on the newborn.

"Farewell," he said, not expecting the least bit of gratitude. If there's anything he'd learned in his travels with Ashtadukht, it's that being a star-reckoner was thankless.

After spending three nights cooped up with strangers, the first thing Tirdad wanted was a bit of privacy, so he headed home, restless legs enthused to stride again, and wondering if Shkarag would have an omelette ready.

What she had prepared would outclass any omelette.

· · · · ·

A hiss penetrated the front door as he approached. "Eat the šo-damned—eat it!" A crash followed, a thud joined by the rattle of something shattered. "Don't spit! Swallow, you star-fucker!"

Dread rising in his throat, Tirdad opened the door. Inside, Shkarag had an elderly man flat on his back, her hand on his mouth with something black smeared beneath. From where she straddled the man's chest, she craned up at Tirdad, mouth agape and eyes darting as if in search of an escape.

Tirdad clammed up, blinking and taking in the scene. The dread that had set in when he opened the door increased by magnitudes. He saw himself standing before Ashtadukht on the night he'd ruined her ritual. The man tried to struggle, which Shkarag dealt with by bearing down on his neck with her other hand. Tirdad parted his lips, and though his thoughts were storm-livened with questions and accusations, none wanted to be the one to take the plunge. He did have the wherewithal to step in and close the door behind him, but only that. He just stared, mind racing.

251

Now faced with the scenario that had, as far as he was concerned, set in motion so much misery, Tirdad was petrified.

Shkarag broke the hush. That would have been all well and good if she hadn't done so by snapping the man's neck. "He . . . wouldn't . . ." She cast at the shards of a ewer that were strewn across the floor, and the wine that pooled around them as if they were an ill-fated fleet.

"They say," she began, "they say, you can only lead a horse to a flight of stairs. But he wouldn't, he wouldn't climb, wouldn't drink." Shkarag went quiet and stared past Tirdad as if in anticipation of a response, but he had none to give her. Minutes passed, tense as heartstrings and precarious as plucking them, before she backed off the man and sat on the floor, scrutiny darting from one thing to another.

"Don't want, was trying to—" The hiss that took purchase on her voice was tremulous. "Don't want you to become like her, so I thought, thought, they say, say you have to break a few eggs if you want to—" She raked one claw over her skull, and the remainder came out in a hurried jumble. "—keep making omelettes for the person you love." Shkarag lifted her hood to hide her eyes, and sat there motionlessly.

The still that poured in was enduring. The sort of still that rallied itself, grew more oppressive for no other reason than because it went on unchallenged. So the longer it endured, the harder it was to disrupt—like grief too far gone.

After a time, Tirdad eased himself to the floor. He'd gone over the scene countless times by now, trying desperately to piece it together, but he couldn't get further than the man whose life had just been snuffed out before him. This wasn't war. This was murder. Shkarag had never stooped so low in all their years together.

An hour must have passed in that mounting still before Tirdad managed to break through his haze of fear. Immediately, the black smear jumped out at him as if it had been primed. Shkarag had been eating black berries recently, had warned him against their toxicity. This was utterly unlike her. It strode against everything he knew of her and her lineage. In poisoning the man, she would have easily deflected suspicion. She'd called him a star-fucker. That gave Tirdad somewhere to start, but it would take many an attempt before he could gather the courage to do so.

"Was this man a star-reckoner?" he asked. Succinct as it was, the question was as stubborn as an onager in coming out.

Her cant was only a few degrees, her reply thin. "Maybe."

Tirdad exhaled. "Did he threaten you?"

"Maybe."

He closed his eyes. Poorly phrased. "Did he attack you?"

"Maybe." Not nearly as certain this time.

It felt as if he were reliving the past, as if he were a single misstep away from repeating it. That constant foreboding maintained his calm by suffocating him with his own mistakes. "Did—" It caught in his throat.

She loved him. She had said as much. Tirdad wanted dearly to be thrilled—he almost smiled!—but no, not yet. This had to be settled, not merely defused.

"Did—" It caught again.

She saved him the trouble by confessing. "Gave Adur-mah the wine. Star-fucker told a golden thread, but . . . I had to. The . . . the others, too."

Tirdad put his head in his hands. The constant pressure of the ritual had drained him, leaving him ill-prepared for what was already precarious. He would have nodded off if not for the anxiety. "I don't understand why," he muttered. "You know these star-reckoners are the only chance I have at getting to the bottom of this conspiracy. So why in the seven fucking—" Tirdad sucked in a steadying breath. That would not do. "All this time I've been so relieved to have you back. I thought we were in this together, and took pride in our path because I was privileged enough to share it with you. Only to find out it was a lie. Why would you sabotage it? Why work against me all this time, Shkarag?"

Her lips moved to an inner monologue that went on so long it became rodomontade. "Not against you," she replied at length. "Not against you. Don't want to stand by and, like some—" Though her mouth moved, the words were once again lost. Eventually, she pressed on. "Never against you," she hissed, which had already softened before she finished the sentence. "Never. Always thinking, thinking, 'Does he want me gone? Is this a šo-biting prank?' But I'm never against you."

Head hung, Tirdad sighed. She was trying in earnest to explain; that much he knew. So he reined in his temper to ask, "Why, then, would you do this?"

Shkarag flexed a claw by her head. "Can't dig up the right word. Eluding me something fierce, like some, like some arch, arch—" Her breathing grew so heavy it dominated the room. "Like some archaeologist poking around without a torch and tossing this or that priceless artifact because they can't see and turns out they had found it only now it's all so much ostraca over their shoulder, off galavanting with the rest, prevailing upon this or that scribe for a turn of phrase. When you, when the—" She croaked, which then engendered a pained gasp. "Haunted," Shkarag said with both finality and triumph. "Being obsessed is . . . not pleasant, but it's, it's not indomitable. Being haunted is . . . I've been . . ." She trailed off, and the claw she held by her head hesitated by the rim of her hood before pulling it back down. She stared dead at him, unblinking and attention hardly fidgeting at all.

"Been haunted all my life. When W—" She drew out the sound, patently trying to force the rest of the word out. When she finally did, it was thick with sorrow. "Waray died, everything, all that, it all closed in. Memories smart, but being haunted is—" Her eyes flicked away to find the term before bringing it back. "A curse. Can't be lifted or cured. Always there, always waiting, always ready to take more and more and more." She leaned forward. "Don't want that for you."

Tirdad returned her stare through the cage of fingers that sheltered his face. His anger had sloughed away. He never could stay angry at her, even when she was prone to the most infuriating of pranks. Especially not now, not after what she'd said. The trouble with which she strove to answer. He wanted only to make sense of her actions, and to find the forgiveness she deserved. But for her to have undermined him in his quest for the truth—that reeked of betrayal. Had she known the truth all along? Why, then, would she set him on this path to begin with?

Shkarag got up, plodding over and reaching back with both hands to undo her girdle as she did. Once she reached him, she tossed it to his feet. Tirdad turned consternation and an appraising eye on the girdle. The craftsmanship was astounding, even with a number of its lapis lazuli inlays missing. Coloured as they were, they reminded him of her, which made the vacant slots all the more fitting. He looked up at her. "What?"

"Don't know what you'll unearth," she said, low and resigned. "Only that, that it'll be a šo-wretched truth. Maybe those star-reckoners placed Ashtadukht on that carpet, they placed her there like some, like some doomed planet in your, in your board game that . . ." She went silent, searching him for an answer.

"Nard?" he offered.

"Like some doomed planet in your nard game," she picked up summarily, "placed there only to be taken in some strategy, to have the carpet yanked from under her."

"Then why—"

"Maybe they didn't," she punctuated. "Doesn't matter. You'll be haunted. Can find nothing, can find everything. That's just as the crow flies. Doesn't matter. Ever since, ever since you found a thread, I knew I'd made a terrible, done a terrible thing to you, bringing that sheaf of leather and scrolls."

Tirdad averted his gaze. As far as she was concerned, disrupting his quest was protecting him. Her reasoning was not unsound. She truly meant well. What's more, she felt guilty for getting him into it. How could he hold that against her?

"Phylactery," she said, nudging the girdle with her boot before about-facing and limping her way upstairs.

Torn between her actions and her motives, Tirdad followed her departure with a pensive frown. His was a fleeting contest, though. A battle that belonged in the past. He had forsaken honour, and in so doing, had freed himself to act not in the pursuit of lofty ideals, but in the best interests of those he held dear. Honour stopped where their relationship began. That was, foremost, by virtue of being in a relationship with a half-div.

Tirdad heaved a sigh that became a groan as he got to his feet. He decided to compromise. With that in mind, he made for the steps, only to draw up short and turn back for the girdle. "Phylactery," he mused as he picked it up. It didn't just belong to Shkarag; it was Shkarag. He ran his fingers over its surface, as smooth and cool and inviting as her scales. All this time she had vouchsafed her soul in a girdle she treated as casually as old rags—perhaps that was all part of the cover. But the significance ran deeper than its nature.

Most significantly, he held it. He held it, knowing fully what it was, and at her behest. For someone so prone to distrust, so withdrawn and caught up in suspicion—

"Fuck," he cursed under his breath, aiming it at the ceiling. She'd worn him down bit by bit, only to save the most trenchant strike for last. After what she'd revealed today, he would suspect her of planning it as such if he didn't know how much of a trial any part of it must have been for her.

Tirdad tucked the girdle beneath on arm. Upstairs then. He scaled them slowly, deliberately, one after the other, and having worked out no part of what he intended to say. Talking from the cuff had never been his favoured saddle; he had long preferred to give his words due regard. She had taught him to speak his mind, so he would do just that.

He drew up short of the last step, having encountered her earlier than expected. Shkarag peered up at him from the landing, where she massaged the splinters lodged in her thigh. She wore her expectance plain and clear. The massage became a strangle.

"Shkarag," he began. She canted ever so slightly. For some unexplained reason, that rapt gaze instilled confidence. "What you said earlier, about needing to break some eggs to keep making omelettes for the person you love, I feel the same, and that's why we'll dispose of the body tonight." He sat on the uppermost step just shy of her outstretched foot and laid the girdle across his lap. "But you already knew that, or you wouldn't have given me your phylactery."

That inspired one of her crooked smiles, exposing her fangs where they curled back into her mouth, but only just. Rare as they were, she smiled more often in the months since her return than he had seen in all their years together. Contented smiles, not those inspired by bloodlust. He wanted more of that. Those uneven flashes were like seeing her surface, if only fleetingly, from a deluge of suffering. He had never been anyone special, never capable of genius or impressive feats, sentenced to obscurity or worse since birth. But that he could bring to her life these pockets of happiness—that was enough.

"Tirdad," she said.

"Yeah?"

"We're . . ." She stared through her foot, and the smile was fleeced away. "We're family," she said. "I think."

"We're family," he agreed. "The two of us."

"Not the goat-fucker."

Tirdad screwed up his face at the mention of the marzban. "If it weren't for Chobin, I probably wouldn't be here talking to you. He supported me when my House crumbled. Chobin is a dear friend, but you're family."

Shkarag inclined her head as if to nod, though Tirdad still couldn't discern a cant from a nod—if the latter ever happened. "Abarkawan," she stated.

"Abarkawan?"

"Abarkawan." Shkarag brought up a claw, sweeping it instead of flexing it by her head. "The land all splayed and sunbathing like some, like some lackadaisical viscera maybe, maybe a liver out there and—" She cocked her head. "Why in the, in the seven climates does a person crane at the šo-smoldering sun and think a bath is in order? Don't get, grasp, understand it one bit."

"Seven climes," Tirdad said.

She canted and went on. "And it's a liver maybe, and it's out there in the ocean, all drawn out for the, it has a long face over being out there, since livers don't fancy being outside of things, and there's a sea of blood around it, rippling and honest."

Tirdad had been following until the mention of honest blood. "Honest?"

Shkarag raked a claw over her scalp, tilting as she did. "Can't explain."

"So what about this viscera?"

"Abarkawan. It's there where the sea thins like alloyed blood."

"Oh," said Tirdad. "I'd forgotten about the island. Abarkawan, then. What of it?"

"We'll go," she said.

"Why?"

"To see your star-reckoner."

"My . . . what?" asked Tirdad, unable to hide his astonishment.

Shkarag deepened her cant. She clutched her thigh. "Can't stop you anymore. Tried something fierce to do the right thing for you. Can't anymore. We'll go to Abarkawan."

"You could've just kept that from me," said Tirdad.

"We're family," she said, as if that were explanation enough. "But you promise me this . . ."

Tirdad waited, beetle-browed, when she trailed off and stayed that way. She didn't seem to have retreated mentally. "Uh, Shkarag?"

"Promise me this," she repeated, insistent.

"I promise?"

"A promise," she confirmed. "When you catch these šo-damned answers, when you've got them draped over the back of your horse, a trophy to end all trophies, you hang it on your wall or wear it or festoon a thing. You hunt it, you seize it, and—" She leaned forward, muscles straining against her caftan as she grasped her thigh as if she wanted to pull it off. "—you fucking stop."

Tirdad meant to reply, but she edged closer, commanding the scene with her intense yet flickering gaze and the checked rage she emanated. "You." She leaned closer. "Fucking." Closer still. "Stop." She had her head even with her foot now, which in turn had it close enough that he could smell the egg on her heavy breaths.

"All right," he said. "You've got it. Once I've found my answers, I'll stop. And if I don't, you'll be there to set me straight. I'm leaving it up to you. I promise."

With that, she relaxed, sitting back and returning to her kneading. "Abarkawan is far," she said.

"Should we leave tomorrow?"

"Maybe. Maybe wait. Finish your apricots. Let your šo-woolen goat-fucking friend know. You wouldn't, wouldn't like to leave him blind. In the dark, maybe. The dark holds you close, smothers you, makes you feel safe, until—" She shivered, and swallowed audibly. "Maybe."

"Huh," said Tirdad.

She canted at him. ". . ."

"Strange."

". . ."

"You know, I was thinking. Here you're suggesting I stay true to my word, and that I wait for a friend whose wellbeing likely means as little to you as a bird."

" . . . "

"I figure it's a mighty thoughtful sentiment coming from a skink-slicker." He'd hardly finished the sentence when she leapt at him, bowling him over and taking him down the stairs in a tumble that could have killed them both.

Tirdad released a drawn out groan from the ground floor where he ended up on his back, which was none too happy, and sure to be furious come morning. Shkarag hissed, and crawled on top of him.

"You're the only one here with a phylactery," he said. "I'd rather not die to a flight of stairs."

"Oh." She threw a glance over her shoulder. "Can only lead a horse to a flight of stairs," she muttered.

"Yeah."

"Oh."

"Skink-slicker," quipped Tirdad, enjoying the wince it engendered in her.

"You're beating it," she said.

"What?"

"That horse. Not even a prized breed like those stallions from Nisaya." She sat up by his side, and posted on palm on his chest. The look she gave him was as enigmatic as any. "Your jokes are . . . they're like you."

"Like me?"

"Flat," she said.

"Thanks?"

"Your jokes, they're flat, steep as hot tea, but your jokes they're . . . they're the sort of company you don't mind. They're good company."

"Thanks." Tirdad meant it this time. No one had ever enjoyed his jokes before. Come to think of it, he hadn't even enjoyed them. He almost felt as if losing his social standing had been liberating in a way. Almost.

"Šo-good company," she added, crawling onto him, her shoulders rising and falling like a mighty beast, the telltale sawing taking purchase on every exhalation.

"Shkarag," he cut in with an uncomfortable grimace. "There's a dead man right behind us."

He should've known that wouldn't have had the desired effect. She sucked in a gasp. "There is," she hissed, and where she simmered before she was now ablaze.

"Shkarag, don't—" She shifted forward to reach for the star-reckoner, and the second thing that came to mind was that she had to be kidding him. The first was that he wished she'd be kind to his back. A meaty rip sounded from above, and she shifted back so that her blood-slathered face was above his.

"Still fresh," she slurred. "Still hot."

Tirdad opened his mouth to object when he realized he didn't actually mind. Somewhere along the line the vileness of her lineage had become commonplace. Beloved, even. So when it was his turn for her to smear the fresh blood over his face, he concentrated on its warmth, on the metallic smell that filled his nostrils as he sucked in a heady lungful. Whatever had changed in him when he took on a part of Ashtadukht reacted to her aura; it bred in him a fraction of what he saw in her. Crimson bled into his vision like paint through water. Without pretense, and without affording it a second thought, he gave her the adrenaline rush she yearned for. He slipped a dagger between her ribs.

• • • • •

Later, after downing his daily apricot, and together with Shkarag under the cover of night, he set out to dispose of the body. He regretted damaging her caftan with the knife, but she didn't seem the least bit bothered, so as he rode out of the city with a star-reckoner slung over his horse, he ruminated instead on the deed at hand. That called for a distraction, which Shkarag so blithely provided. Tirdad stared at the river, the celestial theatre mirrored on its surface, while Shkarag idly pointed out one constellation after another. She seemed livelier than normal, though she always named them with a hiss.

"The Lady of the Throne," she said, pointing and canting at him to ensure he was paying heed. "Those five there, the šo-bespeckled breasts."

"I see them," he replied. And he did with an intimacy she could not have known. They winked in close proximity to his soul.

"The Bearer of the Div's Head," she went on. "Don't see it. Do you see it?"

"No."

"The Snake Charmer," she said, indicating a misshapen polygon of stars with a satellite star at two corners. From where she rode ahead, backward in her saddle, he could just make out the poppy-red slivers she had trained on him. "That's your constellation," she explained.

"I suppose it is," he said, breaking a grin.

After hours of following the river downstream from the city, connecting star signs with star signs as if they weren't mortal enemies of everyone present—everyone alive anyway—they found what they were looking for: a marsh. Between its stench, the paucity of those willing to brave its depths, and the veil of reeds, they figured nature would have plenty of time to destroy the evidence. They bound the star-reckoner with ropes and used those to secure stones that would weigh him down. Then the pair dumped him, Tirdad wearing a scowl all the while.

Decomposing corpses bred more than just disease, they contaminated the land with the influence of the Lie, invited the corpse-feeding Nasu into the world, and seeded the power of divs. This was why dogs were made to follow corpses, for in their noses they carried the power to drive away the Nasu. Only then, and with a priest performing rites alongside, could a corpse be safely relocated without leaving a trail of contaminated earth.

A similar relationship existed between death and those left behind. It always arrived twofold. Taking the deceased was never enough. The loss of a single person could infect with grief the lives of many—even go as far as taking some of them. In that way, there is no respite, no attrition of misery: this is why suicide is selfish. Where one person's suffering comes to an end, their misery proliferates in the lives of those affected. Bereavement sinks its claws into hearts and minds. This is why there is rarely such a thing as a victimless death, and why Tirdad gave pause to needless murder. You're never running through a single innocent. You're running through everyone with whom they share a bond. You're turning that bond into a burden they must bear for the rest of their lives.

Ashtadukht, Tirdad, and Shkarag—they all carried such a burden. With Ashtadukht, a single death had cost the lives of thousands. With Tirdad, it took his family, his identity. What it took from Shkarag was anyone's guess, but there was no mistaking that it had deprived.

• • • • •

Tirdad hadn't forgotten his contract. He strove to take it as seriously as his cousin would have. He owed her memory that much. He owed the people of the city that much. With their resident star-reckoner perished by the hand of a daughter of Eshm, they had no one else to turn to. What's more, they were quick to accept the pair—even if they were unreasonably demanding and not all that grateful.

So he pored by day over the volumes and notes left by the star-reckoner, and though he learned a great deal a part of him already knew, there was no mention of these forty divs in particular. Or any similar situation.

By night, Shkarag would use her unique vision and proclivity for the twilight hours to lead him on scouting missions, all of which ended empty-handed.

Every dusk, he would count another apricot down the hatch, which would remind him he was another day closer to the arrival of the div host. Come every apricot, the same shuffling followed. It seemed to him to be growing in volume, as if it were anticipating the fortieth day, same as him. Here and there, he would check. He even posted Shkarag across the cisterns, but she reported no signs of activity.

The townspeople were equally befuddled. None had actually seen the divs, though each was full of wild ideas as to what horrid sensibilities the beasts must surely possess. Having seen an army of divs, and having shared the road with Ashtadukht, Tirdad knew the truth had the potential to give their imagination a run for its coin.

Every day the same thing. Search, apricot, scout. Search, apricot, scout. Search, apricot, scout. When there were but a few left in the jar, Tirdad had begun to consider running. Shkarag had squashed that the instant he brought it up—had brooked no argument. So when the final day arrived, Tirdad stood before the jar's sole apricot no more prepared than if he'd fought those forty divs upon arrival. He had his sword, his planet-reckoning, and Shkarag. He prayed that would be enough.

Tirdad downed the apricot and said, "That's forty down the hatch."

The mysterious shuffling answered as it always did. Only this time, it was different. It went on as if it had found its confidence; it grew in volume and intensity. Tirdad's palm came to tremble on the ram's head pommel. Shkarag retrieved her spear from where it leaned by the door, and leaned instead into it.

"Forty down the hatch," she confirmed.

Tirdad approached the door, through which he could sense the presence of divs, and caught wind of their reek besides. The bone-penetrating fear that had Tirdad in its grip until then was flushed out by adrenaline. He brandished his starling-black blade and shoved the door open. It complained on its hinges, then rapped against stone.

The shuffling ceased.

"Šo-wretched broom sweepers," Shkarag observed from his side.

Tirdad figured that was an accurate enough description. If he were going for something less pithy, he would have described each div as an assortment of animals and men run through ass-to-mouth by a broom and stacked one on top of the other. They were kebabs. Broom kebabs. The nearest spoke, and when it did, all its mouths moved in unison, some yapping or hissing, with the humans somehow getting words through long-rotted vocal cords. It did so in a foreign tongue like dragging an old broom over stone, but one he understood.

"Please spare us!" it swept. "We repent! We repent each and every one of us to He Who Devours Brooms!"

Shkarag emitted a giggle.

"The One Most Slithered!" it swept again, and the brooms all fell forward to prostrate before him.

"Please don't eat us," they swept as one. "We heard you were a redoubtable star-reckoner, so we visited you nightly to see what we were up against. One, then two, then three, each group coming back with the same story. That you could somehow see through our sorcery, and meant to eat us! Oh, how we repent!"

Tirdad skimmed confusion over the divs, all so much brooms and gore, and ended on Shkarag, whose face was drawn into a grimace that battled to hold back laughter. She grinned at him, broad and lopsided as ever, and he knew he'd been played for a fool.

"Shkarag."

". . ."

"Shkarag."

"After," she blurted, canting toward the brooms and shaking her spear at them. "After."

"All right," said Tirdad, shaking his head at her and addressing the crowd with the same authoritative voice Ashtadukht had so often employed. "As much as I'd anticipated devouring you all like—" He sighed, and threw an exasperated glance at Shkarag, "—like kebabs, I'm not above letting you free. But you must indenture yourselves to me, and leave humans to their peaceful lives."

"We'll do as you say!" swept the brooms. "We'll use our sorcery to hide! To keep alleys free of leaves! We'll never trouble another soul if you but sweep the terrible fate you had planned for us under the carpet!"

"Off with you then!" Tirdad roared. "Don't show your face—your bristles ever again!"

Without another sweep, the divs all winked out of sight.

"Wait," said Shkarag, having anticipated his question. Head askew and leaning into her spear, she pivoted around it, trained on empty space. Tirdad figured she could see the brooms, which meant she could see them all along. "Swept away," she said after following their departure for minutes. "Can rant now."

"I won't rant," he said and hadn't intended to. Whatever her prank, it had achieved the desired result. Curiosity drove him now. "Did you know this would happen all along? Is that why you insisted on the dried apricots?"

She pivoted back around to face him, leaning into her spear and making no attempt to hide just how pleased she was with herself. ". . ."

"Shkarag. What in the seven fucking climes were those divs? How much of this was a prank?"

The more he asked, the more buoyant her toenail-swallowing grin. Unable to suppress it any longer she laughed, unrestrained and full of a rare mirth, to the thump of her spear as she retreated into their home.

"Shkarag!" he shouted, following her in. "Come on!"

XIV

RAKHSH, THE MERCHANT WITH WHOM Tirdad and Shkarag had signed a contract, had been practically jumping for joy when they went to collect their due the next morning. Evidently, a few curious souls had seen fit to spectate, which meant the whole of the city had heard tell of the forty terrifying broom-divs and how Tirdad had sent them sweeping once and for all. That earned him a hefty reward and an invitation to settle in for the winter, which Tirdad declined. He had his sights on his next quarry.

The Gulf, too dense with brine and oppressed by heat to remind him of home, was almost nostalgic—almost. It misted him where he stood at the prow of a small single-mast merchant vessel, its lateen rig billowing just overhead, a crew of three idling by the steering apparatus at the aft.

A steady flow of boats passed in the other direction, all headed for one port or another to offload goods from the empire's booming maritime trade. The monsoon winds would be coming up from the southwest this time of year, which meant a return trip for the merchants who had set out with the favourable northeasterly winds months earlier. Why this particular merchant challenged the schedule was beyond him. But Tirdad was neither a sailor nor a merchant. Leave the experts to their trade, he figured.

The Gulf was nostalgic, he decided. The mist, the whiff of brine overpowering his nostrils, the distant coastlines, each with the childhood promise of adventure to be had: none of that brought him back. Shkarag retched over the starboard side. That did.

"I'll—urk," she spat at the water, convulsing and wiping her mouth on her sleeve. "Dourboat's swimming with the fishes and yet—hck."

It was so far removed that he had all but forgotten their first travels together. "You all right?" he asked, grinning. It reminded him of her pranks, too. "I can't believe you convinced me to eat an apricot a day just to trick those broom divs into thinking I'd seen through their invisibility and planned on eating them one by one."

Shkarag threw herself to the deck and leaned against the curtain, looking as if she were ready to vomit again any time now. "Land," she muttered. "Want to eat dirt."

"You got yourself into this," said Tirdad. He glanced back at the crew. They were giving her a wide berth, trying to act uninterested, and had only allowed Tirdad to join the voyage after he'd handed over the sack Rakhsh had given him.

"So how'd you know about this island?" he asked her. "Wait, no. Don't answer that. How'd you know one of the star-reckoners we seek would be here? This better not be another trick. It's too elaborate, if so. Sometimes brevity is best. And look what it's doing to you, why don't you?"

"Don't you—" Shkarag started, seeming offended, only to be cut off by a dry heave. "—urk. We're family. Told you we're family. If you want to, want to do a thing, family should be there, not run off like some—hrk—like some ترســـو"

"What?"

". . ." Shkarag stared past him, racked by a convulsion.

Tirdad had his hand on the ram's head pommel, keenly aware of the pull of the blade. "What'd you just say?"

"I . . . wrung it out of the star-fucker," she said. "Before you returned from—" She made a gesture as if she were twisting a wet rag between her hands. "I wrung it out of him something fierce. Kept carrying on about how he'd never talk, and that made me think what in the seven climates are you, your mouth parts are doing the thing. But I thought that's just as the crow flies and went to task."

"Seven climes," Tirdad corrected with a sigh. "If you're going to mock me at least get it right."

"Mocking?"

"Never mind. So you wrung it out of him. That simple?"

". . ." She canted.

"Well, that was thoughtful of you at any rate."

"Need to know where not to go."

"Oh, smart then. Not thoughtful."

Shkarag opened her mouth to speak when a dribble of bile seized the opportunity to gurgle out. She'd already emptied her stomach many times over, so it could hardly have been called a puddle. A hiss of a groan petered out after, and she summarily fell to one side to hide beneath her cloak.

"I suppose that's just as well," said Tirdad. "Get some rest." The words had hardly left his mouth when the sky lit up with lightning bright enough to force him to shield his eyes, and to cause Shkarag to cry out. It spread throughout clouds like ominous fissures over the core of a yazata. It singed the sky.

The clap of thunder it heralded was deafening. So awful was the sound Tirdad almost expected the world-ending dragon Gochihr to part the heavens. It was enough for him to check. That thunderclap stirred the Gulf into a frenzy. It threw a shadow so sudden and so dark that Tirdad saw fit to check the heavens again for Gochihr, drawing relief in the soot-coloured billows of stormclouds. Better them than the dragon.

That was all he managed to take in before the boat lurched, tossed on an especially vehement swell, and threw him to the deck. Tirdad hit it with a shout, the world all a blur beneath a sudden and torrential downpour. Before he could react, the boat canted to a sharp, slippery incline that slid him into the mast. He groaned, already soaked to the bone, and hugged the mast with everything he had. Somewhere in the back of his mind, between the unsettling complaints of wood and an ear-piercing scream, Tirdad sensed the telltale signs of star-reckoning—whatever they were. He just felt them.

Thunder swept over the measly vessel again, cruel and tyrannical, pinning him in place as much as the lurch of the ship. It had power, personality; he could have mistaken it for a roar. Over and over it broke his spirit, more blood-curdling than the rain-tended lulls left by a departing roar, and the agonized screams that occupied them.

Around him, the deckhands were doing their part in keeping the vessel afloat. Tirdad didn't know boats. He didn't know seafaring. He'd never been farther out than dinghies would take him on the Mazandaran Sea. He'd rushed into this voyage because it would get them there well before an approach by land. Now, he wished he'd followed the coast until a dinghy could ferry them across the strait occupied by the island.

He clutched the mast, lurching this way and that to an unabated scream, the steady hum of rain, and the piercing thunder that arrived with less and less frequency. Tirdad had no way of knowing just how long he toiled at the mercy of the storm. As far as he was concerned, it'd been hours.

When at last the thunder ceased and the sea calmed, it did not take the screaming with it. Tirdad put his feet beneath him, feeling utterly drained from struggling against the storm, clothes heavy with rain, and squinted across the deck to the stern where the merchant and his help had gathered.

"Shkarag?" he asked, turning a circle to scan for her. Had she fallen overboard? Could she even swim? "Shkarag," he shouted. "Where in the seven climes are you?"

"Over here," called one of the crewman. "Don'tcha hear her?"

"Oh," said Tirdad, hurrying over. Going on as long as it had, he'd assumed it was part of the storm. "Move," he snapped, shouldering between them and shoving one aside. "Get the fuck away!"

She was on her hands and knees, fingernails cracked and digging into the deck, muscles taut with what could only have been agony. He shivered. What he had mistaken for a scream was so much more. To call it a scream would have come up dismally short. It had substance; it smothered the air around him as if the aura of her bloodlust had turned against him. She went on without stopping for breath: shrill, grating, and constantly at the point of breaking. The deck began to splinter under the strength of her grasp. A plank exploded behind her.

"Shkarag?" he asked. "Shkarag, what's wrong?" He got to his knees beside her, and that's when he noticed the thin trail of blood that ran from her ear, which directed him to other such trails from her nose and mouth. "Shkarag?" he asked, anxiety tightening his throat. He took her by the head and raised it so she could see him and—

"Fuck!" he cried, falling on his back but scrambling to get his bearings immediately after. "What the fuck is happening?"

She gazed at him, still screaming, without the faintest flicker to a glare that was not her own. Her eyes were human now, one blind and the other an aged brown. Whoever it was, it saw him. It looked back.

Horror held him in its grip, a combination of the eyes, her unending scream, and an aura unlike anything he'd ever experienced. For a moment, it seemed as if everyone and everything were out to get him, as if the stars themselves conspired to cut him down. His thoughts came all at once, demanding he sort through the clutter. The world tilted without him. He angled his head to compensate, but that only gave the things that did not belong free rein to do as they pleased. He couldn't place what exactly—maybe it was everything. Maybe. His surroundings were off. So, too, was his place in them. He angled again. There were thoughts like faces in the dark reaches of the world into which his mind saw fit to leak. Everything was related, connected. Briefly, in that torrent there prevailed a view of reality unencumbered by perception—one distorted instead by patches of long-sown thoughts where there should have been clouds or sea or boat. They appeared to him as unnatural and unknown as a twilight mirage. And in those mirages, two scenes were locked in combat, flickering between one and the other as if the world could not decide what it wanted to be.

Directly ahead, there was Shkarag. Only she wore the trappings of a div twice her size, flesh and scale charred and bubbling, a starling black mantle thrown against her in a wind he could not feel. She screeched. Tirdad knew then that she had plotted his demise from the very beginning. That she was his sworn enemy. Without another thought, he unsheathed his dagger, and without giving his actions due consideration, plunged it into her skull.

The screeching stopped. The aura disappeared. The world sloughed its indecision. Everything returned to normal. Shkarag collapsed to the deck. Tirdad fell to his knees beside her.

"I'm sorry," he whispered as he tugged his dagger free. Whatever had come over him was beyond explanation, and he was too drained to give it much thought. The deckhands were edging closer as if they were Nasu trying to get at a corpse.

"You . . . the div is dead," said the merchant. "You killed it."

"Give us some space," said Tirdad, an edge to his delivery. When they didn't oblige, he brandished his dagger at the nearest. "Now. Or you're next." That did the trick.

He eased her head into his lap and stared, waiting blank and silent to the slosh of water against hull. The boat rocked lazily, uncanny in how far-removed it was from the tempest they had endured. The sun cast a pleasant warmth over his back. He stroked the ruts of her scalp, where another would soon take shape after the wound had healed.

Hardly a minute had passed before she woke up. Tirdad took solace in the way her pupils contracted to slits, blood-red advancing on and driving out the abyss, to flutter over his shoulder.

"That smarted," she said, inscrutable as ever. "That smarted something fierce."

"Forgive me?" asked Tirdad. "Something came over me and I just lashed out. I really don't know—"

"Not that. Not the, not that." She flexed a claw by her head. "The star-fucker."

"I stabbed you in the head."

Shkarag canted. "Asked you to."

"Asked?"

". . ." She looked away. "Thank you."

Tirdad screwed up his face at that. Shkarag did not typically show gratitude—not in the conventional manner. And he had buried a knife in her brain.

"Star-fucker wanted me to rip this šo-damned boat to splinters and scatter your organs across kingdoms. I would—" She convulsed, and brine streaked with leftover blood bubbled up. Shkarag spat it to the side and sat up. "Urk. I would've. Couldn't hold out much longer. Dagger did me in."

"This star-reckoner, he was controlling you?"

"Maybe," she said. Shkarag seemed as if she had more to say, but she left it at that.

"Well, fuck me with a fishing rod." Tirdad turned a frown on the island, and scratched the side of his head, only to find the itch was on the inside. The island's rocky outcroppings watched the strait that defended the only access to the Gulf. From those far off cliffs a star-reckoner had made the first move. Had ruled out the possibility of negotiation. Until now, Tirdad had wanted answers. Now he wanted answers and violence.

"She's strong," said Shkarag. "Others have tried, but . . . she's strong."

Tirdad's frown deepened at that, but the thought of a challenge had a certain allure. "How do we stop her from controlling you?"

"Not controlling." Shkarag flexed a claw by her head. "Divs are, divs are, she wasn't controlling. Star-fucker was . . ." Shkarag took a moment to find the word, and finished with, "Liberating."

"Liberating?"

Shkarag angled her head away, but kept her eyes on and around him. "Casting off shackles and chains. You don't want that."

"Well—"

"I don't want that."

"Well, you've never been one for restraint, so these shackles and chains must not be worth much."

Shkarag seemed anything but amused. She put her boots beneath her and limped past the crew to the bow, convulsing twice along the way. Tirdad followed suit, drawing up behind her where she stared out at the island.

"She's still in there," said Shkarag. She ran her fingers along the latest scar. "In here. You're still in here. Like snakes in honey."

"Snakes in honey?"

". . ."

"Not familiar with that idiom," said Tirdad. He contemplated the island, wondering how ready this star-reckoner would be for their approach, and whether to expect another lot thrown their way before making landfall.

"Snakes in honey," reiterated Shkarag, trying to impress upon him the importance of the phrase with her tone.

Meanwhile, Tirdad wondered why Abarkawan appeared to him to have changed expressions. He'd caught the island off guard, and now it didn't know whether to maintain its ruse or do away with the pretense. What he did know, looking on as it shifted from friendly to conniving and back again, was that he had been here before. Like some, like some—

Scenery passed in a blur, like a gale through his senses, with him oblivious to its significance, bearing, or that it was passing at all. Only a faraway feeling reached him.

"Like some long-dormant memory," he blurted out. "Biding its time and—"

". . ."

"Oh? I see." Having said that, Tirdad didn't. All he realized was that he was no longer standing by the prow of the boat. A scant few scenes like plaster murals connected their disembarkation to a mangrove forest to this place. "Huh?"

". . ." Shkarag turned around to stare in his direction.

He looked beyond the impatience aimed his way to the shaft of light that gleamed overhead, squinting and shielding his eyes until they adjusted. Only after he limned its edges for a moment did he see it for what it was: the height of fissure. Tirdad drew his gaze down, and found himself at the bottom of a narrow rut that ran between porous, pock-marked sandstone.

"Where—what—how did we get here?" he sputtered, peering into the recesses that littered the rock face. It felt as if he were traversing the inside of a hive. His breathing quickened; he could hear it in his skull. "Shkarag, what just happened? We were on the boat, headed for the island, and I was thinking—"

"Stop thinking," she cut in, gingerly and with a knowing stare. "It's . . . it'll be over soon." Her lips formed what was likely a withheld 'maybe'.

How could he stop thinking? Tirdad turned a circle, trying to recall how he'd gotten from the boat to wherever this was. Even now, select recesses were making themselves unknown. "What the fuck is going on?" he asked, thick with desperation.

273

Shkarag snatched his wrist and pulled him farther into the fissure. "Happens," she said. "Not to you. Shouldn't to you. Star-fucker is, šo-wretched star-fucker is still in here." She threw one of her inexplicable looks back at him and added, "I'm cross with you. And you're a weakling."

"What?"

Shkarag pressed on, leading him effortlessly even when he lost his footing. "Cross with you," she repeated, punctuated by the clack of her spear against stone.

Tirdad was growing more and more frustrated with the situation, and her obtuse answers weren't making it any better. One minute he was standing by the rig of a merchant vessel, the next he was being dragged through the depths of a fissure. "I—"

"—should've taken the direct route," he mused aloud. "Going to sprain an ankle at this rate." The sky was dark and busy with the din of the luminaries. He could feel the planets revolve and riposte. His bones were anchors, his muscles seaweed, his organs inhospitable islands. He leaned against the nearest recess for a breather, boring into its tenebrous depths as he did.

"Tortoise-sodomizing woman had to hole up all the way out here," he complained, light in its feminine carriage but heavy in spirit. Another of Ashtadukht's memories, he half realized, to the familiar sensation of riding a dream. Like a dream, the realization was fleeting. "There's nothing romantic about hermits. Just inconvenient. I swear, brother, if I ever become a—"

He clammed up. Briefly, brittly, he held out. The grief, only months old, was swift and indefatigable. It conquered him. Sorrow, fury, guilt: these were the currents of bereavement that raged through him. Gushnasp was lost. Forever.

He threw a fist at the sandstone. That hurt, but not enough. Tirdad didn't let up. Not even to the crack of bone, or to the barbarous fire that dominated his arm. He went on until he could no longer form a fist. Until his hand fell limp by his side, and instead of sliding down the rock face, he fell into it. Half-standing, he bawled into the stone.

"Come back . . ." he uttered, comprehensible only to himself. "Come back. I'll do anything. I'll do anything."

One hand trembling and useless, he used the other to fish a small packet out of his tunic. He hadn't the faintest idea where he'd gotten it, only that the person had told him it would make everything go away.

"I want everything to go away," he said, as if reaching out to try and shape the world to his desire. "Gushnasp is alive. I didn't kill him." He'd seen the drug time and again during a childhood spent by his father's side in one encampment or another. Administering it was as simple as swallowing. So he did just that.

It was bitter—magnitudes worse than wormwood. He gagged and would've vomited it back up if he weren't so hopeful it would save him. "I miss father," he said to himself, wishing he could just while away his days in the warmth and smell of leather that came with every hug shared with the man. Then the drug set in.

His thoughts thinned, became miasma. He forgot his grief; he forgot he had reason to grieve. He just forgot. Tirdad stumbled the way he'd been headed purely by chance, not knowing why and not questioning it either. The stone was smooth under his fingers; his trousers and tunic were still soaked from the mangrove forest he'd waded through to get here. The sensations reached him, but not their significance. Tirdad could have stumbled like that for hours for all he knew. He just went.

At some point, he fell. Rather, he found himself on the ground. How he got there was anyone's guess, but a reasonable explanation would have been that a fall played a part in it. He made to right himself with the wrong hand. He was on the ground again. Maybe he'd fallen. Probably, the stone had dragged him down. He wasn't frustrated. He wasn't anything. He only existed outside his head. And he was stuck in it.

There arrived a warbling like songbirds held underwater. With it, a figure. He squinted, but not at it. That would have required a more lucid squint. Still, he squinted. The warbling went on, those passerine fighting for air beak and wing, and eventually succumbing to a grim fate. Then he was flying—and how! He soared. He would have been exuberant if he had it in him. Instead, he looked from one thing to another, each only a thing.

The procession of the night cannot take place unobserved. So when the miasma began to recede, Tirdad merely found himself further along the celestial equator. The planets always seemed to be the first to harangue him in the morning—well before drowsiness took purchase. Coming out of a high turned out to be no different. Their battles, their weapons tinkling like cosmic wind chimes, bid him good evening. Then a tended silence filled their egress, ushered them out hurriedly. He wasn't alone.

Tirdad opened his eyes, and wished he hadn't. The headache that often assailed him come dawn redoubled its efforts. His body complained like it had never complained before. The worst part was that he remembered. He found himself wanting more.

"You are awake," said the caretaker of that tended silence, throwing her garden to the wayside. The voice had an unusually high pitch for how rough it sounded. "That was foolish. You are a damn fool. If I had not sensed your presence like a stink come to sully my refuge you might have gotten yourself killed out there."

"Myrod?" he asked, blinking against the drug's lingering daze.

"The same. You stink. I swear, if Mehr-farr got you into fucking divs I am going to have to come out of hiding."

"Fucking . . . divs?" Tirdad groaned, and it finally came to him that the light at the bottom of his vision was from an oil lamp. He was staring at the ceiling. He struggled to sit up, which called for a prolonged hiss when he posted on the wrong hand.

"I did what I could for your injury. Not much, frankly. It may hound you for the rest of your life. Try not to go around punching divs in the future. You will regret it."

Tirdad made a second attempt at getting up, careful for his—he looked, and that drew a grimace—mangled hand this time around. Across an empty room clammy from its environment there sat what appeared to be a woman, betrayed only by the shadows light revealed along her jaw. She was better-looking than he'd expected, especially the sheen like polished obsidian to her hair. He wished he had hair like that.

"Beautiful," he thought aloud.

That inspired a tempered smile. "Well, that is a first," said Myrod. "Cannot say anyone has ever been so desperate as to call me beautiful. But I assure you, flattery will not get you far here. Now," she crossed both her legs and her arms, "why are you here, and how did you find me?"

Right. He had come for a reason. Not just any reason: the only reason that mattered. He reached for his pack, only to find it wasn't there.

"By the door," said Myrod. She'd uncrossed her arms as soon as she'd crossed them. Now, she nursed a wineskin.

Tirdad stumbled over, still uneasy on his feet, and fished around with his good hand for a roll of documents. "These," he said once he found them. "These—"

"Actually, tell me how you found me first."

"The wine."

Myrod leered at her wineskin. "What about it?"

"Bazrang wine. It's your favorite." He made to fidget with his cuff, only to remember his injury too late. A tense outbreath hissed through his teeth. The other cuff then. "You only drink Bazrang. Refuse to drink even Babylonian. When you disappeared, so too did your orders. You knew better than to have them sent directly to the island, so you had them routed along the coast. Made an arrangement with the local fishermen and pearl divers for drop locations all around the Gulf."

"There are many drop locations. Even on the island."

"I really need to talk to you. Can we just—" He held out the documents. "Can we please just talk?"

Myrod's stare hardened. "Have you told anyone about this?"

"No one." Tirdad swallowed. The quiet spoke for itself.

"That was stupid," Myrod said at length. "Do not be so stupid in the future. How you can manage to find me and be so fucking stupid is baffling."

Tirdad had been holding his breath since his reply, and only then allowed himself to breathe.

"So," she asked evenly, "why have you sought out a person who obviously wants to be left alone?"

"I . . ." Tirdad kneaded anxiety into his cuff. He averted his gaze, hoping the dim light would obscure those few tears he couldn't fight back. "You know what they did to me. They're responsible for Gushnasp's—" He swallowed a gasp of a sob, and had to pause to hold it back. "You know they're to blame."

"So?"

"What do you mean by that?" Tirdad growled. The anger that washed over him evaporated his gloom as swiftly as a drop of water in the Lut. "What do you mean 'so'?"

"Speak to me like that again," Myrod replied in a tone as deadly as the worst of threats.

Tirdad bit his tongue, and the chill that swept over his skin was quick to disarm his anger.

"Good. Now, I ask again: So?"

He held out the sheaf. "I connected the way stations, the trades and missives, the code. You disappeared right after I was taken on as an apprentice. You wanted no part of it. Everyone says you're the most powerful star-reckoner of our time. The most accomplished. If you speak up, they'll have to listen. You could challenge them, bring their crimes to justice."

"You assume much."

"The King of Kings would believe you," he pressed.

"You assume much in coming here. Principally, young Ashtadukht, that I would leave my refuge behind for your grudge. Stupid again to allow these romantic dreams of justice to guide you here. You cannot afford to continue this stupidity."

Tirdad opened his mouth, none too pleased with the constant berating, but Myrod's raised palm saw to that.

"In this, you are stupid. You need to do more than hear it; you need to listen."

Crestfallen, he contemplated his dirty boots. He'd staked everything on this quest. Without the support of someone like Myrod, no one would listen. She'd often run aground of one star-reckoner or another due to her unconventional nature. Still, they respected her each and every one, because she was powerful. He heard she once drew five lots in a single day. Went toe to toe with a forty-armed div and survived. Alone.

"You are also stupid," Myrod went on, "to think I could simply emerge from my hole and ruin the reputation of a score of influential star-reckoners. Their power is not mine. They deal in intrigue, in politics, in the prosperity of the Houses."

"But—"

"No."

"Please, just—"

"No. Do yourself a favor and avoid being such a stupid child in the future. You cannot afford that. Neither in your quest or our profession."

"You're a fucking coward," he spat. "A toenail-swallowing coward. A fucking—" Where the room was comfortably bare a heartbeat earlier, the stars bore down on him as if their orbits had brought them in, crowding him in blinding, suffocating divinity. The pressure on his chest was such that he couldn't suck in the slightest breath. He tried to apologize, but that emerged as a whine that cracked half-way through.

"Leave," said Myrod. Her tone was beyond threatening now. She was in the middle of following through. "I will not relent."

Determined, Tirdad matched her stare. His chest soon began to burn; his vision blurred. But he refused to back down. He had come all this way to seek her aid, and he would not be turned away so casually.

"Leave," she bade him. "Once through the threshold you can breathe again."

He didn't so much as glance at the exit. He did, however, swell with pride at the surprise she wore. That's right. He wasn't about to go any—

Tirdad woke up to the sound of a door slamming.

"Good luck," called Myrod. "Try to be less stupid." A pause. "Oh, and never fucking return."

"I'll fucking kill you!" he shouted. "I'll kill each and every one of you menstrual-bathing fucks!"

Ashtadukht's memory didn't evacuate as it had before. Parts of it hung around like smudges on his senses—splotches of night imposed upon day, furious faraway screams joined the celestial theatre.

Shkarag hovered over him, leaning into her spear and looking as if she had been doing so for some time now. ". . ."

"A memory," he explained. "Ashta, she came here and . . ." He remembered her desperation. How she tried to hide it behind anger. How anger was not sustainable, always sputtering through the last of its fuel before capitulating to thoughts of joining her brother in death. A thirst for revenge would always keep her on the precipice, which was crueller than if she had gone through with it. By its nature, that tenuous footing maintained her yearning while never fulfilling it. Only her rites had.

"Cry later," Shkarag said, unusually brusque. "We're here."

"Here?" Tirdad tucked his chin to his chest. Just ahead there waited an adobe house half-carved from a cliff. One he recognized. "Oh." He wiped his face on his sleeve, feeling embarrassed and more than a little guilty.

"Ashta was here," he said. "She visited a woman she called the most powerful of star-reckoners."

"She's strong," Shkarag confirmed, brusque as before.

"What do you suggest we do?"

"Kill her."

"Shkarag, look. I—"

"Later." She jabbed her spear in the direction of the building.

"Right." Tirdad made a futile attempt at wiping the brushstrokes of night from his vision, and approached the door. The starling-black blade was strident in its call to be freed. Whatever was left of Ashtadukht in her aborted phylactery, he felt it now more than ever. He wanted to bellow a heartbroken, mad-at-the-world scream same as she had been doing since the memory receded, out there alongside the planets where they orbited the furthest reaches of his hearing. He drew the sword instead.

Shkarag inserted her spear between him and the door, leaning into it as she leaned it in front of him. "Tirdad, d—" The remainder came out as a strained croak, which threw her into a rage. She smashed through the door, hissing wildly.

Tirdad chased her in, ready to draw a lot or put the blade to work, only to end up confused by the scene. The interior was just as he remembered it: bare but for a table and the woman across the room. Where it differed was in more than her advanced age.

Myrod was slumped over, head balding and crooked between one shoulder and the floor.

"I do not know what is more disconcerting," rang a voice in his head. "Seeing myself secondhand, or what you see now."

"Myrod?" he asked, squinting and edging forward.

"Only in your head. I assure you, I am harmless at present. You would not be strolling so blithely around my territory if not." Her timbre had changed considerably since the memory, grown gravelly in its high pitch.

Tirdad didn't trust her. He didn't have that luxury when dealing with a star-reckoner, especially not this one. "Why're you in my head?" he inquired, sword leveled at her body, though he held no illusions as to how vain it would have been to try and close the distance. "Was the storm your doing?"

There came to him something akin to a disembodied nod. "The story of Ashtadukht's demise reached me only recently. And when her reek, foul and with a puissance that rivaled my own, advanced on my home, I—" She simpered, patently amused by the irony of her blunder. "—I acted in stupidity."

"Well, I won't argue with that. Mighty fucking stupid."

"Watch how you address me or . . ." Her voice trailed off, and that self-deprecating simper returned. "Even a daughter of Eshm should not have mounted such resistance. Unexpected. Her mind is a treacherous one. Still, I would have prevailed had she not invited you in. Now that was unforeseen. And truly cunning. Divs always put up a fight, you see, which may as well be struggling in quicksand. Oh, she fought like the best of them. But in that, she saddled the lot. Used my point of entry to let you in. From there, it was natural that someone like yourself with a weaker mind would succumb to her will. Frankly, I am impressed enough that it dampens the loss of my life. Always worried I would depart in my sleep."

"Weaker mind? Listen here, you fucking—hold on. Loss of your life?"

"That is what happens when you are stupid."

Cautiously, Tirdad crossed the room to stand over the body. It stunk of feces and piss, though that didn't faze him. Not after all the times Shkarag had died in his arms. "You're dead," he said, nudging the corpse. "And yet you speak."

"That is what happens when a man in a craze uses the skull of the div you have possessed as a scabbard. I am stuck; the three of us are . . . crossed, as the Eshm sister put it."

"Can you hear this, Shkarag?" He looked from the body, thinking she'd left until he noticed her sitting against a wall, leg out, and kneading.

" . . ."

"Shkarag?"

"Maybe," she grumbled.

"I am not one for chatter," Myrod piped up, "but I must press on. This will only last until my soul has departed. What have you come for? Justice for my standing idly by when your cousin needed me? To punish me on her behalf? I would not blame you. Since the day I learned the truth of her path, I knew I was as much to blame in not acting as those who had."

Tirdad frowned at that, beetle-browed and chin creased with the onset of guilt. He was perhaps the most to blame. He had turned her away from the stability of her rites; he had run her through. "We came seeking answers," he muttered, feeling as if it didn't matter. She was gone for all eternity, and he could never make amends for his part in that.

"Go on."

"The conspiracy against her." He stared through the dusty carpet at his feet. The memory from earlier still smarted something fierce. Even now, Ashtadukht's cries hounded him. Her morbid fancies of plummeting from cliffs or being torn apart by divs were suggestions worth entertaining. All the disparaging things she called herself. She had thought herself worthless, scum, unwanted, unlovable, hideous, undeserving of her title.

That struck him keener than any of it. She had always seemed so proud, always standing tall and wearing her role of star-reckoner for the achievement he had always believed it to be. A mask she wore for herself as much as anyone else.

"You have it wrong," said Myrod, interrupting his spiraling depression. "There was never a conspiracy against her. What use would there be in that? The conspiracy was meant to bring down the whole of your House. In that, I suppose it did."

"My . . . House?"

"Several other houses wanted yours gone. The why never really concerned me, to be honest. Whatever the reason, Ashtadukht was a convenient tool for those loyal star-reckoners. And cause to find myself a less deplorable circle to run in." Myrod let that fall to a moment of deliberative silence. "I did try to show them the error of their ways. That they were ruining that poor girl's life. Politics were never my strength, however, and that is all they paid heed to."

As it had so many times with Ashtadukht, anger quelled his melancholy. What was saturnine became white-hot. He growled, which transitioned to a shout of rage. "Fuck!" Tirdad paced around the house, fuming and kicking at the single table stationed at the far end. "Fuck!" he bellowed. "Fucking menstrual-swallowing cowards!"

After a few such circuits he addressed her again. "Who?" he demanded, still utterly incensed. "Which Houses are responsible?"

"All of them. Mainly that of the second House."

"Then I'll fucking, I'll rip their livers from their guts and—" The second House. Chobin. Chobin didn't just belong to the second House, he was the son of its patriarch. All this time. For the last decade, Tirdad had been played for a fool. They were probably in some pavilion laughing at him behind his back—they had been all along.

"Chobin," he breathed, seething. It's no wonder the marzban had been so eager to take him in. Though their Houses' territories shared borders, the two had never really been close. There was, after all, a gap in age and standing. Not to mention the fact that Tirdad had been out adventuring with Ashtadukht well before Chobin was conceived. So it should have come as more of a surprise when the marzban invited Tirdad into his inner circle. In trying times, a friend —or someone posing as a friend— was not given second thought.

He faced Shkarag, eyes narrowed. "Did you know about this?"

". . ." She ignored him, focusing instead on her kneading.

Tirdad took a step forward. He felt like flying into a rage. Exploding. That bled into his delivery. "Did you fucking know?"

Shkarag craned to cant at the upended table. "No," she flatly replied.

Those straight answers, elusive as they were, always threw Tirdad off as sure as a lariat yanking his feet from under him. He grimaced, and occupied himself with stowing his sword. "Sorry. You have a habit of keeping these—" That wouldn't go anywhere enviable. "Just, uh, sorry."

"Goat-fucker tread on you," she said. "Tread on you like some, like some crook going around snatching pillows, and you were using those to sit to the right of the, to the, like some vineyard stomping your grapes, and you're thinking I'm into this or that, wouldn't be all that ruffled by a wallop or stropped-iron handshake, but the stomping can go for a saunter on a salt flat." She swiped the axe he'd given her from its holster and gave it a spin. "I'll lob his head clean off." She set hers askew. "Not clean. A šo-messy cleaving, all scorching-hot and—" She sucked in a breath as tremulous as it was wanting.

"Some company you keep," said Myrod. "Now what is she doing? Cease that at once!"

Tirdad watched with indifference as Shkarag limped over and set to hacking at the star-reckoner's corpse. "You're already dead," he reminded her.

"That is not the point. She is desecrating my body."

"I think you saw to that when you shit your trousers."

"Fair point," Myrod conceded. "What do you plan to do now?"

Tirdad trailed his fingers through his hair, blinking against the splotches of night that bridged his vision with that of Ashtadukht's memory, as if the starry sky had somehow done to his eyes what staring into the sun would have gotten him. "They destroyed my family, brought all so much ruin to our lives. Left us destitute. Broke Ashtadukht. All those thousands who fell to her invasion have the second House to thank for it. Then there's Chobin. I thought we were friends. More than that."

"He would not have been born when their ruse was set in motion," reasoned Myrod. "Perhaps he was none the wiser."

"Perhaps," Tirdad surrendered, though he didn't believe it. "What would you do?"

Myrod emitted another of her simpers. "You are looking at it."

"You would have me run and hide?"

"I would not have you do anything. I have said my piece, and am merely entertaining your questions until we are free of one another. Besides, should you not be asking that of the half-div?"

At that, Shkarag cocked her head to regard at him out of the corner of her eye.

"Well?" he asked. "What should I do, Shkarag?"

"You fucking stop." As caustic as it came out, hiss and all, the ease with which she lowered her axe flagged her surrender. "Would like šo-rousing adventures, crossing to and fro, hither and thither, unconcerned with—" She lifted her axe as if for another chop, but suspended it above her head.

"Not worried about this vendetta or that feud. Used to travel all over with, with Waaaaaaaaray. Think you—" She brought her axe down, cleaving through the star-reckoner's neck. There wasn't much blood, which is likely what inspired her pursed lips and furrowed brow. "Left out too long," she said, reaching down to dab a finger with a taste of blood. "Out too long," she affirmed. "Think you might be company worth spelunking with."

Tirdad continued to watch as she wiped her axe on Myrod's robe. Despite her claims to the contrary, it seemed to him she always went for the axe he'd given her as her first choice—whether oiling, sharpening, chopping, or fighting.

He had also given her his word. As incensed as it made him to think about the conspiracy, Tirdad would be a fool to pursue it against her will. While he had forsaken honour, he had not forsaken their bond. Pursuit would mean disregarding his promise and the trust she had placed in it. There was also the prospect of venturing into the unknown by her side, which had an allure all its own. Most of all, she had invited him to take the place of her sister. Not in so many words, but she had at least in part. If they could shore up one another by filling the hollows left by loss, who was he to argue?

"All right," he said. "I've my answer, and I won't break the promise I made to stop. Otherwise, they're meaningless." He shifted subconsciously to open a path toward the door, and withdrew his hand from the ram's head pommel. The blade had been constantly urging him to run the star-reckoner through. More than that, he noted. The exact nature was uncertain, but its urges had become either demands or pleas. "We can venture as far east as the lands of the Chini if you like. You've no doubt travelled far and wide in your years, so I'm leaving our destination up to your experience."

Tirdad sighed. There, he had acquiesced. It hurt more than he thought it would. He felt as if he were betraying Ashtadukht, dismissing all she had endured and lost at the hands of star-reckoners and grandees. All so they could expand their influence, seize another House's dominion. She deserved better; they deserved death. Would that he could give her some justice. A part of him realized he was clinging as she had to the past, unable to release himself from his mistakes or those responsible for their transgressions. That realization was more than she had ever managed as far as he could tell. Tirdad couldn't decide whether he was honouring her death by turning away from her mistakes or desecrating her ossuary by ignoring why she'd made them.

Shkarag saved him the trouble. During his rumination, she had taken up a position by his side, spear bearing her weight with one hand while the other rested on her favoured axe. Had she always done that? Her habitually neutral expression warmed into a short-lived grin that tapered soon after, as if she'd come to a sudden, sobering realization. She aimed her half-smile instead at the ceiling, and reached up to rub his back.

"Had me . . ." she began. "Took me to a clearing all surrounded by worry something fierce. Know it smarts to lose. You're, you're turning your back on her . . . for me. Don't know that I could if it were my šo-beloved sister."

"Yeah," said Tirdad.

The irregular circles she pressed into his back were reassuring, and adamant enough in that reassurance that they almost pushed him forward. "Just wanted to hear you say it," she said. "To know you can. And . . . that you care."

"Yeah," said Tirdad.

"We'll see your goat-fucker," she said, sounding as though she'd reached the conclusion after much consideration.

Tirdad trained a brow knotted with bewilderment on Shkarag. She still watched the ceiling, tilted and pensive. "Why?" he asked.

"You must think I'm some, some šo-indecisive šo-impossible . . ." She trailed off, and dropped her hand, inserting a few steps between them. "I'm those things and worse."

"And worse," Tirdad agreed, endeavouring to sew some levity into his tone. That emboldened in her the traces of a smile, guarded as it was.

"Maybe," she confirmed, still studying the ceiling with her darting stare. "Know it'll gnaw at you. Don't want you to resent me for it. We'll confront the goat-fucker. Catch him testicles-deep in mutton, and he'll be bucking and rutting and we'll give him another cleft to swoon over. Just—" She angled her head away, but leveled her fluttering gaze on him. "Had to be sure you'd stop. That you wouldn't become her."

Tirdad nodded. He knew all too well her meaning and admitted to having felt the pull of whatever was left of Ashtadukht to continue her legacy. "I understand. I'm grateful, Shkarag. That you're here to prevent me from falling into her footsteps."

She mouthed something unintelligible to herself, focusing now on his scabbard. "Maybe," she said. This time it was as unreadable as they came.

"Chobin must be a goat after all," Tirdad mused. Shkarag canted, but didn't raise her eyes. "Because we're going to have him drawn and quartered." When she showed no signs of responding, he added, "Because you can't eat it until it's four."

That inspired a distracted smile.

"After, we'll travel to your heart's content. Until my years are numbered if you so please."

Shkarag reached back to retrieve a sizable egg from her pouch, and bit into it without a care for the yolk that oozed between her fingers, down her palm, over her cuff, and to the floor. Before it could drain entirely, she stuffed the rest into her mouth.

"Are we not going to discuss how she just chopped my head off right in front of me?" asked Myrod.

XV

THE RETURN TO PORT HAD none of the perils the way out had. Myrod had faded shortly after setting sail, but for much of the ride, Tirdad felt as if he were living two lives. Like his late cousin, Ashtadukht's memories were faint yet intransigent. The blotches wherein her experiences imposed upon the present hounded and confused him. To make matters worse, he felt threatened. Endangered. By what, was beyond him. He made connections where before there had been only passing acquaintances. The celestial theatre became the celestial theatres. Each vied for the right angle. Tirdad wasn't certain what the right angle was, only that it was not ninety degrees. That crook had gotten him nowhere. It overwhelmed him such that he spent the ride huddled in his cloak, focused, when he could manage, on the sloshing of waves against the hull. Fortunately, that too had faded before the ship moored to port.

"They're headed east," he said, emerging from the port garrison to find Shkarag leaning into her spear. "Let's retrieve our horses and perhaps we can intercept them along—" He blinked, peering incredulously over her shoulder. "—the way."

A familiar face had caught his attention. Damned familiar. He swallowed, and steeled himself as the face left the crowd to approach him.

"Cousin," he said.

"Some nerve showing your div-fucking mug around here," spat the woman from where she drew up in front of him. The thick layer of soot and grime that clung to her skin made her almost unrecognizable. She had eyes heavy with enmity and laden with bags, clothes so tattered they had lost all semblance of what they once were. She seemed to him a completely different person than when she'd strut around the estate, chin held high and wearing the finest accoutrements. This was his first time seeing her since. "Some fucking nerve."

"I'm . . ." Tirdad swallowed, and worked unease into the ram's head pommel. "This isn't our land."

"Nowhere is!" she shouted. "Nowhere is! Because of you and that div-fucking Ashtadukht! Everyone knew you were born under an ill-fated sky. They should have cut your throats at birth! You have brought ruin to us all!"

She lifted her hand as if to hit him, at which point Shkarag cut in with a deft movement to snatch her wrist and press an axe to her throat.

"Don't kill her," said Tirdad. He frowned at the dagger his cousin held in her upraised fist. "She has good reason to despise me." Shkarag hissed at that, but acquiesced. Instead, she availed the woman of her dagger by wrenching her wrist until she dropped it. "I'm sorry," he said. "I . . ." There was nothing he could say. She would not forgive him, and he did not care. Not anymore. "Don't try that again, or I'll let her have her way with you."

With that, he left for their horses. That was why they'd returned to this port, after all. Tirdad would not leave behind such a prized stallion, even if it turned out that Chobin had a hand in the plot. After the sounds of scuffling and a shout, Shkarag caught up to limp in step with him.

"What'd you do?" he asked.

"Sprinkled rosewater on the battlefield like some, li—" She cut the head off the snake, demonstrating a discretion he'd come to recognize more and more. "Here," she said, offering an egg.

Tirdad cracked it open and swallowed the contents without a second thought. It no longer disgusted him; instead, it'd grown comforting. Whether by virtue of her giving it to him, or the intended effect having sunken in, was anyone's guess.

The trip for supplies and an extra winter cloak was a quiet one. Tirdad wasn't sure what to make of the last few days. It wasn't until they were well on their way that he had found the right questions to which he would seek answers.

Rather than a circuitous course through the marshes to the north, the pair had taken an easterly route along the shore. This afforded them a less nauseating view of the Gulf's glinting waters and busy lanes.

"The King of Kings is dead," he said, meaning to strike up conversation to lead to his question.

". . ."

"Yeah, I don't feel all that bothered by it either. Only heard of it from the garrison, so they must want to keep it quiet until the war is over. King or no king, most of us would go on living same as before."

"Crown-baster will be forgotten. Annals will crumble like so many sweetmeats."

Tirdad nodded. "You'd know, I suppose. The heir apparent doesn't seem all that cozy with the nobility, so maybe it's for the best that I avoided that confrontation. Anyway, he sent Chobin out east. Seems Hrom turned our alliance with the Turks against us, so the goat-fucker is off to defend that front."

"Oh."

"Yeah." Tirdad ran his fingers through his hair, feeling awkward and cursing himself for not bathing while he had the opportunity. "I feel gritty," he said.

Shkarag's hood canted, and she shifted beneath her cloak. "Gulf's there all ready to swallow you up something fierce." She canted further. "Like some, like some šo-horny king off doing heroics, fucking dragons and slaying women, because some fussy princess from Hayk wants trials. But he's got this lake, this waterfall, this offspring from another fussy one, and he's šo-horny, too. So it's patricide, then." She paused to adjust in her saddle, which she rode backwards. "Sounds like a catchphrase. But you're looking at your boots thinking I won't go on as the scabbard to an offspring, so you trot your horse into the Gulf and that's that."

"The Gulf's too salty for a bath," said Tirdad.

A cant. "Oh."

Tirdad felt a bit less awkward after her rambling. As one-sided as it was, it was casual and conversational. "I've been meaning to discuss something with you," he said. "About our, uh, voyage. When our minds were crossed."

". . ."

Tirdad exhaled in an attempt to stave off anxiety. "What was that? It was if everyone wanted to roll me in a carpet and send a cavalcade over me. But it was . . . more than that. More involved. I recall you describing something along those lines. And there were all these . . ." He tried to reach for the description, and it took him a moment to grasp what it was he had experienced. "I could see these threads between what were previously unrelated events, all converging on me, and there were these cluttered ideas." Tirdad was convinced there had been more, but what remained was lost to him. He turned in the saddle to face her. The awkward feeling was coming on again. "Was that . . . was that what you endure every day?"

Shkarag cocked her head away, though he could tell even with her hood and scarf that she was trained on him. "Maybe," she probably confirmed.

"How?"

". . ."

"It would've driven me mad, Shkarag." He couldn't hide his astonishment. "How? How could you possibly live like that?"

". . ."

Tirdad watched her for a time, waiting for a change in body language, but she only rode in her stuffed silence. "I respect you for it," he said at length.

". . ." She angled so he could see her eyes, inscrutable as ever, and lifted a hand from beneath her heavy cloak to form a claw by her head. "Have only known this. So that's just as the crow flies. Only the šo-damned—" She focused on something beyond him. Her lips parted, and for a moment he mistook the trumpeting that blared as pouring from between her lips. When she closed them and the trumpeting persisted, he turned to see what had caught her attention.

Tirdad squinted against the midday sun. Even low as it was on the winter ecliptic, the Gulf lent it a summer glare. In the distance, surrounded by tussocks, there emerged a face that was wider than a face had any business being. If he wanted to make out the details, he'd have to venture closer, but it seemed human. It trumpeted.

"Strange song," mused Tirdad. Shkarag's only response was the creaking of leather. She'd brought her horse closer to his and now had his reins in a vice. "What is it?" he asked.

"Not human. Not div." She angled slightly, gaze still locked on the faraway face. "I think."

"It sure looks human from here," he said, remembering her less than stellar vision. "Should we investigate?"

The reins creaked. ". . ."

"Shkarag?"

"Our fates are sealed," she said. "Misery is the currency, the šo-minted coin of the universe. Stamped right there on the obverse." Her stare darted to his, flickering and intense. "Don't ride gentle into its purse."

"What do you suggest we do, then?"

"Rage."

"I'm not sure what—"

"Rage and bristle and . . ." She trailed off, and though patently uncertain about it, released the reins. "Rage at the road ahead," she finished, then veered her horse away.

Tirdad expelled a sigh—a sure sign of his resignation—but primed his hand on the ram's head pommel all the same. "You're right. We shouldn't swap saddles midstream."

The trumpet-like call grew more and more distant, until at last the calls of crickets and nightjars prevailed. Over the following days they left the open air of the coast for the oak-forested sinks of the adjoining mountains, careful to choose a course that was kind to their mounts. The further they pressed, the worse the chill, until they were each bundled in their saddles.

With each day that passed the trumpeting returned. Oftentimes, Tirdad would spot the face peeking from a far-off copse or tussock. Truth be told, it terrified him. The more he saw it, the more he understood it wasn't human. He could have sworn its mouth opened from ear to ear when baying.

The sole reason he managed to sleep at all was thanks to Shkarag. She never mentioned it, but she was always awake come dawn, and slept more often than not in her saddle. This arrangement made for a dour trip. And having no one to talk to, Tirdad instead occupied his mind with increasingly outlandish ideas about the face, its origin, and its motivation. Chief among those thoughts was the literal mystery behind it: what was the face attached to, if anything?

The trumpeting went nearly unabated, but while traversing a wide trough of pastureland sparse with almond trees and scattered with wildflowers, the face had nothing from which to emerge. This afforded the pair a much-needed respite.

On one such morning, brisk and gloomy beneath a cover of clouds, Shkarag stirred. Tirdad trained a curious stare her way as she adjusted her cloak and pulled down her hood. She stared back.

"You should rest," he said.

" . . ."

"You look exhausted."

"Šo-damned brass misplaced its wind, and . . ." Her stare flicked away to scour the creases of a stone outcropping where it parted the otherwise verdant hill. "Miss this."

"Yeah," said Tirdad. "It's been, what, seven months now? I've grown accustomed to your company, to our shared silence."

" . . ."

Tirdad urged his steed closer to hers. "Shkarag," he asked, "have you heard the saying, 'Don't nourish a viper in one's bosom'?"

That got her attention. "Maybe," she said, leering.

"Well, I've been told as much many times. But just now—" A smile honest with contentment brightened his features. "Just now I was thinking it'd be great if a certain viper nourished mine in her bosom."

Shkarag's leer softened, and mirth overthrew the exhaustion in her eyes. "Jokes are still flat as the constant where you've got this, this—" She tilted her head, face screwed up in thought. "As a mural."

Tirdad grinned, gleaning no small amount of satisfaction from her insult. "Flat as ever," he said. "Much like your humming."

With Shkarag's humming to guide them, and with the trumpeting gone, they navigated sea-green hills like swells rocky with froth. Many such swells passed beneath them before Tirdad gave voice to something that had been nagging him.

"Shkarag," he said.

She ceased her crooning. ". . ."

"Don't bare your fangs."

". . ." She opened her mouth, but stopped at that.

Tirdad averted his gaze, focusing instead on the wool of her cloak where it described the ankle of her boot. "I woke up expecting Ashta to be alive." Shkarag hissed, which further anchored his stare. "I often do," he admitted. That elicited another hiss. Tirdad sighed, finding refuge in the ram's head pommel. He didn't fault Shkarag for her jealousy, or whatever bad blood had led to the half-div throwing herself into a drunken duel. "I tell you not to hurt you, but to be honest with you, and because if anyone would understand, it's you. It hurts, Shkarag. Every time. Like I'm in the estate with her all over again. Like I'm killing her all over again. When will her memory let me go?"

Tirdad hadn't really expected a response, much less a favourable one, but Shkarag refrained from another hiss. Instead, she sidled her mount over and, after draining a wineskin, straddled his horse so that they were facing. As blank as her countenance was, Tirdad wasn't sure what to make of her until she pulled him into a hug that smelled of rotten eggs.

"Never," she said.

• • • • •

Some mornings later, after passing out of the range and into the arid, sun-baked region over which Ray stood guard, a sudden bloodlust roused Tirdad. He rolled over, wiping the sand from his eyes and blinking at the image of Shkarag, sun on her back and standing over him. She seethed. Her axes were in either hand, brandished by her sides.

It took a moment for her adrenaline to find and galvanize his, but once it did, Tirdad burst into action. He grasped the hilt of his sword where it lay by his bedding, and as he slid from beneath her, threw one arm to the side, which sent the scabbard flying. "What in the šo-fucking seven climes?" he growled, assuming a defensive posture alongside Shkarag, starling-black blade out in a flash. Her bloodlust washed over him full force now, pomegranate-tangy and emboldening. "Oh," he said. "Well, fuck."

Shkarag agreed with a hiss. Her fangs glistened in the corner of his eye.

Seven figures approached, each shimmering blood-red and lapis lazuli. Eshm sisters. Remembering his bow, Tirdad flipped his sword over and shoved it into the dirt. He withdrew to snatch up his recurve, stringing it with a practiced hand and returning to Shkarag's side.

Tirdad nocked an arrow. He inhaled, lifted the bow, exhaled as he drew, then loosed what was clearly a warning shot. The Eshm sisters drew to a halt at that. After exchanging glances, one broke off to cover the remaining distance.

"Shot like that belongs to this one," she said, inclining a grin toward Shkarag. "Makes fletching weep, mhm."

"I remember you," said Tirdad, bow ready, and palm itching for the sword. "You were cowering in the palace of the stork."

"And you gave that star-reckoner something to think about, mhm."

"That I did. Have you come looking to have your wit sharpened, too?" Tirdad felt as cocky as he sounded. His chest might as well have been puffed.

The Eshm sister simpered, hiss more prominent than Shkarag's. "Colour me fucking surprised. Reek so strongly of her I could've mistaken you for Waray. That's some bond you share." She stowed her sword in her belt and locked her fingers behind her head. "Mess at the palace was nothing personal. Caught us mending and needing a release. Like rubbing one out but more fulfilling, mhm."

Shkarag's saw-on-wood breathing dominated the silence that followed. She was one misstep away from striking. He could feel it. Tirdad nocked another arrow, and pulled it to full draw. "What the fuck do you want with us?"

"Suppose that's a fair question, mhm. Chased out the palace, in a bad way most of us, and found ourselves stalked by a beast. We're many things, but hunted isn't one of them. Now we're hunting, mhm. Spotted the smoke from your fire, and here we are." She shrugged. "I smell omelette. Domesticating our bloodline are you?"

"Don't think that's possible."

"Probably not." She shifted her weight and addressed Shkarag. "Mean you no harm, sis. Put it to rest. Beast caught wind of your scent, so it's stalking you now, mhm. Figured a warning was in order. Had we wanted you dead, you'd have no recourse." She flashed a smirk at Tirdad. "During the day anyhow."

Though she lowered her axes and retracted her fangs, Shkarag's harsh breathing persisted. "I'll fry some šo-damned eggs if I fucking please," she hissed.

"You've always been backwards and hard-headed—even for us. Like that about you, mhm." The Eshm sister gestured at Shkarag's girdle where it'd been discarded as if it were worthless. "But that's going too far. Will wish you hadn't made that."

Shkarag backed down at that, which was enough to convince Tirdad to ease his draw. She holstered her axes and returned to the fire, hissing instead at the burned omelette. "Existing is, existing is all so many re-grets, like some, like some baggage train and—" She dropped the pan in the fire to raise a claw by her head. "And the horses and donkeys and camels are all passing by and it's just a šo-wretched string of things you wish you hadn't done." She snatched the pan from the flames and threw one of her deadpan stares at her sister. "Like squirrelling away with six of your underlings."

The Eshm sister inclined her head. ". . . mhm." She glanced over her shoulder at the others, straightening her half-destroyed mail. "We'd fare better together. Beast could be a trumpeting dragon for all I know. Suppose I should introduce myself." She extended a hand. "Stahm's the name."

Tirdad's disbelief was plain. Did she seriously expect him to agree to travelling together? "You what now? What are you—"

"Maybe," Shkarag cut in.

"—poppy-addled?" Tirdad knotted his brow at the inflection she'd used: decided, and adamant about it.

Shkarag glanced up from tending the frying pan. This time, an im-passive expression punctuated her will. She would brook no argument. "Maybe," she said.

Tirdad expelled a sigh. He yanked his sword from the ground, noting that its obscene heartbeat was going wild. "Well," he said while searching for the scabbard, "you heard the Queen of Queens here. Hope you like eggs."

"Revolting," said Stahm, smirking and with a thick hiss. "Would rather have mine fertilized, mhm. When you're looking to do the honours just—"

An axe careened end over end by her head.

$$\bullet \ \bullet \ \bullet \ \bullet \ \bullet$$

Tirdad moved his piece along the nard board, unable to find rhyme nor reason in Shkarag's pieces. Knowing the celestial theatre, and the part the planets played in it, hers was a strategy true to form to the chaos at play there. He offered the board, which she exchanged for a flask of spirits. Tirdad took a swig. The distallate's bite was all but numbed by now. "You're—" He clutched the horn of his saddle to steady himself. "You're always riding backward," he observed.

". . ." She focused on the board, eyes swaying from one declination to another. "Nothing worth, worth . . ." She canted, and leaned with it. "No horizons worth looking forward to."

Tirdad grunted his disapproval. "You've been gloomy of late. Something on your mind?"

After a bout of deliberation, Shkarag flung the board. "Fuck!" she shouted in a shower of game pieces. "Fuck! Fuck! Fuck! Fuuuuuck!" With a final shout, she split off to brood by her lonesome.

Wearing a grimace, Tirdad meant to follow when Stahm pulled up alongside. "Best not to bring it up again," she said, returning his grimace. "She can't tell you, mhm. Just making it worse by doing your prying thing."

Tirdad endeavoured to blink through his drunkenness, doing an awful job of it. "I don't understand. Why?"

Stahm nodded to herself, smirking at some unspoken joke. She then set about gathering the game pieces while talking. "Probably think being half human dilutes the blood of our father. Can't dilute our lineage, however—can only make it a trial to endure, to control. As the eldest I'm, I—" She looked away, and Tirdad saw in her what he'd seen in Shkarag all those years ago. She cleared her throat. "Was up to me to reform her, to stomp her into shape. Royally whiffed that one. Father still gets on me over it."

"Why're you telling me this?"

"Because Shkarag isn't allowed to. Because . . ." She stooped to pick up the last of the nard pieces. "Been many centuries since, and I haven't had the opportunity to repay her." Stahm straightened, dusting off the wooden board as she did. The stare she trained on him was tense, and when she finally spoke, it was clear in how she tiptoed over them that she'd chosen her words carefully. "She'd never willingly betray you. You'd do well to remember that. Don't, and you'll have me to deal with, and I've lived long enough to develop quite the imagination." Stahm offered a grin wide enough to expose her fangs, then headed back to the the rest of her group. "We'll do the rounds," she called over her shoulder. "Still have a beast to track."

Tirdad watched their departure with consternation. Back at Castle Dahag, he'd hoped to never see them again. Now, here he was travelling alongside seven and a half Eshm sisters.

"Wonder if this is how Ashta felt," he mused. "Throwing in with divs after a life spent bringing them to heel. Turns out I'm just as backwards as they are." He brought his horse alongside Shkarag's, negotiating her meaningful quiet by occupying himself with the nard board. Occasionally, she'd hack at the air with the axe he'd given her.

Having finished, Tirdad balanced the board on his lap. The pieces weren't situated exactly as before, but he figured they were close enough. He reached back to rummage through his saddlebag and retrieve a small wooden box. It housed a pair of eggs, off-white, splotched with what looked to be dried blood, and generously padded with fleece. Ostensibly, they belonged to an osprey. The merchant had assured him as much, for whatever that was worth. Tirdad did know they weren't laid by kestrels. This was a powerful certainty—the utmost distinction.

"You all right?" he asked, offering the box.

Shkarag ceased mid-chop, axe trembling as if it yearned to lash out. She exhaled, charged as ever.

"Eggs," he said, tilting the box. "I'm told they're osprey. To be honest, they could be kestrel for all I know."

". . ." She eased the axe down.

"Rest assured they aren't chicken," he added.

Shkarag didn't smile. That would have been too much to ask. Tirdad always considered the expectation of a smile nothing short of unreasonable. Sometimes, there is nothing to be but down. She did, however, slip the axe into her weapon belt.

"Put in a general order when we left for the island," he explained. "Honestly didn't expect anything to come of it. Mind letting me know if I've been swindled?"

Shkarag cocked her head and accepted the box. She spent some time contemplating its lid before finally opening it, but once its contents were in full view, her gaze darted to flicker over his shoulder. Meanwhile, she drew an appraising touch over the eggs.

"Osprey," she confirmed at length. "I think."

"You can tell by feel?"

She canted, but only just. "Maybe," she said, unconvincingly. Without taking her eyes off the space just above his shoulder, she crammed both eggs into her mouth. After a protracted round of crunching, she closed her eyes and emitted a hum.

"Well?" asked Tirdad.

Shkarag licked a strand of yolk from her lip. "Maybe the bazdari gloves, the falconry leather isn't so far-fetched after all."

"Sure it wasn't a kestrel egg?"

". . ." Deadpan, she held out her hand. "My move."

Tirdad gave her the board, pointing at the pieces as he did. "Tried to put them back as we had them." He looked on as she tinkered with the pieces, picking each up and putting it back down without making a move.

"Well . . ." He ran his fingers through his hair, and treated himself to another long draw of spirits. "As close as I could manage."

Shkarag's stare flitted from the board to him and back. When she finally got around to throwing the dice, her roll took two of his pieces.

"Oh, nice move!" he said. "You're getting the hang of it. And here I was thinking your strategy was an utter mess."

She held one such piece between her thumb and forefinger, tapping it on the board and moving her lips as if to some internal dialogue.

Tirdad had been working toward an apology, but it seemed to him the right moment wasn't forthcoming. By now, the distallate had relaxed him enough that he didn't need one. "Listen," he began, "you're entitled to your secrets—we're all burdened with the things we keep to ourselves, even the tiny everyday thoughts. And that's just as well. Trust can't be absolute. There will always be something we can't share, or something better left unsaid." He reached out and, when she showed no resistance, placed his hand over hers. "For everything else, I'm here."

Her reply was bereft of emotion. "An utter mess," she intoned. "Only moving from one right ascension to another like some, like some star strolling through the šo-merry celestial theatre, and the star's thinking, it's rolling over its tongue that allies are like an onager. That bringing the right one to a siege will secure victory. Wrong one will make you look like an ass. And it's thinking it hopes its alliance was the siege engine. But really it doesn't know war or allies so maybe there's no onager at all."

She pulled her hand away, and something foreboding leaked into her delivery. "Your game is only strolling to me. No strategy. But chaos . . ." Shkarag made a claw of that same hand by her head. "Can see into it sometimes. Here and there. To and fro. Connections are always there, peeking from behind this onager or that catapult."

"So you're playing without a plan at all then?"

"Sometimes the plan isn't yours," she said. "Can only glimpse it. Make the moves they demand of you. Doesn't mean you aren't, aren't into the game." Shkarag returned the board, which freed her hands to fish for another flask.

Tirdad inclined his head. "There's wisdom to be found in reacting to those whose plans are brazen or foolhardy. Allow them to seal their own fates."

He went on to win the game no contest, which left him wondering whether her one good move was a fluke. That curiosity fell by the wayside, soon to be replaced by her explanation. Tirdad found it odd. Strangely, since odd came to her naturally enough to be anything but.

XVI

IS SNOW-POWDERED HILLOCK AFFORDED TIRDAD a clear vantage of the ambush. A Turkish invasion force had been corralled into a narrow pass, upon which Chobin's humble contingent rained arrows and boulders. Muted as they were by the cover of snow, the cries, shouts, and commands still fought against the walls of the ravine as desperately as those unfortunate souls seeking to flee certain death.

Tirdad's lips were a thin line. Without intervention, the ambush wouldn't be enough to stop the nomads from emerging from the pass. From there, they would no doubt pillage the nearby villages.

He brought his horse about to face those who had joined him on the rise. Over the course of their month-long journey northeast, the Eshm sisters had proven themselves worthy sentinels. Time and again, the trumpeting would return, only to be scared off for a few days thanks to their tireless pursuit. That aside, they kept to themselves. Only Stahm ever addressed him directly, and hers were brief conversations, often meant to impart some anecdote or another when not teasing Shkarag. For her part, Shkarag took it in stride. More relevant to the matter at hand, he trusted she would follow him to the end of the universe. Ultimately, they were all Eshm's stock, which meant he had his answer; asking was at most a formality.

He drew his sword, blade alive as ever with iridescence, and looked them each in the eyes. "Shall we give the sky-obsessed fucks something to dash themselves over?"

Seven grins told him what he'd already anticipated, to be topped off by Shkarag's saw-on-wood consent. He locked stares with her—as much as one could, prone as she was to flitting—and her otherwise inscrutable slits and blank expression, betrayed by her parted lips and anticipatory breaths, were utterly transparent. Her bloodlust swelled. Her thrill became his. He grinned wide, which she returned in kind, uneven as the shuddered chuckled she let out.

Tirdad dismounted, and Shkarag followed suit. Their horses would only encumber them in close quarters combat. "Let's wreak ourselves all kinds of havoc," he said, feeling bolder by the second, as he started off in a trot toward the mouth of the pass.

From afar, the ravine had seemed an off-kilter cleft that violated rolling hills otherwise white with virtue, and went on to defile the adjoining ridge. Passing into it imparted a different perspective altogether—one much like returning from the celestial theatre with a lot drawn and ready. Now, the cliffs towered to either side, acting as insurmountable boundaries to pen in livestock on their way to slaughter. Tirdad grinned, full-toothed and drunk on adrenaline. They were the wolves. And they were quickly closing in on horsemen who were panicked and focused on the enemies overhead.

To his side, Shkarag flung her cloak open to billow behind her with a flourish, axes spinning by her sides, which prompted him to follow her example and unclasp his cloak. Together, at the vanguard of a wedge, they collided with the line.

It must have been a true spectacle for those looking on from above.

In the span of seconds, Tirdad severed the front legs of the leading horse, introduced its falling rider to a bite colder than the blizzard, cut another horseman's arm off at the elbow, gutted his horse, and pressed their wedge deeper into the line.

Their advance seemed indefatigable. Every step he took was one of gained ground. Every stomp into blood-saturated snow another rider dispatched. Arrows pelted all around, but he paid them no heed. It was as if his well-being came second to glory; there was only the thrill of the moment.

Shkarag moved in and out of his vision, axes a blur and cleaving with furious abandon, as if the battlefield bowed to her, fashioned itself such that she could vault from foe to foe, winding and unwinding, in a constellation both unerring and panache.

Meanwhile, her display drew him in sure as a shared orbit. Where she lashed out with her axes in stilted succession to open the chest cavity of one warrior and cleave through the skull of another, he was there. Tirdad bobbed and weaved beneath her left arm and between her victims to bat aside an incoming spear that would have run her through. A curt thrust dealt with its bearer. Another found the heart of a nomad whose back was to him. Shkarag's scales flashed into view, there came the clap of metal, and a downward stroke fell just shy of his forehead. Its owner gurgled.

Tirdad turned, her cuirass to his back, to face their rear for the first time. There, the Eshm sisters were fighting in his wake. Unlike Shkarag, they moved in well-honed unison. That was the only glimpse he got of them before he had to parry an incoming thrust from a straggler. Tirdad's rebuttal had him spin, crack the woman's jaw with a reverse elbow, then uncoil in a swift movement that brought his blade across her throat. Without looking back, he rushed to overtake Shkarag.

Ahead, several nomads had the wherewithal to form a cursory line. That called for theatrics. He skidded to a kneeling halt, and from immediately behind, reacting as if she knew his aim ahead of time, Shkarag bounded off his upper back. Even as he knelt, Tirdad had been readying his bow, and wasted no time putting it to use once she was airborne. With one smooth movement, his trained fingers found the nock, drew, and loosed a single arrow beneath her flight, effectively plugging the opening she'd left. The warrior directly in her path collapsed, which gave her leave to descend upon the next in line.

So progressed their tireless advance. Where before Tirdad had merely supported Shkarag in battle, he became a part of her routine, and she his. Where before he kept an eye on her, he felt her presence as keenly as his own. Where before smoke and firelight screened his vision, pomegranate-red swamped it. Tirdad smiled through it all. He didn't just fight: he belonged.

The paths they carved through the horde overlapped constantly, coiled like a pair of snakes. Together, they might have made it out the other end.

If not for the sudden blaring. A herald blew its trumpet, announced the arrival of the latest predator to join the fray. Tirdad had only the chance to glance over his shoulder before it barrelled through him.

Thrown into a roll, he tried and failed to right himself before the cliff face did it for him. A prolonged groan escaped, and he looked up in time to see the beast skid through swathes of horsemen.

"Fuck," he spat when it turned on him. Parted as it was at the jaw, connected by rows of teeth like haphazard potsherds, playing at humanity but coming dreadfully short, that vulgar face was unmistakable. Their trumpeting stalker had come for them at last. A manticore.

Tirdad fought to plant his feet beneath him, still dizzy from the roll. He couldn't afford to recover. Deathly unnerving though it was, its face was the least of his worries. The manticore had a body like a lion's rife with mange, balding mane grimey as seaweed, and larger than several elephants combined. Worst of all was its tail, which oscillated with bristles like pikes.

Dire. That was the word for it. Not just any manticore—a dire manticore.

Thankfully, the chill was bracing. He snatched up his sword and raced to join Shkarag.

"What now?" he breathed. The burning in his ribs changed; it invigorated him. "How in the seven climes do we take that down?"

The manticore blared its trumpet-damned roar. The Eshm sisters drew up alongside, and Shkarag bared her fangs. Tension hung in the air, taut as hide left out to dry. Then a gale stirred a plume of powdery snow, and with it, everyone into action.

Bristles, hurled from the manticore's tail, broke through the snow in whirling pockets, streaming past like a hail of javelins. Tirdad dove beneath the barrage just as a bristle caught the thigh of the Eshm sister to his right, and ripped her leg clean off. He came up from his roll with Shkarag by his side, and together, they rushed the beast.

"Under!" he yelled, hoping to use the other Eshm sisters as a distraction while he and Shkarag attacked its flank. "And watch for the tail!"

A paw raked through the plume, claws like shark fins leaving eddies of snowflakes in their wake. The first swipe came up short; the second had him diving once more. Snow bit at his face, and when he recovered, it was to another cloud of it, probably excited by the huge paw.

Perfect. That meant a moment's cover. Though it prevented him from seeing Shkarag, it could not obscure their bond. He dashed toward her, only for that terrible maw to lunge into the cloud just in front of him, rows of teeth gnawing and snapping independently of one another to the sound of pots shattering.

He stumbled out of the way, twisting his ankle and cursing, only for the maw to snap shut around his sword. That was a mistake. The manticore reared, trumpeting in pain and in so doing pulling the unnaturally keen blade through its chin.

Tirdad seized the opportunity to rush in beneath its ribcage and swerve to his left, sheathing his sword as he did. With both hands free, he about-faced, slipping in a puddle of blood, but catching himself in time to greet Shkarag. Without thinking, he clasped her forearm in both hands as she ran by, and swung her in a rising arc that flung her into the air.

Half-way up the manticore's flank, her axes struck home. Briefly, her descent could have been likened to ripping a tapestry on a ride to the bottom. That ceased when she began hacking her way down—glorious and wild. The blood that splattered her reeked of sickness, but it smoldered all the same. Her bloodlust glowed, beautiful and alive; it sloshed out of her with Tirdad there to catch the excess. How he revelled in it.

"Yeah!" he exclaimed before the manticore's pounce cut short his triumph. Its back leg caught him mid-bound, and this time, he was knocked flat.

Unwilling to let it gain the upper hand, he hurried to his feet. Or tried to. Bloodlust drowned out the pain, but that didn't stop his leg from buckling beneath him. Chest to the snow, Tirdad craned to look ahead in time to see it land by the exit, whipping its tail. The figure between him and the manticore was out of focus—until it jerked all of a sudden.

Lapis lazuli inlays were the first to come into focus, sharp and damning. A lump rose in his throat as he watched the shards fall to the snow.

"No . . ." he muttered. "Ohrmazd, no."

A bristle had skewered Shkarag just below the cuirass—penetrated her girdle, her phylactery. The bloodlust fled completely. She staggered back a step, her shoulders slumped, and she fell to a knee.

"Shkarag!" Tirdad screamed at the top of his lungs. "Shkarag!" He pressed himself off the ground, screaming as loudly as he could as if it'd somehow undo her fate.

"Shkarag!" he bellowed, even as his leg failed him a second time. So he crawled for her. "Don't you fucking do this to me! Don't you fucking do it!"

Shkarag struggled to look over her shoulder, but couldn't seem to get her upper body to listen. He could feel the dread in her as if it were his own, deep-seated and ancient. A fear that could be neither contained nor overcome. Not a fear of death—she would have embraced death. This was terrifying; this was freedom.

She spoke to him through their bond then. Though only a series of hurried and convoluted emotions, she got the message across. "Don't make me do this to you."

Tirdad was on the verge of crying out when it hit him. If her phylactery was destroyed, if she embraced death, what could she possibly have to fear?

Someone grabbed him by the collar, lifting him as if to carry him away, but he shoved off to fall to the ground again.

"You must leave now," Stahm hissed from where she loomed over him.

"I'm not going anywhere," he growled, teeth gritted at the pain that gripped his broken leg.

Stahm stooped to pick him up, patently impatient. "This is where I failed," she said. "Believe me when I say we must go." She threw a nervous glance at Shkarag. "Now."

Stahm went to heft him, but drew up short when he reached for his sword. "I'm not going anywhere," he said.

"You'll die."

Tirdad stared her down. Whatever was happening, Shkarag would not face it alone. Not as long as he breathed. "So be it. I refuse to leave her."

The Eshm sister shook her head, backing away. "Have it your way," she said, then sprinted off in the opposite direction.

Tirdad sidled against the wall of the pass, thinking he'd find a spear to use as a crutch, when a sudden wave of heat washed over him.

Shkarag straightened her back.

She canted such that he could see the glint in her smile.

She bared fangs dripping acid.

The stone at her feet cracked.

Even from afar, she felt heavier to him—massive at that—but not only in weight. She was magnitudes denser, as if too much were being contained inside her.

"Shkarag," he called, unsure what, if anything, to do. He reached out, not really knowing why, and feeling stupid for it.

Her semi-keeled scales flared, and out rushed a billow of steam so caustic the rock to her sides bubbled. Starling-black rivulets, pearly and livid, described the space between scales.

Shkarag pulled in a breath that filled out what remained of her sizzling caftan. When she exhaled, more steam billowed. Her breathing became more and more frequent; with each, a hiss would feed on those that came before it, to rise in intensity and volume. Until, when it seemed it would come to a head, she screamed. Like cruelty given life, it echoed through the pass. His hair stood on end. He felt at the same time nauseous, euphoric, and scared out of his wits.

Then the stone buckled beneath her. Corpses were thrown into the air. She took a step, then another, and with each a crater gave credence to the immensity he sensed in her. Shkarag bent at the knees and moved so swiftly the haze of steam didn't react until a second later.

The manticore trumpeted its challenge, which took a sharp turn to a high note. Shkarag had appeared directly in front of it, and with a left hook, tore its jaw from its face. Tongue hanging free, it bayed like a trumpet into water. Probably meaning to escape, the manticore leapt, but Shkarag would have none of that. She caught it by the tail mid-leap, and dislodged the bristle from her abdomen with which to stake the tail to the ground.

The manticore scrambled to crawl away. Its claws scraped desperately at the ground, making a high-pitched whine to accompany its muddy trumpeting.

Shkarag gave it no quarter. Her scales vented billows of steam that made the manticore's mange-infested flesh bubble and run. She leaned into its hip, grinned her crooked, half-moon grin, and with what scarcely amounted to a shove, the bone caved in. Wide-eyed and wild, the beast had only begun to thrash its head when she tore the leg off and chucked it behind her. True to form, she was toying with it. When the manticore got it in its head to roll over and swipe at her, another leg flew end over end by her shoulder.

To his surprise, in a timbre that was both hers and foreign, in two languages at once, she sang a discordant tune.

> "What quarry's this,
> whose quarry's that?
> Not marble, not gypsum,
> some šo-damned cat."

The manticore's fight was all but gone; blood stained the snow around it. Its head lolled as she stalked up its remaining leg to stand on its back, still heaving steam, and set to plucking its ribs from its spine. All the while, she went on with her too-merry song.

> "One rib's just fine,
> and two that's plenty,
> but three or four,
> cracks a tease too many."

Her voice became a growl of a hiss, and she cocked her head to turn piercing starling-black eyes on Tirdad. Shkarag ripped out another rib.

"Storm's fresh brewing,
no tea reeks enough.
But your šo-boiling blood
that's the fucking stuff."

Looking on, he realized she had never been just Shkarag. She was Shkarag the Wrathful, Shkarag of Brutality, of Violence in War, of Drunkenness, of the Bloody Club, of the Murderous Spear, of the Raving Axe. She threw anger and malice into the hearts of men, encouraged every evil. Eshm wasn't just her father; he was part of her.

Still, he told himself, she was foremost Shkarag of his Heart. This is what he thought as she turned on him, and the last thing he remembered.

XVII

TIRDAD AWAKENED TO THE TELLTALE crackling and popping of a fire. Soon to join was a rotten egg aroma. With it, a touch of charred wood and old leather.

"Stirring, goat-fucker," said Shkarag, breath tickling his nose.

Chobin grunted. "I can see that just fine, skink-slicker."

Tirdad grimaced at the dull but persistent throbbing in his left leg, and opened his eyes. Shkarag hovered inches above, and Chobin knelt by his side wearing a worried smile. Behind him, the burgundy canvas of their pavilion rustled in an outside wind.

"Nngh," he said. "What happened?"

Shkarag pressed a brief kiss to his lips before sitting back. She found somewhere else to look.

"Skink-slicker almost did you in," said Chobin. "Reckon stopping her is about the only good thing that sturgeon-kissing star-reckoner has done since persuading himself into my campaign."

"I . . ." Tirdad tried to concentrate, but the throbbing in his leg was giving him a hard time of it. "Star-reckoner," he muttered. "Star-reckoner."

"What about him?" asked Chobin. "He's a bit of a prick, but—"

Tirdad snatched the marzban by the lapel, and pulled himself face to face. He remembered why they'd come.

"Did you know?" he asked, bearing a stormy calm that could have belonged to Ashtadukht. Out of the corner of his eye, he noticed Shkarag move to block the pavilion's exit. Chobin must have too, because his uneasy smile became all the more toothsome.

The marzban rubbed the back of his neck. "Never took you for one to show off. Admit to appreciating your flair, though—charging in at the head of a wedge just in the nick of time. Not to mention the two of you fighting side by side like something out of legend. Pretty much stole my thunder what with your—"

Tirdad jerked his lapel. "Don't think I won't kill you here and now, Chobin. Answer me."

Though it persisted, the marzban's smile sobered. "What in the everliving fuck do you think I knew?"

It took everything he had not to reach for his sword. "Don't be coy. What your family did to mine. To Ashtadukht."

Chobin averted his gaze, which was answer enough.

"You knew."

"Only recently. I swear to you, I had nothing to do with it."

"How recently?"

"Father told me while you were in Ray. Said I should know in order to better protect myself should your family discover the truth."

Tirdad released Chobin and laid back. He supposed it could've been worse. He could've had to kill Chobin. Now, he didn't know what to do. A man, especially a good man like Chobin, should not be made responsible for the actions of his father, no matter how reprehensible.

"I should have Shkarag put you down," he said. "The damage can't be undone, but it would inflict upon your family a heavy blow." He then recalled his chance encounter with his cousin during their stop at the port. He allowed himself a self-deprecating chuckle. "I know I should. If my family were here, they would demand it. But . . ." He sighed, shaking his head at his past self. "I really thought I'd do it. Now that I'm here, I can't even entertain the thought."

"I will consider myself lucky then."

"Do that." Tirdad shifted in a vain attempt to make his leg more comfortable. "And tell me something why don't you?"

"Anything."

"Why'd they do it?"

The marzban's smile became a grimace. "Power, to those less privileged. Your uncle had the ear of the King of Kings, and that became an easy scapegoat. Father claimed there was more to it, but refused to tell me outright." Chobin cleared his throat. "Did slip here and there, and well, I think your uncle fucked his first wife. Don't think her suicide was an accident either."

Tirdad couldn't hide his astonishment. "That's . . . news to me."

"News to everyone, I imagine."

"You could've told me."

"Know it wasn't my place to decide, but thought you were better off not knowing. You've been through a lot as is." Chobin's grin vanished. "Truth be told, I was afraid you'd hate me."

Tirdad wasn't sure how to respond to that, so he turned his attention to Shkarag. She wore an overlarge tunic obviously loaned from Chobin, which was bunched at the waist by her lapis lazuli girdle. In defiance of a gaping hole and many missing inlays, it was intact.

He envisioned her transformation, the sheer power and cruelty of it. There was something intoxicating about seeing her like that. As wondrous as any feat of nature. But she'd been terrified of it. He now knew why: it divulged her of control.

"How're you feeling?" he asked.

". . ." She set her head askew, palm resting on the butt of the axe he'd given her. "Here. I think."

It warmed his heart to see her casual bearing. Had she been tense, it might've signalled an uncertainty over what'd transpired. Guilt, if not worse.

"Glad you got a chance to blow off some steam," he joked, hoping to further ease any worries she might entertain.

Shkarag grinned, crooked and glintless.

"She nearly plucked you apart like flower petals," Chobin saw fit to add. "Had you by wrist and foot."

Tirdad didn't take his eyes off her. The marzban didn't know the half of it. With what he'd detected in Shkarag, she could have gone toe to toe with a forty-armed div.

"Better her than some faceless spear," he said, sitting up, and feeling as though his skull were dense with mist. He bunched his face and ran a hand over it, which did nothing for it. "What'd you give me?"

"Something is fucking wrong with you two. Still."

"Roots," answered Shkarag.

After gathering his thoughts a moment, Tirdad reached out to clasp Chobin's forearm. "I've acted like an onager of late."

"Hah!" Spirits so easily lifted, the marzban slapped his thigh. "We're a pair of onagers, you and I, stubborn, packing a mean kick, and, most of all, an ass."

"Yeah." Tirdad tried to run a hand through his hair, but it was tangled and matted with blood. "Did you retrieve my horse?"

"Skink-slicker did."

"That's good; the horse is a treasure. Listen, Chobin." He posted on one palm to lean in, giving credence to the severity of his delivery. "I haven't forgotten the gravity of your gesture. Your offering to restore my status. You need to know that. Haven't forgotten our friendship either. You're a brother to me. All this—" Tirdad sighed and furrowed his brow. Whatever he was getting at was being mighty evasive.

Chobin offered a soft grin, looking wiser than his years, and gripped Tirdad by the shoulder. "You taught me empathy more than my father ever could. You've always cared too much, shown compassion where others would not." He gestured to Shkarag. "Like you do with her. I figure that's a double-edged blade. Something like Ashtadukht happens to you, and no mourning period will be enough. That you've come this far is a testament to your strength, my friend. Lesser men would have lost themselves."

Knowing what he did, Tirdad couldn't make eye contact. Somewhere along the line, he had lost himself. To change wasn't necessarily shameful, but the truth of the matter was that he wasn't the man he used to be.

"So," Chobin continued, leaning back and crossing his arms, "enough of this fucking wallowing! I wasn't done savouring your flair, and you'll let me finish this time whether you want to run me through or not."

"My what?"

"Oh, now you're playing coy, you sturgeon-kissing snake fucker." The marzban stooped to fetch a ewer and a pair of glasses, wasting no time in filling them before handing the ewer to Shkarag. He emptied his before going on. "There I was, nocking arrows as fast as my fingers could manage, which wasn't very considering how fucking frosty it is out there, when I look up and—" Chobin unsheathed his sword, waving it with a flourish. "—there you are all a storm of swords and axes, blades flashing like lightning. I've seen my share of battles, you know that, but—hah! The spectacle of it all. That, well, that's the battle of a lifetime. Fuck me with a fishing rod if I've seen a woman as beautiful, and you know how it goes around bivouacs."

"Yeah," Tirdad chuckled. Shkarag poured him another glass without his asking, which he drank with gusto. "You're busy."

"Youth," said Chobin, as if it were explanation enough. His grin widened at that. "But the two of you fighting alongside one another looked as natural and as awe-inspiring as anything I've ever seen. Meant it when I called you something out of legend. Fucking legendary, that's what you were. Like you always knew where and when the other needed you. Colour me fucking impressed. Dye me awestruck. Slackjawed, sure as fuck." He leaned forward, a mischievous glint to his eye. "What's a man have to do to hook up with one of those sisters of yours?"

Shkarag was not amused. She finished off the ewer and held it in her lap. Were it not for her fangs, menacing and exposed, she would have looked nothing like an instrument of destruction in her absurd tunic. A hiss took purchase on her throat.

"All right, all right," said Chobin, shrugging and patently amused with himself. "You're into some eldritch sort of threshing anyway. Sort of person to look to pinecones for inspiration."

Tirdad grimaced at that. "Please don't give her any ideas. Besides, are you really going to antagonize her after what she did down there?"

"Point taken," Chobin said, grunting. "But now that you mention it, what the everliving fuck was that?" He stooped for another ewer, and offered it to Shkarag, grin wide as ever. "Entertain the question and it's all yours."

Meaning to speak up, Tirdad held his tongue. This was the sort of back and forth banter you'd expect over wine after a battle—even if it was more one-sided where she was concerned. He admitted to being too defensive for her sake, when she seemed perfectly fine with it. Plus, Chobin was treating her like any other soldier. Tirdad respected that.

Shkarag gave him one of her inscrutable glances, tied together by the clinking of her nails on the ewer in her lap. It persisted well into the territory of what would have been awkward if it were anyone else, before breaking off to accept the wine.

"Maybe," she said, proceeding to chug the contents. She set her head askew, deliberating the tarp above. But for its flapping, another bout of silence intervened before she spoke up.

"That," she said, "is the hunt, šo-bloody and šo-pure, searching for how to best be true to your lust like some, like some—" Shkarag leaned back on her hands. The ewers fell from her lap to roll in either direction. "Not pure. Not that." Her face screwed up in thought. "What's the, the— prurient. Šo-prurient. That's—"

"Shkarag," Tirdad interrupted. "He's asking about your . . . transformation during our encounter with the manticore. If you're willing, I'd like to hear it as well."

"Maybe," she replied. Shkarag swept her wavering gaze over the pavilion, finding one ewer then the other. "A pittance, that wine. A šo-damned pittance."

Affectedly exasperated, Chobin held up a finger, then left the tent, soon to return with a jar in tow. After waving away the man who'd helped him carry it over, he returned to his seat. "Have at it, skink-slicker."

Shkarag bared her fangs, though fleetingly; she finished the jar off in no time. After giving it a moment to sink in, she began.

"I'll—" She made to lean back again, but ended up flat on her back. "I'll narrate the, spin the, tell the thing," she went on as if it hadn't happened. Her head rolled to address Tirdad. "For you."

He smiled and inclined his head.

She turned her face to the canopy, followed shortly by her eyes. "They say, they say Eshm is all so much—" Shkarag raised a claw beside her head. "All so much everything. But they don't half the, know the half of it." She let her arm fall limp. "Too much. All so much everything is too much. There's a planet inside of you, raging and bucking and ravening and it's too much for one person." She craned to peer at Tirdad from an odd angle. "Too much for me."

Disbelief and confusion joined in the furrows of his brow. "That's figurative isn't it? You don't mean to tell me there's an actual planet inside you."

"Not the only one cavorting in the celestial theatre. Revolving even now."

"That's fucking absurd," Chobin stated.

If she'd heard him, Shkarag paid him no heed. "Full-blooded sisters can contain it. Turns out, turns out being half human revokes the, makes it tricky. Would've put me down, but Stahm, she pledged to snuff out the human in me."

"W—" The name stretched as if she were reeling it from her cords, a web tangled in the claw of her fingers as they raked the ground. "Waray was šo-fierce. Convinced Stahm she needed that thousand- year torture just so—"

Shkarag clammed up, and the sorrow in her eyes made her audience look away. She made several attempts to reach into her egg pouch before coming to terms with it being gone. When she finally spoke up, it was hard-edged. "Planet storms and thunders like some, like some šo-clattering die too enthusiastic, buoyant and gleaming ear to ear, because it knows, it knows its life is falling apart, and the moment its clattering quietens everything it loves will cease to exist. So you can never let it show you a side. The clattering must go on. Always."

She closed her eyes as if just discussing it was enough to exhaust her, and in that, reminded him of just how ancient she was. "But that's just as the crow flies."

When it became obvious she had nothing left to say, Chobin took it upon himself to fill the silence. "Well, planet or no planet, I'm convinced you're not to be fucked with. Why not do that all the time? You'd be damn near unstoppable!"

"Were you even listening?" asked Tirdad.

Chobin shrugged. "Much as anyone can."

"Goat-fucker," Shkarag grumbled.

Shaking his head and wearing a full-toothed grin, Chobin planted a palm on his knee and leaned toward Tirdad. "So, how about you set the record straight. Did you or did you not fuck forty divs, and were they broom-kebabs?"

Tirdad brightened at the memory of Shkarag's prank, and recounted it fondly. Together, he and Chobin spent the hours that followed drinking and reminiscing until sunset.

Eventually, Chobin cleared his throat, sounding as if he'd concluded some inner discourse and was determined to see it through. "It's been a fucking pleasure catching up, and I hope you choose to stick around this time, my friend. Can't undo Father's sins, can't reinstate your family or clear their name, but perhaps there is something I can do to repay you."

He flashed his trademark grin, pushing off his knees to stand. "Wasn't just any star-reckoner out there: it was the fucking family star-reckoner. The very same who persuaded his peers to turn on you and yours. Same fucker who relays your whereabouts and deeds to the King of Kings. He'll no doubt call for your imprisonment in Castle Oblivion if you don't join my family. But here's the thing: he drew three lots just to subdue Shkarag."

"So?"

Shkarag hissed. "Šo-tyrannical star-fucker."

"So," said Chobin, starting for the exit, "he's old and frail and drew three lots. Three." He stopped with the flap half open to glance back and add, meaningfully, "He's a toenail-swallowing rat, and our nation would be better off without him."

With that, Chobin departed.

Shkarag took a seat by Tirdad's side and immediately set to kneading her thigh. In the course of her task, she regarded him pensively.

Tirdad returned her stare in kind. "What?"

". . ."

"You look ridiculous in that tunic."

She gave herself a once over, then cocked her head slightly. "Maybe."

"Shkarag," he said, and her pensive stare redoubled. "Tonight."

• • • • •

Under the cover of darkness, with his arm slung over Shkarag's shoulder, Tirdad limped through the bivouac.

"Need to heal," she hissed quietly. "Not some šo-strapping legend."

"After," he assured her through gritted teeth. Tirdad knew all too well. Bitter as the cold was, he dripped with sweat. Though the roots were potent, they couldn't dampen the pain of standing.

Shkarag guided him beyond the light of the camp and into the dead of night, between sentries too otiose to notice, and back into the bivouac. Masked by a new moon, their progress went undetected.

Until, out of nowhere, she stopped. ". . ."

Tirdad leaned into her, squinting against the darkness. With his head on hers, the ridges of her scales pressed into his hair, which caused him to wonder whether the starling-black coursed beneath them even now. "What is it?"

"Star-fucking sailor of the skies is there."

It took a moment for Tirdad to pick out the shape of the pavilion in the pitch black. There were no torches or braziers in the vicinity, no guards posted by the entrance. It seemed he'd read Chobin correctly; that, or this was a trap.

"Let's finish this," he whispered.

Shkarag stood anchored in place. She shifted beside him, and her voice grew tremulous. "Sailor of the skies."

"Shkarag?"

She passed him her spear. "Go."

Tirdad deliberated her for a moment, and though he couldn't make out more than her silhouette, he could tell something was amiss. "What's gotten into you?" he asked.

". . ."

Tirdad shrugged it off, deigning to use the spear as a crutch with which to hobble into the tent. Sweat made it difficult for him to get a good grip, but he managed to make it inside. There, illuminated by only a small oil lamp, lay a man in the robes of a star-reckoner, pale and infirm.

This was it then. Tirdad unsheathed his sword, the hilt pulsating as it never had before, runaway as his heartbeat. He swallowed, took a steadying breath, and drew up short of plunging it into the man's chest.

He'd damned Ashtadukht for her rites. He'd known she was unwell—he'd fucking loved her!—but honour had nevertheless bade him to do what he believed to be the right thing. Tirdad imagined her now, pleading and alone, and knew honour had been wrong. The desperation of her memories hardened that conviction. She'd been wronged. By him, by—Tirdad followed the blade's edge to the star-reckoner it ached for—by this man.

As a star-reckoner, he had no doubt done some good. Had furthered the well-being of the nation despite his selfish designs. By virtue of their profession, a star-reckoner need only exist for that to be true. Even Ashtadukht, worst of the star-reckoners and misguided besides, was no exception. But this star-reckoner had spearheaded the conspiracy that ruined her life—never mind the lives of so many others.

The honourable thing would be to turn away. Tirdad could not. He kept reliving her last ragged breaths, the dreadful finality that'd swept in where they ended. Honour had caused his part in her demise, and it no longer had a place in his life.

He plunged the blade into the man's chest.

The starling-black fed ravenously. It rejoiced, and its ebullience drowned out his pain. The celestial theatre raged around him, stars decrying the planets' premature advantage. The constellations were woefully outmanned in the realm of mortals, their chosen hunted and thinned. Someone or something had been freed.

Tirdad extracted his blade, and the starling-black fell content—as if its quest was finally over. He'd never expected to find peace in avenging Ashtadukht, but he had expected something. Presently, he only felt tired.

He'd turned to leave when reddish-brown light like spoiled yogurt oozed through the flaps and into the tent. Tirdad scowled, leaning heavily into the spear. "What in the seven climes?"

He waded through it, feeling as if he were walking through a stuffy ossuary, and was stopped by Shkarag pulling a flap aside to enter.

She seemed to him a specter then, drained of spirit and ready to end herself. "I'm sorry," she muttered, sounding utterly despondent, as if she were holding back tears. "Father made me do it."

Tirdad leaned heavily into the spear, doing his best to soothe his leg. "Made you do it? I don't follow."

Shkarag parted her lips several times, forming the shapes to words but never actually saying anything, while her stare darted around the tent.

He frowned at her apprehension, the fear she wore like shackles. "Whatever you've done, it won't change how I feel about you. But it's dangerous to linger here. Let's discuss this—"

"Tried," she said hurriedly. "Tried to tell you. The more I fought, the harder it became."

"Tell me what?"

"You brought the . . . the šo-damned blade to me. Had escaped the, hid from Father's—" She formed a claw by her head, and raked it over the scales. "His hisses, his—" She hissed. "His commands. Never wanted to, never wanted to betray you."

Shkarag shook, and though he felt them, her rage and sorrow mixed so thoroughly and with such intensity that Tirdad couldn't determine where one ended and the other began. He endeavoured to tread lightly, talking smoothly and calmly.

"Don't worry. I've got your weather. We'll sort it out and—"

"I betrayed you!" Shkarag screamed, fangs bared and dripping acid to the smell of ozone. "I . . ." Her fangs slowly retracted. ". . . betrayed you." She turned untrammeled hatred on his sword. "Starling-black is his."

"I don't . . ." Tirdad stared glumly at the blade. "But Ashta?"

"His. They both wanted, their goals were . . . the star-reckoners only had to become dust."

"That's why you were killing them. Why not let me then?"

"Already explained," she started, and the rage that took purchase on her delivery was quick to subside. "Wanted to save you from being haunted like some, like some—" She sucked in a breath that shivered as she exhaled, reaching back for an egg pouch that wasn't there. "And thought, hoped you'd throw in the, give up. Couldn't resist Father's will. Could kill them first and hope."

"That's . . . clever of you."

"I'm sorry."

Tirdad sighed, glancing over at the figure of the dead star-reckoner. "Were you only manipulating me all this time?"

The words had hardly left his mouth when he realized how stupid and needlessly hurtful they were.

It became immediately obvious that this was the outcome she'd been dreading the most. She seized up, tense as a bowstring at full draw. Her fury sloughed away. Though she formed an unspoken "Maybe", she managed to hold it back to say, "No. More than only, more than that." Shkarag felt for her pouch, and when she couldn't find it, made claws of her hands. "Sister always said blood is honest. Yours reeks of roving, of . . . exploring together. Reminds me of her."

Tirdad would have accepted a simple no. He hobbled up to her, and when she didn't flinch, embraced her. Shkarag bore his weight by returning the hug, which allowed his fatigue to catch up to him. He relied on her strength, took solace in it. "I wouldn't have left you," he breathed. "What matters is that you fought it, and more than most would've managed."

"Trust you, too," she said. "I think."

Tirdad took a moment to rest in her care before asking, "If you're telling me all this, does that mean it's over?"

Shkarag took her spear, and with her help, they limped through the flap and out into a bivouac flooded with a sickly light. All around, confused onlookers emerged from their tents to turn their heads toward the sky. There, snowclouds billowed the same reddish-brown. They crawled with spoiled light.

Tirdad was about to ask for an explanation when a great bulge formed in the clouds. It wafted away like a water over a surfacing whale, and he understood the portent he'd witnessed in the celestial theatre. The world-ending dragon Gochihr descended.

Streamers of smoke ribboned from a thousand forked tongues, between jaws large enough to swallow a forty-armed div whole, and across its serpentine body, which was dominated by glaciers and snow, except where interrupted at times by rounded horns that glowed like magma beneath a thin layer of igneous rock. On its back sat a lone rider: Eshm.

Tirdad swallowed.

"Oh fuck."

www.ingramcontent.com/pod-product-compliance
Lightning Source LLC
Chambersburg PA
CBHW030604180626
46816CB00005B/1666